Romances, feuds and curses echo ~~~~~~~~~ Emerald Station, and lingered to ~~~~~~~~~ dwelled there. Now sudden death and impending doom are threads woven into the tapestry . . . Is the curse of Emerald Station too strong for even the beautiful passionate women and the strong determined men of the Kennelly Dynasty?

Also by Daoma Winston:

MOORHAVEN
THE HAVERSHAM LEGACY

Also in Troubadour Paperback

THE WOLF AND THE DOVE by Kathleen Woodiwiss
THE FLAME AND THE FLOWER by Kathleen Woodiwiss
VOTE FOR A SILK GOWN by Jay Allerton
THE SEVENTEENTH STAIR by Barbara Paul
THE FLAME OF THE BORGIAS by Jean Briggs
THE BLADE OF CASTLEMAYNE by Anthony Esler
THE LADY OF WILDERSLEY by Josephine Edgar
RENDEZVOUS WITH DANGER by Margaret Pemberton
A CROWN IN DARKNESS by Margaret Mullally
NO MARKS FOR TRYING by Stella Allen
MOORHAVEN by Daoma Winston
POLMARRAN TOWER by Charlotte Massey
FALLS THE SHADOW by Regina Ross
THE QUEEN BEE by Phyllida Barstow
LOVE'S TENDER FURY by Jennifer Wilde
THE PRICE OF VENGEANCE by Freda Michel
THE MACHIAVELLIAN MARQUESS by Freda Michel
MORWENNA by Anne Goring
THE HAVERSHAM LEGACY by Daoma Winston
SWEET SAVAGE LOVE by Rosemary Rogers
SHADOWS IN THE FIRE by Eva Dane
WICKED LOVING LIES by Rosemary Rogers
DEVIL'S DESIRE by Laurie McBain
THE DEVIL DANCES FOR GOLD by Regina Ross
DUCHESS by Josephine Edgar
DARK FIRES by Rosemary Rogers
THE BRIDE OF INVERCOE by Charlotte Massey
DISTANT THUNDER by Olivia O'Neill
THE KING'S BRAT by Constance Gluyas
BORN TO BE KING by Constance Gluyas
A FIRE IN THE BLOOD by Mary May Simmons
MY LADY'S CRUSADE by Annette Motley

Daoma Winston

Emerald Station

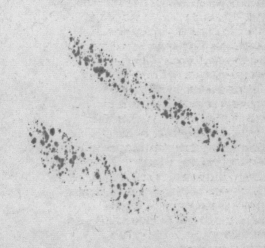

Futura Publications Limited
A Troubadour Book

A Troubadour Book
First published in Great Britain by
Futura Publications Limited in 1977

Copyright © 1974 by Daoma Winston

Published by arrangement with the author

ISBN 0 8600 7589 3

Printed in Great Britain by
Hazell Watson & Viney Ltd
Aylesbury, Bucks

Futura Publications Limited
110 Warner Road, Camberwell
London SE5

DEDICATION:

For MORGAN WILSON

Chapter 1

The carriage wheels jolted rhythmically over the wet cobblestones. A grimy yellow mist smeared the windows, and beyond them, city-gray faces tipped up to look at the bedraggled black funeral plumes and then turned quickly away.

Watching, Nealanna Yarrow observed to herself that all men must turn away from the reminders of their own mortality. Those on this thoroughfare were not exceptions, but in the hustle for survival they would soon forget what they had, for an instant, looked upon.

There was a sudden jerk and skid, with the wheels locked and squealing. The driver shouted in language appropriate to the occasion. Rude voices yelled back.

Nealanna braced her small feet, and clung to the wooden armrest, expecting further calamity.

In her seventeen years she had already learned that it was well to be prepared. But this time at least nothing untoward happened. The angry shouts faded. The black-draped carriage rolled on.

It passed a one-legged man leaning on a heavy crutch, whose faded and tattered uniform afforded him no protec-

tion against the November chill. She looked away from
him quickly, and remembered the gray faces averting their
eyes from the funeral plumes.

Next to her, Mr. Caroway heaved his small bulk and
muttered, "Poor devil. A survivor of Khartoum no doubt.
And if not of there, then some other benighted spot."

"Yes," she answered. "I've seen many such since I came
to London."

Mr. Caroway peered at her over the glasses that rode the
end of his pink round nose. "It is a jungle these days.
Civility has become a lost art and a lost way of life. A
man is no longer safe in the road, nor safe within the
walls of his home."

He was a man in his middle years, portly with good
eating and drink. He had small brown, slightly bloodshot
eyes, and what was left of his hair made a neat brown
ruffle around his mostly bald head. Now it was covered by
a tall black hat. His round chin rested on his stiff white
collar and his round belly made a bulge under his dark
greatcoat.

"London," he repeated in tones of exasperation, "the
hub of the empire . . . and yet we see such sights as make
us wonder."

Nealanna said nothing, but she thought it must be his
profession that led him to such dismal conclusions about
the city that was his home. He was a solicitor, and she
supposed that he dealt daily with the pathetic and sordid
and depressing.

"The trouble is, my dear Caroway, you resist change,"
said the other man in the carriage.

He had been silent for so long that Nealanna had
almost forgotten his presence. His name was Jonathan
Davies. He was a tall and elegant man who was impecca-
bly dressed.

Now he went on, "And change is what is upon us. The
old ways are dead or dying. New ones will come. And it
may be that that's a good thing."

He was a physician, but she suspected that he saw
nothing of the sordid in his Harley Street office. Sorrow,

and pain, and even death, yes. He would see those, but the sordid would never soil the air near him. Perhaps, she thought, that was why he could look ahead with an optimism plainly not shared by the solicitor.

An optimism not shared by herself either. Changes, he said. But there had already been enough changes, and she did not consider that they had brought much benefit to her.

She stiffened again, stretching to reach the floor to brace herself as the carriage made a sharp turn.

"We're very nearly there," Mr. Caroway told her.

She nodded, black curls sliding along her neck under her veil. She recognized the street that would lead to the small mews cottage in which she had spent the past three months. She was glad that the journey was almost over now. But she wondered how long she would stay there, and where she would go when she left.

Mr. Caroway exchanged a significant look with Mr. Davies, then said, "We'll come in with you, Nealanna. There's a matter of importance to be discussed."

Her heart gave a single hard thump. If it was a matter of money, then she would have to tell them straight out. She had nothing, nothing but a few shillings. How these two men were to be paid for their services, she didn't know.

"The future," Mr. Caroway said.

She nodded again, noting that he, and Mr. Davies, too, suddenly appeared uneasy. She wondered grimly just what was to come next, what changes lay in store for her, and why these two men, experienced in worldly affairs beyond her imagining, should be concerned.

The carriage rolled to a stop. Mr. Davies opened the door and jumped out. Mr. Caroway followed more slowly, grunting and groaning.

Nealanna gathered her heavy black cloak around her, and stepped, with his help, to the cobblestones.

The grimy mist was thicker here, and lay like a yellow twilight over the buildings.

Mr. Davies told the driver to wait, and then the three of them went to the small blue door.

Nealanna fished in her reticule for the big brass key, and finding it, permitted Mr. Caroway to take it from her. He unlocked the door, and stood aside to allow her entrance.

She went ahead, and suddenly it was just like the day she had come here for the first time. She had made her way from the station through the misty streets and found herself inside this door. Her heart was beating quickly. There was heat in her cheeks. Her lips were dry with excitement. Then it had been because she had known that soon she would see her mother. Now it was because she knew that ahead of her there was nothing but an aching emptiness.

For a moment, the three of them, she, the doctor and the solicitor, were bunched in the tiny dim foyer.

Then she said faintly, "The parlor, I think," and led the way up the narrow flight of steps, her footfalls soundless on the threadbare carpet.

The odor of emptiness, age, illness and defeat assailed her as she reached the second floor, and over that there hung the scent of her mother's perfume and powder. The combination was very nearly overpowering.

She hurried into the parlor. She took off her cloak and veil, and quickly lit the small coal fire laid on the hearth. She touched a taper to the gas lamps. Now the dingy room seemed cozy, the grimy mist held at bay.

Mr. Caroway stood before the hearth, his plump legs spread wide, his black waistcoat riding up over his plump belly, his round chin resting on his collar.

Mr. Davies sat on the narrow settle, his long legs elegantly crossed, his slim hands folded together. "You might as well begin," he told Mr. Caroway. "I really don't have much time."

The solicitor cleared his throat with a rumble that seemed to shake the walls. He bent a kind glance over his spectacles on Nealanna. "The circumstances . . ." he began. "I confess that I do not know what you know of them. Your mother never told me. I tell you frankly, dear child, I don't know precisely where to begin, or how."

She said nothing. She was not certain just what he knew of what he called the circumstances. She was determined to give nothing away.

Mr. Davies said impatiently, "Stop this beating about the bush." He turned to Nealanna. "This concerns your future, and also, in part, your past."

She thought that, in truth, it could concern only a small part of her past, not all of her seventeen years in Cornwall with Widow Hart and the orange cat called Poo, but only these three months spent nursing her mother in the mews cottage here in London. For she doubted that either the solicitor or the physician knew much about her beyond that very short time.

But she realized that she was wrong when Mr. Caroway said, "Some seventeen years ago, Nealanna, your mother was just about your own age. A young and very pretty girl, come up to London from a village in the south."

Nealanna felt the blood rise into her cheeks. Plainly he knew the facts of her birth, and he was preparing to tell her them. But she did not want to discuss it with him. It was the future which concerned her, not the shameful past with which she was burdened forever but which was hardly a fault of her own.

She said quickly, hoarsely, "Yes, yes, Mr. Caroway. I know. I know."

Mr. Caroway shot a relieved look at Mr. Davies, then answered, "I should have realized that your mother would tell you. Anna was a dear woman, and a loving mother, even though sad misfortune drove her."

Nealanna said nothing.

"She did what she had to do," Mr. Caroway went on. "One may not approve, but one must understand."

"We all know that," Nealanna agreed.

Mr. Caroway cleared his throat with another wall-shaking rumble. "There is someone who wishes to see you, Nealanna."

Her dark eyes widened. She knew no one in London beyond these two men and a few of the shopkeepers in

11

the road below. When Mr. Caroway didn't explain, she inquired, "Well, who is it?"

"You will confuse the girl beyond good sense," Mr. Davies cut in. He leaned forward, smiled at her. "Look here, Nealanna. You know the facts, I gather, then you must know the rest of it, so I'll tell you. After your birth, a friend of your mother's settled a trust on her, and on you, too." Mr. Caroway made some small disapproving sound, and the physician glanced at him, then went on. "It is that trust which supported you all these years, paid for your care in Cornwall, and for your schooling. It paid for the food you ate, the clothes on your back . . ."

Again Mr. Caroway made a small disapproving sound. "I don't wish to speak ill of the dead, Nealanna, but you must know that the fund was substantial, and within your mother's discretion to spend. We all regret that in those seventeen years she spent it unwisely."

"That is not to the point," Mr. Davies said smoothly. "What is is that this friend now wishes to see you, Nealanna."

Mr. Caroway put in quickly, "But, of course, if you have no desire to talk with him, why then, there's no need to. You must understand. You are under no obligation. You have absolute freedom of choice."

She felt the blood drain from her head. Her cheeks were suddenly cold, and her vision blurred. The room seemed to swim. She gathered herself tightly, her small body rigid.

This friend, to whom Mr. Caroway and the physician both alluded so delicately, must be the man who was her father. And yet she had always believed that her father was dead. For that was what her mother had told her.

But he was alive. And she would see him now, the gay lover whom terrible circumstance had torn away before the planned marriage could take place. The man, young and handsome and dashing, who had, in spite of all, loved her mother, loved her, too, without ever having seen her. Why else would he have supported them? Why else appear now?

The solicitor and the physician mistook her silence.

Mr. Caroway said uneasily, "Now, now, Nealanna. Do be sensible. There's no need to be frightened."

Mr. Davies said, "He won't harm you, girl. Why should he?"

She said breathlessly, "No, no. I am not afraid." And then she smiled tremulously, "But it's a dream come true."

Mr. Caroway cut in, "Then you will see him?"

Nealanna nodded so hard that her black curls slid down the curve of her cheek. She brushed them back impatiently. "Of course. When? Where?"

Mr. Caroway pulled his gold watch from his waistcoat, studied it through his glasses, then answered, "Why, if you can be ready in half an hour, I'll take you to him myself."

"I am ready now," she retorted.

Mr. Davies laughed, rose, and reached for his greatcoat.

But Mr. Caroway said, "Not so fast, if you please." He turned back to Nealanna. "I should tell you now that I do not know what the gentleman proposes. It was not something he cared to divulge to me before he had spoken to you. Which is, perhaps, as it should be. Yet I do feel a responsibility to you. I want you to know that you are not alone in the world, Nealanna. You have me. You have Mr. Davies. We stand ready to serve you." He paused for confirmation from the physician. A confirmation, Nealanna noted with wry amusement, which was not forthcoming.

Mr. Davies was plainly anxious to be off to his pleasant Harley Street quarters and his pretty wife.

Mr. Caroway hurried on after a quick look at the physician who was examining his slender fingers, "We have your welfare at heart. Once you have heard the gentleman's ideas, you must think them over carefully. Then, I suggest you discuss them with me. If they are not suitable, why, why, then we will consider further."

"Come, come," Mr. Davies laughed. "He is not going to sell her into white slavery, you know."

"That is not proper," Mr. Caroway retorted.

"Certainly not," Mr. Davies agreed, with a smile.

Mr. Caroway ignored him. "Do you understand, Nealanna? Why, Mrs. Caroway and I would deem it an honor . . ."

She shook her head, smiled. She said, "First of all I must see this gentleman, mustn't I? And if you think he may be waiting . . ."

"He will be waiting," Mr. Davies said.

Nealanna reached for her cloak.

"If you would like to change," Mr. Caroway suggested, "I should be glad to wait. Perhaps . . ."

She looked at him gravely. "This is what I have, Mr. Caroway. This is what I must wear."

He nodded, took up his coat. "Then we'll take you to the Ritz."

"The Ritz?" she repeated.

Mr. Davies laughed softly. "Oh, yes, child, he is a man of great means. He stays only at the Ritz when he is in London."

The hotel lobby seemed wrapped in a golden glow under gleaming chandeliers. The panelled walls had a high sheen, and the embroidered hangings were beautifully colored.

"Ask for Mr. Kennelly," Mr. Caroway had told her. "Just go up to the big counter inside, and say you are expected."

Then he and Mr. Davies had ridden away, no doubt relieved to have disposed of her.

Now she hesitated on the threshold, very nearly bewitched by the golden glow, the rich carpets, and the flower-scented air. She had never in her life seen anything like it before, and never expected to. This was a world peopled by those whose doings were carefully followed in *Town Topics,* her mother's favorite reading. It had nothing to do with Nealanna herself.

But she took a deep breath. She went quickly toward the counter. She was aware of eyes on her, eyes that noted her simple cloak, her well-polished but cracked boots. Among the fashionably dressed ladies there, she

14

stood out like a scarecrow in a marrow field. She didn't care. She raised her chin a fraction, hurried a fraction. She stood at the counter at last. "I would like to see Mr. Kennelly."

She was examined from head to toe by the clerk. He asked finally, "Are you expected?"

"Yes," she said firmly. "I am. And I am somewhat late."

She hesitated. Then, "Nealanna Yarrow."

"I'll have you escorted to the suite," the clerk said with a nod.

The page was ten years old, she thought. Surely not more than that. He had golden hair under the cap he wore, and wide blue eyes. He bounded ahead of her like a green-clad fawn to lead her into the great birdcage elevator. It drifted majestically upward to stop at the third floor, and then he hurried along a narrow corridor to pause suddenly before a mahogony door. "Mr. Kennelly's suite," he announced in a piping voice.

She thanked him, and he gave the panel a single quick knock before he bounded away.

There was a sound from within, and then the door opened.

The man who stood there was in his mid-sixties, she guessed.

He had a thick shock of white hair that waved over a high forehead. His eyes were gray and piercing. He was clean shaven but for a thick curving mustache, and his wrinkled and scored skin was heavily tanned.

"Miss Yarrow?" he asked in a deep rough voice, the two words, and their rhythm, suggesting an accent unfamiliar to her.

She nodded, speechless with the excitement of seeing him for the first time, and bewildered, too. He was so much older than she had expected. She saw nothing in him of what her mother had described.

He gave her a faint and reassuring smile, pulled the door wider. "I'm Neal Kennelly. Come in then. We must have a long talk."

She instantly dismissed what had been the beginnings of doubt. If proof were needed, there it was. Her mother had made for her a name by blending hers, Anna, with this man's, Neal.

Nealanna felt that she drifted through the door, was guided by some sense other than her own, across the thick red carpet.

"Take off your cloak," Neal Kennelly told her. "Have the chair near the fire, and I'll pour us some sherry."

She did as he told her, but he didn't move. He stood quite still, towering over her, looking down from his bulky-shouldered height. His careful examination made her once again aware of the plainness of her black dress, the shapelessness of her boots.

At last he gave up his silent scrutiny. He turned away to the sideboard. She watched as he handled decanter and crystal glasses. His white hair glowed in the firelight, and his movements were slow and definite.

The luxurious appointments of the room seemed to have been designed for a person just such as he was. A man of power, of wealth.

It didn't occur to her to wonder why her life had been what it was until then. She was too taken aback by the events of the last two hours. She simply accepted what she knew must be true.

He returned to her, gave her a small glass, and retired to a low easy chair across from her. He sat down, leaned back, and resumed his long silent scrutiny of her. Finally he said, "No, Nealanna. I might as well tell you straight out. I see what you think in your eyes and in your face. But it is not that way. And you mustn't believe that it is. You are not my long lost bastard, Nealanna. I am not your father."

Chapter 2

The words fell with all the force of a ruthless and brutal blow. They were the last words she expected, and too bald in their meaning to be borne. She gasped with the impact.

Before she could speak, before she could deny, question, or protest, he went on quickly, "No, no. Wait a bit. Let me tell you the facts. And then we will talk."

She nodded, bleak with disappointment, and with a new rising despair. Her mother had told the truth, after all. Her father was dead. She was alone, and with no one to turn to.

Mr. Davies? He had made plain his lack of interest.

Mr. Caroway? She could imagine with what restrained joy she would be welcomed by Mrs. Caroway.

This man who sat before her? He owed her nothing.

Now he said quietly, "I knew Anna Yarrow when she was your age, but I knew her only briefly. You are remarkably like her physically. The same dark hair, the same tilt to the eyes, the same small stature. She was a pretty girl, too. And with some minor grace, a touch of talent for dancing. She worked in a music hall, but she hadn't been long in the city, I think." He turned, looked into the fire on the hearth. The flames jumped, and tiny bright embers flew upward like a swarm of golden bees. He went on, "As you might have guessed by now, I am an American. I was here on business, one of many trips I was making in those days. I was not traveling alone. I'll not speak of the man with whom I was traveling. You do understand me, don't you?"

"Yes. I believe I understand," she answered. The man with whom he had been traveling was the man who had become her mother's lover.

Neal went on, "Later on, when I returned to London by myself, I learned of Anna's plight. She was alone, without help. I was sorry for her. A sentimental reaction that I am not prone to, as you will probably learn. But there it was. I wanted to help her, and I had the means to do so. The trust was established for her." He paused.

Nealanna said through dry lips, "I am grateful for your generosity, to her, and to me."

"It seems not to have been much generosity," he said roughly. "Plainly I should have taken more care to see how it was spent. But it seemed best, at that time, to deal with it that way and have an end to it. I never dreamed . . ."

"She was grateful, too," Nealanna said. "After all, why else would I have been named . . ."

"No. You're mistaken. You are not named for me. And if you saw the two names written you would realize there is no connection. You see?" He pulled an engraved card from his waistcoat pocket, passed it to her.

She saw, in fine black script, Neil Kennelly, and understood. She was named, she supposed, for a man named Neal. But not the man who sat before her.

She said quietly, returning the card, "You mustn't think that I would press a claim where there was none. Nor press one, unwanted, even if I were justified."

"It isn't the claim that concerns me," he said. "It's the truth. You must understand the truth. It is essential. I am

18

not your father. That's an end of it. I did what I could for your mother, but she never named you for me."

"You knew my father," Nealanna said.

"I'll not tell you about him."

She waited a moment, then said softly, "My mother said he was gay, handsome, loving. She said they would have been married, but for his death."

He frowned at her, looked back at the fire. "Then you were told that you were born out of wedlock?"

"I was told that. Yes. And I knew that was why I had to stay in Cornwall with the Widow Hart, while my mother was in London, or traveling in the provinces. There was so little money, you see. She couldn't have me with her . . ." Nealanna's voice faltered to a stop. Something in his rock-hard face gave her words the lie. She asked, "Was it not that way?"

"Go on," he said quietly.

"But . . . there is no more."

"You saw your mother often?"

The chair was suddenly not as soft and welcoming as it had been, nor the fire as warm. Nealanna moved uneasily, and didn't answer.

"Well?" He was impatient, curt. He would have a reply.

She said finally, "I saw her three times over the years. Until . . ."

"Until you came here to London to nurse her in her last illness," he finished. "Is that right?"

She didn't answer him.

"Come, come," he snapped. "There are to be no secrets between us. I must know how it was, Nealanna."

"Yes," she said finally. "I came to London for that. But why ask me? You seem very well-informed about my comings and goings."

"I've spoken to Mr. Caroway, and Mr. Davies," he said dryly.

But she didn't answer him. She was remembering now. The first time she had seen her mother was when she was six years old. The sky was black with Cornish clouds, and the wind wet off the sea. She played on the cottage steps, beating a dented pot as if it were a soldier's drum. It was her only toy.

A conveyance pulled up in the road beyond the stile. She was young enough then to still believe in fairies, and when the lady stepped out in a swish and swirl of ribbons and feathers, she had thought her a fairy princess. She dropped pot and spoon and shrank back against the steps, breathless with wonder.

The fairy princess opened her arms wide, and cried, "Nealanna!"

Widow Hart leaned over her, pulled her to her feet. "Run," she hissed. "Run and hug the lady. It's your Mum, you ninny. Run now."

Nealanna didn't remember what had happened then. But next she was wrapped in warmth and in silken arms, and scalded with tears and shaken with happy laughter. It was her mother, and she never forgot her scent, and the sound of her voice, though she was twelve before she saw Anna Yarrow again.

That time they walked together along the coast. "Oh, it's good to see you again," her mother cried. "Oh, Nealanna, how you've grown." And then, holding her hand tightly, "Are you happy? Does the harpy treat you well? Could you not try to shed the village dialect? After all, you won't be here forever, you know."

Nealanna answered the questions as well as she knew how.

Anna didn't seem to listen. She said quickly, "We'll be together soon. It's difficult, you see. I am on tour in the provinces so much. I have not enough to make a real home for you. But I want you, Nealanna. Oh, how I do want you."

Anna had black eyes, very much the shade of Nealanna's own slanted black eyes, and black curls, too. She had a high-colored feverish look, and was too thin. Yes, even then, she was much too thin, wearing bustles and full skirts, and great heavy floating cloaks.

It was when Nealanna was fifteen that she heard the story of her birth, of the lover who had died. By then she was aware of the sharp odor that always lingered beneath her mother's favorite scent. The sharp odor that was whiskey. By then, too, she was aware of the feverishness in the black eyes, the quiver in the thin fingers.

And then, three months before, a letter had come to her. A letter written in a shaking hand. Anna had said that she was ill. She asked Nealanna to come to her.

Widow Hart packed up her few clothes, and sent them on. Nealanna kissed her goodbye, and hugged the orange cat called Poo, and took the steam train to London, not knowing then that her fourth reunion with her mother would be the final one.

She arrived at the mews cottage to find the elegant Mr. Davies in attendance, and the worried Mr. Caroway standing by.

Anna Yarrow was a ghost of the slim laughing woman that Nealanna remembered. The silks and satins, the ribbons and veils, were gone now. And so was the laughter. Anna was a laudanum addict, and spent hours in drugged sleep, and hours more in long wild ravings about a past Nealanna could not share with her, and soon began to doubt. She would have been a great actress, Anna insisted, but for her weak lungs. Mr. Bernard Shaw had mentioned her once. And others, too. She had been a great beauty, sought after and cherished by important men. But illness had stolen her beauty away. She sent Nealanna on hopeless treasure hunting through the tiny rooms in search of the fading memorabilia which was her proof of the life that had been and was no more. Nealanna found only a few worn and old posters from music hall doors. For three months Anna told tales by night, and slept heavily by day. And then she died.

Neil Kennelly's gruff voice interrupted her musings, to Nealanna's relief. He was saying, "Yes. It was through Mr. Caroway that I learned of your mother's illness, and all that had happened, and that you were here as well."

Nealanna said, "What does it matter now, Mr. Kennelly?" She felt no bitterness, only a vast sadness. Anna was gone.

"Your mother . . . she never mentioned my name?" he asked.

"Never."

"Nor your father's?"

"I've told you," Nealanna answered. "Never."

He nodded, satisfaction on his face. "That was part of the agreement."

"Agreement?"

"When I set up the trust through Mr. Caroway, it was to be a matter just between the three of us. He, your mother, and myself. She maintained it. At least she was reliable in *that*."

The stress in his words told Nealanna that he believed Anna to have been less than reliable in some other way. But Nealanna did not want to question him. She did not want to know. She would have preferred to hold intact the memory of Anna as she had known her, known her before these past three months.

But he would not have it. He said heavily, "You are here, with me, in the Ritz. You see what I am. Surely you've begun to wonder why, since I provided for you, I did not provide more."

She drew a deep and shaky breath, and said quickly, "Mr. Kennelly, it was enough."

"Yours was to have been a better life, I assure you. I have spoken to Mr. Caroway, as I told you, and I know what it was."

"I had food," she said. "And care, and schooling in the village."

He smiled faintly under his heavy mustache. "You consider that ample. I do not. I think you had better know the truth. Your mother was not an actress, nor a dancer. She worked at nothing after your birth, and died destitute because she had squandered everything, beyond the pittance paid for your upkeep, on frills to wear and gambling and drink."

These words, too, had the force of a blow. But Nealanna was silent. She could not say that he lied. She remembered that along with the fading music hall posters she had found a few roulette chips, some loaded dice. She remembered her mother's ravings, which she herself had thought to be dreams.

She wished now that she had never heard Neil Kennelly's name, nor met him. She had only her mother's memory to cling to. But for that she was nothing, and no one. And he was trying to take that away, too. She wondered why.

He said, "I fear I have hurt you by stating the facts of your birth, and what happened after, so baldly. But we Americans are a blunt people, and we speak our minds. We are determined, too."

She was to learn, though she did not know it yet, that what he said was only partly true.

She said, "Mr. Kennelly, I was told that you had a reason for wanting to see me. May I ask what the reason is?"

"I'm an old man, Nealanna," he answered. "You must bear with me. I couldn't change if I want to, and I don't want to. I must tell you my own way." He drew a deep breath. "Yes. We are Americans. But our lineage goes back to sixteenth-century England. My forebears were among the early colonists. We carry a proud name and we are proud of it."

It was unnecessary for him to tell her this. She saw the pride in his face and bearing and heard it in his voice.

He went on slowly, "I have many ties here, mainly through business affairs. Here, and in southern Africa as well. At home, in America, I have a wife, and children."

She sat very still. She knew that he had some reason for telling her all this.

The fire had burned low, and there was an odd chill in the air. She had the sense of being watched by unseen eyes, but there was no one in the room except the white-haired man who sat before her.

His glance flickered at her, gray, sharp, then withdrew. "I explained my interest in your mother, and in you."

"You explained what you did. But not why," she said gently.

Again his gray glance flickered at her. "I told you that sentiment, pity . . ."

"If you wish me to believe that, then I will," she answered. But there was not much conviction in her voice.

He smiled faintly. "The man involved was a man I knew. I did not approve of his behavior. Would you accept that?"

She said painfully, "There was no great love between them, was there? Death did not separate them, did it? He simply left her and went away, didn't he?"

Neil said, "He's dead now."

She nodded. She had somehow expected it. She had known at the moment of her mother's death that she was alone. Now she knew that all that she had believed about herself, her birth and parentage, had been a lie. It was a painful fact to face, and yet she saw that it didn't matter. She was Nealanna Yarrow still. She would continue to be.

He said, "I have a reason for giving you these details about myself, Nealanna. Do you wish to know what it is?"

"Yes. If you please."

"I do please. Thats why I asked Mr. Caroway to tell you about me, and to see that you came to the hotel." He waited, but she said nothing. She was beginning to feel danger. She could not see its outline, but she sensed its presence, just as she still sensed the unseen watching eyes that made the back of her neck prickle.

He said, "I have a favor to ask of you, you see. That is, in a way, it's a favor. And yet, not entirely. It will also benefit you greatly. It will give you a future you don't have."

Now the danger seemed even closer. She had the feeling that she was being pressed into some shadowy corner, held at bay by a ruthless hunter. She said faintly, "I don't understand you."

"No, of course not. How could you? I haven't explained." He leaned forward now. His big shoulders were hunched, his tanned lined face intent.

"I have a son, Nealanna. His name is Gareth. He is twenty-six years old. He has prospects beyond your wildest

24

imaginings. He will be my heir, and the head of the Kennelly family when I die. He is ... I believe that young women find him a comely man. I ask that you ... I suggest ... I want you to consent to be his wife."

When Neil stopped speaking, the room was very still. The logs in the fireplace settled with a series of cracks that sounded as loud as gunshot in the silence.

Nealanna gasped in disbelief. Then she cried, "Oh, no. You can't be serious."

"But I am serious," Neil told her. "I have never been more serious in my life."

She didn't answer him. She lowered her eyes to the hands clasped in her lap, palest white against the rusty black of her skirt. Now she knew with absolute certainty that he must have been telling the truth before. What father would ask that his son and daughter marry in incest? No. Neil Kennelly was not her father. Her father must be, as he had said, in his grave.

Now Neil asked, "Why does it shock you so? You're seventeen. A grown woman by all standards. Surely you've thought of marriage."

She had thought of love, of finding, somewhere, somehow, that other part of herself, which would make her whole. But she couldn't speak of love to Neil Kennelly. She raised her dark eyes to his. "I have not been thinking of marriage, in fact. Nor of marriage to a stranger."

"A stranger? My son?" His lips twisted wryly under his mustache. "Why, I don't see why you should say that exactly. We have had our relationship, have we not?"

"A relationship of pounds and pence," she said softly. "Surely no more than that."

He shrugged his wide shoulders. "It was the best one could do, you know." Then, sharply, "And what are your objections?"

She frowned at him. "They should be quite evident to you, I think."

"I want to hear them nonetheless."

Now she saw the outlines of danger clearly, and knew the shadowy corner in which she stood. She felt a chill at the same time that a warm blush touched her cheeks. She remembered her mother speaking of love through those long drug-induced dreams.

"Well?" he demanded. "If the Jeromes could marry Englishmen, why can't a Yarrow marry an American?"

She said, "But I do not know your son. I do not know him, don't you see?"

She imagined this Gareth to be some monster, comely to women or not. Why else would he need the offices of his father? Why else would his father contract a marriage with the daughter of a low-born dancer, an illegitimate child? If he was what he said he was, then the son should marry high and into greater wealth. Not low, and to nothing.

"You will meet him," Neil told her.

She answered quietly, "I have nothing to offer. I see no reason for such an arrangement."

"You see none. But suppose I do?"

She shrugged, looked into the fire. She said, after a moment, "I'm sorry. I cannot."

He leaned forward, as if the very weight of his body would persuade her. "But you can," he said. "And you will. It is, after all, scarcely more than a few years since all marriages were arranged. In the best families they still are. Among royalty they always will be. I am doing no less, and no more than that."

"But you are not royalty," she told him. "Nor am I."

"I don't know your objections," he said sharply. "Let me hear them so that I may answer them."

"I cannot marry a stranger," she told him. But she was saying she could not marry except for love.

If he understood her, he gave no sign. He said heavily, "I am not asking for what will destroy you, you know. But for what will save you. Where will you go now? What will you do? What life do you see ahead?"

She gave him a sharp look. He was not threatening her directly, nor openly, yet the threat was there. The time of his compassion was over. He would offer help no longer. She had nothing but a few worn garments, the useless contents of the mews cottage. As she weighed that, she realized its unimportance. She owed him much for what he had done for her mother, for her as well. She surely owed him her very life. It was no small debt.

In the face of her thoughtful silence, he sighed. He pulled a leather pouch from his pocket and upended it on the marble-topped table at his elbow. A stream of brilliants tumbled into the lamplight.

"We have much to offer, we Kennellys," he told her.

She raised her eyes to his face. "I am not for sale, Mr. Kennelly."

He shrugged, leaned back. "You must do as I ask."

She drew a deep breath. "I don't care for your gems. But I am beholden to you. And I know of no other way to repay you. All right, Mr. Kennelly, I will marry your son."

Chapter 3

Neil Kennelly rose. He stood looking down at her for a moment. She saw a certain softening in his eyes, and relief in his craggy face. Once again she sensed danger, but he said nothing.

He strode past her, spoke a few quiet words, and then returned to his seat near the sinking fire.

Nealanna, watching him, was at first unaware of the figure in the doorway behind her. But she felt eyes upon her as she had before. She felt the tingle of a direct, and examining stare.

She raised her dark head, and turned, and saw the tall man on the threshold. With the glow of pale light behind him, he appeared to be no more than a shadow, a looming black shadow that fell across her, across her fate, she thought with a shiver.

"This is my son," Neil Kennelly said in a deep warm voice, a voice of pride. "Gareth." Then, "Gareth, this is Nealanna Yarrow, who has just consented to become your wife."

It seemed suddenly to Nealanna that all her known past had been wiped away in this day since her mother's burial.

28

She reminded herself quickly that it didn't matter. The future began now. In this moment. She waited, breath suspended.

Gareth advanced into the room. His dark head was inclined toward her. Green eyes flashed with strange brilliance beneath his dark straight brows. He was as tall as his father, but very straight and lean, his narrow waist accentuated by a tight, thigh-length jacket.

"How do you do?" he said, and without waiting for a response from her, "Is this true? Have you allowed my father to talk you around?"

"Yes. I have agreed." She was startled at the quavery sound of her voice. She made an effort to clear her voice, said, "It is settled."

Now he looked, for a long silent moment, at the gems scattered on the marble-topped table. To Nealanna their brilliant facets seemed dimmed by the green brilliance of his eyes. Then he returned his gaze to her face. "And do you understand the undertaking?"

She gave him a bewildered look. She didn't know his meaning. She couldn't read his impassive expression, nor comprehend his deep uninflected voice. What undertaking was there to understand? She had agreed to marry him. They would be man and wife.

He smiled very faintly, just a tilt at the corners of narrow lips. "There was no coercion?"

"Gareth," Neil interposed. "This is quite unnecessary."

"Forgive me," Gareth retorted. "You will permit her to answer, won't you, Father?"

Neil shrugged, but his mouth was tight under his thick mustache, and his eyes watched her sharply. "As you wish, Gareth."

"Nealanna?" Gareth's bright gaze was on her again.

She found that she couldn't look away from him. It was as if she were mesmerized.

Was this the monster for whom a marriage must be arranged? This rugged and handsome man who could, obviously, have whatever woman he chose, have her and spellbind her with a single steady glance. It was not to be believed that he required his father's offices in such an affair. Then how had all this come about? And why?

"Nealanna?" he repeated. "Can you hear me?"

There was some mockery in his voice that she didn't understand, and that frightened her.

But she said coolly enough, she hoped, "Yes, I hear you. I have been thinking. Was there, you asked, is there, any coercion?"

"And . . ."

"No," she said steadily.

Neil Kennelly had asked of her a favor, a favor was what he had called it, in exchange for what he had done in the past for her mother and for her. He required of her the future that lay ahead of her. But she had had a choice. She could have refused him. She could have ignored debt, and said that she would not marry. They had not really discussed what her life would be without his request. But she had seen a vast yawning emptiness if she refused him. She knew that she had dismissed it, just as she had dismissed his display of the gems. She had decided only that she owed him what he asked of her. There had been no coercion.

Aloud, she repeated, "No."

Gareth pressed, "You're quite sure?"

Neil brought his big hands together with a sharp crack "That's enough of this."

Gareth said, "Then it's decided." He glanced sideways at the winking gems on the table, and turned on his heel and left the room. The door closed sharply behind him.

She didn't know if, in closing the door, he had just closed away the light from the next room, or if it was the absence of himself, of those brilliant green eyes, that made everything about her seem darker, duller.

"He is a fine man, as you'll come to know," Neil said. "You'll never be sorry, Nealanna."

"He seems to have reservations," she said dryly. "I think he is already sorry."

30

"No." Neil seemed to hesitate, then he said, "It is a strained situation for both of you. Time will ease it."

But she wondered. If Gareth had not wanted an arranged marriage, why had he permitted it?

Neil rose to his feet. "Will a day after tomorrow be convenient for you?"

"Will it be convenient for your son?" she retorted.

Neil grinned at her. "I see there's fire in you. You'll do. You'll do very nicely indeed. The Kennellys have always admired fire in a woman."

"But you haven't answered me," she told him.

"It will be convenient," he answered. "Just leave that part to me." Then, "I know that it seems a very short time to you. But I've passage booked on a Cunard ship for day after tomorrow. We will sail immediately after the ceremony."

She stared at him, speechless bewildered. "Sail?" she said at last.

"For home," he told her. "For America."

"But . . ."

"Surely you understood, Nealanna. Where else would you and Gareth live but in his home?"

"I never dreamed . . . you didn't say . . ."

He made an impatient gesture. "I told you that we are Americans. And what difference does it make? You have nothing, nothing to hold you here."

She linked her fingers together, pressed them tight to keep them from trembling. What he said was true, of course. She had nothing to hold her here. Yet the thought of going to a strange land, to live with and among strangers, was frightening.

"You mustn't worry," he told her. "All will be well. Leave everything to me."

There had been no choice but to do so. She soon discovered that he was a man who assumed control, and swept others before him. It made her wonder about Gareth, about the man she was to marry. The brief glimpse she had had of him did not suggest to her that he was so easily led.

She didn't see him again until the very day they were joined in wedlock.

Neil said, "We'll have a cold supper in the dining room downstairs before I return you to your home." He added, "If that suits you," and then, not waiting for an answer, "And there is a couple waiting for us with whom I want you to become acquainted."

Her head turned slightly so that she could see the door through which Gareth had gone before, taking all brightness with him.

"No," Neil told her. "I think he'll not join us tonight." He took up her cloak and held it as if weighing it. "A skimpy and old-fashioned thing," he said. "You'll need a proper coat. And other clothes, of course. Between now and the day after tomorrow, you shall be very busy."

"I have what I require," she told him stiffly.

"Hardly. One look at you says what you have, and what you don't have as well. The wife of Gareth Kennelly must have a complete wardrobe."

"I am in mourning," she reminded him.

"Yes," he answered impatiently. "Yes, I know. But that has nothing to do with it."

Downstairs, in the main dining room, he led her across the thick mossy carpet, under the glowing chandeliers, to a round candlelit table. Two people were seated there.

They were, Nealanna thought, a couple out of a painting. The woman was in her late twenties, stunningly beautiful. The man was just over thirty, and exceedingly handsome.

Neil said, "Nanette, I am happy to present Nealanna Yarrow, who is to be Gareth's wife." And to Nealanna, "This is Mrs. Gordon, an old friend of ours from home, and her husband, Mr. Jason Gordon."

Nealanna managed to murmur a greeting to both of them, though taken aback somewhat by the effusiveness of her welcome.

Nanette Gordon had a sweet, open smile that showed very white teeth. Her carefully-coiffed hair was brown with a touch of russet. She wore a blue gown with a high collar that was elaborately embroidered with tiny pearls. She said in a low gentle voice, "I'm happy to meet you at last. It's been such a mystery to us. But now we know, and with what delight!"

Jason Gordon was a man of medium-height and heavy build. He was clean-shaven but with long brown sideburns. He had brown eyes and a square stubborn chin that softened when he smiled. He smiled now, saying, "Nealanna, this is a joyous occasion for all of us," and rising to take her hand for a moment.

What mystery there was, and why it was a joyous occasion for the Gordons, Nealanna was not able to determine.

Neil seated her, then himself. He gestured for the hovering waiter, and took his time studying the menu. When he had done so to his satisfaction, he ordered without consulting the others.

Then, and only then, he said, "Gareth sends his regrets. He was unable to join us. But I felt it was important that you meet Nealanna now." His gray eyes were fixed on Nanette. "The marriage will be a day after tomorrow, and then, of course, we sail for home. So there is much to be done."

"And it will be, with pleasure," Nanette answered. She smiled warmly at Nealanna, "And meanwhile we'll become acquainted."

Jason asked, "And what can I do to help?"

Neil grinned. "I think it is mainly women's work."

"Just leave it to me," Nanette assured him. "I have been looking forward to it. And it will be very good for me, I know."

She had, obviously, been told about Nealanna. Been told, even before Nealanna had seen Neil. But what Nanette had been told, Nealanna couldn't imagine. She had no opportunity to ask.

Jason began to talk about their travels in England. The conversation went on over salmon and white wine, and then Stilton cheese with great platters of grapes.

After coffee, Nanette apologized, saying to Nealanna, "I must go see my children to bed now. But I'll meet you here as early as you can be ready tomorrow morning." Then, leaning heavily on her husband's arm, she left the dining room.

Neil, perhaps seeing Nealanna's gaze follow the couple, said quietly, "She has been ill. The trip was as much for her health as anything else. But she is quite recovered now, I would say."

Nealanna nodded. She supposed that explained Nanette's pallor and excessive slenderness, and wondered from what sickness she had suffered.

Neil offered no further comment. He rose, led her outside, and helped her on with her cloak.

On the way back to the cottage in a hansom cab, she said, "Mr. Kennelly, I think I would like to speak to your son before . . . before . . ."

"Are you intending to withdraw now?" he demanded sharply.

"No," she said.

"Well then?"

"What are you afraid of?" she asked. "What will happen if I speak to him? What will he say or do that troubles you?"

"I'm troubled by nothing. Or nearly nothing. But you won't have the time. Nor will he."

She wished that like Neil Kennelly she could say that nothing troubled her. But it wouldn't have been true. Nameless fears assailed her through the next two days.

The mews cottage when she entered it that evening was filled with whispering shadows. Even the lamp light did not disperse them. She spent hours examining what there was to take with her, and then she went to bed. But sleep wouldn't come, and she spent hours picturing the lean hard planes of Gareth's face.

The next morning she met Nanette, and was swept into an orgy of picking, choosing, and trying on. That afternoon they dealt with the contents of the cottage. Aside from a few clothes, Nealanna left everything behind except a small silver brooch that had been her mother's, and a small sepia photograph that had caught a happy and smiling Anna Yarrow at the age of twenty-five.

Two days after she saw Gareth Kennelly for the first time, she saw him again in the study of the parson who was to perform the ceremony.

She hadn't quite caught the name of the tall thin blond young man, and she doubted that he had caught hers. She was certain of it when, during the service, he asked, "Do you . . ." and paused, looking suddenly anguished.

Then Gareth said, with a glint of amusement in his eyes, "Nealanna Yarrow, sir."

". . . Nealanna Yarrow," the parson repeated dutifully, "take this man . . ."

She didn't hear the rest of it. She was intent on repressing the shameful laughter that had risen to her lips. She managed to cover her mouth with the white roses Neil Kennelly had given her.

By the time she had control of her wayward emotions, the ceremony was over.

Gareth leaned down to her, pressed his lips firmly to her cheek. It was a public kiss, without warmth or passion. And yet she felt an immediate response to it, a swift deep pang that surprised her so that she pulled back from him.

She did not see his reaction. Nanette and Jason seized her, hugged her.

Then Neil, no longer smiling, said, "Bless you both. Nealanna and Gareth. And may you be fruitful."

"You can hardly be ill," Gareth said, frowning at her. "We've barely weighed anchor."

She set her lips. "I am not ill."

"But you're very pale. Would you like some wine?"

"No. Thank you." She sat on the small gilt chair before the dressing table. In the mirror, she saw her reflection, her white face, her eyes large and dark and shining over prominent cheekbones, the folds of her dark green velvet

35.

gown, her wedding gown. Beyond all that, she saw him standing near the door.

He seemed to dwarf the stateroom, to draw the walls in, to overshadow the luxurious appointments. It was a place like none she had ever seen, nor dreamed of, in her life. She wished that she could appreciate it, appreciate the adventure that lay before her. She had never dreamed that she would be on a ship, that she would sail to America. Yet it was true. It was happening. She felt nothing but a flutter in her chest that made breathing difficult.

If she were alone, she would forget it in exploration. She would open all the small cupboards and drawers. She would examine the fittings. But Gareth stood watching her, dark brows in a quizzical curve. She found that she couldn't ignore him.

Now he said, "It will soon be time to go up to dinner."

"I don't believe that I care for any," she answered. "Perhaps I'll just stay here and rest."

He smiled faintly. "We could do that, of course. It's probably quite customary for a bride and her groom to miss the first meal aboard. I'm sure no one would remark on it."

She felt the blush rise in her cheeks. She said quickly, "No, no. I imagine that your father, the Gordons, expect us. We should go."

"That doesn't matter," he answered. "We're grown people. We can do as we please."

She nodded, though she wondered.

She had gone to see Mr. Caroway at his office, and told her plans to him. His pudgy face had seemed relieved as he listened to her. He peered at her through his glasses, resting his round chin on his collar. But at last, he asked uneasily, "Will it be all right, Nealanna? Does this arrangement please you?"

"I chose it myself," she had answered him. "And you, Mr. Davies, too, will be paid for all your help."

"That's done," Mr. Caroway protested. "Mr. Kennelly . . . this morning . . ."

She bade him goodbye, sent her regards to the elegant

36

physician. She wrote to Widow Hart, explaining all, but thinking of the cat called Poo. She took nothing with her except for the brooch and the picture. And now she was here, on the way to America. Had all this been of her own choosing? Or had she been guided, mysteriously, through every step? Had Neil Kennelly led her to this very moment?

Gareth said, "I do think you might begin to get ready now."

"Yes," she said, and took a deep breath. "I would like some privacy, Gareth."

"Do you realize that that is the first time you've used my name?" he asked.

She blinked at him. "What? What do you mean?"

"I had begun to think I would be 'you' and nothing but 'you' for the rest of our lives together."

"I hadn't realized it," she answered. "I'm sorry."

"You needn't be. It doesn't really matter." He went to the door. "I'll give you the privacy you require."

She changed quickly, aware of the slow heave of the boat, but untroubled by it. She was just fastening her gown when he was back.

He offered her, dangling from the tip of his forefinger, a string of green stones set in small gold links. "Your wedding gift," he said.

She touched it, held it, and then realized that it was not made of the colored bits of glass she had supposed. These were emeralds, a clear shining and unflawed green, emeralds the same color as his eyes. These must be as precious as those stones that Neil had flung so casually on the table the night of their meeting.

She thrust the necklace back into Gareth's hand. "No, no, thank you," she said.

His dark brows rose. "No, thank you? Is that what you say to your wedding gift?"

"I'm sorry again." She drew a deep breath. "They are too fine, Gareth. Too valuable. Suppose I lose them?"

"Suppose you do."

"But how would I ever replace . . ."

"You wouldn't need to replace them. I would do that."
He moved close to her. Before she could stop him, he
slipped the string around her throat. His fingers brushed
the back of her neck, her piled-high black curls, as he
fastened it. "There." He gave her an approving smile as
she turned. "Gareth Kennelly's wife always wears jewels.
You'll have more of them than you'll know what to do
with."

She slid a glance at the mirror, saw her face, too pale,
still, and below them, the glow of the stones. She
whispered, "Thank you," knowing that wasn't enough to
wipe out her previous refusal.

But he had already turned away, to reach for the door.
With his hand on it, he swung back, "Before we go up, in
order that you may enjoy your evening, let me relieve
your mind. You have nothing to fear from me, Nealanna.
Nothing at all. Do you understand me?"

She wasn't sure that she did understand. But she nodded
all the same.

He waited a moment, then went on, his eyes glinting
with amusement, "It is something that would never occur
to my father, of course. And if it did, I doubt that he
would discuss it with you."

She let her breath out in a long sigh. Now she was sure
that she did understand him. He meant that she must not
fear that he would make a husband's demands on her. A
kind of blankness settled over her mind. Why had he
agreed to marry her? Why did he need a wife who was
not a wife? But she said quickly, "Yes, yes, and *you* need
not discuss it with me either."

He laughed aloud at her retort. "Why, you sound like
Queen Victoria's own. But it is much more interesting to
talk about sex than about politics or culture or anything
else. Especially since, for the first time since we met, I see
some signs of life in you."

She raised her eyes to his and said coolly, "We are married now. You ask me to wear your jewels, and I am
wearing them. If you ask anything else of me I will try to
please you. That was part of our bargain, and I will live
38

up to it. But I will not talk to you on this subject. Even though it amuses you. Because it does not, and cannot, amuse me."

He laughed again, said lightly, "Why, then, it's all settled, isn't it? Then let's go up to dinner."

Chapter 4

By the end of the crossing, Nealanna felt that she knew Gareth no better than she had the first time she saw him.

He was unfailingly courteous, though sometimes she found his sardonic humor trying. He had been, on those days when the rough seas brought her to bed in anguish, quietly kind in looking after her needs. He allowed her the privacy of the stateroom when she wanted it, and complete privacy of her person.

She found herself remembering the touch of his lips on her cheek when they were wed. To her embarrassment, she felt a certain pique that he made no approach to her. She couldn't believe that he intended to live as a celibate, yet he gave no sign that he intended otherwise. So she understood even less, as the voyage ended, why he had permitted his father to arrange his marriage. That Neil Kennelly had some ulterior motive, she was certain. That it was a motive Gareth shared, she was also certain. But she could not, for all the time she spent in idle speculation, figure out what that motive might be.

Neil, and Gareth, too, had both prepared her for what was to come.

They had, together, and separately, gone over her life with her in such detail as made her head whirl, and made her suspicions even more intense. She had had so little to tell them. Hers had been quiet days with Widow Hart in Cornwall, days of chores, and school in town. She had met no one in London aside from Mr. Caroway and Mr. Davies in the three months she had cared for her mother. But it seemed that Neil and Gareth felt they must know all of it. Neil's dour face, as she told him, reminded her that he had intended to provide more than she had received, but she felt no bitterness for her mother. Anna Yarrow had done what she had to do.

And then Gareth told Nealanna that it was not necessary for anyone to know that she and Gareth had only just met. Therefore she would say they had become acquainted roughly a year before, but she, being only sixteen then, and still in school, had not been ready to consider marriage. She was to say her mother had recently died, her father many years before. For the rest, she could tell the absolute truth in all things.

"In all things?" she had asked Gareth.

"Why not?"

"Do you know the facts of my birth?" she demanded, still remembering the sound of Neil's voice when he denied that she was his bastard.

"That is your business," he retorted, "and I don't care about them. Nor should you. For neither will anyone else."

It was a good thing that she had been prepared.

Nanette Gordon was determined to be friendly. By that, she meant, as women often did, Nealanna supposed, that they must exchange confidences.

Nanette said, smiling over the head of her five-year-old son, Jason II, who was always called Jay to distinguish him from his father, "Jason and I fell in love at first sight," and waited.

Her pallor-touched face was animated now, and the droop to her lips, the heavy look of her blue eyes, some-

41

times seen that showed the ill health of which Neil had spoken, was gone.

Jay, chubby and square jawed, with his father's brown eyes, sat quietly listening, and playing with the long strand of pearls at his mother's throat, shielded by a heavy plaid blanket from the sea wind that blew steadily.

"Love at first sight," Nealanna repeated. "How exciting. When did you meet? And where?"

"Oh, we met at Emerald Station. It must have been seven years ago. And what about you and Gareth?"

"Emerald Station? And where is that?" Nealanna asked, ignoring Nanette's question.

Nanette's blue eyes widened. "You mean you don't know? They didn't tell you?" She leaned back in her deck chair and laughed. "That's the Kennellys . . . Emerald Station is their estate."

"An odd name for an estate," Nealanna commented.

"Not so odd as you may think. It's named for the place in Kasai where Mr. Kennelly made his fortune out of the diamond mines."

Nealanna thought of the gems tossed on the table the first time she had met Neil Kennelly, of the emerald necklace Gareth had insisted she wear. Emerald Station.

Nanette said, "You have an experience before you. It is quite a place."

"In what way?"

"You'll see." Nanette paused. Then, "And how did you and Gareth meet?"

"It was in London. At the home of a Mr. Caroway. He was my mother's solicitor, and knew Mr. Kennelly. That was last year some time."

"Oh," Nanette said. "You met just last year, was it?" And the smile was quite gone from her lips.

Jay wriggled within her tightening arms, and kicked out in mute protest.

Noting Nanette's face, Jay's sudden restlessness, Nealanna wondered if she had already made some mistake. Could she have managed somehow to say the wrong thing?

42

"Poor Gareth . . . was he broody when you first laid eyes on him?"

"Broody?" Nealanna glanced at Nanette sideways, seeking a clue in the pretty but pale face. "Broody?"

"Well, you know. He can be very withdrawn at times, can't he?"

"It's his nature," Nealanna said firmly. "I expect he's always been that way. Thinking of other matters. And, at least, he was no different then from now. Why should he have been?"

Nanette did not answer directly. She said, as if thinking of something else, "Yes, I remember that trip. They did a whole tour of Europe. Three months." Then she smiled again, "And you, I suppose you always dreamed of falling instantly in love with a tall dark American who would carry you away from all your kith and kin . . ."

"I have none, as you know," Nealanna answered.

"Of course." Nanette's face sobered. "I do know. I was teasing a bit." She hurried on. "He's a good man, Gareth. And I know you'll both be happy."

Nealanna did not reply to her assurance. She wondered why Nanette felt impelled to make it to a bride. As if she knew of some reason why it might not prove to be so.

Instead she asked, "What of the other Kennellys, Nanette?"

"But Gareth has surely spoken of his brothers and his sister," Nanette protested.

Nealanna made herself smile. "You know how men are. They say the names and think they've said it all. And I should so like to have some idea . . ."

"Men, yes. And especially Gareth, I suppose." Nanette laughed softly, and ruffled Jay's brown hair. "I hope to train my boy differently." Then, "Well, let's see. There is Alicia, the only girl, very much attached to Gareth. She's nineteen, a bit of a madcap, and a tomboy, from having grown up among the three boys, I suppose. She's sweet, of course, poor thing, but unpredictable. And then there are the boys. Faran is next after Gareth. A quiet boy, who has just discovered romance, I suspect. He's twenty years old.

Jennings is the youngest, and seventeen, though some days you might think he's only seven. He's that changeable and always in conflict with his father. Faran is rather bookish, and greatly interested in the flying machine. He predicts it will be accomplished, though everyone knows that if God intended men to fly He would have provided them with wings. On the other hand, Jennings is a bit of a wanderer, like his father in that, I suppose, and settles to thinking of nothing." Nanette smiled. "Now. Is that sufficient?"

But Nealanna asked, "And Mrs. Kennelly?" for though Gareth, and his father, too, had mentioned the lady, they had said little about her.

Nanette answered, "Mary Kennelly is very sweet, very quiet. If you fear her as a mother-in-law you make a real mistake. She will trouble you in no way."

But again Nealanna sensed something withheld, some private thought which Nanette was not putting into words. That made her wonder even more about Mary Kennelly.

But now Jay said plaintively, "I'm cold. I want to go down. I want to play with Doe." And his jaw squared with his father's stubbornness.

Nanette laughed, but held him firmly, "No, Jay. Doe is with Lolly. When Lolly comes then you'll see Doe."

"Is the baby napping?" Nealanna asked, referring to Doe, four years old, more properly named Dora, who was the miniature image of her mother.

"Supposedly. But I think that Lolly is a somewhat indulgent governess." Nanette grinned. "So far at least she indulges me. Which is more than many a mother can say about the woman who raises her children for her. We are lucky to have found her." Nanette's grin faded. "And she is lucky to have found us, I think. She was a scullery maid at the hotel. Just sixteen, you know. It will be a great opportunity for her to come with us. And as for me," she sighed, "I find it taxes me . . ."

Jay wriggled from beneath the blanket, thrust out his small arms, "Neala, take me?" he inquired.

She laughed, allowed him to scramble from his mother's lap to hers.

44

Nanette looked at her, at Jay nestling his brown silken head to her shoulder. "How good that looks, Nealanna. As if, already, you had your first son. I hope it will happen soon. It would bring much joy to the Kennellys. And they deserve it. They need it."

Once again Nealanna noted the odd tone of Nanette's voice, but, more important to her, was her struggle for composure. She could hardly think of having a son. Not now. Perhaps never. Suddenly Jay's warm weight was unbearable to her.

And then a shadow fell over her.

She looked up.

Gareth was there, the wind tousling his dark hair into unruly waves.

Nanette cried, "Why, Gareth, won't you join us?"

"No," he said absently.

He stared down at Nealanna with a gaze so intense that she became uncomfortable. Her arms tightened around Jay, though she wished him gone, and the boy squealed his displeasure.

Nanette asked, "Did you wish to speak to Nealanna alone then?"

"Yes," Gareth said.

She rose, laughing, and held out her arms for her son. "Come along, Jay. We'll go find Lolly and Doe. I believe the groom has designs on his bride."

Nealanna gave her a stiff smile as she moved away down the deck, but Gareth hardly noticed that she was gone. Except that he sat down in the chair she had just vacated.

"That was neatly done," Nealanna observed. "You might have hurt her feelings."

He shrugged. "She knows me."

"But I do not."

"You will."

"And what are you staring at, Gareth?"

He dropped his green gaze to his hands. "You're no longer as pale as you were."

"The sea air," she retorted.

"It becomes you."

"Thank you for the compliment."

He shrugged again. Then he raised his eyes to hers. "That was a nice sentimental little picture you made. You and the boy."

"He is a lovely boy," she answered, knowing what he meant, but refusing to acknowledge that.

"Was it deliberate, Nealanna?"

"Was what deliberate?"

He leaned back, his eyes bright with amusement. "You're fencing with me. You know just what I mean."

"I do not," she said hotly, "and I would appreciate it if you would not always talk in riddles. I wouldn't like to think that I shall spend the rest of my life being puzzled by what you say to me."

"It could happen," he said softly. "I've seen it before."

"Only if you are determined that it should," she told him.

"The picture ... you and the boy ... did you do that deliberately?" The glint of amusement was gone from his eyes now. His mouth looked tight, the corners drawn in, and muscles showed suddenly in his jaw.

She folded her hands in her lap, and the diamonds in her wedding ring winked at her like small tear-filled eyes. "Are you suggesting to me that if I take a strange child in my arms I am offering a reproach to you?"

"Reproach? No. Not quite that."

"Then what, if I may ask."

"You may ask." He got to his feet. "But I shall not answer."

She glared at his retreating back. She knew perfectly well that he had asked her if she were reproaching him for maintaining a marriage that was not a marriage. But was he suggesting that she had tried to seduce him by offering him the image of her as a mother? This reminded her that Nanette had said the Kennellys would be filled with joy at the birth of Gareth's son, that they needed such joy and deserved it. All felt happy to have grandchildren. But why need? Why deserve?

She sighed to herself. These were more vexing questions to which she had no answers, and saw no way of learning them either.

The following day the ship made its way into New York harbor. A gray mist shrouded the Statue of Liberty's upraised arm and head.

She stood on the deck with Gareth, straining for her first glimpse of the famous city.

Far far below there were masses of people. Men in caps, women in shawls, weeping, laughing, gesticulating, shouting in languages she didn't understand. She had not even known they were on the ship. She mentioned it to Gareth.

He said, "Immigrants from Europe. They think the streets are paved with gold, but they'll find that gold hard to come by."

"But it will be better than what they left behind," she said softly.

He looked down at her. "Yes. And I hope it will be the same for you."

The ship soon docked. The Kennellys and Gordons moved quickly through the landing formalities. Two carriages carried the party and its luggage across the bustling city to the railroad yards where it boarded the Kennelly private car.

The sights and sound of America had made her dizzy, and the wealth which surrounded Neil Kennelly startled her.

She was relieved to sink into the upholstered seat of the car, to look from the draped window, sipping a sweet wine, as the miles went by.

Gareth sat beside her, pointing out the sights, but she retained nothing of what he said. Soon the city gave way to the stillness of countryside, and the rolling hills and neat forests and gray sky reminded her of the journey when she had come up to London from Cornwall for the first time.

"We'll be there at twilight," Gareth said. "And then you'll meet the family."

"Are you looking forward to being at home?" she asked.

"No." He folded one long leg over the other and leaned back.

It was a relaxed posture, but she felt tension in his body.

"Have you been away long, Gareth?"

"Not very long. What do you ask?"

"I'm making conversation," she retorted. "Would you prefer that I be still?"

"No. Go on. You have a pleasant voice." He didn't smile, but she saw something flicker in his eyes.

"I can hardly go on when you say 'no' to whatever I ask, and then contribute nothing of your own."

"Perhaps I have nothing to contribute," he suggested.

She gave a vexed sigh. "Never mind then. Let's have no conversation. I find that I'm tired anyway."

"Tired," he said. "Barely married, and my dear wife already confesses to being tired. How then will you feel after a year, or ten, or twenty?"

"I can't look ahead that far," she told him. And then, somehow, before she could stop herself, "Gareth, why did you allow your father to make you marry me?"

"Be quiet," he said. He leaned so close to her that she felt the hard tension of his shoulder, the warmth of his breath on her cheek. She thought of his kiss. "Never speak of it. Never think of it." His voice was rough, frightening. But it was very low, too low for the others, gathered now at the buffet near the end of the car, to hear. "Never. Do you understand me?" he went on. And then he laughed, "Why, my dear, I married you for love. What other reason could there be?"

For love . . .

They should have been sweet words, and sweet sentiments, spoken by a man to his young wife. They fell on Nealanna's ears like a curse.

She shrank back from him and shut her eyes. "No," she whispered. "That's cruel. And there's no need to be."

She felt his hand settle on hers, clasp her fingers tight

enough to make her wedding ring pain her. She felt his bulk shift closer to her. She opened her eyes to find his face inches from her.

"If I intended cruelty, there was need for it," he said very gently. "But forget it, Nealanna. You'll learn that I often speak without thinking."

"Is that when you speak the truth?" she asked.

"You'll have plenty of time to learn that, too," he answered, and got to his feet and walked away.

The two carriages had pulled up before a low sprawling white house that was set in a huge grove of towering blue spruce. Light glowed behind lace-curtained windows. The drivers were busy unloading sea trunks and carrying them up the narrow brick walk that led to the front door.

Nanette was saying, "Oh, Jason, I am so glad to be home at last. It was a lovely journey, and I do thank you, my love," but her mouth had begun to droop and her pallor deepen. Then, with a forced smile, she turned to Nealanna, "You will visit soon, of course. It's an easy trip by carriage. I'll arrange with my dressmaker . . ."

Gareth interposed, "It will take time for us to settle in, Nanette. But we will see you soon."

Nealanna took Nanette's small cold hand in hers. "Thank you. Thank you for everything."

"We're not saying 'goodbye," Nanette cried, and stepped, with Jason's help, down from the carriage, while Lolly, slim and hardly larger than her charges, it seemed, led them toward the lighted house.

Nealanna looked back, waving. The last she saw of the Gordons they were bunched at the front door, with Nanette leaning on Jason's arm.

Moments later, the carriage, turned into the main street of Bellingham. It was called Maine Avenue, Gareth told her. She saw a few shops, several short blocks of neat white houses, a brightly lighted public house, which Gareth explained was called a saloon. Then they passed a place called Angler's Inn, a narrow four-story building, from which shouts of laughter trailed them along the road. It was the town's only hotel, Gareth explained, a stopping place for drummers who paused overnight in Bellingham, but respectable enough for all that, though the Kennellys, he made it quite clear, never went there.

Then they were in the open countryside, the horses trotting uphill, so that the baggage thudded, and their bodies jolted.

Neil said, "This is the beginning of a new life for you both." He divided a long steady gray glance between Gareth and Nealanna. "I want you to remember that. Forget the past. That is what we must all do. We must forget the past."

Gareth nodded, without speaking.

To Nealanna, there seemed some special urgency in her father-in-law's words, a menacing urgency she didn't understand. She wondered at it, and peered at him sideways. But his hard brown face was expressionless and he said no more. He sat quietly, his big head sunk between his wide shoulders, his hands in their leather gauntlets folded into fists on his knees.

The carriage sped along the roadway under lowering dark skies. Clouds thick and black had gathered in the twilight. They crossed a ring of small hills and entered into a valley. Vast fields, brown and sere, rolled away into the distance.

They slowed, then made a turn past two huge pillars of granite, gate posts without a gate. Like a huge banner hung between them, there was a scrolled wrought-iron sign, saying Emerald Station.

Emerald Station, Nealanna thought, with a sudden shiver. Emerald Station. Yet there was nothing of green here. Only a long curving avenue, over which tall trees arched, like black skeletons against the darkening sky.

It was a fancy that did not divert Nealanna. She turned her eyes, and her thoughts from that, to consider the spreading dun of the fields, and then the house came suddenly into view.

It was very large, of a dark gray stone that could have been cut from the sky that hung over it. It had three storeys. It was a fortress without battlements or gun emplacements, but a fortress just the same. Its windows were spaced wide apart, and were long and narrow, unrelieved by any decoration. Blank glass seemed to glare down at her. Its wide door was heavy, of some dark wood she didn't recognize.

The carriage rolled to a stop.

"We're home," Gareth said.

The door swung open. Neil stepped down, then Gareth.

He offered her his hand in assistance. But she paused, half-bent in the narrow opening, to look again at the house that loomed above her, cast its dark shadow over her, as if in evil omen.

"Come down," Gareth said. "Why are you staring? Doesn't the place suit you?"

She accepted his hand, stepped lightly to the ground. She didn't answer him. She couldn't. Words would not form on her dry lips. Breath would not pass her throat.

She wished only that she had never come to Emerald Station.

Chapter 5

It was a wish that she was to make to herself silently, in fear and anguish, many times. But she did not know that then. She banished the dread from her conscious thought, and went with Gareth up the eight stone steps to the door.

It jerked open, reminding Nealanna of a great mouth ready to engorge the unwary.

That was another fancy that didn't please her. She shivered a little and braced herself for what was to come.

What did come was a slender young woman in flying skirts, bursting with joyful laughter.

It was, Nealanna knew at once, Gareth's sister Alicia.

She was taller by several inches than Nealanna, and had Gareth's long, lean, bony frame. Her hair was dark, too, brushed high off her forehead, and fell to her shoulders in undisciplined waves, a style that would, at home, have been inappropriate to her age.

She brushed a quick kiss on her father's cheek, and then threw herself at Gareth, crying, "You're home. You're home at last. I began to think it would never happen. I . . ."

Gareth seemed to evade her sweeping gestures. He

smiled, stepped back, holding her away from him by one bony shoulder.

"Leave off," Neil said irritably. "Where are the others?"

But Gareth continued to smile, and reached for Nealanna's hand now. "Alicia, I want you to meet Nealanna, my wife."

The joyful laughter faded out of Alicia's face. She stood frozen. Only her eyes moved, eyes as gray as Neil's, but shadowy, with strange depths to them, Nealanna thought. Momentarily, there was no expression on her long narrow face, the high cheekbones graven, the long mouth still. But then, she smiled, though the gray eyes did not. "Your wife, Gareth. My sister. What a charming surprise this is."

She flashed an odd look at Gareth, then turned away, and went running back through the foyer toward where there was light. "Mother," she cried. "Mother, come quick. And where's Faran? Where's Jennings? You must all meet Gareth's bride."

Nealanna's memory of the next few moments always consisted of fragmentary impressions. There was the chandelier which was suddenly alight as she stood beneath it, as if it had flashed on of its own accord. Yet she knew that must be impossible. One of the servants must have been there with a taper to set all those prisms aglow.

There was the rich carpet under her feet, a soft warm brown, and laid over it, large rugs of green and red, forming pools of contrast in the light.

There were the panelled walls, dark, heavy, and the mirror that seemed to hold all their reflections, to hold them imprisoned within its thick gold frame.

Strange carvings leered down at her, elongated black faces with blind eyes and jagged teeth. A great shield painted in odd designs, smelling of cured leather hung among them. And in the corner, a heavy tree trunk slowly resolved itself into a carved figure of a grimacing man.

But mostly, there was the touch of Gareth's hand on her shoulder. His touch freeing her from the reflection, and freeing himself, too. The touch of his hand as he guided her down the hallway, past the wide curving staircase, to the big room, where, beyond Alicia, she saw a group awaiting her approach, a group that was as motionless as if cut from stone. A group that was faceless, without expression, and without life. Two young men, and an elderly woman.

But then, Alicia cried shrilly, "Mother, Faran, Jennings . . . look! Isn't she pretty? Isn't she a little doll? Look at her, look at Gareth's wife."

Neil said gruffly, "Alicia, will you be still? The din you make would awaken the dead."

It was his voice that seemed to melt the frozen group, to touch it with sudden life.

Mary Kennelly gave a small cry, and hurried forward, making quick gesture of welcome at Neil and Gareth, but directing herself at Nealanna.

"My dear girl . . . I am so . . . so overwhelmed to meet you. So happy. It is such a wonderful surprise. Gareth never said . . . my husband didn't write . . . we never dreamed . . ."

She was a small, frail woman. Her gray hair was braided into a neat coronet that seemed to suit the shape of her head. Her eyes were dark, and shadowed by dark rings. She wore a high-necked dress of gray silk and over it a black shawl. Tiny red rubies dangled from her ears, reminding Nealanna of the Kennelly gems.

"You are not only overwhelmed," Neil said dryly, "but you are overwrought. You leave our Nealanna speechless."

"Nealanna," Mary Kennelly repeated. "A lovely name." And then, "Welcome, Nealanna."

But the younger girl wondered if she heard, or only imagined, a faint question in Mary's tentative voice.

"Jennings," Neil said.

Gray eyes met Nealanna's, crinkled at the corners. Jennings grinned broadly, "Pretty bad, I know, to be trotted out for family inspection. But it won't take long, Nealanna. Then you can relax and forget about us, and concentrate on Gareth again."

He was of medium height, and very plump, with round

rosy cheeks and a rosebud mouth. He looked as if he might not have lost his baby fat as yet but some time would. He wore a red embroidered vest and narrow black trousers stuffed into riding boots.

She managed to smile at him, to say she was glad to know him.

"Faran," Neil continued then.

Faran was not quite as tall as Gareth, but built along the same lean lines. He had the same dark hair, too. But his eyes were tawny, almost yellow. Already there was a noticeable frown line between his brows. That accentuated his serious look. But he smiled, said, "Hello, Nealanna. You've come a long way, haven't you?" as he looked her carefully up and down.

With the introductions done, the group was wrapped in silence, an odd waiting silence. It seemed to Nealanna that they were like actors who had, each one of them, forgotten, or never known, their lines. Or as if they had once again been captured as reflections in the foyer mirror.

She allowed her eyes to move from face to face. Alicia's. Mary Kennelly's. Jennings'. Faran's.

She saw no joy, no welcome, in spite of the words that had been spoken. She saw nothing but that odd, disconcerting pause.

Then Mary said, "Oh, we must have you settled at once." And turned to Neil. "Your things?"

"Henry has moved the carriage into the courtyard, I should think. He'll be unloading from there. It will be a little while."

"Of course," she murmured, and looked at him, as if awaiting instructions.

Gareth said, "I'm sure Nealanna would like to have a wash, and a rest."

"Of course," Mary repeated. "If only we'd known ... we'd surely have prepared ... as it is, I don't quite ..."

"My apartment is ready, isn't it?" Gareth asked.

"Oh, Gareth," Alicia laughed. "It has been ready since the day you left, and surely you know that. Why, I've aired it three times weekly myself, lest the mustiness set in."

He smiled at her. Once again he touched Nealanna. "Then suppose we go up," he said. "Dinner at seven as usual?"

"Oh, yes, as usual," his mother answered. "And Brooke and Avis will be here. Oh, how pleased and excited they will be . . ."

"Why pleased?" Alicia demanded. "I should think they would be pained. It will be a terrible reminder to them. I . . ."

Gareth's fingers tightened. He led Nealanna into the foyer, past the grinning black masks, and toward the steps, having totally ignored Alicia's question.

Nealanna wasn't even certain that he had actually heard it. But she had. She had heard it very clearly, and as she went up the steps with Gareth, feeling the blind eyes of the carvings follow her, she wondered who Brooke and Avis were. And why they would be pained rather than pleased at news of her marriage to Gareth.

He said, nodding at the black masks, "Mementoes of Africa. My father brought them back. There are all sorts of things scattered through the house."

"Does he still take many trips there?"

"No. It's unnecessary now."

"But how . . ."

"The mines are a part of the combine. That's what it was set up for. To deal with the business. We leave it that way."

She nodded. But as she went with Gareth down the long, gaslit hall, she asked, "Brooke and Avis? Who are they? Friends of yours, Gareth? Or of Alicia's? Or . . ."

"The Maradines," he explained. "Friends of the family, and our nearest neighbors, the only ones in the valley. Why do you ask?"

"But Alicia . . ."

"Never mind my young sister."

He stopped before a white door, cocked his head, listening to the sound of bustle from within. "That will be Henry with the trunks, I expect."

He pushed the door open. "Henry?"

A woman came out of an inner room. "Gareth! It's you! And how fine you look, too."

She had red hair, with wings of white at her temples. Her eyes were a blazing blue in the pink curves of her face. She was about thirty-eight years old, but her manner was young. She wore a black cotton dress that was relieved only by a small white collar and white cuffs at her wrists. She turned to Nealanna, examined her frankly from head to toe, and then her smile widened as if she liked what she saw. "I'm Evanne Borden, in case Gareth hasn't yet told you. I am the housekeeper here. Henry and Moira, my children, help out. A small staff, but sufficient. We're all glad to have you here, Mrs. Kennelly."

"That won't do," Gareth laughed. "Mrs. Kennelly indeed. She'll never know who you're talking to if you call her that."

"Why, she must have practice at it, as does any bride," Evanne retorted.

Nealanna smiled, said, "You will call me Nealanna, I hope." She liked the woman at first sight. There was warmth here, and a fullness in the smile and the voice. And more, there was something in Gareth that responded in a new way to what Nealanna had seen before. She decided that she must learn what it was.

"We'll make you comfortable, never fear," Evanne said. "Though it may take some time. She surveyed the room in which they stood together. "Just you ask, my dear girl. Whatever you wish. And if my Moira can serve you, dress your hair . . ."

"Oh, no," Nealanna protested. "I certainly need no personal maid, but thank you."

Evanne's smile broadened even more, showing both approval and appreciation, "There now, I won't argue with you, and I won't even pretend that I'm not relieved as well. We're just the three of us, me, Moira and Henry, you see, to run this big house. So that you understand, one chore less is one chore less."

Gareth said, "Thank you, Evanne."

"For nothing," she bridled, "What nonsense." She winked at Nealanna. "And if you're lonesome for home, child, then come and seek me out. I guess you're no more than seventeen, a year older than my Moira. So I know girls. Just find me if you want help or company." On that note, and chuckling, she left, closing the door gently behind her.

"A good woman," Nealanna said. She unpinned her flowered hat, put aside the coat with its trim of fur at collar and hem that Nanette had chosen for her.

"Yes," Gareth agreed shortly. He jerked his head toward an open dorway. "Your bedroom is in there."

She waited, breath held.

He jerked his head to a doorway opposite. "Mine is there."

She nodded, crossed the room to the door he had indicated, and turned back. "We are fortunate, aren't we? That you have such wealth, I mean. How would we manage otherwise?"

"Why would we need to otherwise?" he asked her.

She said, "I don't know what you mean, Gareth."

He slipped off his coat, loosened his tie. "No," he agreed. "Of course you don't. And I don't know either. It was again a matter of words, words without meaning. Forget it, Nealanna." He went into his own room, and closed the door between them.

She stood still, staring first at the closed panel, the wall that was between them now, a physical one, instead of that other barrier, which she didn't understand and couldn't see, but sensed was there between them, too.

Then she surveyed the sitting room which separated their two separate rooms. It was a fairly pleasant place. Its single tall window was covered with green damask over white lace. Its fireplace, in which flames now danced, was of black marble. The carpet was green, too, as was the loveseat covered in velvet. A big mahogany desk stood against one wall. Over it gaslight flickered in a wall sconce. Bookshelves lined with leather-bound books covered another wall.

It was a comfortable place, but not highly decorated. A man's place.

She sighed, and went into the bedroom. It, too, was a man's place, she saw at once. The furniture was large and dark, the draperies a deep warm burgundy, the rug the same. The four-poster bed was canopied with the same burgundy as the rest. There was no dressing table. No mirror.

She sank down on the edge of the high bed, closed her eyes briefly. She was dizzy with fatigue. She felt as if she had travelled an infinite number of miles from what had once been familiar, but now seemed no more than a distant dream, to what might have been the landscape of the moon, so strange were her surroundings, so strange her feelings, too.

There was a sound, and she opened her eyes.

The burgundy draperies billowed out suddenly, and from beneath them, there came ambling a small orange kitten with tawny eyes.

Nealanna went down to hands and knees in a single gentle movement. "Why, kitty," she whispered. "Kitty, you look just like my Poo. I don't feel homesick any more. How could I with you here?"

The kitten mewed, arched under her stroking hand.

There was another sound and Nealanna looked up. She saw shiny black slippers behind the drapes. She asked hoarsely, "Who is it? Who's there?"

A giggle answered her. Then the draperies were flung dramatically back. Alicia stepped from between them, grinning widely.

"I thought you might allow, and perhaps welcome, a guest," she said brightly.

"Why, come in then," Nealanna said helplessly. "But tell me how . . ."

"Oh, don't be frightened. I'm not a witch to materialize out of thin air. There's the balcony that you don't know about. Come have a look."

Nealanna went to her, and saw that when the draperies were open the window looked out on a narrow balcony,

59

enclosed by a plain wooden rail. It ran the length of the back of the house.

"There's one on each floor," Alicia said. "And the real entrance is from the various galleries. But we Kennellys are an agile lot. It took us only a day after moving in to discover that we could use our own windows as well."

Alicia went inside, plumped herself on the bed.

Nealanna followed, pausing only to close the window against the November chill.

"You're not yet dressed for dinner," the younger girl said accusingly, as she nudged the kitten away from her ankles.

"No," Nealanna agreed. "And I had better begin, or I shall not be ready in time."

"And Gareth won't like that. Nor would he approve of my invasion of your room." Alicia grinned again. "But what he doesn't know . . ."

Nealanna smiled. "He probably will know."

"Will you tell him?"

"If he asks me I will."

"Then you're going to be a good wife to him, are you?" Alicia tipped her head to one side, eyed Nealanna thoughtfully from shadowy gray eyes.

"I hope so," Nealanna answered.

"I expect you do hope so." Alicia paused. Then, "But that won't be as easy as you may think."

"Oh? Why not?"

"Surely you already know that much. You were married in London before you came over, weren't you?"

"Yes. But . . ."

"And where did you meet?"

"In London, too."

"And when was that?"

"Why," Nealanna hesitated. "We met for the first time last year. At a solicitor's house, and then, more recently . . ."

"Your accent," Alicia said, "It's not quite what I'm used to from the England. Are you really . . ."

"I'm from Cornwall originally," Nealanna said. "We

60

speak somewhat differently there." And she remembered her mother asking, 'Couldn't you learn proper English? You won't always live in Cornwall.'

"And it was a romantic whirlwind courtship, I suppose," Alicia went on.

Nealanna nodded her agreement, but she was listening with her heart as well as her ears and head. She sensed a purpose in Alicia's visit, and wondered what it was.

"We find that hard to believe," Alicia said. "Those of us who know Gareth, and love him, find your marriage hard to believe, too."

"Why . . . what do you mean?" Nealanna stammered.

Alicia smiled sweetly, nibbling her underlip. "Why, surely Gareth told you . . ."

"Told me what?"

But Alicia didn't answer. She tapped a grubby broken nail against her front teeth, stared thoughtfully at Nealanna. "He didn't tell you. I see that now."

Nealanna waited. She saw that Alicia would do the telling more quickly if she was not questioned.

"We know Gareth so well, you see. He is deep. A man of intense and real feelings. He doesn't love and forget, you know. He loves forever and ever. Which is why we were all so startled before. When we found out who you were, I mean. But now I begin to understand. It's Gareth, but not really. There's my father's hand in this. The two of them. They're both equally mad in that way. You wait, you'll see." She paused.

Nealanna held her breath.

At last Alicia said, "And that's why he married you, of course. Out of their combined madness. For that's what it is. Madness."

"And why must Gareth be mad to fall in love with me, to marry me?"

"He couldn't have fallen in love with you," Alicia said firmly. "There's Deborah, you see."

61

Chapter 6

Nealanna clung to her shaky composure, hoping that nothing of what she felt, thought, showed in her expression.

Deborah. There was someone else. Another girl, beautiful beyond imagining certainly, with all the charms and graces to which Nealanna had not been born . . . a girl who Gareth . . .

It was too painful to dwell upon somehow, and it taught her that what she called pique at sharing a mock marriage with him was not that at all. It was a deep and anxious yearning to love and be loved. By Gareth. By this man who remained a stranger to her. And then the question burst into words, but silent ones, throttled before they could hang on the still air. Why did he marry me, she asked herself. Why?

Alicia smiled faintly. "No. I see. Of course. He never told you about Deborah." She bent in a swirl of pale green velvet, and picked up the kitten. "Oh, well . . . I'm sure it doesn't matter. You mustn't take my ravings seriously, you know."

But Nealanna remembered how her mother would come

up out of laudanum-induced lethargy to rant through the long nights. Spread through her wild outcries were small kernels of truth. Nealanna had come, at last, to believe that if one recognized them, one would in all ravings find some element that was fact. The gambling that Anna had talked of, once considered a disordered dream, had happened, and been true. But what truth was there in Alicia's words?

She asked quietly, "And who is Deborah?"

Alicia's pink lips parted. Her throat pulsed, and her breasts rose as if with a deep breath. She was surely about to answer.

There were footsteps in the sitting room.

Alicia drifted back against the draperies, holding the kitten to her, absently tickling it behind its small ears with a thin forefinger. "Oh," she smiled past Nealanna, "I've had a visit with your wife, Gareth. But now I'll leave you two alone."

"But who . . ." Nealanna stopped herself as Alicia glided between the draperies, allowed them to fall into place behind her, as she withdrew.

Nealanna turned to confront Gareth who stood in the doorway.

He spoke first. "Not ready yet? We mustn't keep the family, and our guests, waiting."

"You heard Alicia?" she asked.

He didn't answer.

"Gareth, tell me. Your sister mentioned someone named Deborah. She didn't identify her further. But . . ."

He looked at the luggage stacked in the corner. "Henry did bring it up then, but you haven't unpacked."

"I didn't notice it there," she answered. "Not two minutes after Evanne Borden left me, your sister . . ."

"There's no time now, and you'll do. You'll do remarkably well in fact. So shall we go?"

"Gareth. Gareth, you haven't answered me."

"I have no intention of doing so," he told her. His voice was flat, toneless. His green eyes were narrowed.

She knew the expression, the barrier between them that it reflected.

But she said, "It's all so mysterious, Gareth. Yet I married you in good faith. Have I no right to understand?"

"I married you in good faith as well. And here you are, complaining already. In this short time have you come to regret your bargain?"

"I have no regrets," she said stiffly.

But it wasn't true. She regretted the deep searing jealousy she felt for an unknown woman. A woman named Deborah. She regretted the weakness in herself that had brought her to this feeling for Gareth. And more than anything she wished that they had come together freely, by chance, in some other place and some other time.

He was offering her his arm, saying, "That's fine, Nealanna. And now, shall we go down?"

The immediate setting was different, but the scene, she thought, was exactly the same. She knew that she should have been prepared for it.

Instead of the big shadowed foyer, it was the drawing room, a huge high-ceilinged place with a great fireplace built of the same gray stone of which the house was made. Instead of the big, gold-framed mirror to catch and hold reflections, there was only the gleaming prisms of the chandelier spilling a glow on the Oriental carpets.

And instead of the family, these were friends, neighbors.

But the reaction to her was the same.

When Gareth presented her to Avis and Brooke Maradine, the sister and brother who sat side by side on the brown love seat, there was a moment of silence.

It went on and on until Nealanna thought she could bear it no longer, just as she could bear no longer the so-evident shock in the two faces before her.

She said on a choking breath, with a faint hopeless smile, "I'm happy to meet you both," and the spell was broken.

Brooke Maradine rose to his feet, put out his hands to clasp hers, and smiled. "Welcome, Nealanna."

At the same time, Avis turned up her heart-shaped face, and said, "I'm happy to meet you."

With an inward sigh, Nealanna saw that the too-familiar moment was over.

The Maradines had mastered their shock, and what she sensed was their displeasure at meeting Gareth's bride.

Brooke insisted that she sit with Avis, and went to join Gareth and Neil near the hearth, and began speaking about the journey.

Brooke was a slight man, and not very tall. He had pale blond hair that curled on his collar, and deep-set dark eyes. He was twenty-six, Gareth's own age.

Nealanna sensed that though he was speaking to Gareth and Neil, his attention remained firmly fixed on her.

Now Avis said brightly, "You must tell me all about it, Nealanna. Where did you meet Gareth? And when? And when did you marry, and . . ." She smiled. "I do hope you understand. We are such old friends, you see. And it is a surprise."

That was the careful introduction to the careful catechism that followed.

Nealanna answered each question as it came with equal care. Neil, and Gareth, too, had told her just what she must say. She did as she had been directed. But it was obvious to her that Avis, did not, no more than Alicia or the others, really believe her. And there was still a trace of shock in the wide dark eyes that searched Nealanna's face, as if learning it feature by feature, and still a quiver in the lips that smiled.

It occurred to Nealanna then that in the case of Avis, she might know the reason. Avis' dark eyes went frequently to Gareth. She was twenty-four, a good age for him. It might be that Avis had hoped that Gareth would marry her. Was she jealous, then, of Gareth's new wife? But there was Deborah . . . surely Avis had known her, or about her. Then why this strange repressed surprise?

And what about the others? What about Alicia, Jen-

65

nings, Faran, and Mary Kennelly? What about Evanne Borden? Surely none of them could be in any way jealous that Gareth had married. Then why should each of them have gone frozen, blank-faced, blank-eyed, at Nealanna's appearance? Was she so extraordinary a choice, so dim, so young, so unaccomplished? Was it that that was wrong?

She looked sideways at Avis, who, with her questioning done, had fallen silent, and was watching the door expectantly, for whom Nealanna did not know.

But Avis was an attractive person, with the same coloring as her brother. Dark eyes and blonde hair. She wore hers very simply. It was drawn back from her heart-shaped face, parted in the middle, and looped on her neck in a loose chignon wrapped in a net of brilliants. She had on a gown of heavy dark blue silk, cut low to expose her smooth white shoulders. Small earrings glistened when she bent her head.

She must have caught Nealanna's glance, for she touched them. "My father gave me these. They are from Emerald Station, of course." She responded to Nealanna's look of surprise. "Oh, not here. I mean the real Emerald Station. The one for which this place was named. Surely Gareth told you." At Nealanna's nod, Avis went on. "My father and Mr. Kennelly were in business together, you know, founded their fortunes together, too."

"I didn't know that," Nealanna murmured.

"Just as Brooke and Gareth studied law together. Not to practice as attorneys, but to be prepared to deal with our interests."

Nealanna said nothing, but noted that this, too, was something she did not know. She supposed there would be more to come.

Avis hesitated. Then, "My father died just ten months ago."

"I'm very sorry," Nealanna said.

Avis didn't reply. There was no expression now in her dark eyes. Her lips trembled.

Hoping to distract her, Nealanna said, "Gareth tells me that you live in the valley."

Avis made an obvious effort. She drew herself together. Her lips curved in a new smile. "Yes. Just across the river. There's a short cut over the meadows, well-worn over the years. I'll show it to you one day so that you can come to visit on foot if you like."

"I would," Nealanna said quickly.

"The Kennellys bought the land for Emerald Station from my father," Avis went on, as if once launched she was unable to stop, though her eyes had once again sought the door. "We've always lived here. The Maradines and the Gordons, you've met Nanette and Jason, I know, were the town's founding families. So when the Kennellys decided to relocate ten or twelve years ago, they came here."

"Then this house is fairly new," Nealanna commented.

"Oh, yes. Some ten years old only. And that's new for a house." She gave a mock shudder. "And somehow . . . not quite finished even yet. But of course . . ." She stopped, her lips closed tightly.

Nealanna wondered what it was that she had not permitted herself to say, but there was no time to speculate upon that.

Avis said quietly, "I hope it will be all right. I hope you'll like it here." And then, quickly, "Or perhaps you won't be staying. Perhaps you and Gareth plan another sort of life in another place."

"No," Nealanna answered. "We have come home."

"It might be better," Avis said, "if you . . ." Once again, she stopped herself.

But now it was because Faran and Jennings entered the room with Mary Kennelly.

Greetings were exchanged, and Mary took a seat in the corner. Jennings and Faran joined the other men at the hearth, but Faran's eyes returned repeatedly to Avis, Nealanna saw, and saw too the eager smile Avis gave him.

Soon after Alicia came in. She carried the orange kitten under her arm, a splash of color against her dress. She wore a tiny bandage on her finger, and when Avis asked about it, she gave the kitten a mock shake. "She did it, the

67

little fool. She was playing and forgot her claws. It's in the nature of the beast, I suppose, so I forgive her for her wickedness." Then, dropping the kitten to the floor, she exclaimed, "Oh, good. Here's Moira. I'm starving."

Moira Borden, Evanne's daughter, was sixteen, a slim, elfin type, with her mother's red hair. She wore a long black dress, and over it a frilly white apron. A small white cap rode her curls. She pushed a huge mahogany trolley laden with a group of decanters and trays of small sausages and olives.

Gareth served sherry to the ladies, whiskey to the men, while Moira offered the savories.

There had been, Nealanna thought, no need to hurry down. She and Gareth could have dawdled, and still kept no one waiting. But she knew why he had insisted. There was the question between them that he would not answer. There was Deborah to be explained.

Now Brooke said, musing over his glass, "What do you think, Gareth. All this business about temperance? Is it talk? Or will it develop?"

"I doubt a few fanatics can change the habits of the nation," Gareth said.

"It might be a good thing for the working man if they did," Neil observed.

"But you can't have one law for them," Gareth answered, "and another for us."

"What a pity," Brooke laughed. "That would solve the problem, wouldn't it?"

"It might make even greater problems," Gareth told him.

Mary, silent until then, asked, "And what about London, Nealanna? Is there much talk of temperance there?"

"Some I suppose. I read about it," she answered. "But I saw so few people while I was in London."

"Oh?" Mary's voice required explanation.

Nealanna smiled. "You see, I spent only three months there. My mother was ill. We had no guests. And I didn't go out."

68

Neil picked up her last word. "Our world is the same there as here. And with the same opinions."

There was a certain finality in his tone. The subject was dropped.

A few moments later, Moira announced that dinner was served.

It was a long and abundant meal, with two kinds of meats, great platters of vegetables, and several wines.

Nealanna, too tired for hunger, picked politely at the food, left the wine untouched, and half listened to Faran describe something called the Waterman automatic pen which would make quill and ink obsolete forever, and Jennings urge on his father a hunting trip the next morning. Once she felt Gareth's green gaze on her, but when she looked at him he turned away.

After dinner, the men withdrew to Neil's study for brandy and cigars.

Mary Kennelly, looking wan, excused herself, and went to her rooms, a habit, Nealanna learned, that was rarely broken.

Alicia and Avis remained with Nealanna, making desultory conversation in which she did not join, and to which, again, she only half-listened.

She was glad that the evening was nearly over. She was exhausted by the journey, by the tension of her arrival. She wanted nothing more than to creep into her bed, to pull the satin quilts over her head, and to escape into the release of forgetfulness.

" . . . Deborah . . ."

The name caught her attention. She raised her dark head.

Avis was pale to the lips. "No," Avis cried. "No, Alicia."

"But we should tell her," Alicia was saying. "She ought to understand. It's not fair."

Avis rose stiffly. Her heart-shaped face had gone as red as her lips were white. "Alicia . . . please . . ."

"I realize that it's painful," Alicia said gently, her gray eyes shadowed. "But don't you see . . ." She leaned toward Nealanna. "You've felt it, I realize. And it hurts,

69

of course. But tell the truth, Nealanna. You've been troubled these hours since you came here, haven't you? You want to know about Deborah, don't you?"

Nealanna hesitated. She saw torment in Avis' face.

But Alicia went on quickly. "Deborah was Avis' and Brooke's younger sister."

"Was?" Nealanna asked in a dry whisper.

Avis made some soft whimpering sound, and hurried from the room.

Alicia said, "Deborah and Gareth ... well, nothing had been announced yet, but they were madly in love. He will never get over it, of course. Just as her father didn't. Mr. Maradine died just two months later. His heart was broken, you see. And Gareth's was, too."

Then that hot searing jealousy had been for a dead girl. For someone loved and lost. And Gareth had married her because there was no Deborah to marry. But then, why marry at all?

"Don't you want to know?" Alicia asked.

"And how did Deborah die?" Nealanna whispered finally.

"She was murdered," Alicia said. "She was brutally, terribly, murdered."

The gas heater burned blue and steady in the dark of the room.

Nealanna lay abed, watching the pinpoint flames, while Alicia's words still echoed through her mind.

There had been no opportunity to question her new sister-in-law. The awful sentence had hardly been spoken when Gareth came in.

He said, "I'm sure that you're quite exhausted, Nealanna. I know that I am. Shall we go up?"

She had risen silently, silently followed him from the room.

Avis and Brooke were in the foyer, donning their coats.

They exchanged farewells, promises to meet again soon.

Then Nealanna and Gareth went up the steps. She fancied that the black masks grimaced at her as she passed them. She thought that the hallway was more dim than before. But she said nothing.

Within their apartment, he told her, "Moira will have unpacked your luggage by now. I spoke to her about it."

Nealanna thanked him, said good night, and he, his face unreadable, had gone into his room and closed the door.

She had done the same, and now, lying still, listening to the silence that enwrapped the house like a shroud, she wondered if Avis had told him of Alicia's outburst. She wondered how Deborah Maradine had come to be murdered. It was with a peculiar ache that she accepted the truth of Alicia's words. Gareth had loved Deborah. He would love no other. He lay now, staring into the dark, and thinking of that love.

He would have married because men of his age and station must. Fortune and family pride required that dynasties be founded. Neil Kennelly, and Gareth, too, labored under the burden of that pride. But Gareth had never touched her, nor given any sign that he would. Dynasties are not founded on unconsummated marriages. It was a lie, based on a lie. But what was its purpose?

A kitten mewed, whined, and was still.

There was silence again.

She raised herself on her elbow, wondering if Alicia's kitten had somehow found its way into the room. She surveyed the shadows, but nothing moved that she could see.

The frantic little sound came again.

She rose from the bed, stood listening. She thought it might come from beyond the draperies, perhaps from the balcony Alicia had showed her.

She pulled the draperies open, peered out. But it was dark, an empty blackness. She pressed the window open, and through the slight complaint of wood against damp wood, she heard the kitten's plaintive cry once more.

She drew up her gown, stepped over the low sill, and then onto the balcony. The cold of the night air chilled her. The empty blackness was virtually blinding. Under her bare feet the boards were damp, slippery with slime.

"Kitty," she whispered. "Where are you? Come here now."

There was a stillness, then a new whimper, a sound of claws scrabbling.

She moved that way, toward the balcony edge. There was a railing there, a narrow board of carved wood, a few posts. Beyond it, more than a yard away, well past arm reach, there was the slant of the roof, an angle of dormer eaves. Green eyes glinted at her. The sound of slipping and scrabbling claws became louder as she approached. The kitten's plaintive cry became louder, too.

She whispered wordless comfort, and stretched, reaching out for the small hunched body. But, though her cold fingertips grazed its fur, she could not seize it.

She held herself against the railing, leaned her full weight upon it, and stretched again.

That time she caught the kitten. She drew it toward her.

She heard no sound but the kitten's own. Yet, suddenly, the railing was gone from beneath her body. She was arched, hanging on empty air, and then she fell forward.

The kitten leaped from between her loosened fingers, and with a despairing shriek fell into the dark below.

Her hands caught the rim of the eaves and froze there, while the empty night swirled around her in a blaze of stars.

Chapter 7

Half fainting, she still felt the sharp slate cut her flesh, and her blood-slick fingers begin to slip. She felt the arch of her clinging body begin to break and knew that she would fall. She would fall in the trail of the kitten to disappear into the dark.

Then she believed that she was dreaming. She imagined that she had fallen and died without knowledge of pain. There were strong arms around her. She supposed that they were the arms of God Himself, holding her, and lifting her from black emptiness into safety.

But the arms were Gareth's, and the voice was Gareth's too. "Let go," he said softly. "I have you fast, Nealanna. Can you hear me? Let go I say."

She willed her frozen fingers to release the slant of eave to which she had clung so desperately, and felt welling pain in them as they opened wide. Sagging against him, she felt the hard beating of his heart, and her own heart, too.

He carried her indoors, and set her, shivering and trembling, in the big chair. He swooped the quilt from the bed and wrapped it around her. Moving quickly and silently he turned the gas heater high, and lit the lamp.

Then he stood over her, regarding her shivering figure while she bit her lips to keep her teeth from chattering. At last he asked, "What did you think you were doing?"

"The kitten," she whispered, and her teeth audibly clicked together. "The kitten like Poo that I left at home. I'm afraid it's dead."

"What kitten?"

"Alicia's, I think."

"You don't make much sense. I suppose you can't help it." He turned abruptly away, disappeared for a moment. When he returned he thrust a glass of brandy at her. "Drink it. It will warm you so you can explain."

She raised her eyes to his. "I'm all right, I think."

"So I see," he said dryly. He put the glass into one of her hands, took the other and examined it, his face stern and cold. "You have some fine cuts, for all you're all right. And what of the other hand?"

She shifted the glass, opened the other hand, and blood ran between her fingers.

"Drink," he said.

She sipped, and choked, and saw him smile suddenly.

"You're not much accustomed to spirits," he told her. "I'll have you tipsy before you're warm." With that, he left her.

That time when he returned, he had a basin of warm water, some white cloths.

She had put aside the half-full glass. He made no comment. He took her hands, worked over them silently, his dark brows drawn in an awesome frown. When he was finished washing them, binding them, he dropped them to her lap, and she pulled them beneath the quilt to hide them. Then he sat back on his heels, looked up into her face.

"Now do you want to tell me?"

"It was a miracle that you came, Gareth. I could never have managed to hold on much longer."

"A miracle?" Amusement shone briefly in his eyes, then

vanished. "Not quite. I was unable to sleep. I sat up, reading, having a last brandy. I heard you open the window and wondered why you did. And then I heard you cry out."

She saw now that he was half-dressed, still wearing his dark narrow trousers. But he was collarless, and cravatless. His shirt was open nearly to his waist. His bare chest showed, brown and smooth. She averted her eyes and said, "It was still a miracle."

"I want to know what you were doing," he said impatiently.

"It was the kitten." She began to shudder anew, remembering what it had been like. To hear the soft helpless cry, and see the tiny body, its eyes glowing, on the ledge, to hear the minute claws strive for safety, to feel the heart beat within her fingers for an instant, and the body arching up and away from between them. And then that last awful wail . . .

"Yes. Go on, Nealanna."

"I couldn't help it. I knew I had to save it, so I tried. She was on the ledge, where the dormer eave comes down, not quite within reach of the balcony, for me at least. I stretched, and the railing . . ."

He rose, went through the draperies and outside. He was gone for only a few minutes. When he came in, he closed the window and locked it. He pulled the draperies securely shut.

"The wooden railing broke at the joint. It's still hanging there," he said. Then, "You must be more careful. There is a courtyard below, paved with stone."

"And the kitten?"

"I'll attend to it when you've returned to bed."

She closed her eyes against sudden tears. It had been so small, so unoffending. Now it was surely dead. She drew the quilt around her, and looking at him, she got to her feet. "I'll go to bed now."

He waited until she was settled, then he lowered the lamp. He bent over her. "You are all right?"

"Yes."

"Then go to sleep."

The moment the door closed behind him, she was up, back at the window. She clumsily unlocked it and eased it open. She stepped out onto the chill balcony. She stood firmly, carefully, near the wall, and peered at the broken railing.

Had it broken under her weight?

Or had it already been broken when she leaned against it?

How had the kitten climbed to the eaves? Was it natural for a kitten to go higher than it could climb, and to land in a place from which it could not retreat? She supposed it was. She had taken Poo down from an apple tree once.

Yet she was obscurely troubled.

She had had an odd welcome here in Emerald Station. Already she had been told that it would be better for her if she had never come, better if she were to go away.

And now, tonight, her first night here, she had had this strange accident.

Was it an accident really? She couldn't tell.

She heard sounds below and knew that Gareth was dealing with the small broken body that had been this night's victim. She retreated inside and crept back to bed.

An hour later, when he quietly opened the door, came to stand over her, she pretended to be sound asleep.

"Your hands," Faran said. "What happened to them?"

"It's nothing." Nealanna shrugged, folded them under the table. "A small accident."

"An accident?" He stared at her, his face intent. "You've not been here twenty-four hours. Surely, when you went up to bed . . ."

She sighed to herself. She had known there would be questions. She had unbandaged her fingers, thinking that they would be less conspicuous that way. But they had immediately begun to bleed again. She could not go down, she knew, trailing blood wherever she moved, so she had bound them again.

She had dressed slowly, wearing a blue gown that Nanette had helped her choose. She had put up her hair twice.

Still, by the time she had left the apartment, she had not seen Gareth, nor heard him stir. She decided to come down alone, thinking to have a quiet breakfast and then retreat upstairs again.

Instead Faran had been helping himself at the long buffet, and though she had started to withdraw, he had made that impossible, saying, "Stay. I insist. I want to talk to you. We had no time to become acquainted last night."

He had pressed her into a chair at the big table, brought her coffee with a small, serious bow, then brought her sliced bacon of a kind she had never seen before, and a heap of scrambled eggs to go with them. After he had seated himself, he explained, "We arise at different hours. Evanne sets up the buffet and we attend to breakfast ourselves. I suppose that's very different from what you're accustomed to. But we live our own way at Emerald Station, as you'll learn."

"It is different, yes, from what I'm accustomed to," she agreed dryly. "I've done my own cooking, and my own serving."

He was staring at her hands by then, and that was when he demanded to know what happened. "How did you cut yourself?"

She told him briefly, "Alicia's kitten was trapped on an eave near the balcony beyond my window. I tried to get her down."

"And she managed to scratch the palms of both your hands?" Faran frowned. "I don't see how."

She swallowed, her appetite gone, remembering the last pathetic wail as the kitten fell to the courtyard. "I wasn't able to save her," she said finally.

His face went still. "I'm sorry. Ought your hands to be attended? I could ride into . . ."

"No. They're all right. In an hour or two I'll take the bandages off."

His face cleared. He attacked his food with gusto. When he had finished, he asked, "Is Gareth up yet?"

She very nearly said she didn't know. She caught the words back just in time. She said, "I think not," which she considered to be equivocal enough.

"I envy him the trip to England. I would like to have gone."

She said hastily, "Perhaps you will. Some time."

"Of course," he agreed. "But perhaps I shouldn't envy him too much."

"Oh?" she raised her brows, leaned forward encouragingly. Gareth was one subject on which her attention was immediately fixed. "What do you mean?"

"He's the oldest," Faran told her. "It isn't a position necessarily the most comfortable in this family."

"I don't know what you mean."

"But you will. As a matter of fact, you'll feel the strain of it yourself since you're married to him. But, of course, perhaps just being in his boots makes it different for him. He has always been the oldest, you see. And he and my father are much alike. They think alike, feel alike. Now, you take me, or Jennings ... we aren't all that whole-clothed Kennelly. We take after our mother. She is a sweet woman, though you don't know her yet. And she won't be easy to know either. But you'll see that she is. Sweet, in the same way that Avis Maradine is sweet." His face was suddenly red. "Of course," he went on quickly, "my mother is not a Kennelly. That's the answer."

"And are your father and Gareth made of stone then?" she asked.

"You'll have plenty of time to see for yourself," Faran answered. "But watch their faces when they take you to the family room. Which they'll surely do today some time. Just watch them when they talk of the Kennelly family. Then you'll know what I mean."

She did know. She recollected Neil Kennelly speaking of his family line the night she first saw him. She remembered thinking of his pride.

Faran took a last sip of coffee, rose. "I'm off to the Maradines this morning. I'll see you later."

She nodded, asked that he convey her regards.

She had only a moment or two alone, a moment or two in which to consider his words. Then Neil Kennelly came in.

He wore a riding habit of dark brown, and dark brown boots. His tanned face looked tired. He seemed startled to see her. He asked, "Down so early? I thought surely you'd take today to luxuriate in bed, and have your food brought up to you."

"I'm not used to such amenities," she told him.

He took coffee, bread, and cheese on a fine china plate, and seated himself across from her. "I hope you rested well." His gray eyes, she saw, were on her hands.

She answered, "Not very well, I'm sorry to say."

He put down the cup, stared at her. "Why not?"

She held out both hands to him.

He eyed the small bandages without a change in expression. "What is that from?" he asked finally.

She told him in a few, very brief sentences. She omitted any mention of her terror, of the emotions that had burned through her. She told him the bald facts. And then she said, "I find it very hard to believe that the kitten climbed to that particular place on its own. Somehow it seems odd, wrong. I just . . ."

He cut in, his words measured, even, his voice level, "My dear child, what are you saying? Do you think someone has made an attempt to injure you? To hurt you, here, in this house? And who are you accusing? Of what crime? For what reason?"

"I don't know," she said. "And I don't mean to accuse. It just seems . . ."

He leaned back in his chair. "The kitten, I gather, climbed to the eaves, was stranded there. You heard it, went out, reached for it, and the railing unfortunately broke under your weight. How can there be a foul plot against you in that?" he demanded.

She knew that she had made a mistake. She ought not

79

to have told him what happened. She ought not to have mentioned her doubts. There was no reason for those doubts except her own perhaps faulty intuition. Now, no matter what she said, he would think her foolish, hysterical. He would hardly listen to her.

And she saw that it was exactly as she had feared. She made herself go on, but she soon realized that though he listened, answered, his attention was elsewhere. His mind was not on her words, nor even on his own.

She said, "If you will concede the possibility that someone tried to do me an injury, then you must know that came about only because you brought me here. And I am here because you arranged my marriage to Gareth. Why did you make such an arrangement? Why was it necessary?"

"I explained all that beforehand," he replied.

"You did not," she said quietly. "You simply said that it was what you wished."

He shrugged.

"I have no illustrious name to bring with me, nor a fortune. I have nothing to offer. Yet you wished Gareth to marry me, and he did so. There must have been a reason."

Neil brushed his mustache carefully with his linen napkin, then laid it beside his plate. At last, he said, "It was time for Gareth to marry. He is twenty-six. He will be heir to the Kennelly fortune, to everything we own and control, and he is prepared to deal with that. He must have his own family, his own sons."

"I understand your feelings, and his," she said. "But why me? Why not someone from here? Avis Maradine, for instance." She watched him closely. She saw that when she said that name, he winced, and knew that he must be thinking of Deborah. Of Deborah Maradine whom Gareth had loved, perhaps still loved.

Neil said, "You've heard about Deborah, haven't you?"

Nealanna nodded, waited.

He drew a deep breath. Then, "It has nothing to do with you. There is no connection between your silly adventure last night and that ... that other thing. You only im-

80

agine you're in danger because you heard about her. If you had not, you'd never have thought such a foolish thing. You chose to marry Gareth of your own free will, and you can not now change your mind, if that is what you're leading up to. In the first place, let me remind you of what you've apparently already forgotten. Every bit of bread you've eaten in your life was paid for by me. Every small comfort you had, your schooling, your clothes, each of your necessities, I paid for. And I was in no way obligated, either legally or morally to do so. You are, as you admitted a while back, in my debt. I would not recall it to you except for one reason. To protect you, and to protect my son, I would do anything. Anything at all. If debt doesn't matter, then let me remind you that it is too late to change your mind. You have no money, no where to go. It is settled. Have I made myself clear?"

She nodded and looked down at her hands. What was most clear of all to her was his ruthlessness. She saw now why Faran had said his father was made of stone.

Neil said, "Then let's have no more of this, shall we?"

She didn't reply because she knew that he expected no reply, and wanted none.

He drank off his coffee with the distracted, half-attending look still on his face, a look unaltered by his speech to her, then excused himself and left the room.

81

Chapter 8

It was two weeks later.

The cuts on Nealanna's fingers had healed. The accident which had befallen her so soon after her arrival was no longer mentioned. Alicia never spoke of the disappearance of her small orange kitten. The night might have never been.

By now, Nealanna knew her way around the great stone pile that was Emerald Station. She could go, no longer losing her way, from the apartment she shared with Gareth, along the three level galleries up into the empty rooms of the dormers and through the small dim cul-de-sacs of the eaves to see from their windows the low hills that ringed the valley. She could go down the broad curving staircase, under the black carved masks that stared at her from blind eyes, past the drawing room, and the dining room, into the kitchen. She knew the ground floor place where the hunting guns were kept, racks of gleaming weapons which had made her shudder, and seeing her shudder made plump Jennings laugh. "There's sport here in all seasons, and of all kinds, but no tigers, Nealanna. Nothing to be afraid of." She knew, too, the room which

Neil Kennelly kept as a chapel to his family, and she had seen and measured the depths of his pride as he showed her the family crest, gently touched the records that went back the more than a century and a half to when the first Kennelly set foot on New England soil, and further back to England itself. And at the same time, she had seen in Mary Kennelly's worn face the look of a child punished too often, as she listened to her husband's words.

Gareth had shown her the three doors that led to the paved stone courtyard where the kitten had died, and taken her out to the meadow where he had buried it in the dark.

She knew her way to the carriage houses, and the stables where five beautiful horses were kept, and where Henry Borden, slight, and red-headed like his mother, but much more shy, would give her a grin, and duck his head, in a manner inappropriate to his twenty years. Alicia had pointed out the path that went beyond the slanting roofs of the outdoor storage sheds across the fields through the grove of trees near the river, and the foot-bridge one took to go to Maradine Mansion.

Twice in the past two weeks she had been to visit Jason and Nanette Gordon. That had been a pleasure, though she had been concerned to see the increased pallor in Nanette's face, and wondered.

She had played with Doe and Jay, and chatted with joyful Lolly, while Nanette smiled from her lounge chair, and Gareth walked with Jason under the blue spruce.

The first time she had met Mrs. Moody, who Nanette recommended as seamstress, and whose name so well suited her. The woman, middle-aged, and gray-haired, had grumbled through pursed lips, "All right. I'll do it. But here. Here at the Gordons. I don't go to Emerald Station." The second time the woman had begun the fittings, and said through a mouthful of pins, "Well, Mrs. Kennelly, how do you find it there?" in a strange tone.

Nanette had pretended not to hear Nealanna's queries about these two comments, so her questions went unanswered. They were hardly important when compared to the others that plagued her.

Why had Neil Kennelly wanted Gareth to marry her? What purpose had he had in bringing her here? She was sure now that he had had some purpose, and she had begun to be certain she had made a mistake in trusting him, even in being grateful for what he had done for her.

It was, partly at least, the depth of feeling for Gareth that she had discovered in herself, that troubled her. For he maintained the cool distance between them, and she was determined to hide from him that he had a wife in spirit, if not in flesh, and each time she looked down and saw the diamond-decorated wedding ring he had put on her hand, she thought herself a fool and a fraud, and worst of all, unwanted.

The family's shock at the marriage was no longer evident. But it was there, she suspected, although hidden now. Each one had begun to pretend that what had happened had been expected, though somewhere within them, she was sure, the embers of disbelief still burned.

Now, two weeks after her arrival at Emerald Station, she sat in the Maradine morning room. It was a bright place, full of books and games, though there was snow in the air outdoors.

She liked to come here because the atmosphere was so different from that of the place she now called home. The house was big, white, with four great columns upholding a portico. The many windows were wide and draped in pale green.

Avis had told her that the house was probably designed after one that her father, soldiering as a young man in the War Between the States, had put a torch to and never forgotten.

Nealanna liked to come to Maradine Mansion even though from where she sat she could look at the portrait of Deborah, loved by Gareth, and dead for a year. The brown eyes in the heart-shaped face seemed to offer no reproof, nor had Avis or Brooke ever spoken of her to Nealanna.

84

Brooke was saying in a light voice, "I had thought Faran would bring you over instead of Jennings, Nealanna."

"Faran went with his father and Gareth. So Jennings had to do the chore. I thought to walk over alone, but Mr. Kennelly insisted that Jennings drive me. He wasn't much pleased either."

"There are days when he could stand a good kick," Brooke said with a grin. "And where did he go?"

"To walk a bit. He'll come back later, he said," Nealanna answered.

But Avis was still thinking of Faran, for she tossed her head, murmured, "When he wants to come to Maradine Mansion, he will."

"And does," Brooke drawled. "But is that often enough for you?"

"It'll do," she snapped. She bent her blonde head over her embroidery hoop, but Nealanna saw the blush on her heart-shaped face.

She said hastily, "I believe they all went into town this morning."

Brooke looked surprised, but said nothing.

Nealanna leaned forward, peering at Avis' work. "Do you think you could teach me that stitch?"

"Why not? Come closer. I'll show you," Avis told her, plainly pleased that Faran was no longer the subject of conversation.

"But first, Avis, wouldn't our guest like some refreshment?" Brooke asked. "I would."

"You would, of course," his sister retorted. "You always would. Watch out or you'll be plump as Jennings."

That made Nealanna laugh. Brooke was slight and spare, and she thought it probably in his nature to be so.

"Cocoa," Brooke suggested, ignoring Avis' promise.

"You're spoiled, Brooke Maradine," she told him, but she was smiling, and she hurried out, calling ahead to the housekeeper.

Brooke waited until her voice had faded away. Then he said, "It's the first time I've been able to speak to you

85

privately." His brown eyes regarded her warmly. "I hope that it won't be the last."

She smiled. "Why should it be?"

"I heard of your mishap. Your hands are all better?"

"Of course. It was nothing." Easy to say, she thought. But not so easy to convince herself of the truth of the words. Still, nothing further had happened. Perhaps Neil was right. It had been an accident. Perhaps her sense that malice had led her to that spot was mistaken.

Brooke lowered his voice, said anxiously, "I know that Alicia told you about Deborah." His dark eyes glanced briefly at the portrait, then returned to Nealanna's face. "She ought not to have done that. But you mustn't think that Avis and I do . . . could . . . in any way resent . . ."

She said hastily, "I don't, Brooke."

"You must understand how we feel. It's a good thing that you did for Gareth."

"Good for him?" she asked.

"Because of Deborah," he answered quietly. There was a pained look in his eyes now. His hands were linked tightly on one bent knee. "Ever since she died . . ."

"How did it happen? Can you tell me? Alicia said only that she had been murdered . . . brutally murdered were the words used. But I . . ."

He looked at the door quickly. Then, "She was struck down on the path between here and Emerald Station."

"No one said. How? Is it known . . ."

"Nealanna, Bellingham is a very small town, as you've learned by now. It has no proper police force. Just two constables. They had the aid of a county policeman, a stranger here. They are convinced that it was some wanderer. A tramp, perhaps . . ."

"And was he . . ."

"He was never found. No. And now, after a year, it's very doubtful that he will be."

"I see," she said, feeling a chill touch her.

"The police believe that, but there are many in town who think otherwise," Brooke said heavily.

She raised her head sharply. "Otherwise, Brooke?"

He said gently, "Now ... listen. You must understand why Gareth is ... the way he is. Which you certainly do know, being his wife. I, Avis ... we all know the truth. It was a tramp most certainly. There is no doubt of that."

But then why did Brooke sound so troubled? Nealanna asked herself. Why did he sound less than certain? There must be more. She saw that he was nerving himself to put some other fact into words.

At last he said, "Some folks in town insist that Gareth ..."

She drew another shocked breath. Gareth. She gasped, "Oh, no, Brooke. No one would believe that Gareth could have murdered your sister."

But that was what some did believe, she realized. Hadn't Mrs. Moody, the seamstress, said she would not go to Emerald Station? Hadn't she asked how she herself liked it there, in so odd a tone of voice?

"Some do," Brooke said, and after a hesitation, "You see, the Kennellys are newcomers to this place. They've only been here for ten years. And there are many resentful, jealous people ..."

"Resentful of what?" she asked. "Jealous of what?"

"Oh, well ..." He shrugged. "Money, position, power. Surely, in England, it's much the same."

"Yes," she agreed. "There's always been some of that. The common folk against the gentry. Class feeling."

"Here, one wouldn't call it class feeling," he smiled. "Rather call it the opposite. There is so much egalitarianism that no man will admit he has his betters."

"And perhaps he doesn't."

"You see?" He grinned at her. "You're an Englishwoman, and you mentioned class, but you don't believe in it yourself."

"I suppose I don't. Nevertheless, that's off the subject. What of the Kennellys?"

His grin faded. "They've explained so little to you," he said thoughtfully.

"Nothing," she told him.

"They should have done." Brooke paused. "But is it my place to do what they haven't?"

"If we're friends, then it is," she told him firmly.

He looked down at his hands. "We're friends, Nealanna." His serious voice stressed the words.

But it need not have done so. She had felt, since they first met, some closeness to him that she had known was reciprocated, some unnamed warmth in him and in Avis, too.

He said quietly, "The Kennellys, I've told you, came here about ten years ago."

"From where?"

"A small town in the north of New England. They left it . . . the whole family . . . because . . . because . . ."

"Yes?"

"Neil's brother, Nealanna. Mr. Kennelly's brother. His name was Holten. He was called Holt though." Brooke's eyes refused to meet hers now. He lowered his voice. "It was a pretty awful thing that happened. About twenty years ago, perhaps a bit more. Holt went mad one day. It was a fair on the grounds of their home. He killed ten people, women and children and men, and then he blew his brains out."

She sat frozen, still. Then she whispered, "But, Brooke, why?"

"No one knows," Brooke answered. "He simply did it, then killed himself. It was terrible for the family, of course. For the Kennellys and Gareth, The others were not yet born, and I doubt they know of it. But the Kennellys were virtually destroyed. Neil spent everything he had in compensation to those injured, and it took him ten years to re-build his fortune, traveling with my father, doing God knows what besides the diamond mines, and then he brought his family here. They built Emerald Station. But somehow, what happened in that town up north has followed them here. And there were other complications, too. And then, when Deborah was killed . . ."

"But they can not say that Gareth . . ."

"They don't. Not in front of me, nor Avis. Not in front

of the Gordons either. We all know, you see. We wouldn't allow . . ."

"But then they think it?" she demanded.

"I suppose some few trouble-makers keep alive the old tale. But I believe very strongly that now he's married, now that you're here, it will end of itself."

"Yes," she breathed. "I hope so. I hope I can do that for Gareth at least."

She understood at last. To lay the gossip about him Gareth must have a wife. It was as simple as that. Then why hadn't he found one himself? Was it because he had been still too much in love with Deborah's memory to look for someone else?

At that moment Avis came in with a tray. Her cheeks were pink with anger, and she was breathing hard. She set the tray down on the mahogany table with force enough to make the cocoa cups dance, and the liquid spill inelegantly over the fine china rims.

"Stapelton," she told Brooke grimly. "Tom Stapleton. In the kitchen, lounging about, and gossiping. I won't have it. I won't. Not in this house."

"Avis," he said warningly. "Never mind now. I'll have a word with him a little later."

"And tell him that I said I won't have it. It will stop. Now, and forever. Or I . . . I . . ."

He laughed. "Come. Nealanna will be wondering why you're breathing fire. Serve us and forget Tom Stapleton and the kitchen, too."

She smiled faintly, "You're right." She gave Nealanna an embarrassed look. "Forgive me, I'm quite ashamed. It's too a small thing to raise so much temper." She passed the cocoa, then cookies. She settled herself on the sofa, and began to chat about Christmas plans, though Christmas itself was a month away.

A few minutes later, Jennings came in.

Avis cried out, and Nealanna jumped to her feet.

"What happened to you?" Brooke demanded.

Jennings carefully lowered his plump body into a chair. He loosened his coat and leaned back his head, closing his eyes. The light fell harshly on his face. His rosebud mouth was swollen and blood-stained. His plump cheeks were bruised and beginning to color. There were cuts over both his gray eyes.

He said wryly, "I had words with Tom Stapleton on the road."

"No. Oh, no," Avis said bitterly.

Jennings' swollen mouth twisted. "You should see him, Avis."

"Was there no one about?"

"No. I don't think so. Except for Alicia. She was at the edge of the meadow, going away. I doubt that she knew what happened." He winced, then added, "I did manage to knock Tom Stapleton down."

"You shouldn't have," Brooke said. "It'll do no good, Jennings. Can't you see that?"

"There are things I won't have him say to me, and he did." Jennings raised his head. "I'll fight them all. I'll fight them forever."

"For all the good it'll do," Brooke answered. He got to his feet. "Let's clean you up. If your father sees you like that . . ."

"For all he cares," Jennings said. But he got to his feet.

He and Brooke left the room together. Nealanna turned immediately to Avis. "Who is this Tom Stapleton? Why should Jennings fight him?"

Spots of color suddenly appeared on Avis' cheeks. "It is . . . hasn't Gareth mentioned . . ." She stopped herself, eyes on Nealanna's face.

Nealanna shook her head slowly from side to side. "I've never heard the name until today when you first spoke it."

"A family in Bellingham," Avis said. She paused, seemed to consider. Then, "They had the land where Emerald Station now stands. My father's tenants. He put them off it so the Kennellys could build there. Tom was only a boy then, but it still rankles in him."

"So he hates the Kennellys," Nealanna said. "That seems hardly enough to . . ."

"Unfortunately, there's more," Avis said. "The sister

worked as a maid for the Kennellys for some time. A long while ago. She's gone now. She ... ah ... Tom Stapleton is a very hard man. She ran away, it's said. Perhaps with someone she loved. No one knows."

"And what has that to do with the Kennellys?" Nealanna asked. "Why should her brother speak ill of them, and fight Jennings?"

"He blames the Kennellys, you see. For everything. For taking the land that was once theirs as tenants. For Jane Stapleton's disappearance ... for everything."

"I see," Nealanna said thoughtfully. But, in fact, she did not see. Avis was so plainly being uncandid. There was a secret she didn't want to divulge. She didn't want to lie, but she didn't want to speak the truth either. It involved Gareth, of course. Why else would Avis be so hesitant to say what she knew?

Soon after, Jennings returned. He looked a bit more presentable now, his hair brushed off his bruised forehead, the bleeding wounds staunched and washed.

He walked with a slight swagger as he led her to the runabout. There he asked, "Do you suppose you can drive it, Nealanna?"

"Why, of course," she said. "But aren't you coming home with me?"

"Not just yet. I'll be along later." His round face looked hard. "If you're sure you can go home alone."

"I'm certain of it." She gathered her skirts and coat in her left hand, and with his help, climbed up to the seat.

He unhitched the reins, brought them to her. The black horse moved in the shafts, and snorted, and flung up his head.

"You'll be careful, won't you? And you'll go directly home?"

She laughed down at him. "Jennings, of course I will. Where else would I go?"

He stepped back, and she gave the reins a flick. The horse moved briskly down the lane, its breaths making great white plumes in the frosty air.

She sat back comfortably as they rolled across the valley.

It was hard to believe, in that peaceful moment, in the turmoil with which she had to contend, the confused and swirling emotions that beset her, the questions that gave her no rest.

Why had Neil Kennelly wanted her to marry Gareth? Was it because of the gossip that had attached itself to him after Deborah was murdered? Why had Gareth accepted the arrangement, yet not completely accepted it? Why did he seem in some very few moments to share some brief unspoken intimacy with her, then to withdraw into a chill amusement? Was she right to suspect malice intended as she tried, unsuccessfully, to rescue the orange kitten? Or should she rather doubt her own intuition? Why did Tom Stapleton blame the Kennellys because his sister had run away? What was it that Avis had not mentioned?

The miles rolled by. A thick bank of clouds gathered around the distant hills, and the watery sun grew even more dim.

She thought ahead to Emerald Station, set in its dun meadows, and wondered if, in summer, it lived up to its name.

The runabout gave a sudden jolt. She thought that one of the big wheels had slipped over a stone. But the jolt came again, and then again.

She straightened, pulled at the reins with all her force to slow the horse. But before it could respond, a wheel snapped free and went rolling wildly away.

The runabout careened on, skittering, tilting, turning, for another few yards, and then Nealanna was thrown free of it.

She saw the sky spinning around her, and felt the breath-taking impact, and the heat of pain.

After that, there was only darkness.

Chapter 9

The first sound she heard was the drumming of hoofs. For an instant, she imagined that she was asleep, dreaming. But then she remembered. She had watched helplessly when the wheel spun off and went dancing erratically away. She had seen the countryside flash past as the horse bolted and the shattered runabout dragged on behind it.

The drumming came closer, vibrating the earth under her head, and echoing in her body. She knew that she had to move quickly. She supposed that the maddened horse had somehow turned, was coming back. It would trample her if she lay in the road.

So she forced herself up to hands and knees, and rested there, waiting for breath to return to her. The clouds on the hills had moved closer, and with them, a cold thin drizzle that seemed to penetrate to her bones. She shivered. She rose to her feet.

Behind her, the empty lane led back to Maradine Mansion. Ahead, a long walk on foot, at least by road, lay Emerald Station.

She limped a few steps toward it, unwillingly though it

was the only home that she had. Where else was there for her to go but to Emerald Station?

The drumming was loud now, then louder still. She moved cautiously off the lane, into the high damp grass of the verge, and stopped to wait.

From the curve just ahead, a horse exploded into view. A horse and a single rider.

It reared as it was pulled up sharply. The rider leaped down. It was Gareth.

"Nealanna!" He was with her, his arms around her, his dark head bent, and green eyes aglow in his drawn white face. "What happened to you?"

She felt her bruised and aching body continue to tremble. She was aware of the torn folds of her gown, and the long rip in her coat. Her hat lay somewhere nearby, and was forgotten now, and her hair had come down in a cloud of damp black curls.

"The runabout lost a wheel," she said through chattering teeth.

And it was then, as he held her, that she was suddenly struck by the strangeness of it. In all her seventeen years she had driven in carriages many many times. Nothing like this had ever happened before. Not until she came to Emerald Station as Gareth Kennelly's bride.

How had it happened that the runabout lost its wheel? Why had it happened just then, to her, when she was driving alone?

"I know that much," Gareth was saying. "The horse came racing in, dragging what was left by the shafts, reins trailing and all. I thought that you must be dead, Nealanna. I thought . . ."

"Well, no," she said. "You can see that I'm not. I was terribly frightened, but . . ."

"We'd better get you home. You must have attention."

"I'm not hurt, Gareth."

"Then you're more hardy than you look," he told her.

He led her to his horse, lifted her to the saddle, and seated himself behind her. His arms came around her waist, holding the reins.

It was good to be held thus. She felt safe now. His wide chest was at her back, bracing her, his chin was near her hair. She knew that her blowing curls must touch him lightly.

He set the horse into a slow walk.

After a moment, he said over her shoulder, "You were a fool to marry me, Nealanna. A child, and I understand that, but a foolish one. Why did you listen to my father? What good is his wealth? How will it mean anything to you if you don't live to enjoy it? What sense was there in trading your life at the sight of those worthless stones he threw on the table before your dazzled eyes?"

"Stones," she said. "Stones?"

"Those precious gems . . ."

She protested, "But it wasn't that, Gareth."

He didn't seem to have heard her. He went on. "And I was a fool, too. And don't have the excuse of being a child. I should have known better. I did know better. But he is persuasive, my father. And he had a strong ally in that part of myself that presumed to suppose resolution would make anything possible, and that the end would justify whatever risks were involved."

She couldn't see his face. She could go only by the sound of his voice. It was troubled, angry.

"What risk did you take in marrying me?" she asked quickly.

"Never mind." Now his voice changed. "It was all wrong. That much we both know."

She tried to turn. She wanted to read his eyes. She thought that if she saw him, saw into him in that moment, she would understand him at last.

But his arms tightened, held her prisoner. "Be still," he said. "We'll soon be there."

In his voice she heard the same unwillingness that she felt. An unwillingness to return to Emerald Station.

That was what led her to say, "I did not marry you for what you, or your father, could offer me. It wasn't the gems. I was under a deep obligation to your father. And still am."

95

She wouldn't allow herself to go on, to say that the obligation no longer mattered to her. Everything but her feeling for Gareth himself was washed away. Instead, she asked, "Why should I not have married you?"

"That must be evident to you by now."

"If you had no intention . . ."

"No intention of what?"

"You know as well as I do," she retorted. And she thought of Deborah Maradine. Did he still love her, dream of her? Was that why his family had seemed so shocked when he brought Nealanna home with him? Had he actually married her so that the evil whispers in Bellingham might be stilled?

He had, instead of answering her, kicked the horse into a hard gallop. It jolted her bruised and aching body mercilessly. It was impossible to speak then, impossible almost, to think.

Within moments, they raced under the big iron-work sign between the massive stone pillars.

Henry, leaning forward in the saddle, was waiting. His red hair looked like flame under his cap. Relief lit his thin face and fired his blue eyes.

"You've found her," he cried.

"Take a message to the doctor to come at once," Gareth told him, ignoring her protest. "And then find Jennings and bring him back with you."

Henry nodded. "That's why I was ready here. Your father sent me to see . . ." He bent his head into the thin cold drizzle, and with another blue flash of his eyes at Nealanna, he set the horse running.

She and Gareth went on at a walk now, up the curving driveway, and to the front door, his arms still tight around her. There, at the foot of the steps, he slid down, tied the horse to a ring, and lifted her to her feet.

She looked up at his grim face. "You shouldn't have done that, Gareth. I don't need a physician. I need only a bath and a change of clothes."

Gareth's mother was standing in the foyer, her hands anxiously clasped before her, obviously waiting. She seemed smaller now, thinner. The lines scoring her face looked more deep, and the vulnerability even more intense.

She said, through pale lips that hardly moved, "You must lie down at once, Nealanna." And then, "Your father is in the study, Gareth. He wants you there. Did you see Henry . . ."

"He's on his way." A faint smile moved his mouth. "But it's all right. I think she'll do."

"If so, then your father would want . . ." Mary Kennelly stopped.

Neil had come down the hall into the foyer. He stood tall, his wide shoulders hunched in his dark coat, his head bent to study Nealanna. At last he said, "Are you able to tell me what happened?"

She nodded, and Neil turned, strode down the hall to his study. He waited there at the doorway until she and Gareth were inside with him. Then he carefully closed the door.

She sank gratefully into a soft chair, suddenly conscious of her trembling knees.

"Tell me," he said.

"Well, you know I went to the Maradines for a visit."

"Jennings took you," Neil put in.

She nodded. "And then, when I came home . . ."

"Where is Jennings?"

"I don't know," she answered.

"He was to bring you back," Neil said.

"Oh, but I can handle a runabout, and I told him so. I've done it many times before. There was no reason for him to come with me."

"There was a reason," Neil said. "I told him to. But go on. What happened?"

"Why, he was going to do something else." She paused then, thinking of his fight with Tom Stapleton. Should she mention that? Would that soften his father's anger against him? She decided it might be better to let Jennings' face speak for him. She went on, "I started out alone. A wheel came off. The horse bolted, and the runabout tipped over.

I was thrown clear fortunately. And then Gareth came and found me and brought me back." She stopped, set her lips. This time she would not make the error she had made before. She would not say aloud what good sense told her. Whatever doubts she had had before were quite gone. She knew that a second attempt had been made on her life.

Neil's face was expressionless. To Gareth he said, "I'll see the doctor, and have Jennings come in here the moment he arrives."

"But you mustn't blame him," Nealanna protested. "It wasn't his fault. I assured him . . . and besides, the wheel . . ."

"Take her upstairs," Neil told Gareth.

"But I tell you . . ."

His gray eyes touched her, softened. "You're persistent in defending the boy," he said. "But it will do no good."

She saw that was so. When Gareth touched her shoulder, she went with him.

On the stairs, he said, "I'll send Evanne to help you."

"I don't need any help," she answered. Then, "Gareth, don't let your father blame Jennings for this. I don't want to be the cause of trouble. And the poor boy isn't to blame."

"He should have been with you," Gareth answered. "He should never have left you alone."

"You'll do," Dr. Robinson said. "The bruises will fade, and the scratches heal. But from what I'm told, you've had a lucky escape. You must mind your actions in the future, I would think."

And it was not the first lucky escape, Nealanna thought, but didn't say aloud. There had been another one. There had been the kitten, whimpering on the eaves, and the railing that fell away when she went to rescue it. There had been that terrible dangling moment in the dark before Gareth's arms came around her to draw her to safety.

And now, just two weeks later, she had been flung suddenly, dangerously, from the runabout. She had thought that surely she would die then. Instead, she had ridden back to Emerald Station, cradled in Gareth's arms. And she had heard Neil say that Jennings had been told not to leave her alone, and Gareth reiterate it. Those words suggested to her that both her father-in-law and her husband had expected something to happen from which she must be protected, implied that they had known she walked with danger in Emerald Station.

She looked into Dr. Robinson's whiskered face, and smiled a little. "I'll be careful."

He was a small man, as unlike Mr. Davies of Harley Street as a person could be. There was, instead of elegance, a roughness to him that was somehow pleasing. His smile was meager, his eyes hard.

"All right, then. A day or two of rest, as you like. If you feel unexpected pain, have Henry come to me. But I think it won't be necessary."

"No," she agreed.

He rose from her side, stood regarding her. "You're a stranger to these parts."

"I'm from England."

"So I've heard." He picked up his bag. "Mr. Kennelly will be waiting. I'll go down to him."

She asked quickly, "Do you know if Jennings is home yet?"

"I don't. It's not part of my job to keep track of the Kennellys." He left her before she could answer, left her wondering at the sudden hostility she had heard in his voice, wondering if that small bewhiskered man shared the aversion of the people in Bellingham for those for Emerald Station.

She rested, eyes closed, breathing shallowly, for just a few minutes. Then, driven by the need to know if Jennings had yet returned, she got up.

She paused at the dressing table Gareth had moved into her room. In its three-sided mirror she saw her pale face and disheveled hair. She took a brush to her wild curls and smoothed them. She put on a dark blue robe and knitted slippers. She found, next to the old picture of her mother, the brooch brought with her. She didn't know why, but she put it on. Then, moving slowly and stiffly, she went down the steps past the leering black masks and the great leather shield.

Jennings stood just inside the closed front door, his plump shoulders set against it.

Gareth towered over him, demanding, "What do you mean . . ."

Until she said, "Gareth, please . . ." they were neither of them aware of her presence. When she spoke they looked up at her.

Jennings said through his swollen lips, "You had an accident. I'm sorry. I shouldn't have . . ."

She cut in, appealing, "Gareth, don't you see his face?"

"I do," he retorted. "We'll discuss that later. Go upstairs, Nealanna. You shouldn't have come down."

Neil spoke from the study doorway. "Get in here, Jennings."

The tone of voice was much the same as that Gareth had just used to her.

The boy glanced up at her, the cuts over his eyes streaked red.

She guessed that Dr. Robinson had already departed, and wished he had not been in such a hurry to be gone.

But Jennings' battered face suddenly eased into a smile. Then he went to his father. The door closed behind him.

In the silence, she heard the rattle of hail against the windows, and the thin whisper of the wind.

And then she heard Neil's voice raised in a terrible anger. "Why? Why can't you obey me? You left her alone against my express instructions. You went to town. Haven't we had enough trouble? I want an answer. I want it now!"

Gareth said quietly, "Upstairs, Nealanna," and again his tone was like his father's.

She returned to her room. She sank into the blue chair near the hearth, and listened to the thin threatening song of the wind.

If only she understood. She never doubted that there

was a connection between what had happened the night of her arrival and what had happened today. Someone had tampered with the balcony railing, baited a trap with the kitten. Someone had tampered with the runabout wheel.

Who would go to such extremes? Who hated her? Who had hated her on first sight? Or to whom could she be a threat?

She had been in the place only hours when the first accident occurred. Only hours. She had met the members of the family ... Faran, Alicia, Mary Kennelly, young Jennings. She had met the three Bordens. She had meet Avis and Brooke Maradine.

Which of those could be determined to destroy her? She could not suspect the Maradines. She felt from them a warmth that could not be pretense. And of the others, only Jennings had been at their home today. But then she remembered that he had said he'd seen Alicia running toward the meadow.

Jennings ... Alicia ... her thoughts made no sense.

She could hear nothing from below now. Was Neil still shouting at Jennings? Why had he told him she must not be left alone? Was it because he had expected something further to happen to her?

Was that why he had arranged her marriage to Gareth? Was she to be the bait in some trap he had set?

It was terrible to believe, and worse when she realized that Gareth must be a party to it. Gareth, too, had planned that she be brought to Emerald Station, used in this most awful of ways.

She closed her eyes, but felt the hot sting of tears behind their lids. Did this then explain Gareth's manner to her? Was he determined that they live out their lives together in this extraordinary way? Or was she simply a temporary expedient, one which he expected to be removed when some other problem was resolved? Would he then be free for another marriage?

Brooke had said, and she found herself believing him, that her marriage to Gareth would save him, would wipe away the stigma cast upon him by Deborah's murder. But she saw now that she could be, as Deborah had been, a victim. Was that why, each in his own way, had warned her to leave Emerald Station? And what would be the consequences to Gareth, if she were to heed such advice?

She lay back in the chair, pressing her face into the fabric for a comfort that was not there.

The door opened with a faint sound.

Her heart began a sudden drumming. She looked up.

Alicia asked softly, "Am I disturbing you, Nealanna? Mother wants to know if you need anything."

"I need nothing," she answered.

"Gareth told me. I'm sorry. I hope you're all right."

"Yes," Nealanna said.

The younger girl sat down on the edge of the four-poster bed, the canopy shaded her face. "You're lucky you're here and out of earshot."

"Why?"

"My father, and Jennings . . . but mostly my father. He is enraged."

"I'm sorry," Nealanna said helplessly. "I wish I . . ."

"I'm sorry, too. But mostly for Jennings. He is very defensive when he is angry, and that drives my father wild."

"But it wasn't his fault, Alicia."

"So he says. My father feels otherwise. And Jennings is a bit of a fool, too, which makes matters worse. He *will* go to town where he's not wanted. He will fight with Tom Stapleton. And then try to make friends with him as well. When he knows how they hate us and always have and always will."

"But why?" Nealanna asked. "Why should anyone hate the Kennellys."

"They've cause enough, I imagine," Alicia answered, and shrugged. Then, "How was your visit to the Maradines?"

"Very pleasant."

"Avis and Brooke are nice," Alicia agreed, "and Deborah was so beautiful. You saw her, of course."

"The portrait. Yes."

"She didn't look like that when they found her," Alicia said thoughtfully. And added, "I fear she didn't. She was badly beaten."

Nealanna shuddered. "It was a terrible thing to happen."

Alicia agreed with a nod. "And I'm afraid Gareth will never get over it."

Nealanna had no reply.

But she remembered the feel of Gareth's arms around her, the sense of his chest at her back, bracing her. She remembered what it had been like to safely lean against him. That, and the expression of fear on his face, when he first beheld her standing on the verge.

But those moments had lasted but a short time, and then he had become again the Gareth she had known since she first saw him standing in the hotel room doorway. The cold Gareth, who smiled with his mouth, but never with his emerald eyes. The Gareth who had brought her to danger, to death.

Chapter 10

"He's gone," Neil said heavily. "He went some time this morning, and I doubt that he'll be back very soon."

It was two days since Nealanna's visit to Maradine Mansion. Soon after her accident in the runabout, they had learned of it, and now they had come to see her.

Neil's remark had been made in answer to a question of Brooke's about Jennings.

Mary Kennelly's sigh could be heard in the small silence that followed. When she raised her eyes, Nealanna saw accusation in them.

She said, "But why, Mr. Kennelly? What happened?"

"We'll not discuss it," he answered.

"But we must. Is it my fault that Jennings has run away?"

Gareth stood near the graystone fireplace, hands clasped behind his back. He said coldly, "You take too much on yourself, I think. Jennings has nothing to do with you, Nealanna."

She bit her lip, choked back her words of protest. She had not seen Jennings since the afternoon when Neil had called the boy into his study, and begun his tirade against him. She had found it difficult to ask after him, but finally she had mentioned the boy to Gareth.

He had said sourly, "Jennings is banished to his room for now."

"Oh, Gareth," she protested. "It isn't fair."

"That's not for you to judge. But don't worry about it. He's healing, though too soon for my taste. It means he'll fight again. When he shouldn't. And he'll not be beaten, nor starved."

"He's too old for such punishment," she snapped. "And what happened can't be his fault."

But she still wondered. Jennings had been at Maradine Mansion. He had had ample opportunity to tamper with the runabout wheel. But then, the same was true for Alicia.

"Forget about it," Gareth had told her, with a cold finality that warned her there was no use speaking of it further.

But now Jennings was gone, and there was such terrible accusation in Mary Kennelly's eyes.

Brooke said quietly, "You'll find him. Or he'll turn up."

"Of course," Faran agreed, but looking at Avis.

"We should *do* something," Nealanna said.

"We'll not discuss it further," Neil told her.

Later, in their sitting room, Gareth said, "He'll manage, you know. He's one who lands on his feet."

"But he's only seventeen," she protested. "How can your father let him go, not knowing where, not caring . . ."

"Seventeen is your own age," Gareth answered. "Is that so very young?"

She refused to be teased though she knew it was his intention. She said seriously, "But I'm a woman. And women grow up much sooner." Gareth's face showed nothing of what he thought of her argument. She went on, "And my life has been different, too."

"Has it?"

"You know it has. Jennings has always had his family around him. He was treated as a child, the youngest child. He can't be prepared for the world."

"Then we'll see if he learns."

"But where will he go?"

"Knowing him I would guess that he'll go out West."

Her eyes widened. "Out West. Where the Indians are."

Gareth's stern face suddenly broke into a grin. "Nealanna, you've read too many stories. This is 1890, not 1790."

"But there are real Indians," she told him.

"Of course. Still, I think Jennings will be safe enough to hold on to his hair."

She gave him a puzzled look.

"The favorite means of killing was to scalp," Gareth explained.

"It isn't funny," she cried.

"No, I don't mean that," he answered. He went on soberly, "But you must understand. Jennings is at the age when he must find his own way. He's trying to now. He'll be all right."

"He was punished because of me, and unjustly so. He'll never forgive me."

"There's nothing to forgive. You simply don't understand."

"Then explain it to me."

He considered her thoughtfully. But at last he said, "There's nothing to explain."

She didn't answer, but she thought that there was much to explain. If only he would. If only he would allow her his confidence.

She felt his eyes on her. She heard him take a deep breath.

Then he rose, went into his room, and left her alone.

She had awakened when Gareth left. Cold pink dawn had filled the room when she rose, opened the draperies.

She heard the voices below, the footsteps in the courtyard. Soon Gareth and Faran, all three of them carrying guns, had ridden out with Neil. The night before they had talked about this hunting trip.

Alicia had asked that she be allowed to go, too, and

suggested that Nealanna accompany her. But Gareth had said firmly, much to Nealanna's relief, that he didn't believe she wished to hunt. Which she did not, in fact. Alicia had pouted. *She* enjoyed it, she insisted. Nealanna would, too.

But Gareth had been adamant, without asking Nealanna's own opinion. It was, she had thought then, quite typical of him to assume that she would agree with him. And, in this case, she did. But she would have liked it if he had consulted with her. In any case, the three men had ridden out alone.

Nealanna dressed in a black skirt, a long-sleeved white blouse. She wound white and red ribbons in her hair, and tied the same ribbon at her throat.

She found Evanne clearing the table in the kitchen, with Moira helping.

There was unpleasant tension in the room.

But Evanne refused to acknowledge it, though Nealanna asked if anything was wrong, and saw Moira wince.

"Nothing. Except that it's a cold morning. The men have gone. I'll have the buffet in a minute or two. Will you have coffee while you wait?"

"Just coffee, thank you," Nealanna said.

Evanne poured a full steaming mug. "That will start you." Then, "Yes. Cold indeed. It wouldn't surprise me if there were snow by dark."

"I can do without it," Moira told her, her elfin face tight. "I don't like to think of winter coming."

"Consider Christmas. Maybe that'll sweeten your temper. Or," Evanne added with a laugh, "stop winter, if you can."

"If I could, I would do a lot of things," Moira answered glumly. "But I can't."

"That's right," Evanne said, with no laughter in her voice. "You can't. But you can put those dishes into the sink, if you like."

Moira flushed, obeyed, and Evanne sighed, "Children."

"Is something wrong?"

"Nothing except the usual. My Moira is growing and

107

wants her freedom, not much different from Jennings, I suppose, but she's not ready for it. Not judging by the company she tries to keep unbeknown to me." The white wings at the temples of Evanne's red hair seemed to bristle. "Imagine. She tells me that she's visiting Lolly Raines at the Gordons. And then Henry says she walking out with a stranger, some drinking friend of Tom Stapleton's."

Nealanna smiled. "Oh, that's not so much of a crime, is it?"

"We work for the Kennellys," Evanne said. "To be anywhere within ten miles of Tom Stapleton, or his friends, is a disloyalty. I'll not have it, Nealanna."

"It's hard not to have friends though."

Evanne gave her a sharp blue look. "Never mind that. Tell me, are you preparing for Christmas?"

"Just by thinking. I'll have to start soon."

"You'll find little in the shops in town. But Mrs. Moody has a good hand with small things, if you catch her in time."

"I'll see her as soon as I can."

"Well," Evanne said. "I have my work to do. And I'd better see to Moira."

Alone, Nealanna sighed. It would be hours until Gareth returned. And when he did, he would probably retire to his room, or else to the study with his father.

Alicia had apparently stayed abed since she was not allowed to go hunting with the men.

Mary Kennelly had not yet come down, and perhaps she would not until much later. She seemed to spend most of her time in her rooms.

Nealanna supposed she would have to amuse herself one way or another, whether Gareth was here, or whether he was not. She must find some occupation for herself. She was not accustomed to having so much time to spend aimlessly, and she doubted it was good for her. She would, she decided, start reading. There were plenty of books in the house. Perhaps she could surprise Gareth with what she learned. More likely he would tease her, as he had

108

about the Indians. And perhaps, later, if Henry could be spared to drive her, she would visit Brooke and Avis.

She finished her coffee, called out her thanks to Evanne, and went into the hallway. She had started up the steps when she heard the clatter of hoofs in the courtyard. Instantly her heart began to pound. She jumped the steps she had just climbed, tripped over her gown, and ran for the kitchen. Just as she reached it, the door was flung back.

Faran cried, "Evanne, send Henry for Dr. Robinson. And say that it's urgent."

"But what's urgent?" Evanne cried. "Faran! Tell me!"

Now, closer, Nealanna could see his face. It was white, strained. There was a great streak of something dark and moist on his heavy hunting coat.

Evanne stood still, rocking on her boots, her hands pressed to her mouth. "Oh, no," she moaned through her fingers. "Oh, no, Faran."

Nealanna stared at the dampness on his coat. It was blood. She knew that it was blood.

The room seemed to darken. There was no air. Then Evanne's arms went around her, steadying.

"It's my father," Faran said. Then, "Get Henry, Evanne."

But it was Moira who slipped out, crying, "Henry, Henry, we need you."

They soon heard the horse galloping away.

Faran leaned in the doorway, trembling.

"What happened?" Nealanna asked.

"He . . . he was shot," Faran gasped.

"Shot? But how . . . who . . ."

Faran stared at her. "I don't know," he said slowly. "I can't think how it could have happened. We separated as we always do. The three of us going our own ways. I heard firing from different places. And then it was quiet, too quiet. I knew something was wrong. I called out for Gareth. And after a while, he answered me. Then we met. We kept calling for my father. He didn't come in, nor signal. There was nothing. Nothing. We started to look.

109

We found him in the brush. He's bleeding terribly, Nealanna."

"You'd better come in and sit down," she said. "It'll be a little while before Dr. Robinson arrives. And if Henry has trouble locating him . . ."

Faran pressed against the doorframe, shaking his head. "Gareth is with him. We were afraid to move him. He couldn't talk, you see. He couldn't say . . ."

The two of them were quiet. There seemed to be nothing to say. Into that silence there suddenly came the sound of hoofbeats. Very slow hoofbeats in ominous rhythm. Nealanna listened. She couldn't understand. Henry had just gone galloping away. Then who . . .

Faran turned, made a strangled sound.

She looked past his shoulder into the gray of the courtyard.

Gareth was coming slowly toward the house. He was on foot, leading his horse. He was leading his horse, and Neil's big body lay dangling across the saddle.

She made some small whimpering sound in her throat for she knew what must have happened.

Faran put her thought into words. His face tightened even more. He said, "He's dead then. He's dead, Nealanna."

They stood in the small cemetery outside of Bellingham.

There was snow on the ground, and a cold wind tore through the grove of young trees.

The minister's voice came to a stop. He closed the Bible, and raised his head.

Nealanna trembled, and felt Gareth's arm tighten around her. He bent his grim face. "It's over."

She blinked back tears, and looked at the group around her. Faran and Alicia held up a near-collapsing Mary Kennelly, whose face was invisible through her heavy black veil. Close by stood the Bordens, Evanne with Moira and Henry. Nanette leaned heavily on Jason Gordon's arm, and Avis and Brooke were with them.

Now the group broke. Faran and Alicia led their mother to the carriage.

It was big, Nealanna thought, and black, but it had no funeral plumes. She remembered briefly the day of her own mother's burial when she had ridden back to the mews cottage with Mr. Carowy and Mr. Davies as escort, and heard, for the first time, of Neil Kennelly. And now he was dead.

The Bordens followed after Faran and Alicia, and then the Gordons went to their own conveyance.

Gareth released her, moved to the minister's side, and spoke to him. She was alone. She moved slowly on the snowy path, but her boots slipped, and she caught herself against a large granite monument.

Even as she regained her balance she saw, in big carved letters, the name NEAL DAVID MARADINE.

Neal. Whose name with Anna's had made Nealanna's own. Nealanna knew that she had at last found where her father lay. Neil Kennelly and Neal Maradine had been friends. They had lived side by side, and had travelled together. They had been in England seventeen years before.

Brooks and Avis were suddenly on either side of her. She raised burning eyes. Brooke was her half-brother, Avis her half sister. And they must have realized it the moment they heard her name. Did that explain the warmth, the kindness, they had shown her? Was that the reason for the affinity she had felt for them?

She saw the answer in their eyes. Yes. They had known. She supposed they had wanted to protect the memory of their father. Then she would protect it, too.

The mystery of her identity was solved. That was enough. And it seemed, now, compared to the other mysteries which surrounded her, unimportant.

Why had Neil Kennelly wanted Gareth to marry her? And why had Gareth been willing to? Why had her life been twice endangered in Emerald Station? Why had Jennings run away? Why had Neil died?

111

Brooke's hand closed gently on her arm. He led her, with Avis following, to the carriage.

They were silent on the way home through the snow-covered countryside.

The house was cold in spite of the warm log fires.

Evanna and Moira served cold meats and bread and butter, and small slices of cake with steaming coffee.

The men spoke quietly in a group. The women, sitting close to the hearth, were silent, staring into the flames.

Mary's thin hands trembled in her lap.

Alicia sat next to her, cuddling for comfort, as if she were still a child.

Avis and Nanette had positioned themselves on either side of Nealanna, offering silent support.

"Jennings," Mary said at last. "We must find him. We must let him know what has happened. He must come home."

No one answered her.

Nealanna looked away from the older woman's anguished face.

She didn't want to see the pain there. She couldn't bear it. She wondered if, somewhere in Mary's mind, there was the same awful thought that was in her own.

Neil had quarreled with Jennings, imposed a punishment against which Jennings had rebelled by running away. But had he actually run away? Was he really gone from Emerald Station and from Bellingham? Could he and his father have met in the valley? Could they have exchanged words, and struggled? Had Jennings killed his father?

In the days that followed, no one mentioned Jennings again. And he did not return.

Dr. Robinson, Nealanna learned, had reported Neil Kennelly's death as he had said he would. A constable from Bellingham had questioned Faran and Gareth. They had told him what they knew, and he had said, "Such accidents occur. We'll put it so," and ridden away.

Through Evanne, Nealanna learned that the townspeople were less than willing to believe it was an accident. They scoffed at the theory that Neil had tripped over his own shotgun. Remembering Deborah's death little more than a year before, and not far from where Neil had fallen, they clustered to speak in sneering whispers about Gareth, who was heir to Emerald Station. Among those who spoke the loudest, Evanne said, was Tom Stapleton.

Nealanna was disgusted and frightened by such talk. But she forced herself to pretend that she did not know it went on.

A week after Neil was buried, she went to Gareth in the room that was now his study. She said to him, "Do you want me to leave you? We have no marriage. Nor shall there be one, it seems to me. So shall I go away?"

He sat very still at his desk, his big hands spread wide on the dark polished wood. He stared at her for a long time, then said, "Why do you suggest that, Nealanna?"

A pulse beat in her throat. Her breath seemed too shallow. She couldn't say that she loved him. She couldn't say that if Neil had forced him into a marriage he didn't want, then he was free now. She told him, "You have no need of me. Yet if you are to continue your line, and surely you plan to, then you do have need of someone, Gareth."

Was he still mourning his murdered Deborah? If he had married only to fulfill his father's determined dynastic ambitions, then why did he behave so? She waited.

He said quietly, "You made an arrangement with my father, Nealanna. It does not die with his death."

She heard herself ask in a whisper, heard with horror, "Then does it die with mine?"

"You'll not die," he said gruffly, his face cold and empty of any feeling.

"Then you still require something of me," she answered. "That thing, whatever it was, for which you married me."

"Yes," he told her. "I still require it."

Chapter 11

But whatever it was that he required, he didn't say, and she knew it was pointless to ask.

A week passed.

They had a quiet Christmas, exchanging visits with the Gordons and the Maradines.

Another week passed, and with it, the turn of the year.

Snow fell from the leaden skies, feathering the valley in a thin blanket at first, and finally burying it under great white, wind-ruffled quilts so that Emerald Station seemed to hang in an empty landscape, suspended between earth and sky. The heavy stillness in which it was wrapped seemed to further the illusion that it was not quite of this world, nor yet of another.

Gareth left her mostly alone, and went about his concerns, as quiet as the place itself, and as grim. She had no way to read his thoughts, no way to understand what drove him. She would sometimes notice that his eyes sought her out when they met at meals, or when they passed in the sitting room of their apartment. But if she returned the look, he would instantly shift his eyes away from her.

Mary Kennelly rarely came down from her rooms. She was, Dr. Robinson explained, suffering from a depression, which only time, and perhaps prayer, would cure. Neil's death, so soon after Jennings disappearance, was too much for her. Only rest would do her any good. Or word from Jennings. But there was no word from the boy.

Gareth had placed advertisements in many newspapers across the country. But if Jennings saw them, he ignored them. No one knew what had happened to him. And it would be years, though Nealanna didn't guess it then, before they had news of him.

Meanwhile, Evanne said, "The poor lady, she thinks that he's dead, too. And who can blame her?"

"Oh, no," Nealanna cried. "Why would Mrs. Kennelly think that? There's no reason."

"There is," Evanne said softly. "There's reason enough."

But when Nealanna demanded to know it, Evanne refused to answer.

One evening in mid-January, the Gordons and Maradines came for a visit. They brought with them a huge decorated box of bonbons, and two cakes. Evanne filled the silver urn with coffee, and she and Moira served.

Mrs. Kennelly refused to come down, but all the others gathered in the drawing room, chestnuts heating in the fire, to talk.

Faran stood close beside Avis, his hand on her shoulder, while she, smiling up at him, was plainly content.

Brooke teased Alicia into a game of hearts by swearing that she could never beat him.

Jason and Gareth engaged in low-voiced conversation, their serious faces bent close together.

Nanette, seeing Nealanna's eyes on them, said, "Why are you worried about Gareth? It will be all right, you know. He has been well-trained for what he must do. You can be sure of that. And he can take good care of himself as well."

"Yes," Nealanna agreed.

"Then why do you look ... look so sad?" Nanette asked. "Forgive me, but I do see it, you know."

"Sad, Nanette?"

"My dear, you seem no older to me at this moment than my own little Doe. Can't you try to trust me? Can't you tell me what troubles you so?"

"But nothing does," Nealanna said quickly.

Nanette shook her head. "If you don't want to confide in me, then you mustn't. But I know what my eyes see. I realize that Neil's death was a shock to you, but this isn't proportionate." She paused. Then, "Or perhaps you should see Dr. Robinson. He might be able to set your mind at rest."

Nealanna felt heat in her cheeks, and wished that she would not blush so freely. It gave her away, of course. It made her seem young, gauche, without experience. And all three were true. But must she have all three written on her cheeks as well?

She gathered herself, said quietly, "It's not that I'm expecting, Nanette." She stopped herself just in time from adding, "Nor am I likely to be."

Alicia left the game of hearts to bring fresh coffee. Faran served extra bonbons. Avis brought more cake slices.

The interruption didn't deter Nanette. When she and Nealanna were alone again, she went on. "It may be Mary's depression affecting you. Dr. Robinson . . ."

Once again there was an interruption. This time Brooke came and sat beside them, which was just as well, Nealanna thought.

It should have been a pleasant few hours, but somehow there was a heaviness in the air, a lack of breath. And she sensed a certain watchfulness in Gareth, in the others.

She could suddenly endure it no longer. There was a strange leaden dizziness within her. Her hands felt numb, her feet, too. A deep driving pain assailed her some place within.

She rose, interrupting what Brooke had been saying, without knowing that, and murmured an apology at large that was hardly audible. She walked stiffly from the room. She grasped the bannisters tightly and pulled herself upward past the grinning black masks that seemed to shrink and grow in alternating rhythms. One step. Another. Two more. Midway she knew that she could not make it to her room, her bed. A peculiar black haze had begun to form before her eyes. What she saw through it was dark and shadowy and distant. A sudden cold sweat broke out over her body, chilling her flesh and her blood, too. The steps beneath her feet began to dissolve into nothingness. She fought to remain conscious, and screamed, "Gareth, Gareth, help me," as she fell.

The next hour forever remained blurred moments in her memory.

Afterward, she could recall that she had fallen on the steps. There were voices, cries, murmurs. Above all sound, though, she heard Gareth. She heard him swear terrible oaths as he lifted her into his arms.

It seemed to her then that she drifted in pain for a long time. Gareth was with her, and Jason and Brooke, too. She was forced to drink warm water and mustard, forced to be sick. She was agonizingly and wrenchingly pummelled and pounded and held over a basin until she had managed to empty herself. She was aware of the other two men, but her eyes, when they could, always sought Gareth.

At last she was allowed to lie still. She was covered warmly. She couldn't speak. She couldn't open her eyes. She was limp with exhaustion, shivering with a cold that wouldn't leave her.

Jason was saying, "You can check with Dr. Robinson, of course, and should. But I'll stake my life there's no doubt of it, Gareth."

"Yes," Gareth said.

"What will you do?" Brooke asked.

"I don't know yet."

"Do you have any idea of how ..."

"No, Brooke. How could I?"

"It's a terrible risk that you take, Gareth." Brooke's voice was heavy, disapproving. "Do you want the girl's death on your conscience for as long as you live? Is pride so strong ..."

Gareth cut in, "Leave it to me, Brooke. You, too, Jason."

The two men left the room.

Gareth leaned down. He pressed her hand, and then touched his lips to her forehead. She opened her eyes and saw anguish in his face. She summoned all her strength to whisper, "But I'm all right now, Gareth."

His face emptied. He said, "Go to sleep. I'll stay right here."

He was there when she awakened. The room was bright with sunshine, and she winced against it.

When he heard her move, he turned to look. He had been at the door, speaking in a whisper she couldn't understand. He closed the door, crossed the room to her side.

She said tiredly, "I'm afraid I made a peculiar spectacle of myself last night, Gareth. I'm sorry."

"Don't be sorry. Though you did. You were very ill."

"What happened to me, Gareth? Do you know?"

He hesitated. Then, "It happens sometimes. But you're fully recovered now, aren't you?"

"Yes. But what happens occasionally? Why should I have been stricken so suddenly, and so terribly?"

He didn't answer her.

Remembering the blurred words she had heard the night before, she became certain that her illness, like her two other escapes, had not been caused by accident. Once again, malice had been planned and executed.

She whispered, "Gareth, haven't we had enough lies?"

Again he didn't answer her.

She said, "I think I was poisoned, Gareth. Brooke and Jason thought so, too. Is that candid enough for you?"

He said, "And I think that you're quite delirious still. You only appear recovered." He started for the door, "I'll send for Dr. Robinson after all."

"There's no need to," she told him bitterly. "You know perfectly well that I'm not delirious. I'm weak, yes, and sick at heart. I'm frightened, too. But I'm not ill. Not any more. And you don't want Dr. Robinson to see me, and speak of this in Bellingham, do you?"

It was two days before she was allowed up, and another two before she could leave the house.

She waited patiently, determining that as soon as she could, she would go to Bellingham, on whatever pretext she could. She would go to Dr. Robinson, describe how she had been affected, and ask him what it would mean. She would go to Jason, too, and make sure that she had not misunderstood him. And if Jason wouldn't help her, then she would go to Brooke.

In her mind, she repeatedly went over that night. Nanette had been sitting beside her most of the time. Brooke and Alicia had played hearts. Alicia had served fresh coffee. Faran had brought bonbons. Moira had brought cake. Evanne had been in and out. Avis had moved from one place to another. Any one of them could have put some noxious preparation into her coffee. But it was impossible to accuse anyone when she didn't know whom to accuse.

Could Avis or Brooke, always so kind to her, actually hate her because she had taken Deborah's place in marrying Gareth? Or could they hate her because she was their secret half-sister? Had Nanette or Jason any reason to consider her a threat to them? What about Alicia and Faran?

Hour after hour, she speculated on who had attempted to poison her. Hour after hour, she asked herself when that hidden hand would strike against her once more. Finally, the four days passed. She dressed warmly, and went downstairs in search of Gareth.

He was, Evanne said, at the Maradines. He would return later.

"Could Henry drive me into town?" Nealanna asked.

Evanne hesitated, an uneasiness in her eyes. At last she said, "He has chores, and there's a great deal of snow on the roads."

"I want the air so badly," Nealanna told her.

119

"When Gareth returns . . ."

"It will be too late. And besides, I should like to go now," Nealanna answered.

With a sigh, Evanne said, "All right. I'll have Henry bring the carriage down. And I'll send Moira with you for company."

"I don't want company," Nealanna retorted.

Sighing again, Evanne went out.

Nealanna grinned to herself. It was a small triumph, but at last she felt, she had asserted herself. She was Gareth's wife. She must be treated as such.

She waited outside on the steps. The cold air was bracing. The sun was bright. She was delighted with herself, but hoped that Gareth didn't return before Henry had driven her away.

He brought the carriage around, smiled shyly at her from under his cap, and helped her up. He carefully tucked a warm fur rug around her, saying, "You mustn't take cold."

"We'll go to Dr. Robinson's house," she told him.

He gave her a quick look, but only nodded, climbed to the seat, and they set off across the snowy valley.

They passed no one on the way, and soon they climbed the last slope and rolled down the other side of it and into Bellingham.

Henry stopped before a small white house that was not two blocks, Nealanna saw, from the Gordons.

"Shall I wait?" he asked.

"No. I'll surely be here an hour."

"Then I'll come back," he said. "And pick up the mail meantime."

He waited until she had gone up the steps, pressed the bell as directed by a sign, and entered as also directed by the sign. Then he drove the carriage away.

A small woman, with flour up to her elbows, covered by a long apron, came into the hall to ask her business.

When she explained that she wished to see Dr. Robinson, the woman said, "He's off on a conference. And will be for two days. Is it urgent?"

Nealanna said that it was not. Then, not knowing what else to do, she asked that Henry be told she was waiting for him at the Gordons, and went out into the sunshine. She slowly walked the two blocks through snowy sidewalks to the Gordons.

There, Nanette exclaimed over her. "How good to see you. I wanted to visit, but Jason said Gareth wouldn't have it. Are you all well now?"

"Isn't Jason here?" Nealanna asked.

"He's off to Boston for a day or two. He just left this morning. But never mind, we'll have a nice visit."

Nealanna followed her into the living room, a pleasant place full of indoor plants and books and childrens' games. Small Jay immediately left his book on the floor and climbed into Nealanna's lap. Tiny Doe crawled across the rug and rested her cheek against her leg.

"Lolly's shopping," Nanette explained. "She'll return soon. I couldn't do without that girl, you know."

"It's pleasant here," Nealanna answered, thinking of the chill, quiet, watchful air of Emerald Station.

"Then come more often."

"Yes," Nealanna agreed. "I ought to."

But she thought that there was no way now for her to confirm what was already very nearly a certainty in her mind. If Jason was away, and Dr. Robinson, too, who could tell her if she had been poisoned? Who could tell her how to protect herself?

Nanette excused herself, saying that she would have some coffee brought in. But she had hardly left when she was back.

"Nealanna," she said nervously, "Tom Stapleton's at the door, asking to see you. Shall I send him away? Do you know him?"

"I don't know him. But I'll speak to him." Nealanna set Jay on the floor, patted Doe's head, then rose.

"Perhaps you'd better not," Nanette told her. "I have the feeling . . ."

But Nealanna went into the hallway. She saw a big silhouette through the frosted glass. She pulled the door open.

"Yes?" she said. "I'm Nealanna Kennelly."

"And I'm Tom Stapleton." He swept a cap from his blond head, made her a mocking bow. "You sound more like the Queen of England than Nealanna Kennelly, but so be it. I'm at your service, no matter what you've heard of me, and I'm performing a service now."

He was the man with whom Jennings had fought, the man who hated the Kennellys because they had been sold land on which he and his family had been tenants, and perhaps because his sister who had worked for the Kennellys had run away from there to marry.

Nealanna studied him carefully. He was tall, heavy. She guessed him to be about twenty or twenty-two years old. By his hands, he was a workman of some kind.

At last she asked, "And what service are you performing now?"

"If you'll come down to the sidewalk, I'll show you," he answered.

She held back for a moment, but he urged her on, a hand at her elbow. The cold air bit into her body.

She shivered, wishing immediately that she had not gone with him.

But she was there. She looked up and down the empty street. "What trick is this?" she asked.

"No trick." He put two fingers to his lips, shrilled a whistle. Then he grinned at her and walked quickly away.

A man stepped from a nearby alley, stood staring at her. He was a stranger, no one that she knew or had ever seen. Her heart began to beat very quickly. She turned to go into the house.

She had taken only a step when his voice stopped her, his English voice.

He stood at her shoulder, smiling at her from dark, deep-set eyes. "Nealanna," he said. "Don't you know me? Don't you really? I'm your own brother, your twin. I'm Dale Yarrow."

122

Chapter 12

Shock held her frozen, speechless. She had had no brother. Yet he was dark of eye and hair, slight, and not very tall. Still, she could not believe it.

He watched her, his lips twisted in an odd leering smile. At last he asked, "Is it true then? You never knew? Our dear mother Anna never told you?"

"It can't be true," Nealanna said at last. "Surely I'd have heard of it before."

"Would you?" An unmistakable sneer was in his voice. "How? When? Why should our dear Anna have told you that you had a brother who was a twin? She refused me herself remember."

"It's impossible," Nealanna stammered. But by then she had begun to wonder. Why was it so impossible? She had first seen her mother when she was five years old. She had seen her twice in the years that followed, and then, when she was seventeen she had had those last three months, being nurse, daughter, confidante, and listener. What did she know of Anna Yarrow? What had she ever known that was true? But wouldn't Mr. Caroway have told her? Wouldn't the physician have said? Mr. Caroway might have known. But now she recalled that Mr. Davies had not seen Anna Yarrow in those days.

"I see that you realize it is not so impossible after all," Dale was saying. "Let me tell you . . ."

But she had rallied. No. She would not believe it. Possible or no, it was not so. He was not her brother. She said, "What proof do you have to offer me? And what do you want? Remember that we're strangers whatever you claim."

"Proof? Is that what you want?"

"How did it happen that we were separated? That I never heard of you before this?"

"Our Anna was seventeen when she was delivered of twins. One boy, one girl. She had no husband, no where to go. The boy she gave away. Yes, Nealanna. Gave him away as if he were a bit of unused furniture. The girl she would have given away, too. But it was not so easy. No one wanted a girl. A boy would work, in a few years past infancy. But girls were always a burden." He shrugged. "And then great fortune befell our Anna. So she decided to forget her only son. And you benefited by the fortune, and continue to do so. While I," he shrugged again. "You can see me. You can tell."

"You cannot be seventeen," she said, though what he had told her of her mother, her life, rang true. "So you cannot be my twin."

He said sourly, "Oh, how do you know? My looks are from the life I've led. Just as yours are from the one you've had."

She had no answer. She saw in his face something that was familiar, though she didn't know what it was beyond his dark hair and dark eyes. He was thin and wiry as a sparrow, a man who worked, she judged by his hands. Could he be her brother? Could he be her own flesh and blood? Should not her own flesh and blood tell her if it were so? She thought of Brooke and Avis. It was true that she hadn't recognized them, but she had felt their warmth for her to be unusual; she had sensed a closeness, though she had determined never to speak of it to them or anyone else. She looked into Dale's thin face. She didn't know him. She saw only that he was staring at the rings on her fingers. Her wedding band that sparkled. The other ring that Gareth, just the other day, insisted that she wear.

Now Dale said, "You struck it, my lady. I know all about you, I might as well say. I met Stapleton in a pub here the day after I arrived . . ."

"We call it a saloon," she said absently.

"How far you've come," he laughed. "But no matter. I followed you from London on what was only a hunch, and I was right, so Stapleton tells me."

"What do you mean?" she demanded.

"We should share, should we not? You've had the benefit all your life until now. I want some of it, Nealanna."

"But I have nothing," she said.

He grinned at her. "Perhaps. But the Kennellys have a great deal, and you're a Kennelly now."

"That doesn't signify."

"It does, my lady."

"Stop sneering at me," she told him. "You have no reason."

"You're a bastard," he said quietly. "Excuse me for reminding you. But you're a bastard as I am. Our mother was a common . . ."

"That's not true," Nealanna cried.

But it was no use. She knew too many of the details. What her mother had told her had all been a dream. No more than that. Neal Maradine had used her, and left her, as he had perhaps used other women. Only Neil Kennelly had pitied her, helped her. There had been no love, no romance, and no inopportune death. Anna Yarrow had dreamed it all, along with her acting career. And the money left to provide for her had been thrown away on drugs, and drinking, and gambling.

Nealanna drew a deep breath. "What does it matter? She's dead now."

"It matters to me. And even more to you," he retorted.

"No," she said.

He put his hands on her shoulders, fingers biting cruelly through the thickness of her coat. "You've married into a fine rich family. But one with a history, too." He smiled a little. "Remember. I have friends here in Bellingham. Stapleton, and others, too, closer than you know. They take pleasure in their hatred for the Kennellys. Can you imagine what would be if I were to tell him about Gareth Kennelly's wife?"

"But you wouldn't," she said faintly, a pleading in her voice.

"Surely not. Why should I?" He waited, then added, "Unless I was forced to."

"But who would force you to? Why? Surely you can forget you've found me."

His small smile became broad and ugly to look at. He said, "I've no desire to forget it. Not when I've come all this way. A long trip, and in steerage, too. Suffering, hungry, I came just to see my sister with these eyes of mine. Just to see her. So why would I want to forget her?"

She stared at him. She knew now for certain that he meant her ill in some way. He had uttered the threat clearly enough, and he had seen her weakness. He would follow up his advantage.

She said briskly, "All right. What is it that you want?"

"Why, you've so much, and I so little. A few dollars to start me off in this great land. I work with Stapleton now, carpentering. But I'm a smith, you see. Perhaps a hundred dollars, for a start, or two hundred, if you were generous, and then . . ."

She cried wildly, "But I have no money. None. Where would I get it? Where? How?"

"A clever girl, and well-educated, I'm told. Surely you can manage, in a house so fine, to locate a few hundred dollars."

"No," she said. "It is not possible."

"You'll make it so. Or everyone in Bellingham will know that you're a bastard," he said thinly.

She shuddered. She didn't know what Neil had told Gareth. She didn't know if Avis and Brooke had ever

126

spoken to him of their knowledge of the facts of her birth. That she could face, she supposed. But should the town know ... here, where already they spoke of the Kennellys in ugly whispers. Here, now that Neil was dead, Gareth would be brought low, shamed, perhaps destroyed.

"I'll try to do it," she said at last. "If I can, where shall I find you?"

"I'll find you," he said. He touched her cheek in a gesture full of the mockery of tenderness. "Sister, I'm a happy man today."

He was a man, yes, she thought. He was seventeen, if what he said was true, but he was ages older than Jennings at the same seventeen. Dale Yarrow knew evil. She was sure of it. Jennings, she was equally sure, did not. But Dale was here, and Jennings wasn't.

She said faintly, "I'll try, Dale."

"Then succeed."

Past his shoulder, she was aware of movement. A horse snorted and stamped as it came slowly down the cobblestone street, and under the bare trees stopped beside where she stood with Dale.

Gareth stepped down from the saddle. He stood still, his face hard as stone, his green eyes as brilliant and blank as the emeralds for which his home had been named. He let the reins drop from his gauntleted hands, and came toward her.

It was like some evil nightmare from which she could not awaken. Gareth, with that frozen look on his face, and Dale suddenly whispering hoarsely, "Do it. I'll find you," and striding away, to leave her alone.

Then Gareth stood close to her, so close that she had to tip her head back to meet his eyes. He asked softly, "Who was that man?"

It was on the tip of her tongue to tell him, to say the truth, and let come what may. But too much had happened. She was afraid for him. What would Gareth do if he heard of Dale's threat? What would he do if the truth were known. She must not chance it. She dared not.

She swallowed, said, "I don't know him, Gareth."

"Then why were you speaking to him?"

"He ... he asked me for directions. He is a stranger in Bellingham."

"How odd that he should ask you. And you, yourself, a stranger, too. Or have you somehow managed to slip into Bellingham more often than I know?"

"Of course not," she said.

"How oddly you behave. You told Evanne you wanted to come to town. At least that's what she said when I returned home. I came in, and met Henry by chance. He dropped you at Dr. Robinson's. I went there, and you had left word that he was to pick you up here at the Gordons. I arrive here, and find you ..."

"A chance meeting," she said. "Gareth, you must believe me. I do not know that man." Here, at last, was the truth. She did not know Dale Yarrow. She must cling to that fact, think of nothing else. Yet there was, in her mind, the memory of his threat. What would it do to Gareth if it were said in town that his wife was ...

Gareth shrugged, turned toward the house. "I suppose I shouldn't blame you. I suppose our life isn't much conducive to loyalty. And perhaps there is, through no fault of your own, a taint in your blood that cannot be denied."

So she became certain he knew of the facts of her birth. Neil had told him. But still he mustn't know about Dale Yarrow, and Dale mustn't let the facts be known in town.

Softly she said, "I am not disloyal to you, and you mustn't think so."

"Very well. I won't think so." He moved ahead of her up the snowy path. But she stayed where she was, refusing to follow.

He turned back. "Come in, Nealanna. We'll tell Nanette that you're coming home with me. By then Henry will be here to pick you up."

"You have no reason, and no right, to accuse me," she told him.

"I accuse you of nothing," he answered tonelessly.

128

"Now, I insist. You must come in and say goodbye to Nanette."

That night, in the sitting room of their suite, she tried again. "Gareth," she said, "you misunderstood what you saw today. Please believe me. What you think is wrong."

He raised his head from the book he was reading. His face was shadowed by lamplight. He answered, "I think nothing, Nealanna. But it would be wise if you never saw that man, whoever he is, again."

"I don't ... I don't plan to," she said in an agonized whisper.

"Then we'll say no more about it." He bent his head in abrupt dismissal.

She went into her room.

One hundred dollars, two hundred dollars ...

She ground her hands together. How could she find such a vast sum of money? She didn't dare ask Gareth for it, didn't dare ask anyone. Why didn't Dale see that there was no way for her to give him what he asked? How did he expect her to do what could not be done?

She went to her dresser, examined its contents. There was so little here that belonged to her, to her alone. So little that she had had before Gareth married her. She touched the strand of emeralds. They were worth much, but they were Kennelly stones, just as the rings she wore were Kennelly stones. She could not give them away. She remembered when Gareth had put the emeralds around her throat and insisted that she wear them.

She turned away, her eyes burning with tears. She had been, then, a foolish and hopeful bride. Now she was without hope. She was trapped in an invisible web. In every direction she looked there was danger. Dale was only part of it. The other was here, here in Emerald Station.

"Why, Nealanna," Mary Kennelly asked, "whatever is the matter? Are you ill again? You seem so pale this morning."

"No," she answered. "I'm fine."

129

She knew that Gareth was watching, listening. She could feel his stony eyes on her face, sense the tension in his body, though he was apparently concentrating on his food.

Mary sighed. "I wondered when we came here if we could find happiness in this house. I wonder now, so many years later."

Gareth said nothing.

Nealanna held her breath.

But Alicia laughed, "Oh, Mother, what do you mean?"

Mary passed her hand over her wrinkled brow. "I don't know what I mean." She rose and walked out of the room.

Alicia said, "She worries about Jennings, her baby. And I suppose she should. Where can he be, Gareth?"

He looked at her over his coffee cup.

She flushed, lowered her eyes. "I worry about him, too," she said sulkily.

He glanced at Nealanna, then got up, and left the room.

Alicia said, "I am beginning to feel like Mama. There is no hope for the Kennellys. We're all doomed."

Nealanna said nothing.

Alicia went on, "Since you came, Nealanna. Do you know? I believe that you are the cause of our problems."

"I?"

"Gareth is unhappy, and you are his wife."

Again Nealanna said nothing. She finished her meal, nodded at Alicia, and went into the hall. She climbed the stairs slowly. She told herself that she must not listen to Alicia. The girl was nineteen, but flighty. She had the mind of a child, a malicious child, perhaps.

Yet she was right in sensing the threat that hung over Emerald Station. Nealanna herself had sensed it the moment of her arrival. She had looked under the great scrolled sign at the big stone house, seen its blank windows reflecting only the black clouds that hung low in the sky, and wished that she had never come.

And Alicia was right, too, in imagining that Nealanna

130

had something to do with the troubles. But it was not she alone. Too much had gone before. Deborah Maradine had been murdered. The whispers about Gareth had passed through Bellingham. All that had taken place before he brought Nealanna home with him.

And since then . . .

Three times there had been attempts on her life. Three times death had reached out for her . . .

She had just reached the door of her room when Evanne called from the foot of the steps. "Nealanna, there's a man here to see you."

She went to the bannister, leaned over to look.

Dale Yarrow stood there. He held a canvas suitcase in one hand, a checked cap in the other. He smiled up at her. "I've come on business, ma'am," he said.

Chapter 13

It was impossible to believe, yet it was so. Dale Yarrow had come, to the one place beyond all others that he must not be.

She went down the steps as fast as she could, her dress flying out behind her.

Evanne, waiting, was plainly puzzled, and not quite certain what to do.

Where was a place she could speak to him in private? Nealanna asked herself despairingly. But there was no time to think or plan.

"He's a peddler," Evanne told her. "He has needles and pins. We have need of neither."

"Yes, yes," Nealanna answered. And then, "But this way. The drawing room."

Grinning, Dale followed her.

Within the room, she closed the door. She stood there. "What do you want here? How could you dare come here?"

"A man must eat," he said. "I sell needles and pins. You heard." And his tilted black eyes scanned the shadowed room, touched the prismed chandelier and the gray stone fireplace, admired the Oriental rugs and the hangings.

She saw that, said hurriedly, "You should never have ..."

"Your husband's gone off, sister. I waited until I saw him ride away."

"I have nothing for you. I can not help you," she said. "I've thought and thought. It's just no good. You must believe me."

"You wear diamonds on your hands," he retorted. "And it's said in town that you have a queen's ransom in jewels as well."

"None of that is mine," she said.

She was wearing the brooch that had belonged to her mother. Her fingers trembled as she touched it. She knew that she mustn't say from whence it had come. He would reject it if he knew. She told him, "This is all I can give you, Dale."

He held out his hand.

She unpinned the brooch, and gave it to him, making sure that their fingers in no way touched. She thought that she couldn't bear it if he should touch her. He might be the brother, twin, he claimed, but she detested him now for the man he was.

He turned the brooch in his hand, peered at it, and grunted his disapproval. He flung it away from him. It fell to the rug, and lay there like a single staring eye.

She trembled when she thought of that and asked helplessly, "You don't want it then?"

"For two hundred dollars?" he laughed.

"But it's all I can give you."

"You live in this fine house, and wear beautiful gowns. You're mistress of a fortune. I have a hovel to myself, and that's all I've ever had. I wear what you see, and that's all I've ever worn. You must share with your brother, and not turn him aside."

"I cannot. There is no way, Dale. You must leave me alone, and go away."

"Go away? I think you're mad. I came here only to be

133

near you, and here I stay. As long as you're in Bellingham, then I am, too. And wherever you go, I'll follow!"

And at that moment, the door opened.

Gareth stood there. He asked in a low hard voice, "What are you doing here?"

Nealanna clasped her shaking hands before her. "He ..." she began. "He ..."

"I'm a peddler," Dale whined. "I sell needles and pins. You can ask in town, Mr. Kennelly. They know me there. I'm a smith by trade, and I do a bit of carpentering, too. But I sell what I can for the extras. Just ask them. My name is Dale Row."

Nealanna let her breath out in a long silent sigh. She had thought that Dale would betray her. She had expected him to say he was Dale Yarrow and go on from there. But she saw at once that he couldn't. If he once told Gareth what he knew then his blackmail was blackmail no more. He was silent for his reasons, she for hers.

Gareth looked down at him, then glanced sideways at her. "Get out," he told Dale. "We don't want your needles and pins. And if I see you in this house again ..."

"A man goes where his business takes him," Dale answered. He hefted his canvas suitcase, sidled toward the door.

Gareth caught him by the shoulder, spun him around as if he were a child. Small and slight as he was, he seemed a child to Nealanna.

"You're to stay well away from my wife," Gareth said through his teeth. "And from this house." He shoved Dale through the door and down the hallway. In the foyer, he thrust Dale from him, went on, "Perhaps this will help you remember."

"No, Gareth," Nealanna cried. "No, don't."

But he raised his hand, struck Dale two hard slaps.

Beyond him, she saw slender Moira watching, elfin face aflame as her hair, eyes glittering with tears.

As Dale scuttled away, Gareth turned, walked back to Nealanna. "Do you have an explanation?" he asked.

"You heard him. I . . ."

Gareth picked up the brooch, gave it to her.

She accepted it, blushing.

"I believed that I had the right to expect more from you," he said quietly. "I believed that I owed you something as well. Since I can expect nothing from you, and since I consider that I now owe you nothing, I shall do as I please."

She couldn't answer him. She didn't know what he meant, but she couldn't summon the strength to tell him so.

He stared at her for a long cold moment, and then he left her alone.

It was late the same afternoon. Early twilight had fallen, and from it, a light veil of snow drifted down out of the darkening sky.

Nealanna stood on the balcony, wrapped in a heavy shawl. The snow touched her cheeks, and from her own warmth, melted and slid down like tears. Like the tears she would not allow herself to shed.

A runabout pulled into the courtyard below. It was a new one, bought to replace the one shattered in her accident. The orange kitten, she thought, had not been replaced, and she was glad of it.

She watched as Gareth handed down a small boy to Henry, then climbed down himself. For a moment the three of them seemed to disappear into a swirl of snow. Then she saw Gareth and the boy plodding around the side of the house.

She wondered who the small boy was, and why Gareth had brought him to Emerald Station. She went to the sitting room door, stood waiting.

Soon she heard Alicia's outraged cry, "Gareth, what are you doing? Why have you brought him here after all this time?"

He answered, "Be still, Alicia. I'll have no questions from you, nor comments either."

Nealanna opened the door, stood watching.

Gareth, holding the hand of the boy, came up the steps slowly.

She waited, breath held.

The boy paused, looked at her, and smiled. She found herself smiling back, helplessly touched at the bright warmth in his face.

But Gareth said quietly, "Not now, Storr. First we must see someone else for a few moments."

He led the boy past her, then down to Mary Kennelly's apartment. Within moments, she heard him say, "Mother, here is Storr. Keep him with you for a little while. Say hello to your Grandma, Storr."

Nealanna's face burned. She shrank back into the sitting room, huddling within the shawl, though the place was stifling hot.

Gareth came in, closed the door. He stood still, looking at her. At last he said, "You heard? You understand?"

She said faintly, "Yes. I understand. The boy is your son."

He sat in a chair, stretched out his long legs. He said, not looking at her, "Yes. The boy is my son. He has been boarded outside of the valley since he was born some six years ago."

She nodded. Gareth's son ... Who had been his mother? Where had she gone? What had happened to her?

"I've decided to acknowledge him, raise him here."

"Yes," she said. "You should."

The boy's mother didn't matter, Nealanna thought, remembering what her own life had been. The boy's would be a better one. If she could help it, it would be.

Gareth said dryly, "I'm grateful for your opinion. Though I didn't ask for it." Then, "I think we must have no secrets between us." He paused, waited. But she said nothing. He smiled faintly, continued, "So I'll tell you about it, and then we'll not discuss it again. I was twenty, home from school for the holidays. The girl was a maid here in this house. She was older, and knew what she was

136

about, and when I found the way to her bed easy, I didn't struggle, I assure you. I returned to school, and forgot her, and supposed that she had forgotten me. And perhaps she would have but for Storr. In any case, when she learned that she was expecting, she told my father. He would not turn her out, of course."

Nealanna thought of what Neil had done for her mother, for her herself. No, he would not turn out the maid who worked for him.

Gareth went on, "He kept her and made plans for her future. The child was born here. A day later she left Emerald Station. With a new lover, my father believed. She has not been seen since. Her name was Jane Stapleton."

"Stapleton," Nealanna repeated.

This then was the second reason why Tom Stapleton hated the Kennellys. They bought the land he considered his own. And his sister had run away from here.

"You know the name," Gareth said. "I supposed that you would."

"And what does Storr know?" she asked. In the moment that seemed most important to her. To protect the boy.

"That he is my son. That his mother is dead."

"Nothing more? Nothing about his kin?"

"He has none but me and my family. That's what he believes. And he'll never believe anything else."

"But what of Tom Stapleton?"

"He knows nothing, except that his sister left Emerald Station."

"Very well," Nealanna said. "If it can be kept from Storr, then let it be."

"It can be, and it will."

"He'll never learn the truth from me," she promised. "And I'll be good to him. Believe that much."

"I do. And we both know why. But remember that it doesn't matter. Neither you, nor Storr, were the first children born out of wedlock. Nor will you be the last."

137

He paused, waited. "Now do you have anything you wish to tell me?"

She thought of Dale. It was because of Dale, of what he considered to be her interest in him, that Gareth had brought Storr to the house. It had been to punish her for an imagined disloyalty. But it was no punishment to have seen the small boy's smile, and it would be none to make him welcome. Dale couldn't hurt Gareth by telling him the facts of her birth. But what if Dale talked in town? Would Gareth be able, after all that had gone before, to bear it?

She said softly, hoping her decision was the right one, "I've nothing to tell you."

He rose, said, "Then I'll bring Storr to you now."

She nodded.

He left the room, but within moments, he was back.

Storr was tall for his age, a big six-year-old, she thought. He had a sweet face, thin, but very comely. He had Gareth's bones, cheek and brow, sculptured and firm. But his hair was a thick mop of blond curls. She forced back the memory of Tom Stapleton's curls.

"Here is Storr," Gareth said, by way of introduction.

"Are . . . are . . ." The boy's lips writhed, and his throat grew taut with effort. "Are . . ."

"Slowly," Gareth said. "There's time."

Storr tried again, straining. At last, flushed but triumphant, he said, "Are you my new Mama?"

"Your second Mama," Gareth told him.

Nealanna went down to her knees, to his own size. She opened her arms wide, and laughed. "Oh, yes, yes. Come to me and let me hug you."

Storr examined her gravely through eyes that were as green as Gareth's own. Then, at last, he hurled himself against her.

There was suddenly life and joy in the place where there had been nothing but fear and death before. The frightening months were over as if they had never been. The shadowy mysteries had receded, as if once imagined and now forgotten.

It was Storr's doing, Nealanna thought.

Since he had come three days before, the darkness had been chased away from Emerald Station. His laughter seemed to fill the big rooms. His footsteps pattered up and down the halls. He was open, warm, loving. When his eyes touched Gareth, adoration lit them with the glow of a hundred stars. When he looked at Nealanna, it was the same.

If Gareth had brought Storr to Emerald Station to hurt her, then his desire had not been fulfilled. For she never allowed herself to think of Jane Stapleton. She thought only of the boy. And the boy was a pleasure to her. He was totally trusting, totally loving. He had always wanted to live with his father, to have a family. And now he did. He gave love in return.

It was only after he'd been there a day or so that Nealanna began to see that he avoided Alicia. It piqued Nealanna's interest that he should do so, since Alicia actually pursued him. She brought him games from town, and sought to interest him in them. But he refused to join in. She built for him, with her own clever hands, a cart and a windmill, but he refused to touch them. She offered to tell him stories, and he retreated to sit beside Nealanna. He even, in her presence, refused to play with Gareth.

That very afternoon, having considered carefully, Nealanna decided to discuss it with him. They had settled in the kitchen for hot cocoa, after a romp in the snow. They were alone.

She asked, "Storr, why don't you play with your Aunt Alicia? She would like it so. She likes you."

He drew a deep breath. His throat grew tight. He said, "No."

"But she does like you," Nealanna insisted.

"She ... she ..." He drew another deep breath, controlling the stammer that frequently disrupted his speech. "She wears two faces. I've seen them both. She ... she hates me, but smiles and ... and laughs to cover it."

"Oh, no," Nealanna said. "You mustn't say such things. Alicia is your father's own sister. She loves you."

"She ... she loves him," Storr said simply. "She loves him, Mama. And she hates anyone that he loves. She hates me. And she hates you."

"No, Storr. Pray for forgiveness that you have such thoughts, and pray to love Alicia."

But he looked at her with Gareth's own eyes, and turned his face away. "I ... I ... I know," he said stubbornly. "I know, Mama."

She considered how she could discuss the boy's feeling with Gareth, but she saw no way.

Though she knew he was grateful for her kindness to Storr, she knew that the abyss that yawned between them had not been bridged. Nor was it likely to be.

She had not seen Dale, nor heard from him. But she lived in constant fear that he would approach her again. She did not know what she could do except avoid him, and hope that he would give up his attempt to blackmail her. And yet she was certain this must be a vain hope. Whatever little she knew of the world had taught her that people like Dale were not likely to give up.

Now, having read to Storr, and heard his prayers, and tucked him in, she bent over and kissed him. She said, "Sleep well," and leaving him, went into the hallway.

Alicia was just passing by, and said, "He's gone to bed finally, has he?"

Nealanna nodded.

"Peace reigns at last," Alicia laughed. "You'd hardly think one small boy could disturb the whole house. But never mind. I came up to tell you that Avis and Brooke are here. Gareth wants you to go down at once."

A touch of cold wind seemed to blow in Nealanna's face. She wondered if the memory of that afternoon, Storr's words, had made her imagine an odd gleam in Alicia's eyes.

"And what of you?" she asked. "Won't you join us, Alicia?"

"Oh, yes. But I'm going to ask Mother to come down, too. If only she will."

Nealanna went slowly down the steps. She was suddenly

filled with trepidation. Storr was in bed, sleeping, his laughter stilled. There was a darkness settling all around her. She remembered that the last time the Maradines had visited, she had eaten bonbons and had coffee and later fallen deathly ill.

Chapter 14

But within the drawing room there was a pleasurable air of excitement.

Avis and Faran sat together, their hands tightly entwined. She wore a dress of pale green, and pale green ribbons were threaded through her low blonde chignon. Her dark eyes glowed, and her heart-shaped face was pink. Faran smiled at her dreamily.

Gareth leaned at the mantel, his usual place, looking very much at ease.

Brooke laughed softly to himself.

It was hard, seeing the ambience here, to believe that only moments before, Storr had stammered and whispered about hate.

"We've something to tell you, Nealanna," Avis said. But then, she stopped herself, sighing. "I guess I'd better wait for Mrs. Kennelly, and for Alicia, too."

"It won't be long," Nealanna answered. "I passed Alicia in the hallway. She's sure to be down with her mother in a moment." It wasn't, Nealanna thought, too difficult to guess what was to come. She had observed Avis and Faran exchanging looks since her arrival.

Evanne and Moira came in, pushing large mahagony trolleys. It seemed to Nealanna that Evanne was somewhat grim, and then, though Moira tried to keep her face averted, Nealanna saw that the young girl's eyes were swollen. There was no time to think about it, however, for as Gareth served champagne, Alicia came in with Mary Kennelly.

They were no sooner seated, each with his champagne glass, when Avis said, "I can't wait any longer. I must tell you. Faran has asked me to marry him, and I've accepted."

There was joy in her voice, but a tentative sound, too.

Mary turned her wrinkled face toward Gareth, and he nodded slowly.

It was obvious that it was his consent that Mary asked for. But neither Avis nor Faran had done so. That much was obvious, too.

Then Mary said softly, "If only Neil were here, too. If only Jennings would come back."

No one replied to her, and after a moment, Gareth raised his glass in a toast.

Through the cries of congratulations and best wishes that followed, Nealanna resolutely attempted to keep the remembrance of her own betrothal from her mind. But she could not. She recalled Neil Kennelly's deep voice, and her refusal. She remembered Gareth, standing in the doorway and staring at her across the room. She remembered the sparkle of gems on the table, and the gleam of the emeralds he had given her on her wedding night.

It all seemed so long ago now. But it was hardly three months since she had stood beside Gareth and taken her vows.

Avis came and leaned near her. "I hope you're glad for me, Nealanna."

She smiled into the girl's face. "You know that I am."

"I've wanted this for a long time." Avis' smile faltered for a moment. "But there were ... I am four years older than Faran, you know. It seemed, until now, an insuperable barrier. But he says it doesn't matter. So I suppose it doesn't." Her face suddenly glowed again as Faran came and slid an arm around her shoulder. "Do you know what I'm going to do, Nealanna? Instead of the usual geegaws I'm going to buy an electric brougham for Avis, and teach her to drive it."

"As long as you buy it for her," Nealanna answered, "and not for yourself to play with."

It was a relief when the festivities were over, the Maradines gone, the house locked up and still once again.

Nealanna followed Gareth up the stairs, then into the sitting room.

That same darkness that had settled around her when she went down to hear the joyful news was still with her. She thought once again of discussing Storr's fears with Gareth, of repeating what Storr had said.

But Gareth gave her no opportunity to collect her thoughts and then begin. He simply said good night and went into his room, closing the door behind him.

After his prayers, Storr had laughed with her and seemed to settle down to sleep, his blond curls like ruffles at the edge of his sleeping cap.

She sighed now, decided that she would take a last look at him before she herself went to her lonely bed.

She went down the dim hallway, eased his door open. The room inside was dark, still. She stood listening for a moment. Something about the quality of the silence led her to cross the threshold, lean over his bed.

It was empty, the quilts thrown back. Storr was gone.

She stared wildly for an instant. Then she quickly lit the lamp, held it high. She checked the bed again, and then, sweeping the dust ruffles aside, she looked beneath it. She examined the huge wardrobe that he called a cave. She ran into the hallway, calling his name in a whisper.

A small sleeping cap lay on the first step of the narrow flight that led to the third floor. She gasped aloud when she saw it, and ran up the stairs, and then up those, narrower still, that went to the attics and dormer eaves. She had been that way only once before, exploring, but she

144

remembered all those small cul-de-sacs in which a small boy might hide.

She found him crouched in dismal darkness, his eyes filled with the wild gleam of terror. "Aunt ... Aunt ..." he croaked.

She set the lamp down before the open doorway and went to him, sinking down to his level. "It's Mama," she said softly. "Why have you left your bed, Storr?"

"She came to me in the night," he whispered. "She ... she ... came and said ... that I would die. I would die like my first Mama. That's what she ... she ... said."

"Speak slowly," Nealanna told him. "And don't be afraid of a dream. For surely that's what it was."

He drew a deep breath. "It was no dream." His lips jutted in a stubborn pout, white with fear. "Believe me, Mama. I heard her. She stood over me and whispered. She said to hide. She said to run and hide here, otherwise she would find me."

Nealanna rose, cold with a horror that she could hardly bear but trying to conceal it from him. "No one will hurt you. I'll protect you, Storr."

She drew him with her from the cul-de-sac toward the lamp she had set down in the open doorway.

When she reached the place, she stopped. Her dark eyes widened. The lamp was where she had left it, but now a black cord was looped around its base, and one end of it disappeared behind the door that was now closed.

As she watched, the lamp tilted.

Storr screamed, "Mama. No!" and hurled himself at her legs.

It was as if his movement triggered a vast conflagration. There was a crashing explosion, a vast leap of flame. The small area was filled with the stench of black smoke.

Her gown seemed to dance with light. Pain seared her legs.

She ripped the smoldering fabric away, and caught Storr into her arms, retreating before a blinding brilliance.

Storr whispered, "She was there, Mama. She did it. We'll both die as she said."

Nealanna crouched against the stone of the wall, the boy's face turned into her shoulder. She couldn't doubt him now, and, even in that moment of terror, memories flickered in her mind.

Alicia's bright face dimming when Gareth said, "This is my wife ..."

Her visit with the orange kitten that was so like the cat Nealanna had left at home ... The torn place on her finger just hours before the loosened balcony rail fell away under Nealanna's weight.

The hands able to make small wooden toys for Storr could surely have loosened the balcony rail, and surely, loosened the runabout wheel. And Alicia had fled across the meadows that day, Jennings had said.

Coffee had been poured into Nealanna's cup, handed to her by Alicia, the night she became so ill from a noxious substance.

Alicia had pouted because her father and brothers had refused to take her hunting, insisted she belonged with them, the day Neil Kennelly died.

Memories flickered through Nealanna's mind, and she listened to f ounds below, the screams and shouts.

Why had Alicia done this? Where was she while the flames danced here?

The two of them, she and Storr, were doomed, Nealanna thought. They were cut off from the steps, walled in. She choked, coughed, and threw her head back. It struck a wooden knob. She reached up to feel it. It was part of a window. A way out.

She rose, holding Storr in her arms. She eased the window partly open, and felt the heat leap at her back. She screamed into the darkness, and raised the boy to the ledge. "Storr," she pleaded. "Be brave now. Stand here and reach up high as you can. Feel for the eaves, and hold tight. Then I will come out beside you. Can you do it, Storr?"

His teeth chattered, but he nodded.

She set herself to hold him while he rocked back and forth on the sill, his thin arms straining upward. And then, suddenly, the strain was gone. He was laughing into the dark. "Daddy!" he cried as he seemed to fly straight up into the shadows above.

She leaned from the window, the heat at her back even closer now, and heard Gareth say, "Hold him, Faran. I'm going down."

She straddled the sill, her scorched gown whipping around her, and reached up. A warm tight grasp at both wrists steadied her. Gareth hung head down from the slanted roof, his body held by ropes. Another rope came down to her. He loosened one wrist, slid it over her. He settled the rope at her waist and made it fast.

He whispered words to her that she didn't understand. Then, slowly, delicately, she was raised to the eaves.

She gasped, "Storr?"

"Safe," Gareth said. "Thank God. You're both safe now." His arms closed around her as she fell.

She always remembered the slow journey down the slant of the roof, Gareth holding her, and Storr cradled in Faran's arms. Somehow they got to the third floor balcony, and then down the steps to Mary's apartment.

Gareth put Nealanna down on a sofa. Faran lay Storr into her arms.

Mary stood over them weeping as the two men left the room.

The black cord . . . the lamp tilting . . .

Nealanna asked through dry lips, "Alicia?"

"With the others. Helping . . ."

Moments later, Gareth and Faran returned, and Alicia was with them. Her gown was torn and stained and burned in some places. Her face was smudged with smoke and her hair wild. She flung herself into a chair, and in her gray eyes Nealanna saw the reflection of the flames in the attic.

"It's out," Gareth said. "Evanne and Henry were able to smother it in the passage way. What's damaged can be rebuilt. Emerald Station will go on." But there was a strange note in his voice.

Then Storr roused himself. He climbed from Nealanna's

arms. His face was dead white, his green eyes wide and blank. His small body shook with a convulsive seizure. "She ... she said ... said ... she would kill me, like she killed my first Mama," he cried. "She said she would kill my second Mama, too. She told me to hide ..."

There was a moment of silence.

Then Alicia said hoarsely, "The boy needs a doctor, Gareth."

He didn't answer, but only stared at her.

Storr said, "It was you ..."

Gareth said quietly, "You were standing there at the top of the steps before the closed door, Alicia. I saw you when I came out to find Nealanna. I saw you, with your head bent, listening. When I called to you you turned and screamed that you smelled smoke, but that no one could be in the attic. I didn't believe you. So Faran and I went up to the roof. You intended that they die, Alicia."

Her white face darkened and grew haggard with the shadows of hate. She turned her head stiffly to regard Storr. "You devil! I might have known she'd live on in you. Your mother Jane Stapleton was a witch, and she set a spell on Gareth. So he was never the same thereafter. Before, he was mine. But never after."

Gareth asked quietly, "And what did you do to Jane, Alicia? What did you do six years ago?"

"She's in the quarry. Did you think that she would have left here, having what she wanted? Having you, and her son? I gave her a message. I said you'd returned secretly from school and needed to see her. She went there and I followed." Alicia paused. "I killed her. But you would not be the same. Do you remember? You turned more and more away from me. Then there was Deborah. You'd have married her. I followed her across the meadow one twilight. It was so easy to smile into her eyes while I beat her down so there was little left of the face that you loved instead of me."

Nealanna made a sick whimper in her throat.

Mary gathered Storr into her arms and fled the room.

But Alicia laughed. "Then you came, Nealanna. Gareth

couldn't love you, I am sure. But he was stuck with you. My father's work, no doubt. He suspected one of us, you know. From the day of Deborah's death on, he did. And thought of Holt and what he had done. So he watched us, and didn't believe. I put the kitten out, and fixed the railing, but you didn't fall with it. I fixed the runabout wheel, too, and you saved yourself. My father blamed poor Jennings, I fear, and the boy ran off because of that. One more reason to hate you, Nealanna, if I needed it. My father watched me, watched me. And watched over you, too. When he went hunting that day, I slipped from the house, and met him. He suspected but he wasn't wary enough. I used his own gun on him. Yet none of it was enough. For Gareth brought Storr home, and you loved him, and loved Gareth. And he began to love you. I wouldn't have it. And so there was tonight." She turned to Gareth. Suddenly all haggardness was gone from her face. She smiled at him, a flirting, beguiling smile that was a mockery of love.

Gareth's eyes narrowed. He didn't speak. He gestured at Faran, who stepped into the hallway, and waited there. Gareth took Nealanna from the room, paused at the door for an instant, then locked it carefully from the outside.

"What will you do?" Faran asked, his eyes sick.

"She's mad, Faran. We'll have Dr. Robinson here in the morning."

He put Nealanna to bed in her own room. When she tried to speak to him, he kissed her forehead and left her.

When they went to Alicia in the morning, they found her dead. She had hanged herself with a rope of drapery torn from the window in her mother's room. Her cold body dangled from the end post of the bed.

But Dr. Robinson had another patient to treat.

Mary Kennelly, some time during that terrible night, had suffered a cerebral stroke.

She lay speechless, senseless, staring wide-eyed at the ceiling, when Evanne found her in Storr's room.

The boy was wrapped in blankets and sound asleep. Mary lay on the floor beside him.

Dr. Robinson could do nothing for her. She hung between death and life for a week, and then, without speaking a word, she died.

Thus there were two funerals, and two more deaths for those in Bellingham to talk about. The double burials were attended not only by the family and its few friends but by the curious and the cruel. Among them Nealanna saw Tom Stapleton and Dale Yarrow. That time when she left the cemetery leaning on Gareth's arm, she didn't so much as glance at the stone under which Neal David Maradine lay.

She was concerned only for Gareth. A day passed, then another. She saw his face grow more lean, and his eyes more hard. She heard him walk through the night like a man possessed, and knew that the fire that had burned in the attic had seared his very soul.

A night came when, listening to his footsteps, she could bear them no longer.

She rose, wrapped herself in a velvet robe. She went, for the first time since their marriage, into the room where he slept.

It was a small place, with room only for a bed, and a chair near a narrow window. He sat there, looking into the dark.

When she opened the door, he asked, "What do you want, Nealanna?"

She stared at him. "Gareth, will you tell me what I have done?"

"You? You've done nothing. It's I who have. I, and my father before me."

She drew close to him. "It's in the past now. Have we no future together?"

"I don't know."

She was so close that her slender body touched his. "Gareth, I love you. If you can not love me, then say so now. If we can't be man and wife, tell me. We can't continue to live as we have. It's unnatural and wrong."

The words so long held back were out. She was warm with triumph and courage.

But he demanded, "And what I did, my father did, wasn't that wrong, too?"

"But to live by that, whatever it was, is only to compound it."

" 'Whatever it was,' " he repeated softly. "As if you didn't know. Didn't understand. Are you offering me the mercy of that pretense?"

She knew what Neil Kennelly's pride had led him to. He had arranged the marriage so that Gareth, with a bride, would be protected from the town's malice. And Gareth had acceded to it. She knew that Neil had suspected a madman in his house, and used her, risked her, to identify him.

But it was Gareth that was important. So she said, "I owed your father my life, you know."

"And he very nearly accepted it in payment for what he had done for you."

She thought there must be a way to ease Gareth. She told him, "You believe he deliberately risked me, don't you? But I don't, Gareth." She made her voice very firm. "I think he couldn't accept what he suspected. I think he hoped it wasn't true, and brought me here to prove it."

Gareth laughed softly, bitterly. "Nealanna, you do him an injustice if you don't recognize the ruthlessness that was in him. The same as in Alicia, but for different ends. The same that was in my uncle, too. Holt, who years ago went mad, and killed so many innocents, and ruined us all."

"You're not the same. It's not in you, Gareth."

"I married you, didn't I?"

"Did you? Did you really? Or did you protect me always, against yourself and against me, too?"

"I wanted you," he told her gruffly. "Never think that I didn't. From the moment I saw you, sitting in the chair before the fire, your eyes wide and searching on me, I wanted you."

"And you have me," she said softly.

He rose and folded his arms around her. He whispered, lips to her hair, as he took her to the bed, "Nothing will ever hurt you again, Nealanna. Nothing ever. I promise."

Chapter 15

The stairwell and galleries picked up the sound from the third floor and poured it down into the parlor. There were shouts, and mingled laughter, and the gramaphone played "Shine on Harvest Moon," for what, Nealanna thought, must be the millionth time since the song had come out the year before.

She considered that it was a very good thing that Gareth had completely redesigned the top story of the house when the attic had burned sixteen years earlier.

She passed quickly over the memory of the night when the lamp had been pulled over and the flames exploded before her.

She tried never to think of it, but she knew, always, when it was in Gareth's mind. And, too often, it was, though he rarely spoke of it directly.

But it was there when he watched the children. His thoughtful eyes studied them, each one, as they grew. He was observing them, measuring them, and in some hidden sense, testing them. It terrified her, lest in a mysterious way, the fear in his mind would become, in them, a fulfillment.

Yet each of them, from Storr, now twenty-two, to baby Judd, only two, seemed all right to her. She sighed, telling herself not to think of possible blemishes.

Brooke, sitting in a big chair across from her, settled himself more deeply. He adjusted his wooden leg so that it stuck out straight before him, and absently twitched his trouser into place. "Troubled, Nealanna?" he asked.

She raised her eyes to his. He seemed older than his years, and had grown thinner. They had never yet spoken of the blood relationship between them, but the original closeness remained, was even stronger. She felt an intense sympathy for him and for Avis.

It was that which had led Nealanna to accept the care of Avis' and Faran's children for three months while the two of them traveled to California in the private railroad car. William, now twelve, and Jennifer, ten, were amenable enough. But added to Nealanna's own four, it was a lively menagerie indeed. And Gareth's attitude created an additional burden.

"The children are vocal this afternoon," Brooke went on. "I suppose that's enough to make you sigh."

She took a careful stitch in her embroidery. "I was just thinking how wisely Gareth planned the upper story. At the time, I thought it unnecessary."

"You didn't look ahead." He laughed softly. "Little did you know that you'd have four in sixteen years. Plus Faran's two, to house. Have you heard from Avis recently, by the way?"

"Last week. They're in San Francisco now."

"April in San Francisco," Brooke said. "Nice. When do they start for home?"

"In a week or two, I should think." She bent her head over her hoop again. There was silence between them as she wondered about Faran and Avis.

She hoped that Avis had not put too much reliance on this trip to draw Faran back to her. Avis was forty now, the Maradine good looks oddly withered by her fear of aging. She should have been a young woman still, but she was not. While Faran, at thirty-six, was in his prime. He

153

was handsome, and too much of what her own father had been for Avis to have confidence in him. His frequent trips to New York had preyed on her mind until it seemed that she would lose it altogether. She spoke to no one but Nealanna of her fears. At last, she badgered Faran into the three month trip, believing that she could recapture him. Nealanna was not sure that it was possible. The problem lay in Avis' fear, rather than in the surroundings, she suspected. What Avis feared, she brought out. Could it be the same with Gareth?

Brooke leaned forward, and when Nealanna looked up at him, she saw that he was suddenly tense.

He asked, "Nealanna, would it surprise you if I married?"

"Surprise me? It would delight me, Brooke."

"And if I married Lolly?"

"She's a wonderful person," Nealanna said quickly.

She smiled to herself. She had known Lolly since she boarded the ship that brought them both to America. Lolly had been with the Gordons ever since, nursemaid to Jay and Doe, then governess, and now that Jay and Doe were both grown and away at school, and Nanette virtually an invalid, she was still a fixture in the Gordon household.

"I wonder if she'd have me," Brooke mused.

"Why not?" Nealanna managed to hold back a laugh. That Lolly had been in love with Brooke had been evident for years. When he went to Cuba with the Rough Riders, she had been disconsolate. When he returned, without his right leg, she had concealed her pain behind a façade of stiffness. It had taken Brooke nearly eight years to accept what had happened to him, but at last he was beginning to.

He tapped his cane on his leg. It rang woodenly. "That's why not."

"Oh, Brooke, no. She's been waiting for you, hoping, all this time. She's had offers, I know. Nanette told me."

"Of course she's had offers," Brooke said.

Nealanna wondered if Brooke could be troubled by the

fact that Lolly had been nursemaid, governess, and was now housekeeper, for the Gordons. Was it Lolly's social background that held him back? Did he think that a Maradine should marry higher? Or did he fear the talk such a marriage might create? If so, he would never mention such thoughts to Nealanna. He wouldn't want to hurt her. What had she been, after all, when Gareth married her?

There was the thud of feet on the rug outside. There were shouts, screams.

Brooke winced, pushed himself to his feet, and leaned on his cane. "What's this?" he demanded in a voice of mock sternness.

Jennifer burst in, flung herself at Nealanna's feet, and drummed her fists on the floor.

Dolores, Nealanna's only daughter, six, and small for her age, stood over her older cousin.

"She pulled my hair, the wretch," Jennifer screamed. "She has no right. I want my mother. I want my mother and father to come home."

Dolores, red-faced and shiny-eyed, spaced her words carefully. "That cousin of mine is a beast, Mama. She keeps calling me a baby. I'm not. Judd is a baby. But I'm not."

Nealanna put her hands over her ears. She waited until the din of the accusations subsided. By then, the others crowded the doorway.

David, with his shock of dark hair, and her own dark eyes, was too tall for his fifteen-year-old weight. George was two years his junior, marked by the red strawberry at his throat. William was a miniature Faran, except that he lacked Faran's interest in inventions. He jutted out his jaw, said, "We are the guests here. None of them realize that."

"Isn't this a tempest in a teapot?" Nealanna asked.

The shrieks began again.

Hands over her ears once more, Nealanna said, "I'll not listen. None of you have said hello to Uncle Brooke."

Brooke waited until the dutiful greetings had been hurled at him, then said, "You're a bunch of savages." But he was smiling. "Go and tell Evanne that you need your tea, and behave yourselves for a little while."

The group filed out. Jennifer looked back, asked, "When are my parents coming home?"

"In a few weeks," Nealanna answered.

"I'm going to tell them," Jennifer warned. "I'm going to tell them how awful everybody has been to me."

Brooke no longer smiled. He said coolly, "You'd better march, or I'll do now what you father will do if he hears such talk from you." He briskly slapped the air with his hand. "You know what I mean."

"You wouldn't dare," William snarled.

"That goes for you as well, young man." Brooke looked him up and down. "Do you think you're too old to be spanked? Continue trying me."

Jennifer sniffed and stuck her small chin in the air, and started from the room. Dolores looked at her mother, then put her arm around Jennifer's waist.

The others followed them out.

"No wonder you sigh," Brooke said when the children were gone. "They need a firm hand."

"They have it. In Gareth at least."

"When do you expect him?"

"Any minute. I hope the restored order lasts until then."

"And Jennings?"

"In town with Storr."

"The library, I suppose."

Nealanna nodded. "I hope it'll be all right. I try to think so, Brooke. But somehow I'm not sure."

"And Gareth?"

"He has his doubts, of course. But Jennings was so . . . so enthusiastic about it. And, of course, Storr was, too. It's his first real job as an architect, and since those days when he trailed Gareth helping to plan the new top floor, and since the changes he made himself, when he was grown, he's longed to do something larger. So . . ."

She allowed her voice to trail away. She was talking about Storr, but her mind was full of Jennings. She thought of the portentous midnight of 1899, when the new

156

year and the new century were ushered in. The grandfather clock in the hall chimed twelve. A cheer went up. A cheer went up and faded into silence.

Jennings stood in the doorway. He was laughing. It was like seeing a ghost return after nearly ten years.

"I couldn't resist it," he said quietly. "Ever since I knew I was coming home, I planned it this way, for this night."

He was not quite so tall as Gareth, but much heavier. His face was full and whiskered, the rosebud mouth concealed. His eyes were the same as they'd been when he was seventeen. They soon learned that he had not changed much in other ways either. He was still headstrong, obdurate. He never spoke of why he had left, nor mentioned his parents, having known, it seemed, that they had died. He settled down in Emerald Station. While the Kennellys had always kept much to themselves, avoiding Bellingham, he refused to. He had done a variety of things during his travels, and become interested in construction. Storr's training delighted him. Jennings had determined that Bellingham must have a free library, given by the Kennellys. He set out to organize the project. Storr had designed it. Now it was nearly built.

"You mustn't worry," Brooke was saying.

"I try not to, Brooke. But as time goes by I begin to believe that nothing actually changes. There are small things, material things, I know." She paused, and her eyes sought the electric lights that Gareth had had installed, and then shifted to the large radiators that heated the big house. "But we mistake those things for real alterations. It isn't so. At thirty-three, I am the same girl that I was at seventeen, you know."

"And you look the same," he retorted.

But she didn't smile.

"It's Tom Stapleton, isn't it?" he asked.

"Yes. It worries me that Jennings and Storr have let him build the library."

"He's the only builder in town, Nealanna. You know that."

"Yes," she repeated. From being a carpenter, Tom

157

Stapleton had gone into construction work. He had accumulated some wealth since the electric interurban cars had come to Bellingham, bringing people who needed homes. But he was unchanged. She trembled now, remembering that day, a few weeks after Mary and Alicia had been buried. She and Gareth had been at the Gordons, were driving away, when Tom stopped in front of the carriage, and sneered, "Can you tell me why my sister Jane is gone so long and when she'll be back?"

It would have been the time, Nealanna thought, for Gareth to explain. He should have gotten down, and told Tom Stapleton the truth about Jane's death. Alicia was buried. No one could harm her. Instead, Gareth had said through gritted teeth, "Stand aside, man. Or I'll run you down," and had the carriage rolling before Tom could jump away. It had been the Kennelly pride in him, she knew. The Kennelly pride that had made Gareth conceal the truth which should be known. She had covered her face with her hands, and sobbed, and wondered what further damage that same pride would wrought.

Aloud she went on, "He is the only builder, and the whispers still continue."

"They'll be forgotten."

She nodded, but she knew better. Evanne brought back the tales from Bellingham these days, from Bellingham and Dale Row's house as well.

It had been the day after Gareth made their marriage a real one that she said, "I must tell you about Dale Row."

Gareth had protested, "No. It was my own shame speaking. I never believed what I said."

She said steadily, "I want you to know who he is, and what he is. We start fresh, the two of us." She drew a slow breath. "He is my brother, my twin, Gareth. His name is really Dale Yarrow. He was given away at our birth, and I never knew he existed until he came to me demanding money."

"He demanded money from you? Why?" Gareth asked, his face darkening. "How could you owe him?"

She said tiredly, "I owe him nothing, but he insists . . .

158

that I do. Your wealth troubles him, I think. He wishes a small piece of it, Gareth. He . . . threatened to tell you about my mother, not only you, but the town as well."

Gareth laughed softly. "Did you urge him to broadcast it to the wind? I don't care what you were born. How could I?"

"But the town," she said. "And now, after all that's happened. I couldn't bear for you to be hurt any more."

"Just leave Mr. Yarrow, or Row, or whatever he calls himself, to me," Gareth said grimly.

"You mustn't do anything to make matters worse," she cried.

"I shan't," was the answer. "I'll see that he holds his tongue. Holds his tongue now and forever."

Some weeks later, Dale Row approached her. "What about it?" he asked. "I'll take the brooch if that's all you'll offer."

"I've told my husband," she answered. "I'll give nothing to you so leave me alone."

She described the meeting to Gareth that night. He smiled and went to his desk. He took from it a sheaf of papers. "I've been waiting only for this," he told her. He sat beside her, took her hand. "Nealanna, you did have a twin brother. That much is true. He was given away. It was before my father's offer of help reached your mother. As far as is known, no effort was made to trace him. My father never knew of his existence. Don't think too much of that though. For the infant died in its early years. The man you have seen here is several years older, in fact, and with a prison record in England. He is the son of the woman who took your twin. That's the only relationship. He intended to defraud you for what he could. And almost did. But he'll never come near you again."

"But how . . ."

"Caroway," Gareth said. "He's known for years about the death of the boy. He was able to establish Dale Yarrow's true identity quite easily. Dale is here on false papers, under a false name. One move from me and he'll be deported."

"Oh, Gareth, you wouldn't . . ."

"Not unless I have to," Gareth said. "I'll go and see him tomorrow." After that meeting, Gareth said only, "It'll be all right. He'll not trouble you, believe me."

Gareth had been proven right. But one night Moira slipped away. She married Dale Row within the week.

Evanne had been stunned. She would neither see Moira nor speak of her. Henry became the only source of news, and it was he who told Evanne when Moira was expecting a first child. When the child was born, Evanne could stay away no longer. She had gone to Moira, made it up with her, and had become, over the years, a means by which Nealanna knew that the feeling against the Kennellys in Bellingham did not fade. It was there, grown even less rational with time.

For that reason she was troubled that Storr and Jennings should have any contact with the town, with Stapleton. If she herself was so little changed, if she did not forget, then she feared that they, too, had not changed, had not forgotten.

Now Brooke rose stiffly. "I hear an automobile." He limped to the window. "Yes. It's Gareth." His voice sounded strange. She saw that his back was tense. He was leaning forward.

"What's the matter, Brooke?"

"I don't know," he said thoughtfully.

She went swiftly down the hall, and to the big door. She opened it wide, and waited, knowing that Brooke was limping behind her.

Gareth climbed down from the car. He took off his goggles, dropped them inside, then strode toward her.

She saw that his face was white to the lips. There was a dull anguish in his eyes. She jumped the steps, as agile as she'd been as a girl, and ran toward him, ran under the porte-cochère that Storr had designed and had built at the front of the house. She stumbled, and nearly fell on the hem of her dress, but she caught herself.

"What's the matter?" she called. "What is it, Gareth?"

He took her into his arms. "Bad news, Nealanna." And

160

he raised his eyes to Brooke. "I'm sorry. It's Avis and Faran. I've just had word on the telegraph. There's been an earthquake and fire in San Francisco. Their hotel was completely destroyed. They're both gone."

Chapter 16

Nealanna had been waiting for word since November 11th. Now it was Christmas Eve. She clung to patience, and to a surface calm, with a fierceness born of fear.

For days, any sound in the courtyard had brought her to the window, just as any movement in the big bed brought her to Gareth's side.

He lay very still, his long body shrunken under the heavy quilt. His eyes were open, and a glittering stony green, touched with the fever that had hollowed his cheeks.

His lips moved, and instantly she offered water. He sipped, whispered his thanks.

She sank down beside him, took his hand. "How do you feel, Gareth?"

"The same." The words were hoarse, a hardly-heard murmur. "Is there word yet, Nealanna?"

"Not yet. I'll tell you. Try not to talk."

His eyes closed. His breath was shallow and uneven, and when the cough suddenly took him it seemed to shake the very walls of the house.

"Influenza," Dr. Robinson had told her gravely a week

162

before. "There's a lot of it in town. I suppose Gareth picked it up there. You must be careful, Nealanna. It looks as if it's going to be an epidemic."

He had aged greatly since the first time she had seen him nearly twenty-eight years before. His bulldog face was just as square, just as lined, but his whiskers were gray. His hand shook when he took up his bag. She was, she suddenly realized, young at forty-five, compared to him.

"What can I do?" she had asked desperately, "is there anything you know?"

"Nothing beyond what I've told you." And then, "Is there news of your sons?"

She had shaken her head. The dark hair had thin strands of silver in it, but not very many. Her thick fair skin was remarkably unlined, and her dark, tilted eyes still had the embers of her youth in them. "No news yet," she said unwillingly.

Her first born, David, had joined the American Expeditionary Force as soon as it was formed. He had been just twenty-four then, trained as a lawyer, like his father before him, and exalted at the opportunity to be a soldier.

George, at twenty-one, was always striving to keep up with his older brother. He had followed David by a few days. Nealanna had felt a mixture of pride and terror. Pride that her sons would fight for her homeland, the England that she hadn't seen for so many years. And the terror any woman feels when her sons go off to war. Through the several years that followed, she thought of Brooke. Would they return as he had, maimed? If so, would they be able to overcome their handicaps as he had finally? Would they, after three years, after the Armistice, come home at all?

Now there were angry whispers beyond the door.

Jennifer . . . Dolores . . . It was always the same, Nealanna thought wearily.

She rose to her feet, slipped outside. "What is it?" she asked quietly.

"Jennifer took my picture of David," Dolores said in an angry whisper. "I want it back." She was the picture of

163

what Nealanna had been herself at eighteen, slim, narrow-waisted, with dark curls and dark eyes.

Jennifer cried, "The one I have is mine, and not yours." Jennifer had the Maradine blonde hair and blue eyes, and was, at twenty-two, still a bit plump.

Nealanna shushed them wearily. "This bickering is terrible. And now ..."

"I don't care," Jennifer answered. "She can't have everything. She has no right ..."

But Dolores asked, "Is he worse?"

"The same. Go downstairs now. Please. Settle this foolishness between yourselves. I've had enough of it."

She closed the door softly.

Gareth asked in a hoarse whisper, "The girls?" Then, "I'll speak to them. As soon as I'm well."

"Rest now." She forced herself to laugh. "They're worried about you. That's how they show it."

"Children," he agreed, smiling faintly. "Grown up now, but children still in some ways."

She touched his lips with her fingers, and he kissed them. His eyes closed. He breathed shallowly.

The grandfather clock in the lower hall chimed seven. In five hours it would be midnight, and then Christmas Day. The tree, the gifts were ready. She supposed that Brooke and Lolly would come, and perhaps Jason. She hoped he would. He was gray now, tired, and had been since Nanette had slowly drifted into death from the blood disease that had threatened her for so long. Doe was married and lived in Boston. And Jay, a physician now, was studying further in Edinborough. Whoever came, though, would sing their carols without her. She would stay with Gareth.

"Storr?" Gareth asked suddenly.

"He'll be back soon."

"Where is he?"

She didn't want to upset Gareth, but she couldn't lie to him. At last she said, "He's in town with Jennings and Judd."

"Why?"

"Some plan. Don't think of it."

"To rebuild," Gareth said bitterly.

"I don't know. I've not talked to them about it."

Gareth gave a choking laugh. "Poor Jennings. Doesn't he know now that we can't win? He can't end it?"

"Never mind," she said.

She touched his cheek, felt the fever in his flesh. It was as if the fire that had consumed the library just a week before, had begun to consume him, too. Was it the fire that had seized him? Or had it been the chill he got as a result of the wild ride into town when they learned that the library was in flame.

She, Gareth, Storr, and Jennings had stood there, staring, while the volunteers passed their buckets, dragged their hoses and pumps, fought the wind. Within half an hour the twelve-year-old building was reduced to ash.

"Arson," Gareth had said gruffly, turning away.

Storr, white-faced, had cried silently into his hands, and later she saw the memory of another night, another fire, in the wildness of his eyes.

It was something they had never talked about. She wasn't sure that he remembered their danger except in small flashes. Gareth had forbidden her to discuss it with Storr, believing that time would heal his scars, destroy his memories. But the night of the library fire, she had thought she had seen a wildness in his eyes.

She forgot her uneasiness the next day, for Gareth had been gray and coughing. That night, he had collapsed.

There was a tap at the door.

Evanne stood there, her face incandescent with happiness.

Nealanna's heart leaped.

"Go down," Evanne said. "I'll stay here until you return."

She looked back at Gareth. He seemed to be sleeping, but she returned to his side, whispered, "I'll be right up."

She hurried downstairs.

Two tall men stood in the foyer. Two men in boots that shone, and uniforms, and tipped-back caps.

She cried, "David! George!" and opened her arms wide to them.

She had barely kissed them when she heard the shout from above. She raced up the steps, and burst into the room.

Evanne stood at the bedside, face streaming with tears that had washed away the joy. Nealanna brushed her away, and bent close to Gareth.

His eyes opened wide, wider, the brilliant green of emeralds. His lips moved on a breath. "Care," he said clearly. "Watch them. Take care, Nealanna," and then he was still.

Two years later, Nealanna was seated in her sitting room. She raised her head to listen when the telephone rang. It had taken until the end of 1920, a few months ago, to bring the lines in, and she had become well-accustomed to the sound of it, yet it still seemed to her a peculiar invasion of her privacy.

She remembered when Gareth had laughed at her, said, "All man's civilization is unnatural," when she complained that to fly in airplanes would be unnatural. She felt the same about telephone, the automobile, now part of daily life. One came to take these inventions for granted, she told herself, but with a certain reservation, a certain uneasiness. As if what was gained must some time be paid for.

Now Evanne appeared in the doorway. "It's for you."

"Who is it?" Nealanna asked as she rose.

"The school. Mr. Preston. He says it's important."

"Judd," Nealanna murmured.

"No doubt," Evanne observed tartly.

Nealanna went quickly into the study. This would be the third time. She was almost certain that it was happening again. Why else would Mr. Preston call her?

She sighed as she picked up the receiver. What would Gareth have said? What would he have done this time? These past two years without him had been difficult in so many ways beyond her own never-ending longing for him.

Judd was deliberately misbehaving, she was certain, so that he would be sent home from school. Doing now what he had done at ten, at fifteen, but having learned nothing since the last time.

And George, having come safely through the war, developed infantile paralysis soon after Gareth died. He suffered a damaged hip, but bitterness warped him more than his infirmity. He was ungrateful that he had managed to survive the war at all. Brooke said that would wear off with time, and new interests, but meanwhile, she saw only the young tormented face of her twenty-seven-year-old son, and wept inside.

David was healthy enough, but he troubled her, too. He had been engaged once, and broken it off without telling her why. Now he spent more time in the family room, examining the Kennelly memorablia, staring at the Kennelly portraits, than she liked.

William and Jennifer did very little but hang about. He rode the horses, hunting in season and out. She primping before the mirror and playing the radio.

Dolores was moody, showing occasional flashes of temper, which were unlike her usual self. Nealanna would have thought that she was suffering the pangs of love, but there was no one suitable in the vicinity. That might be the very trouble, she decided.

Now she said into the telephone, "This is Mrs. Kennelly," in her gentlest voice.

"Ah yes." Mr. Preston was embarrassed, but plainly determined. He went on quickly, "Mrs. Kennelly, I'm sorry, but I must ask you to remove Judd from the school. He is two years behind, larger than the other boys. And now there's been a fight. A boy is badly beaten. I can't overlook it. When will you arrive?"

"But what happened?" she asked.

"I neither know, nor care, Mrs. Kennelly. We've had David here, and George, and they were no trouble. All I can tell you is that Judd is. I must ask you to take him home."

"But can you advise me? Can you suggest . . ."

167

"What you do is your province as parent," she was told. "May I expect you today?"

"Yes," she answered. "I'll be there today."

She put down the phone, stood motionless, frowning in thought. She knew that she must not panic. There would be a way to deal with Judd. She had to think. But fear crawled in her. Was this problem with the boy a sign of what Garth had always feared? Was this what he had watched for so anxiously in all the children? Was it what he meant when he told her, with his last breath, "Watch them. Take care, Nealanna."

She went into the hallway where Evanne stood anxiously, twisting her hands in her apron. "Is it bad?"

"As always," Nealanna said tartly. "I must go for him today. Do you know where David is?"

"Down with Jennings for a change," Evanne said disapprovingly. "I told them it was a fool's job when they started it. And it will be a fool's job when they finish, too."

Nealanna's lips tightened. She agreed, but she would not say so. For her part, the town of Bellingham could fade from the face of the earth and she would not miss it, nor the townfolk who lived there either. Precious little she owed it, and precious little it had given her over the years she had lived in Emerald Station. She remembered the night the library had burned to the ground, and Gareth's face lighted by the flames, and Storr's wild eyes.

Hardly a week later, Gareth had the influenza that killed him. Soon after Jennings, who would win with bribery what he could not win with charm, decided to rebuild. Storr was delighted, of course. It had taken them two years to begin.

She sighed deeply. "Then is William about?"

"Yes. But . . ."

"But what?"

Evanne bent her head. The white wings at her temple had spread through the red of her hair. Her face was wrinkled and stubborn. "Nothing."

"Ask him to come down please. I would like him to drive me," Nealanna said.

Evanne hesitated, then went up the steps past the carved black masks that still hung there.

Nealanna took her heavy coat from the foyer closet that Storr had designed. She put on her hat, pinning it snugly in place and adjusting the veil over her eyes. She drew on her gloves.

She waited, tapping her foot impatiently until William came down. She knew, as soon as she saw his too-bright eyes, why Evanne had hesitated.

"You wanted me?" he asked.

"We must go and fetch Judd. There's been trouble at the school."

"Again?" William grinned. "He needs a strap taken to him. I always said so."

"I never asked, William," she told him tartly.

"True, Aunt. Anyway, I'll be glad to take you."

She turned toward the door. Then, "Would Jennifer like to go with us?"

"She and Dolores are in town at Jay Gordon's."

"Alone?"

"The two of them." William grinned again. "Aunt Nealanna, this is 1920, you know. Not 1890."

"That doesn't matter to me," she retorted.

"I shouldn't worry. Uncle Brooke and Lolly will be there, too."

She nodded, allowed him to lead her to the car. When she was seated he took a flask from his side pocket, sucked at it in what was to her a distasteful way.

She said nothing, but she winced inside. She knew by his eyes that he was having not his first drink of the morning, but one of many. It happened too often.

He drove down the driveway past the two huge stone lions that Storr had had cast, and then installed in the green of the front lawn, past the fountain that spewed a high glittering stream into the sunlight.

As the automobile passed under the big iron sign that said Emerald Station, between the gray stone pillars that

169

now were carved with leering gargoyles, she said gently, "William, what do you plan to do with your life?"

"Live it," he answered promptly. "Enjoy it."

"There must be more. You must *do* something. You're twenty-six years old. You've been out of the university for nearly three years. Surely, by now . . ."

He laughed, pressed his foot to the floor so that the car leaped ahead. "I play a pretty good banjo, Aunt Nealanna, and do a good two-step. I'm much in demand with the debutantes of New York and Boston, and . . ."

"When will you marry?"

"When it suits me."

She was silent for a long time, braced against the speed. She feared it but she refused to say so.

"I think idleness is not good," she told him at last.

"I'm not idle. I play, I hunt . . . and that reminds me. We have more and more poachers, and picnickers, too. We'll need to do something soon."

They *would* need to, she thought, but said aloud, "That has nothing to do with idleness, William."

"We all are, and why not? We're Kennellys," he answered. He slid a glance at her, then reached for his flask again. He raised it to his lips.

The automobile hit a pothole. It jolted hard, then slewed wildly. She heard his startled oath as a wheel spun away.

She saw it as large, large as a runabout wheel. She saw it spinning off into the trees. And then the sky dropped in a million gleaming fragments.

Chapter 17

"I think," Brooke said deliberately, "that with the circumstances as they are, I could arrange it for you, Judd. I'd go and speak to Mr. Pearson myself. You'd have two months this term. Then go on to college if you applied yourself with tutors in the summer."

That was reasonable enough, Dolores thought, and not too much to ask of Judd.

But Judd said, "Thanks, Uncle Brooke. Only I don't want to," and his hazel eyes surveyed the room, lingering on her, Dolores saw.

She felt quite certain that he was waiting for her to deflect the attention of the others from him. He shifted in his chair with that air of restlessness that presaged an emotional explosion. She hoped that he wouldn't embarrass everyone, and most of all himself, by giving in to the pressure he must be feeling.

Lolly put in gently, "Why, Judd, is that all you can say? 'No thanks.' You know you must finish school."

She was slight, with sandy hair going gray, but her eyes had a very young look. She still had faint traces of the accent she had brought with her from England. The sound made Dolores' heart twist. It reminded her of her mother. Nealanna, too, had retained traces of the same rhythm in her speech.

Judd's big hands became fists on his knees. He shook his dark head slowly from side to side.

Brooke said quietly, "Education is the most important goal of man. For a man to know himself, is to know the world."

Dolores knew that such a rational approach would never reach Judd. He couldn't think that way, nor react that way. Most especially he couldn't do it now.

"Why don't you let him alone?" William demanded, his mouth white-ridged, and jaw hard. "Give him some time, can't you?"

"I can hardly believe it's happened," Jennings mused, as if he had heard nothing of what had gone on before. "It's two months, but I still expect to hear Nealanna's footsteps in the corridor, and to hear her voice."

There was an instant of shocked silence.

Then Judd cried, with his face aflame, "Why can't you shut up!"

Jennifer said sharply, "And that will do, Judd Kennelly. If it hadn't been for you . . ."

Dolores felt the familiar pain clutch her heart. In the two months since her mother's death all stability had departed from Emerald Station. The big house had become a dark place, full of shadows in unexpected corners. Dolores had come to see more and more that those shadows had always been there. But her mother had kept them at bay. Something her mother had been had held back the darkness. But now, with her gone, it was here.

The family sat in the drawing room together. Each wore a black band or ribbon as a mark of mourning. Each one missed Nealanna. Yet they were, every one of them, as separate and distinct as strangers. As far apart as strangers, too.

She said quietly, "What good is bickering?" and turned to Judd. "We only want what's best for you."

"Then leave me alone," he answered sullenly. His fists

172

relaxed. He looked up. "Okay. I appreciate the convening of the clan to discuss my case. But it's not necessary. I've had it with school. I don't want to go to college. I'm going to stay here. At home where I belong."

"But Judd . . ." Dolores began. "You . . ."

David stopped her with an abrupt gesture. His dark hair was ruffled by the restless passes he made at it. His dark slightly tilted eyes were narrowed. He said, "I don't like your manner, nor what you have to say. You're only eighteen, remember. With three years before you reach your majority. Until then you've not quite as free as you think to make your own decisions."

"I'll make them and damn you," Judd cried.

David rose, said tightly, "You're forgetting the facts. I'm head of the family now. And you'll do as I say."

Brooke cleared his throat, adjusted his bad leg. "It's not a matter of doing what anyone says, David. It's that what Judd decides now will affect the rest of his life."

Judd got up, stood at bay. To Dolores he seemed like a cornered animal, as his head moved slowly from side to side. His hazel eyes burned.

He said, "I'm not going back to school."

"Then stay here and rot," David retorted. He sank into the chair, leaned his head back, plainly dismissing the subject and Judd.

But George said, "Judd, you must think of what Mother would have wanted for you."

Dolores winced again.

Judd set his mouth, and his face flamed red.

"You *should* think of that," William agreed silkily.

They were made allies by a senseless guilt, Dolores thought. And that made them enemies, too. It was frightening to think about. For now, one of the shadows that had always hung over the house was taking shape. She saw it, dreaded it.

Storr, silent until then, abstracted as he had been lately, suddenly proved that he had been paying attention after all. He said, "Oh, let the boy alone. Why worry him? He can stay at home if he likes. He can work with me. He

173

has some facility for drawing and scale. Later, when he feels better, he can study, if he likes."

Judd asked, sounding like a child again, "Would you really let me, Storr?"

"Why not? I'm suggesting it." A faint grin touched his mouth. "I'd suggest very nearly anything to stop this useless discussion."

"It's easy for you to say," Jennifer told him. "It's not your responsibility."

"You know nothing about it," David told her sharply. "Though you should."

"But you're Uncle Gareth's heir. Not Storr, though he's the oldest. Not Uncle Jennings. Not . . ."

David shrugged, "Storr is our older brother, true. But I was trained for the law. And that explains it."

Dolores remembered when the will had been read by Brooke. They had sat together in this room, her mother, small, white-faced, grieving.

"You understand," Brooke had said, raising his eyes from the papers. "It goes on as always. There is the principal invested. The profits from the mines. The investments. David, you will handle it all."

Storr had sat in frozen silence.

Now he said, "It was Gareth's wish, and we had discussed it. I wanted to be free to pursue my own calling. I have my own work. And if Judd works with me, I think we'll both be content."

But Dolores wondered. Ever since Nealanna's death, she had sensed the deep strain in Storr. He was the oldest of them, and yet, somehow, she suspected that he missed Nealanna more than the others did. He was the oldest, yes, and he wasn't really Nealanna's son, although he never discussed it. His mother had died at his birth. Gareth had married Nealanna several years later in London. But Storr considered Nealanna his mother, Dolores knew, and Nealanna had considered him her oldest son. And something about him had changed when he lost her. The recognition troubled Dolores, but she didn't know why.

Jennifer crossed her long legs, and sat forward. "Do

you know what I think? I believe we're all mad. The whole thing is ridiculous. Head of the family. Leader of the dynasty. Why, Gareth Kennelly was medieval, and the rest of you just carry it on. As if ... as if you really had to."

"Well said," Jennings applauded. "But it wasn't Gareth. It was your Grandfather Neil. He had a one track mind on the subject. He's the one that built the family room. He gathered all those moldy papers together and hung the first of the portraits. Take a good look at him, and especially at his eyes, and you'll see the dynasty-builder in person. Gareth went on for him, yes. And now David will do the same."

David spread a bewildered look between Jennings and Jennifer. "What are the two of you talking about? Of course I'll carry on. I'm a Kennelly. What else is there to do?"

Jennifer gave a hoot of laughter. "It all went out with handlebar mustaches and high buttoned shoes. Well, just for your information, David, we're all Kennellys here, and share and share alike, and can do as we please."

"Why, yes," David said softly. "You're quite right, of course. It is share and share alike, and we are all Kennellys. And you can certainly do as you like. But remember that I am the one who signs the checks."

She drew a breath that was like a gasp. "David, we've always been friends. But if you attempt to control me by threatening to tighten the purse strings, then you'll find we're friends no longer."

He smiled faintly. "We'll remain friends, and cousins, as we've always been. But I'd like to remind you that you're twenty-four years old. You'll be expected to act your age."

He was so like Gareth in that moment, Dolores thought. He was too like him, in fact. For Gareth had had the authority of age, and David, at twenty-nine, somehow didn't have it yet.

But Jennifer remained silent. So did the others. It was as if a cold wind had suddenly blown through the room, and Dolores wondered if the others were sharing her memory of Gareth now.

Brooke rose, nodded at Lolly. "I'm ready to go home."

She moved quickly to his side, relief evident on her face. Lolly didn't like contention. She didn't know how to handle it. She was always afraid that Brooke would be hurt.

When they had left, William went straight to the decanter. He filled a gleaming glass with whiskey, raised it. "Anyone else?"

"I'll join you," Jennings told him.

"And I will, too," Jennifer said. "Only make mine gin. And let's do try to be civilized. I'll ring for Henry to bring us some ice."

Dolores rose, silently left the room. She paused when she heard a car pull into the porte-cochere.

A moment later, Evanne opened the door, and Jay Gordon came in.

She deliberately repressed the joy she felt at seeing him. She greeted him as casually as always, and thought that one advantage of being taken for granted was to avoid being studied too carefully.

He had his father's hard square jaw that was softened only by the same warm smile. His eyes were gray, sharp, and very perceptive. His hair was a chestnut brown, shot through with glints of red. He wore a tweed jacket and trousers that looked as if he had had them a long time.

"How are you?" he asked Evanne.

"Dragging," she told him, and marched away down the hall.

He turned to Dolores. "What's bothering her? Anything special?"

Dolores shrugged. "Oh, you know Evanne. They've been having one of those family conferences. Awful."

"But what about?"

"Judd. He won't go back to school."

Jay nodded. "It's hit him hard, Dolly. It'll take time for him to get over it."

"I think that's beginning to sink in to David and the rest

of them. But it took some shouting. Now they're making up over whiskey and gin."

Jay frowned slightly. "William, of course. And who else?"

"See for yourself, if you want to," she told him. "I was about to take a ride."

"That's a good idea." His grin softened his jaw. "It might bring roses to your cheeks. And you could stand them."

She asked, "Jay, would you like to do me a favor?"

"Anything. Just name it. You know that I'm always at your disposal."

"Then stop being another older brother to me. I already have Storr, and David, and George. That's quite enough." The words were out before she could stop them, or, oddly, before she had even thought them. She felt her face burn. What a thing to say. What a thing to admit to having thought. She was astonished at herself, and mortified, too.

He stared at her blankly, "Dolly, what's the matter with you? I am like one of your older brothers. There's fifteen years between us, and I've known you, the family, all my life."

She looked down at her feet. "I'm ... I'm very sorry, Jay."

"You might try to explain."

"There's nothing to explain, Jay. And we haven't really known each other if you stop to think of it. I've been mostly away at school. So have you for that matter. At school, or in hospitals, and laboratories, just about everywhere, and ..."

He came close to her, looked down into her eyes. "Never mnd that. What's really bothering you?"

The irrational anger rose up again. It seemed like a flame in her chest. She choked it back, knew that it would continue to smolder.

"It's just everything," she said softly.

"Everything, and me, too? Is that what you mean?"

The drawing room door opened.

Jennifer looked out, grinned. She held a glass in her

177

hand, waved it at Jay. "There you are. I was hoping you'd come out from town."

Dolores deliberately kept her eyes away from him.

He said, "Dolores and I are going for a ride."

"Oh, good. I'll join you," Jennifer said.

He gave her a wide grin. "You'll wait until you're asked."

She sighed loudly. "Oh, all right." Then, "Am I asked?"

"Not this time," Jay told her.

She turned, glared at Dolores, "Thank you very much, cousin," she said thinly.

The car drifted down the driveway past the stone lions and the fountain and between the granite posts.

Dolores held her dark head up, facing the wind, enjoying the tug of it at her curls. She didn't look back toward Emerald Station, but ahead to the open road that wound toward the ring of hills and toward Bellingham.

Jay said, "Want to talk about it now, Dolly?"

She glanced at him sideways. Her anger was gone. Instead she had an irrational need to touch him. She kept her hands folded primly in her lap. It seemed to her that she had known that need for such a long time. At last, she said, "I don't know what it is for sure, Jay. It's just ... it's. . . Oh, Jay, what's going to happen to us?"

"What's going to happen?" he repeated. "Why, Dolly, you're going to live, and ... get married, all of you. Have children ..." He paused. Then, "But that isn't what you mean, is it?"

"No," she said slowly. "That's not what I mean at all. There's this feeling I have, and I know it doesn't really make sense, but there's this feeling of ... of something hanging over us. Something bad. Not just me. But all of us. The Kennellys. A sense that something terrible is going to happen."

He pulled a pipe from his pocket, stuck it between his lips, and chewed on it, saying, "It's what's already happened that's bothering you, Dolly. Your father's death two years ago. Then your mother's more recently. You're feeling the shock of it."

"Maybe," she said doubtfully. "But I just . . . think of it, Jay. David spends so much time with the old papers, the portraits, studying those grim old faces as if they meant anything any more. And you know how George is. So bitter. Buried in his philosophy books as if they'll take the place of everything else he wants and thinks he can't have. And Storr . . . lately he seems so changed. He . . ."

"He'll get over it. They all will," Jay assured her.

"But will I ever get over the feeling that we're . . . we're just dangling over a pit, and at any time . . . It's something I think I've known all my life. And now it's so very strong."

He was quiet for a long time. Then he said, "It'll go away, Dolly. It's just a matter of time. And of being busy, of course."

"There speaks the doctor," she smiled.

"Not the kind of doctor you mean," he answered. "As you know I work more with test tubes than with people."

"Is that what you'll be doing when you leave Bellingham? Working with test tubes?"

"Didn't you know, Dolly? I'm going to stay. I'm going to build a laboratory in the house instead of an office suite."

"But your father . . ."

"He's disappointed, but he'll survive it. And he's going to travel as planned. So it's all settled. I'll be doing my work in Bellingham. Now what do you think of that?"

"I think," she said honestly, "that that's the most wonderful news I ever heard."

Chapter 18

"Now that's what I like to hear," he laughed.

She changed the subject abruptly, afraid that her child-like enthusiasm had given her away. She had loved him ever since she could remember. She had been heart-broken at ten when he was engaged, and though pained for him, too, over-joyed at twelve when his fiancée eloped with another man. It was true, as she had told him earlier, that they had met infrequently, both of them away at school for so long, yet holidays and vacations had presented plenty of occasions for her and Jennifer to vie for his attentions, as they had for those of her brothers. If Jay knew of it, he had given no sign. But he had remained single. She clung to that for comfort.

"About Judd," she said aloud. "What do you think we should do?"

"Leave him alone. He's troubled about what happened, and blames himself. Not very justly, I think. After all, your mother might have been going anywhere when the accident took place. That she was going to pick up Judd at school was nothing more than chance. He'll feel better after a while, I'm sure. Time will help."

"Maybe," she agreed thoughtfully.

"It does most things."

She turned sideways, drew her feet up under her. She asked, "Do you really think so? I wonder." Then, "Were you here when the library burned down, Jay? I don't remember."

He shook his head, and his jaw was firm and square. That small clue told her that he didn't care for the question. Such knowledge was a sign of how intensely she had studied him over the years.

She said, "But surely you heard how it happened?"

"Not any more than anyone else did, Dolly. Why should I have?"

She knew why. It was because he lived in town. He heard the talk, more of it than she would ever hear through Evanne, who had, Dolores suspected, a way of forgetting what she didn't want to repeat.

Instead of explaining, though, Dolores blurted, "Jay, why does everyone in town hate us so? What have we done? The Kennellys have never hurt anyone, have they?"

"No," he said curtly. "They've hurt no one. Except, perhaps, in some way, themselves."

"Then what is it?"

The car seemed to pick up speed then. The newly leafed-out trees flashed by, and the winding road flung up patches of sunlight, then of shade.

The burst of speed meant Jay was troubled. The sound of it was in his voice, too, when he answered, "It's just nonsense. Old rumors. Old jealousies passed on from one generation to another."

"But there must have been something in the beginning, Jay. Things like that don't start spontaneously. How can they? And without any reason, they would have died out. And we would have ignored them."

He asked sharply around the pipe clenched in his teeth, "What do you mean, Dolly? Your family has always ignored those old . . . jealousies."

"No," she said. "Not really. Our behavior has been

guided by the town's attitude. Our lives have been affected in many ways."

"I don't see that at all," he told her.

"Yes, you have. And so has your family before you. The Maradines have, too. It's just something that you, and they, and none of us, has ever talked about. As if to put it into words would make it unbearable."

She was finding, as she spoke, that the words were true. Half-memories became real. A look that had flashed between her parents. The expression on her mother's face when she saw David standing before the family portraits. The high ornamental railings, with the connecting steel ladders, on the balconies, which made the house look like a fortress. The stain of smoke on the granite wall left by the top floor fire that had damaged the house years before she was born.

And Jay asked, "Aren't you being somewhat dramatic, Dolly?"

"I don't think I am. There's something. I know."

He sighed, sucked on his pipe, didn't answer her.

She said, "The fire at the library was arson. I'm sure of that much."

"Oh, are you? And how can you be? I'd like to know. Since nobody else was ever sure of it."

"My parents were, Jay. Though they never said so in my presence. And, of course, when my father became ill . . ."

"I think," he said deliberately, "that you're making a big mistake. You must let the past die. It's over. Done with. Finished. Whatever happened is quite finished."

"Jennings and Storr are rebuilding the library. It's taken them all this time to get started. But they'll do it. You know that. So it isn't finished. Nothing is. And nothing will be."

He slowed, turned the car, and headed back toward Emerald Station.

After a long silence, he said, "Perhaps you'd better tell me what's really in your mind. And I know it's not the library."

182

"I mentioned it before, Jay. The ... the feeling that something is wrong. We're different. We Kennellys are different. Why else were all of us sent away to school?"

"Oh, Dolly, what stretching. The children of the wealthy are generally sent away to school. Wasn't I myself? And Doe, too?"

"Of course you both were, and I understand it. But you lived in town, and were a part of it. And we were never permitted to be. Any time that the boys went in to town, my father frowned. My mother was uneasy. It was noticeable. There was such disapproval, you could cut it with a knife. And they watched us. They ... yes, Jay, don't shake your head at me. They both always watched us. As if they expected us to ... to ... well, I don't know what."

"And that is just normal for parents who care," he told her.

"They had no friends," she said softly. "It was just the two of them. And your folks, and the Maradines. That was all. They never traveled. They ..."

"All that is a matter of taste and style," he said firmly. "And if you don't find that sort of life suitable for you, then you can change it, you know. You have the youth, the means. You can do whatever you want to."

But she wondered. She felt bound to Emerald Station, though she didn't know why. It had always been that way. Leaving for school was a painful wrench, yet, she realized suddenly, returning had been painful, too. The first glimpse of the house, the black masks on the foyer walls ... It was the same now. A trip to the dressmaker in town was an ordeal. A trip to the post office was, too. She didn't quite know what made her feel that way, except that eyes seemed to follow her, examine her, stare at her. She didn't know if Jennifer felt the same. Even though they had grown up together, living like sisters, the rivalry between them had been too intense to allow any closeness. She had always believed that when she and Jennifer were adults it would be different, but she saw now that it was, and would always be, exactly the same. She supposed Jay

183

was right that she could live as she pleased. She could travel, go to England. Would she feel any affinity for the country in which her mother had been born? Would she find something there that she did not find here?

She looked up as Jay slowed for the turn between the grotesquely-carved pillars and under the big sign that read Emerald Station. The house loomed long and high on the landscaped slope, its windows gleaming brightly in the sun, but blankly, too. She wondered if she only imagined the outline of a dark cloud hanging over the slanted roofs.

Jay swore, jammed on the brakes. A car, battered and windowless, with peeling paint, sat squarely in the driveway. And up the slope, past the stone lions that stood guard there, near the fountain that sent a sparkling stream into the air, a young couple had spread out a blanket, and were having sandwiches and drinking something out of paper cups.

"Stay here," Jay said. "I'll see about that." He got out, walked to the people, and stood over them.

She could hear him speaking, but not what he said. She only knew, by his tone, that it was forceful.

The man rose, and she realized that he was young, a boy in his teens. She had seen him before, lounging in Moody's drugstore, or hanging about the post office. He had thick blond hair, shaggy and uncombed, and wore brown work pants and a tan shirt. He ambled to his car, and with a bang and a rattle, moved it aside, while the girl, who was small, thin-faced, with cropped hair and spit curls, stared curiously in Dolores' direction.

Jay returned to her, drove by, and then up to the house, and parked under the porte-cochere. "Stapletons," he muttered, as he turned to look at the young couple below.

"Who?" she asked. "Did you say Stapletons?"

He shot her a quick look. "Yes. I did. Why? Does the name mean anything to you?"

"Of course it does. I couldn't have lived here all my life without knowing that name. He's the builder. Jennings and Storr both know him. But that boy and girl, why are they out here?"

184

"That boy is Stapleton's youngest, I think. He's about seventeen. The young lady is his girl friend. For reasons they didn't bother to explain to me they decided to have a picnic in Emerald Station. I told them they were on private property. Which, of course, they already knew. I won't repeat what Tim Stapleton said. I told them to pack up and get out, and I want to see if they do."

The couple was making a leisurely retreat. They finished their sandwiches, left a brown, grease-stained bag on the immaculate grass. They rose, brushed themselves off thoroughly, then gathered the blanket. They climbed into their car, smoked a cigarette between them, and then banged and rattled out between the pillars with a long derisive blatt of the horn.

Jay said, "I'd better speak to David and Storr about it. And have a word with Jennings, too. It seems, according to Tim Stapleton, that Jennings said they might make free with the grounds when they liked."

"Jennings would never say that," she answered.

But Jay merely frowned.

When they reached the door, they found Jennifer waiting. Her blue eyes were very bright, her cheeks flushed. Her blonde hair had begun to wisp around her head. "And what," she demanded, in slightly slurred words, "was that all about?"

"I'll tell you inside," Jay answered.

"And Jay has some news, too," Dolores said.

"Good news, I hope," Jennifer laughed. "I've a definite surfeit of any other kind."

Jay laughed. He slid an arm around both girls, and went with them into the drawing room.

Dolores didn't know, couldn't guess, and didn't want to, what it was that Jennifer felt at his touch. But she, she was swept by a strange wave of longing, of hunger. Her bones seemed to melt within her flesh. If only she and Jay were alone in the world, she thought. If only they lived in a place without family, town, and Emerald Station.

"Drink?" Jennifer asked, and went toward the sideboard.

"Not for me," Dolores told her.

"Not me," Jay said, and went on, "And you've had enough."

Jennifer pouted, grinned, and deliberately dropped ice cubes in a glass, then poured gin over it.

Jay ignored her.

David asked, "What was that down there, Jay? What were they doing?"

"Stapleton's youngest. He claimed that Jennings had given him permission."

Jennings grinned in his whiskers. "Kids. No. I did not. And I would not."

"Then he came out to see if he could get away with it," Jay said.

"For which we can thank Jennings and Storr," David said sourly. "And I'm not going to have it. Emerald Station is not a park for Bellingham trash."

Jennings' rosebud mouth puckered with disapproval. "You've no reason to say that, David. Tom Stapleton is a respectable man on the way to creating his own barony."

"Which means nothing to me, nor should it to you, Uncle Jennings."

"I think," Storr said quietly, "that it's time to bury the old hatchet."

"That's true, of course," Jay agreed. "But I have the feeling that will be more difficult than you think. Meanwhile Storr, I believe you and David had better put your heads together and consider what's to be done."

William lifted his flushed face. "Thanks, Jay. Maybe you can move them. Every time I go hunting or riding, I find trespassers. I've been saying so for I don't know how long. But nobody'll listen to me."

"A wall," David said thoughtfully. "Why can't we have a wall?"

The suggestion seemed to bring a certain brightness to Storr's abstracted face. It was the thought of designing, building, Dolores knew.

"You're carrying it too far," Jennings said. He heaved

186

his bulk out of the chair, paced restlessly before the gray stone mantel.

Storr didn't appear to have heard that comment. He smiled. "We could do it, David. It's quite feasible. There's plenty of stone in the quarry. All we need is workmen."

"Bring them in from New York," David said. "I won't have anyone from Bellingham out here."

Dolores shuddered. It seemed to her that no matter which way her thoughts went, or what subject was discussed, the old mystery was suddenly there. The Kennellys were anathema in the area. Not just to the Stapletons, who were obvious in their dislike, as she had just seen when Jay spoke to Tim, but to everyone. Why? she asked herself. How had it begun?

"Yes," Storr agreed. "We can bring in men."

"Oh, do what you like about your silly wall," Jennifer said. She turned to Jay, "What's your news? That's more important to me."

Jay grinned. "I wondered when you'd get around to asking me. I told Dolores earlier. You know my father is planning to move. Well, I'm going to stay on in Bellingham, take over the house, and turn it into a laboratory for my research."

A thought occurred to Dolores. She voiced it aloud. "But where will you live, Jay? Surely not in a laboratory with mice and monkeys and I don't know what else."

"Probably with the Maradines."

Jennifer chortled, "Wonderful. Then you'll be closer than ever."

"Yes," he agreed, but he looked at Dolores. "Yes, I'll be closer than ever now."

She dreamed about him that night. It was one of many dreams she had had. She saw him walking toward her, the sunlight bright on his chestnut hair. He was smiling, and his arms were opened wide. She ran toward him, laughing . . .

It was the laughter that awakened her. She lay still, staring into the dark, listening to it. Slowly, as full consciousness returned to her, joy was replaced by a vague alarm.

The room was still, and yet she heard laughter. But there was no happiness in the sound. It was made up of a strange sour horror. It went on and on, softly, terribly. Close by, but not so close that she could identify its source, it still seemed to fill the room.

She threw back the sheets, and slipped from bed. She went across the big room, barefoot, her gown as pale and light as a cloud around her.

She eased open her door, listened. The sound was fainter now. The sound of laughter which was not really laughter.

She closed the door again, listened once more.

Now it was gone. It left a terrible silence behind. A silence that still seemed to hold the lasting echoes of menace, drawn-out sour amusement, bitterness too deep to be imagined.

She stood irresolute. Had that laughter been part of her dream? Was it a warning against Jay? Was it a part of her whispering that she must not allow herself to love him? Or had it been real? No dream at all?

She went back toward her bed, but then paused. She knew that she would not sleep. She would not rest until she had set her mind at peace. Either the sound had been real, or it had been part of her dream. Part of the dream that had begun sweetly, but ended in a strange bitterness.

She pulled on a robe, stepped into slippers.

She went into the hallway. There was nothing there now, no sour laughter. The shadows lay still and unmoving, brilliantly outlined by the moonlight that came in a great white beam through the high window on the top floor.

She paused on the landing. The carved black masks seemed to stare at her from blind eyes. She had the feeling that if the laughter had been real, it had been within the house, but not quite within it. Close by, and muffled ... the balcony ...

She returned to her room quickly. She threw back the

188

draperies that covered her window, and peered out into the fragrant night.

The moon silvered the heavy decorated railings. Small gargoyles leered at her from the capped posts.

She stepped outside into pale shadow, and walked slowly down the long balcony. There were chairs here, and potted plants. But nothing living moved, except below, in the back gardens, there was a whisper of night wind among the plants.

She went through the silence, not breaking it, toward a darker patch of shadow where building and balcony formed a corner.

Forever afterwards she would believe that she had sensed something, that she had been drawn that way for a reason she couldn't identify, a reason that existed only deep within herself.

She had heard nothing since that bitter laugh had entered her dream and then echoed away into silence.

She had seen nothing but the shadows, some dark, some moon-touched, but all as unmoving as the house itself.

The shadow gleamed up at her faintly from the corner. She drew close, then closer.

A body lay in the angle of stone. A face turned to the sky, eyes empty and staring . . .

"David!" she screamed. "David, what's wrong?"

Chapter 19

"There are several cigarettes here," Jennings said quietly. "He must have been standing here, having a smoke. When he turned to go in, he tripped over something. Perhaps he bumped into one of the chairs. Anyway, he staggered, and fell back, and hit his head. It has to be that way. It has to."

As long as he was talking, Jennings seemed himself. His voice as robust as always, his eyes bright. But when he became silent, his bulk seemed to shrink. He looked older than his years, and his whiskers masked his face.

Storr and George were down on their knees near David's body.

Jennifer, leaning against the wall, sobbed softly. William, standing close to her, whispered for her to be quiet without much conviction.

Judd asked suddenly, "But what were you doing out here, Dolores? How come you found him in the middle of the night? Did you hear him cry out?"

She drew a deep breath. She wouldn't mention the laughter. She couldn't explain her feeling that she must not mention it. They would think her mad to have

190

dreamed of a sound in the night. A sound that had led her outside to find David's terribly still body. Yet it had been the laughter alone that sent her looking in the dark.

She said, "There was something, I think. I was asleep. I must have heard a sound of some kind, though I don't know what it was. Anyway, I got up. I stepped outside, and . . ."

Judd said, "You didn't see anyone move, did you? Or hear David talking?"

"No," she said stiffly. "No. Of course not! He must have been alone."

"Yes," Jennings said firmly. "Of course he was alone. And he fell backwards. He hit his head on the rim of the railing. You can see . . ."

Jennifer cried, "Oh, will you stop talking about it? Will you just . . . just not say . . ."

Evanne came out through the window that opened into David's dark room. In a quavering voice she said, "I've called Brooke. And Jay."

"They can't bring David back," Judd said bitterly.

"As if that matters to you," Jennifer told him. "You spent half the day fighting with him."

Judd's hazel eyes gleamed in the dark. "What does that mean? What are you hinting anyhow?"

George rose stiffly, held the railing to steady himself. His voice shook as he cut in quietly, "That'll do. Both of you. David fell somehow. It was an accident. Nothing will bring him back, you just said, Judd. And you're right. We'd better stick together nor. Talking wildly won't help David, nor will it help us."

Dolores wished that she could see George's face, read his thoughts. But his head was bent. It was almost as if he were speaking to David, instead of to those who could actually hear him.

She realized how little she really knew of him in that moment. He spent most of his time reading, and when he didn't have his nose in a book, he was limping alone on the terraces with his eyes fixed on the sky. He seemed uninterested in the things that attracted most men of twenty-seven. Like David, he ignored girls, cars, music. But David had had his interest in the family and its history. And all George had was his books.

Now she imagined that she heard the awful laughter again. She listened to its tone, timber, mood. She tried to identify the throat from which it had come.

David? Had he, alone in the dark, suddenly burst into laughter?

Had it been someone else?

But no one had admitted to being awake, outside. No one had admitted to seeing David.

She pressed her fists to her temples. She wondered what was happening to her. Why was she so determined to read meaning into an unexplainable incident? What difference did it make?

Perhaps David, too, had heard the sound, come out onto the balcony, drawn by it, just as she had been.

Perhaps, half asleep, clumsy, he had tripped, fallen, struck his head. But then what about the cigarettes?

There was the sound of footsteps, footsteps running on the steps. It would be Jay, she knew. And Brooke would probably be with him.

She couldn't face Jay or Brooke. She didn't dare look into their eyes. She was afraid of what they might be able to see in hers.

She turned quickly, left the others standing with David, and went through the silver moonlight, down the balcony, and then into her room.

It was a week later.

She sat in the Gordon kitchen.

Jason Gordon sat across the table from her. At sixty-two, he was white-haired and more trim than he had been as a younger man. He still had the firm jaw and singularly sweet smile she remembered from when she was a child. But some light had gone out of his face when Nanette died, and it had never come back. Now he said, "You're very peaked, Dolores. Are you having trouble sleeping these days?"

She shook her head.

He smiled faintly. "You mustn't lie to me, you know. I can see the marks of it in your face. And I'm old enough to be your father, even grandfather. So if there's anything I can do . . ."

"Nothing," she said. "But thank you." Still, he frowned at her thoughtfully. She went on, "I really am all right. It's just that it's been . . . well, rather hard to take. You do understand."

"Of course, Dolores. The death of a loved one always is hard to take. But it's over. You must forget it."

She thought of the laughter in the night. Had it been an odd coincidence that she heard it the night David died? Or was there some connection she didn't see?

She changed the subject, because in continuing it she might blurt out what remained in her thoughts no matter how she tried to banish it.

Was David's death an accident?

He had quarreled with Judd and Jennifer. He, rather than Storr, had been named heir to Emerald Station. Had one of these three argued with him again? Argued quietly, unheard by anyone? Had one of them pushed David so that he had fallen? It would be easy, she knew, to go to the balcony, and easy to leave it in any direction. The narrow ladders led from floor to floor, balcony to balcony, a fire precaution installed when the balconies had been rebuilt before she was born. Those same ladders made any of the balconies completely accessible. From within, or even from without the house. With a start, she realized that someone, anyone, could have come into the house, argued with David. Even someone from town.

Aloud, concealing these thoughts, she asked, "When are you leaving?"

"In another few days. I'm just about packed. I shan't be taking much with me."

"I can't imagine Bellingham without you," she said.

He laughed. "I know that I'm a fixture. And I'll miss you, your family. I'll miss Jay, too. But I've grown restless these last years. I'll travel a bit. And then I've heard that there's development going on in Florida. I'll have a look at that. It might interest me. Though I think I'm too tired, and too old to undertake anything new."

"Old," she scoffed politely.

There was something she couldn't define in his face, some gentle musing that struck her.

Then he said, "While I was clearing up, I found myself remembering your mother as she was the first time I saw her. It was in the dining room of the Ritz Hotel in London. And now, looking at you, it's as if I were seeing her again."

"Am I so like she was then?"

"Seventeen. That's how old she was. Her hair was black as coal, and her eyes black as coal, too, and gleaming with life. And with a certain sweet pride as well."

"It comes through in her portrait," Dolores said.

"Yes, it does. But, in life, in those days it was even stronger. Pride and strength. She needed both." He looked at Dolores. "As all Kennellys need them," he added.

She waited a moment, then she said, "Jason, I'm very worried about Judd. And I don't know what to do."

"Judd?"

"You know that he was expelled from school. David wanted him to go back, and he refused. Now all he does is ride in the fields, or visit in town."

"Yes. I've heard," Jason said dryly. "I've wondered about it."

"It troubles me. Because ... well, we both know how feelings run here."

She stopped. She knew it was unnecessary to remind him of what had happened after David's death.

Jay and Brooke had come as quickly as they could. Jay, since he was licensed to practice medicine in the state, though he had no office there, filled out the death certificate, and listed the cause as a skull fracture due to an accident, and filed one copy with the coroner and one with the mortuary which handled the funeral details. From one or the other of them, word spread through the town. When David was buried, a crowd of strangers attended, avid eyes fixed, not on the flower-decked coffin, but on the remaining Kennellys. It had been for Dolores a shattering experience, though she controlled her face with a strength she didn't know she had.

Now she said, "And all that, following on what happened the day David died ... the Stapleton boy coming out to picnic on the grounds so near the house ..."

"I had a word with Tom Stapleton about it, and so did Jay."

"And ... ?"

Jason shrugged. "Useless. More than useless. Perhaps it was even unwise. He laughed at me. He also claimed that Jennings and Storr were friends of his. So ..." Jason spread his hands. "There was nothing to say really."

"Why does he hate us so?" she asked hotly. "What did we ever do to him?"

"Oh, it goes back a long way, Dolores. It's nothing to do with you."

"But why?"

"It doesn't even bear repeating."

"But if I understood ... if I did, perhaps I could change it. We're prisoners of Bellingham, of the Stapletons, and those like him. We, the Kennellys, are bound by their hatred. Do you know about the wall? David and Storr talked about building one. And now Storr is determined to build it. And he will. A granite wall surrounding Emerald Station."

"Walls don't matter, Dolores. It's the spirit within that counts. The Kennellys aren't bound by Stapleton hatred."

"Then by what?"

But he didn't answer her. He rose, took a coffeepot from the stove, refilled her empty cup, then his. When he seated himself, he took a sip and said, "I think you may have heard the story. But I'll tell you if you haven't. About Stapleton, I mean. This goes back to your grandfather's day. The Maradines owned the whole valley. Stapleton's father was a tenant farmer. There were five bad years, and then a panic in Wall Street. The Stapletons couldn't manage. Maradine decided to no longer farm. He put them off. They had to move to town, and the old man became a carpenter, and died in some sort of accident. The Maradines sold the land on which Emerald Station was built, and all the surrounding property right up to the river, to your grandfather. Tom Stapleton blamed him, not the Maradines, for he thought the Stapletons would have been able to keep the land if it weren't for the Kennellys. The truth is, they were probably right. Maradine didn't need the land, nor the money for it. But your grandfather wanted to relocate here, and did, so that was that. Then, later, there unfortunately was something else. Tom's sister worked at Emerald Station, and ran away with someone. And Tom blamed the Kennellys for that, too."

"It doesn't make any sense to me," Dolores said.

"Sometimes what begins as rational ends up no longer rational," Jason answered. He emptied his cup, rose. "I'd better get on with it, I think."

"May I help?" she offered.

"I don't see how." He took a round gold watch from his vest pocket. "I expect Jay will be back any minute for you."

"When does he start remodeling the house?"

"The day after I get out, I suppose." Jason chuckled. "I won't let him touch it until them. I don't want to see it changed."

There were footsteps outside.

Jay opened the door and came in with Jennifer hanging on his arm.

She shot Dolores an openly-triumphant look. "We've been shopping," she said. "We've done all of Bellingham. And not once, but twice. From Moody's on."

But Dolores merely smiled. "Shall we start for home now?"

"I don't see why we should," Jennifer said. "We just got here."

Dolores looked at Jay.

"You've probably both had enough of town for one day. I'll drive you back," he said.

196

Jason said, "I'll be out before I leave. I won't go away until I've visited Emerald Station to say goodbye."

George was standing on the threshold of the family room. He leaned against the door frame, favoring his bad hip as always. His thin face was grave, his eyes hooded.

She glanced past him. "What is it, George?"

He touched the strawberry birthmark at his throat, then ran his fingers through his hair. "Dolores, I don't understand. I've been going through the papers, all the old stuff. It just doesn't make any sense to me. I've been staring at the portraits. Neil and Mary. Our parents. William's father and mother. The whole bunch. None of it makes sense to me. Not the way it did to David."

"It doesn't have to be the same for you," she said.

"But ... but I keep thinking that I want to run away. I don't want to deal with it. I never did. I never thought I'd have to."

She said, "It worked out different from what you thought, George. But ..."

"I don't care, you see. Maybe something's just worn out of me, something that was in the blood before. In Grandfather Neil, and in Father, too. Something I don't have any more."

"Storr will help you," she said. "You mustn't be afraid. He will, and the rest of us, too."

"Storr's already concentrating on his wall, Dolores. And he won't even step into the family room, you know that. So ..."

"He'll help," she insisted.

George was silent for a long moment. Then he said, without looking at her, "I've asked Jay to move in with us, Dolores."

"Jay? You have? How come?"

Again George was silent for a long time. Finally he said, "It seemed a good idea. There's no reason for him to stay in town alone after Jason leaves."

"No reason at all," she agreed. "Except that he wasn't going to. He had arranged to live with the Maradines."

"Not exactly arranged," George said quickly. "He had been thinking about it. When I suggested he stay here, he decided that it would be better. Lolly isn't too well, you know. And Brooke's getting on. Jay will be much more comfortable here with us."

"I expect he will," she said.

She hoped that George didn't know what elation the news gave her.

It was only later, when she was alone in her room, that she suddenly began to wonder what lay behind Jay's change in plans, what had led George to extend the invitation that would bring Jay to Emerald Station.

Chapter 20

"You don't want to do that," Henry said, his blue eyes sliding away from Dolores to examine the gravel of the driveway. "Why, your brothers wouldn't like it. And neither would your Uncle Jennings."

"I'm a big girl now," she answered impatiently. "I know how to drive, and I'm going to, Henry."

He rubbed agitated hands in his red hair. He was fifty years old, and he'd never married. She suspected it was because he was too bashful to approach any woman long enough to develop an interest in her or to get her interested in him.

Knowing his shyness, she softened her tone, "Now, Henry, you know it's perfectly all right."

"But not for you to go alone," he protested. "You never know what'll happen. I tell you what. I'll take you in myself. Okay?"

She smiled at him. "Henry, no. It's not okay. I want to go by myself."

He gave her a helpless look. Then, "It doesn't make sense, Dolores. You were raised to know better. Yes, you were, too. I was here. I saw it. What would your mother and father say, if they were to know?" He cast anxious little glances at the windows, plainly wishing that Evanne would notice and come out, and resolve his dilemma for him.

But Evanne didn't come out, and Dolores said, smiling still, "You worry too much. "There's no reason why I shouldn't drive into Bellingham alone, and I'm going to."

"No reason why you should either," he retorted stubbornly.

She wondered if he would actually refuse to give her the keys, and if, once she had taken them, he would lie down in the drive before the car, refusing to yield, no matter what.

He shifted his weight from one foot to another. "If they were here . . ."

"I'd be arguing with them, I suppose. I'm going, Henry."

He sighed, took the keys from his pocket, and put them into her hand. "You be careful, will you?"

"Just what do you expect to happen?" she asked.

But she remembered the ordeal it was to go to the dressmaker, the post office. The ordeal David's funeral had been. And then, she had been with members of her family. That didn't keep her from sensing the stares, the whispers. She was determined now to face them down herself. She would no longer avoid them. And, if there was some way, she would find out more about what was behind them.

She drove slowly, carefully, between the two granite posts at the entrance.

Storr had already brought in workmen to start digging the foundations for his wall. Some dug here, bending over long trenches. They looked up to wave at her as she passed. Others spent hours blasting in the quarry across the meadows. At the rate Storr was pushing them, the wall would not be long in the building.

She had gone only a few miles when she saw a familiar automobile coming toward her. She slowed, lifted her hand, and tapped the horn button.

Storr, driving by, didn't acknowledge the tune it sang out or acknowledge her wave. His big blond head was raised high over the wheel, his eyes, so very like their father's in color and shape, fixed straight ahead.

Bewildered, she considered going back to the house to make sure he was all right. But then she decided to go on. He had probably been thinking about the wall, or perhaps about the library. He had simply been preoccupied with his own interests. Thinking it over, she decided that it was more than that. He had been abstracted ever since Nealanna's death. It was as if, even when he was talking, listening, his mind was not quite present, but going off somehow to examine its own concerns.

When she reached town, she drove directly to the Gordon house. She had expected there to be some activity, but the place was quiet under the tall blue spruce that surrounded it.

She parked, went up the brick path to the door, assuming that Jay would be home. But no one was there. She walked around to the back garden, and, finding it empty, she returned to the car.

At first she didn't realize what was wrong. It simply looked odd. As if it might have shrunk in the little time since she had left it there.

Then she saw why it seemed so much closer to the ground than it had before. Each tire had been carefully slit, and the car now rested on the wheel rims.

She bit her lip, wondering what to do. Henry would be utterly outraged, and blame himself as well.

The Gordon house was empty, locked. She couldn't phone from there. The only thing to do was to locate a garage. There couldn't be very many in town. There just not that many automobiles as yet, though George and Judd agreed that very soon everyone would own a car, and not only the wealthy.

She was sure that she had seen a garage on Maine Avenue, converted, if her childhood memory was right, from a smithy that had once stood there. It was not big she was sure, but it would do, if she could find it.

She walked down the street, turned right at the corner for Maine Avenue. There were shops here, and the post office. Along the block, she saw the garage where she had thought she remembered it.

She approached it cautiously, though she didn't know why. She was wearing a white middy blouse, and a dark blue skirt. Her black curls were rolled and stacked at the back of her head. She gripped her navy blue purse tightly in both hands.

A man came out of the shed, rubbing greasy palms on his dirty overalls. He had pepper and salt hair that showed signs of thinning. His face was lean, black eyes prominent. "What can I do for you, Miss Kennelly?" he asked.

She gave him a startled look, and he grinned.

"Why, I know you, Miss Kennelly. Everybody in town knows you."

There was something in his speech that reminded her faintly of her mother. She said, perplexed, "And you are. . . ?"

"The name is Dale Row." He seemed to wait, an expectant gleam in his black eyes.

"Well, of course," she said, smiling now and suddenly relaxed. "I know your name. Though we've never met before. You're married to Evanne Borden's daughter, aren't you?"

"So right," he chuckled. "To Moira, that is. To Moira who used to work at the castle . . . I mean at Emerald Station, of course." But, oddly, he looked disappointed.

Dolores wondered just what it was that he'd expected her to say.

"I came here because I have four cut tires," she told him. "On Gordon Street. Just in front of the Gordon house."

"Cut tires? Is that what you said?"

She nodded.

"Now how could that have happened, I wonder."

"I don't know. Would you be able to do anything for me?"

202

"I don't know how I can. Not now. I couldn't leave my place alone, could I? If you wanted to wait for a little . . ."

"I've errands to do, Mr. Row."

"I suppose they'd have to wait, too, Miss Kennelly."

"But wait for what?"

"For my boy to come. When he does, he'll go and put new tires on for you."

"But how long would be that, do you suppose?"

Dale shrugged. "Half an hour maybe. Maybe less."

"I'll come back then," she said.

But he didn't answer. He stared at her with a strange, slanting smile.

She started to turn away.

He said, "You look just like your mother, you know."

She swung back, "You knew my mother?"

"Of course. Who in this town didn't? I knew her better than most though. I first saw her when she was just a few years younger than you are right now. A bonny girl she was, too. I still find it hard to believe that she's already dead. We're about the same age, you see. Just a few years different. Forty-seven she would be, but for the accident that killed her."

Dolores, nodding, wanted to leave, but found that she couldn't.

"*If* it was an accident," he said.

"What?" she cried in a strangled voice. "What did you say?"

Once again he gave her a strange slanting smile. "Well, you know it as well as I do. William was driving, wasn't he? And he was drunk, wasn't he?"

"He was not drunk," she said angrily. "That's just not true."

"Maybe. Maybe not. But it's in the blood, my little Dolores Kennelly. Though you may not know it. It's there all right. After all, there was the old man's brother, too. Up north that was. Holt was his name. And what he did was no secret, even if the Kennellys tried to make it one. And then there was Alicia. Hanged herself she did. That was thirty years ago, but there's plenty of us around here who remember that."

Dolores asked in a harsh whisper, "What do you mean, Mr. Row? My Aunt Alicia . . ."

"Hanged herself. And it was just as well, too. And what happened before she managed that? Did anyone ever tell you?" He didn't wait for her reply. He went on, "The old man, Neil Kennelly, he fell over his own gun and died in a hunting *accident*."

She took a step back from him. She saw now that the strange slanting smile covered a hatred so deep that it burned at her from his eyes. Here was what she had come to Bellingham to discover. And now she was sorry.

"The killer Kennellys," he said softly. "Surely you've heard it by now, Miss Kennelly."

She had never heard it in words before, but she knew that she had read the words in ugly stares. It was this that she had felt when Tim Stapleton looked at her. It was this that she had sensed at David's funeral.

Now Dale Row was saying the words to her. The killer Kennellys. A wave of cold moved through her flesh, and made her feel as if her blood had frozen in her veins. She took a step back from him.

"Wait," he said. "I didn't really intend to upset you. Why, you and me, me and your family, we have old links, you know. More than just through Moira and Evanne. Good old links, just between us."

"I didn't know," she whispered, seeing hate in his eyes, hearing it in his syrupy voice, though the words belied it.

"We were both from the old country," Dale said. "Your mother and me. That's right. From England. And we came not too far apart. Your mother first, and then me, soon after. Of course she traveled first class, being married to Gareth Kennelly. First class, with diamonds on her hands and in her ears, too. I see you don't wear them." He waited.

She said automatically, "I'm not that fond of them for daytime."

He grinned. "And I came steerage, a sorry, sick, and

204

messy voyage it was, too. I landed with hardly anything in my pocket, and ended up here in town. I was a smith then, thought you mightn't think it to look at me. And now I've this garage."

She licked her dry lips. "I see," she said.

"I've got a son, Dylan. He's the one we're waiting for. He's three years or so older than you."

"Yes," she said. She summoned all her strength to tear her gaze from his. She said, "Well, thank you. I'll be back."

He laughed aloud. "We're visited so long that here he is now. Here's Dylan. He'll go right along with you, and take care of your four tires."

Dylan Row was dark-haired, and dark-eyed, a few inches taller than his father, a few pounds heavier. He smiled at her, and she saw something of Evanne in his face. The thought was vaguely comforting.

"Mind your dress, Miss Kennelly," he said, leading her to his truck. "You'll be all over grease if you're not careful."

She thanked him for the advice, then for the hand in he gave her. He smiled again and disappeared into the shed. He made two trips to get the tires, and told her, as they pulled away from the garage, that she was lucky they had that particular size in stock. Very often they didn't, he assured her.

It took only moments to pull up behind her car. He unloaded his tools. She stood by, watching as he worked.

"You like it," she said after a few minutes. "Being a mechanic is what you want to do, isn't it?"

"Yes," he agreed. "But that's just the beginning of it. You've got what, four or five cars out at Emerald Station, haven't you? And there's maybe ten or twelve in town. And in twenty years there'll be double or triple that number."

"My brother says the same thing," she told him.

"That's it. To be in on the growing. I talked my father into the franchise. We'll do more than fix cars when they need fixing. We'll be selling the new ones. One of these

205

days I'll be as rich as the Kennellys." His face suddenly flushed. "Now listen, I didn't mean anything by that. We just say it, you know, instead of saying rich as Croesus." He looked at her anxiously.

She smiled. "I think I understand," and she thought that at least it wasn't as bad as saying the killer Kennellys.

He looked down at the tires. "The only thing is, how did you get these?"

"I don't really know. It just happened."

"It just happened with a sharp knife," he retorted.

"Yes," she said, shuddering.

"You don't know who did it?"

"No."

But he was no longer listening. His gaze went past her shoulder. There was a frown on his face, and his hand suddenly tightened around the tire iron.

She turned to look.

Three young men stood behind her now. They had come up so silently that she hadn't realized they were there.

She recognized only one of them. Tim Stapleton. She knew what he was going to say almost before he spoke.

He grinned at her, "Well, here's one of them, boys. One of the killer Kennellys."

"Knock it off," Dylan said.

"And here's Prince Charming, too," Stapleton sneered. "Why, you'd better be careful, Dylan. If you're not, I'll tell your girl on you."

"Say what you want. But get along. I've work to do."

"It's a public street," Tim said. "And I'm a friend of yours. I'll just stand here and make sure no harm comes to you while your back's turned on her."

Inside Dolores felt the trembling begin. She would not allow it to show. What was wrong with Tim Stapleton, with Dale Row? Why did they refer to the Kennellys in that terrible way?

Dylan said under his breath, "Never mind him, miss. I'll get through as fast as I can."

"Does your Dad know you're working on a Kennelly car?" Tim asked.

"You can bet he does," Dylan answered. "We always care for them. Henry brings them in."

"Oh, yes. I forgot. You're practically related to the Kennellys, aren't you?" Tim sneered. "I mean, Henry works at the castle, at Emerald Station, of course, and he's your uncle, isn't he?"

Dylan ignored Tim that time.

Tim went on, "You've got to choose up sides. You can't carry water on both shoulders. It's either your father, and mine, or it's them."

Dylan muttered, "It's nobody. I'm my own man. I can think for myself, and I . . ."

He stopped because Jay drove up, parked. Frowning, he came to Dolores. "What is it? I didn't expect you."

"I thought I'd stop by to see your father. And then I . . . then I had some flat tires."

Tim Stapleton and his friends made an interested audience. She was aware of their grins. Jay swept them with an impatient glance, then ignored them. "Come into the house, Dolores. You can wait there."

Dylan straightened up. "I'm just about finished, Dr. Gordon." Then, "Your father still around?"

"Yes. He was supposed to leave a couple of weeks ago, but he was delayed. He'll be going tomorrow."

"Tomorrow?" Dolores asked. She had known about the delays, known that was why Jay had not yet moved out to Emerald Station. But she hadn't heard that Jason was leaving the next day.

"Yes, Dolly, tomorrow. He called and asked your family to meet him at Maradine Mansion. We'll all get together there tonight."

Dylan said, "You'll give him my good wishes?"

"I'll do that," Jay said. He bent suddenly, stared hard at one of the tires Dylan had removed. "These were cut, weren't they?"

"No doubt of it," Dylan agreed.

Jay straightened. He grinned at Tim Stapleton. "Now who do you suppose would do a thing like that?" he said. "A man could find himself in jail for less."

Chapter 21

The men had gone off together to have their brandy and cigars.

Lolly and Jennifer sat on a small satin love seat on the other side of the hearth, facing Dolores.

The big room showed Lolly's touch. A display of early spring roses on the mantel scented the air. There were more roses and daffodils on the low tables. The filmy curtains allowed the blue twilight in, and a touch of breeze, so that the crystal chandelier tinkled softly.

There were none of the shadows here that seemed always to linger in Emerald Station, Dolores thought. Yet it seemed to her that when Jay had left with the others all light had gone from the room. She found herself anxiously watching the door, awaiting his return with Brooke and her brothers.

She wondered if he would tell them about the four destroyed tires on the car, and how Dylan Row had helped her. She didn't know what she would have done if Tim Stapleton and his friends had continued to harass her, and if Jay hadn't arrived just in time. She could still see, in her mind, the knuckles of Dylan's hand tightening around the tire iron. That she might become the cause of some violence terrified her. And she couldn't forget, either, the look of hatred in Dale Row's eyes, his sneering smile. Yet Dylan was plainly of a different fabric. As he had told Tim Stapleton, he had a mind of his own. Did he see her, the Kennellys, differently because he was Evanne's grandson? It was odd, Dolores decided, thinking of it now for the first time, that Evanne, who was a fixture in the life of Emerald Station, who had loved Dolores' mother, helped raised the family, never spoke of her only daughter Moira. She visited Moira in town, returned with the local news but never mentioned the Row family. Dolores decided that she would ask Evanne why, what had happened to create so peculiar situation.

"Don't you think so?"

Dolores started at the words directed to her. She hadn't been listening. And now Lolly, with raised brow, was waiting.

"Think about what?" Dolores grinned. "I didn't quite hear . . ."

"We're talking about women's suffrage," Jennifer told her. "Now that the amendment has been ratified, women will vote, and everything'll be changed. We'll make our influence felt all right." For emphasis she drew a deep drag on the cigarette she held, and blew a great blue plume in Lolly's direction.

Lolly openly winced, turned her sandy, gray-streaked head away, and blinked her eyes rapidly. She wore a gray dress of chiffon with long bell sleeves and a round neck. Small diamonds sparkled at her ears. Once she had made her disapproval quite clear, she said, "The vote is only a sign of the changes in the world. A sign. No more. We'll know what substance there is to it in the future."

"You'll see," Jennifer retorted. "Now that's behind us, there's more to come."

"It's the same as with the temperance movement," Lolly said, smiling. "If it hadn't been for men it would never have happened. Nor the Volstead Act either."

"I don't care about that," Jennifer answered. "The vote's more important. It will make women free."

Lolly smiled. "But do we agree on what being free means?"

"You wouldn't understand," Jennifer retorted. "How could you?" She stopped, her sulky red mouth tight.

Lolly laughed, glanced over at Dolores. "I'll say for you, Jen, what you're too polite to say. I'm too old to understand. Is that it?"

"Have it your own way." Jennifer tossed her blonde head. "But this *is* 1920. Everything's going to be different from now on."

"I don't quite see how," Lolly rejoined. "As long as men remain men, and women remain women."

"Perhaps they won't," Jennifer suggested. "Perhaps as time goes on, each of them will change."

"Perhaps. But I think that women will remain dependent on men as long as women have babies."

Jennifer hooted. "You see? There speaks an older generation."

"There is more and more work that women can do. I agree with that. But are they doing it in any number?"

"They will," Jennifer answered, blowing another plume of cigarette smoke.

Lolly ignored it that time. "They might," she amended.

"All I know is what I see," Dolores said. "*We* aren't doing such work. *We* depend on our fathers and husbands to protect and support us."

Jennifer gave her an outraged glance. "But I'm not speaking of women like us. We're Kennellys. Naturally we shan't go into the factories, or the offices."

Lolly said, "But it's we who are the leaders, Jennifer. Women of our class set the style, and tone, and pace."

But Jennifer ignored that. She told Dolores, "You're the kind of girl who would hold time back. You're the dependant type. But not me."

Dolores didn't answer. Her dark eyes went to the door. She wished that Jay and the others would come in now. Jennifer was preparing to go on the attack again. It was an old story. They had been at loggerheads for as long as Dolores could remember. She supposed it would always be that way. Always, until Jennifer married and left Emerald Station. If she ever did.

Lolly, too, sensed the coming explosion. She said quickly, "Oh, you know, we were so sorry to hear about Jay's change of plans. It would have been lovely to have him here." She paused, a faint flush touched her cheeks. "It would have been like the old days for me."

It was, Dolores knew, a reference to when Lolly had been, as a young girl, Jay's and Doe's governess, in the days before Dolores and Jennifer had been born.

"Your loss is our gain," Jennifer told her, a brightness coming over her plump face. "I'm glad he decided it would be handier if he stayed with us."

"Do you know why he did?" Dolores asked, hoping that she sounded no more than politely interested.

"Why, no, I don't really. It was all arranged with Brooke. It was . . ." Lolly paused. "Something of a surprise to Brooke, as a matter of fact, when Jay dropped by to tell us. I hope that Brooke doesn't . . ."

Jennifer cut in disgustedly, "Oh, Lolly, don't you start that. Brooke realizes as well as anybody that it would be much better for Jay to be with us. After all, we *are* younger."

"Jay is thirty-five years old," Lolly said gently.

Was that, Dolores wondered, a subtle suggestion that Jay was too old for Jennifer, too old for Dolores? But surely there was a ten year difference between Lolly and Brooke and no two in the world could be better suited to each other.

"Being thirty-five," Jennifer said, "doesn't make Jay an old duffer. At least not to me." She glanced sideways at Dolores. "Of course, to you . . . since you're just twenty . . ."

Dolores laughed. "A disadvantage I'll rectify by next year."

"It won't do you any good," Jennifer cried, her face

suddenly blazing. "Let me tell you, miss, this is one time you're not going to get your way. Jay Gordon is mine."

"Oh, no, Jen," Lolly protested. "You mustn't . . ."

But Jennifer went on, "And I give you fair warning. Don't you try to take him away from me. Because if you do, I'll . . . I'll fight you all the way."

Dolores said coolly, "Jay has some say in this."

"Then you admit it!" Jennifer hissed. "You *do* want him."

"There's nothing to admit. But I do think . . ." Dolores stopped because Jennifer had jumped up from the love seat.

"Ever since my father and mother died, it's been this way," she yelled. "William and I are Kennellys, just as much as the rest of you, but we've always been the outcasts at Emerald Station. Last, never first. We . . ." She stamped her feet, and her heel caught in her dress. It tore with a whisper of silk.

Lolly said hastily, "Do stop that, Jen, dear. Tantrums are very unbecoming in young women of twenty-four. And if Jay should come in . . ."

Jennifer abruptly subsided. She flung herself down on the love seat, but her eyes, pale blue and alive, flickered with points of light as she looked at Dolores.

Dolores ignored her, asked, "Lolly, why is it that Jennings never married?"

"I don't know. But he was away for many years. He might have fallen in love and had something go awry."

"That was so long ago," Dolores said. "And since then . . ."

"He could marry, if he wanted to," Jennifer told her. "With the Kennelly money behind him, he'd be sure to find a woman who would have him. Even at his age."

"Perhaps he will one day," Lolly said. "If he wants to. But I see no signs of his being anything but a confirmed bachelor."

"Yes," Dolores agreed. Then, "And David didn't marry either." She wished, immediately, that she had not expressed her thought aloud. She didn't understand why

212

she had mentioned David. The loss of him was too fresh to accept. And it was much too late to speculate upon his bachelorhood.

"He was too interested in the family to notice anything else," Jennifer said. "That's what held poor David back."

Dolores nodded agreement. That was probably true. Jennings had remained single. So had Storr. It was unlikely that George, who kept his nose in his books, who hadn't shown the slightest interest in girls, whose bitterness about his infirmity kept him at war with himself, would ever fall in love.

It was as if Jennifer had been peering into her mind, watching her private thoughts unreel. For her cousin said suddenly, with a snicker, "I guess the dynasty depends on you, Dolores. You. And me. And maybe Judd."

The men, returning, interrupted that conversation.

Dolores was relieved. She hadn't wanted to continue it. Nor had she wanted to think about it any more. There was something about the fact that the men in the family hadn't married that was obscurely troubling to her. Did they feel that they were safe only when they remained within the confines of the large estate? So much was happening out in the world, yet none of them seemed drawn to join in, to see, experience, learn. Instead of going out, they brought in what they wanted. Their gramaphones, their radios, their automobiles. There must be some reason for their withdrawl into the tight confines of family life.

She rode home from Maradine Mansion with Storr.

William and Jennifer had gone with George and Judd. Jennifer had suggested that she ride with Jay and Jason, and had departed pouting when Jay refused her, saying he would take his father to town and stay a while.

Now Storr's profile was hard and strong, the image of her father's, Dolores thought, as she looked at him sideways. The very image, barring his blond hair, of course. What mattered, though, were the bones, and they were the same. And yet, he seemed different now. She couldn't quite put her finger on what the change was, but something had happened to him. There was a strange rigidity in his face, a stoniness in his expression. All the Kennellys had it to a certain extent, it seemed to her. But particularly the Kennelly men. A look of being braced, controlled, wary. But it was most pronounced now in Storr. She wondered if it was because he was beginning to show signs of aging. He was only a year older than Jay, she knew, and Jay didn't seem old to her.

Hardly that. Jay was young, vital. She longed to have his arms around her. She longed for the touch of his lips in a kiss, a real kiss, not a brotherly peck pressed to her cheek, then transferred to Jennifer's.

It was hopeless to think of it. He considered her a child, and always would. And also there was Jennifer. She was a young woman who always got her way, Dolores had learned, just as, when a child, she had been a child that always got her way.

Storr said huskily, "You're quiet tonight, Dolores."

"I was thinking."

"I guessed that." He turned his head for a moment, looked directly into her eyes. "Is something bothering you? Something you want to talk about?"

She was touched, and startled, too. She had never felt particularly close to Storr. There was the age difference, of course. But also, when she was growing up, he had been away at school a great deal of the time. And since he had come home he had been busy. Busy building, and designing, and building again.

She asked suddenly, "Storr, listen, did you ever want to go away? I mean, to live somewhere else? Or travel? The way Jennings did?"

"No. I belong here." Storr softened the quick positive words by adding, "And Jennings came back, didn't he? He found that he belonged here, too."

"Why did he go away, Storr? Do you know?"

"He had words with grandfather."

"And stayed away for years and years because of that?"

"I suppose," Storr said indifferently.

"Mother never spoke of it."

"No," Storr agreed.

"Do you remember Grandfather?"

Storr didn't answer her. He was gripping the wheel so hard that she saw his knuckles whiten. The automobile began to swerve. It spun off towards the side of the road, then, at just the last possible moment before crashing, it swung back in the other direction.

Storr cursed under his breath, and jammed the brakes on. The car jerked to a stop in a whirl of dust.

"The steering's not right. We'd better walk, Dolores. I can't see what's wrong in the dark," he said. "It won't be too far if we short-cut across the valley." He got out, waited for her to join him. He put a hand on her shoulder, turned her toward the darkness of the trees, toward the shadows where the moon could not penetrate.

She said, "No, Storr. I'd rather go the long way. If you don't mind. My slippers . . ."

He laughed softly. "Women and their clothes," he said. "Walk three miles to save a pair of slippers. But, oh, all right. Let's go."

They went side by side along the dark empty road.

It was so silent. An odd chill touched her. She wished that they weren't alone. She wished that someone would come.

She stumbled, and nearly fell.

Storr caught her, his fingers biting into her arm. For an instant, he held her. She felt the tension in his hand, his whole body.

She was frightened without knowing why. She broke away from him, began to run.

"Dolly," he yelled. "Dolly, wait," and came after her.

The chug and rattle and bang of a car came through the stillness. Headlights flipped over the rise, bathing her in pale light.

She lurched to a stop by the side of the road, waved and called.

215

A tomato sailed through the air, exploded in sticky wetness against her shoulder.

"That's for the killer Kennellys," Tim Stapleton yelled as the car went by.

Chapter 22

"It was," Storr said, "absolutely idiotic. We were walking home from where I had left that confounded car. And she just started to run. I couldn't imagine what struck her. She took off down the road like a chased rabbit. I yelled at her to stop, and followed, and then Tim Stapleton drove by. He threw something. I didn't know what until I reached her. At first I thought it was blood. But when I saw it was a tomato, just a tomato, she collapsed."

"You'd better talk to Tom Stapleton about it," George said. "You or Jennings. Or maybe both of you. "We're not going to have that, you know. Words are one thing. An attack like that is another. I'll have the constables in if I have to."

"Never mind that now," Jennings said. "What happened to the car?" The question was directed at Storr.

He shrugged his head shoulders. "The steering went. I was afraid to drive any further. It might have meant a wreck. And I just didn't want to take any chances. Not with Dolores there, too."

William said harshly, "I suppose that's a dig at me."

"Not at all," Storr answered in a deep, warm and weary

voice. "I wasn't thinking of you, William. You must stop blaming yourself for what wasn't your fault. I was thinking only of Dolores. If I'd hit a tree, gone off the road . . . well . . . I was afraid. I'll admit that I was just afraid."

He was still afraid, Dolores thought. His hands were trembling and his face was white. She supposed that he had had a terrible moment when she screamed, when he saw the stains on her dress.

Judd's hazel eyes were narrowed, studiously fixed. "But whatever made you run that way? You'd have been all right if you'd stayed with Storr."

They were all staring at her. All those eyes. Questioning. Judging. Weighing. Accusing, too. It was frightening. She felt a wave of dizziness sweep her. The walls seemed to be melting around her. The very floor beneath her feet seemed to be moving in uncontrollable spasms. She gripped the arms of the chair in which she sat, holding on, as if it were the only fixed point in a dissolving world.

Then Jay put his hand on the back of her neck, pressed hard. "Get your head between your knees," he ordered. "Hurry, Dolly. Do as I say."

She cried out, but it was useless. He held her that way, while the blood rushed into her head, and the room darkened. After what seemed to be a long time, he drew her up.

He was smiling. "Feel better?"

"I think so," she whispered. "I think I'm all right."

"Of course, she is," Jennifer said, in a voice laden with disgust. "She's just being dramatic. After all, nothing happened. At least nothing to faint over."

"It *was* startling," Storr said judiciously. "But . . . well, I mean . . . not as bad as all that. And if she only hadn't started running . . ."

Dolores closed her eyes. How could she explain to them that she didn't even understand herself? She had been assailed by terror. That was why she ran. There was no other reason for it. She ran because she was frightened, needlessly, senselessly frightened. And if she hadn't run, Tim Stapleton would have passed her by, let her alone. He

218

would never have shouted at her, assaulted her with the tomato when he knew that her brother Storr was so close by. So she had, she supposed, brought the unpleasant incident on herself in a way. But it was just that. Storr was right. An unpleasant incident. Only what of what had come before? Why had she run so mindlessly from Storr?

"I think you'd better go to bed," George told her. "You're still as green as an early apple. And there's not much sense in saying you're all right when your hands keep shaking."

"You should," Jay said quietly.

She felt his eyes on her, and looked up. His face was expressionless, his eyes thoughtful.

She rose. "I will go to bed, and I'll probably forget all about it by morning."

"You're sure it was Tim Stapleton?" he asked.

"Yes. I'm sure," she told him. "But don't . . ."

"Don't what?" Jennings leaned forward, smoothing his whiskers. "Go on, Dolores. Don't what?"

"Don't make any trouble," she answered.

"But are you *sure*?" he demanded.

"I told you," she cried. "And besides, Storr heard his voice, too." She turned to Storr, "You did, didn't you?"

"I'm not all that certain," he answered, surprising her. "I thought it might have been. And you said it was. So . . ."

Her surprise faded as swiftly as it had arisen. She suddenly saw that Jennings and Storr both had dealings with Tom Stapleton over the rebuilding of the library. They wouldn't want to antagonize him by accusing his son.

George fingered the strawberry birthmark on his throat, looking relieved. "If you're not sure, then there's nothing to be done," he said.

She clung to the chair back. "All right. Let's forget that it happened."

"Yes," Storr said. "After all. It's not exactly something new. We've always had words with those people in Bellingham. This isn't different."

219

Judd sneered, "All the more reason for doing something about it. If I had my way . . ."

"But you won't," George put in. "We'll ignore it, as the Kennellys have always ignored it."

Dolores paused at the door, turned back. She looked at Jay. There was a disapproving expression on his face. She wished that she knew what he was thinking.

"A terrible thing," Evanne said. "I just can't bear the thought of it." She shook her head back and forth in open disgust. "You could have been hurt, Dolores."

"But I wasn't." She was curled in a rocking chair, allowing her weight to move it slowly.

It was her favorite place in the house. She liked to sit in the kitchen, to watch Evanne work, to talk with her.

"I guess," she went on, "I was more scared than anything. And angry, too. If I'd had any sense I'd have laughed at him. I don't know why I . . . why I got so upset."

"It would be enough to make anybody upset." Evanne's white head, streaked with fading red, seemed to bristle. "All this time, all these years . . ."

"But why?" Dolores ask. "Oh, I know the old story about the Maradines selling the Stapletons' land to us. But it's too long to carry a grudge for that."

Evanne was silent for a long time. At last she sighed, "Oh, well, child, don't think of it. It doesn't matter."

"But it does matter. Hate begets more hate. And it's wrong. It's so wrong. We've none of us done anything to them. But they call us killer Kennellys, Evanne. They . . ."

"Nonsense," Evanne said briskly. "All nonsense."

Dolores took a deep breath. "Evanne, I met Dylan yesterday."

Evanne's blue eyes brightened. "You did. And how did that come about?"

Dolores explained about the slashed tires, her meeting first with Dale Row, then with Dylan.

Evanne listened, the brightness still in her eyes, but her mouth going tight and hard. When Dolores had finished,

Evanne said, "Yes. He's a good boy, Dylan. And for all that she's been a great fool in her life, Moira is a good girl, too."

"But what happened, Evanne? Why doesn't she ever come here to see you? There's some estrangement. I feel it. And I don't understand."

Evanne sighed, looked down at her hands. "Oh, it's a long story. Dale Row was never a friend of your family's. He ... well, he's a Kennelly hater, I suppose you'd call him. Like Tom Stapleton himself. But Moira met him in town. And when I forbade her seeing him any more, she ran off and married him. I was very angry, knowing the man for what he was, and what he still is, I might add. But then she, my Moira, became pregnant. I ... oh, I couldn't lose my grandchildren. And your mother urged me to make my peace. So I went to Moira, and I made my peace with her. Not with Dale Row, mind you. But with my daughter, and, of course I love my grandsons. And that's how it is to this day."

"Dylan was kind to me, Evanne."

"He would be," she said simply. Then, "When exactly is Jason Gordon leaving, Dolores? Do you know?"

"Today, I think."

"Jay hasn't said exactly when he's moving in. Would it be tonight, do you think?"

"I suppose so."

It was then that Jennifer came into the kitchen. "Oh, there you are. I can't imagine why you insist on hanging around here, like Cinderella or the scullery girl. Excuse me, Evanne," she added as an aside. "You've your job to do. But Dolores ... well, really ..." She stopped then. When she went on, her voice had lost its irritation. It was level, serious. "William's just had a call from Jay."

"What's the matter?" Dolores stopped the rocking chair, got to her feet. She had seen the look in Jennifer's eyes, and knew that something had happened.

"It's Jason," Jennifer told her. "He's ... he's not going to Florida after all. He's ... dead."

221

Evanne cried, "What? How? What do you mean? Speak up, Jennifer. Tell us."

But Dolores could only stare, dry-lipped, and dry-eyed. Jason Gordon had been a part of her life for as long as she could remember. She had accepted him leaving town, but she had assumed that he would come back, visit. She would write to him, and he to her. She couldn't imagine that he was dead. That he, like her mother and father, and David, were no longer a part of her world, a part of the living.

"It happened during the night. That's what Jay told me," Jennifer said. "They'd known for some time that there was trouble. They'd just not talked about it. But that was why he was going to take that trip, and then go South. And then his heart just gave out."

"Is there anything we can do to help Jay?" Dolores asked.

Jennifer shook her head. "Not us. He said not. But William and George are going in with Storr right now." She drew a deep breath. "We'll have to be especially good to Jay from now on. We're all he has left."

"Has anybody phoned Doe?" Evanne asked.

"Lolly did. As soon as she heard from Jay."

"Will she come?"

"Yes. She and her family," Jennifer answered.

"I haven't seen Doe for a long time," Evanne said thoughtfully. "I wonder what she's like now."

She had just paused when a blast, following by a long rolling echo, shook the kitchen. She shook her head from side to side in slow disapproval. "The quarry. I'll be glad when they finish the wall."

The sun was bright, the air sweet with the scent of flowers.

The chapel had been crowded, and now the area around the grave was crowded, too.

The Gordons were well-loved. They had been one of the original families in Bellingham, and had always given of themselves.

222

Dolores didn't listen to the minister talk about the Gordons. She was afraid that she would burst into tears if she allowed herself to hear his words of praise. Her eyes strayed from the coffin near the opened earth that had been prepared to receive it. She looked along the hillside to where Gareth and Nealanna were buried side by side, and David next to them.

When she had been here last, there had been only the family, the Maradines, the Gordons, and some avid-eyed strangers. Now the Kennellys stood alone, in a tight-knit group, while sad-faced townspeople surrounded Jay. His bright chestnut head seemed to stand out above all the others.

She yearned to be with him, to touch him, to smile at him. She yearned to tell him how sorry she was for his loss. But all of Bellingham stood between her and him. She could do nothing but watch him bend his head in prayer, his lips moving. She could do nothing but watch as he straightened up and raised his eyes.

Across the heads of the others, her gaze met his. He nodded slightly.

Her heart began to beat very quickly. He had thought of her then, sought her out where she stood. She found herself wondering if now he would change his plans. She didn't see why he should. But perhaps, with his father dead, Jay would decide to leave Bellingham, leave the Kennellys behind.

She saw Dale Row with Moira and Dylan. The older man stared at her with eyes as hard as black marble. But Moira, who was twin to what Evanne had been when younger, smiled. And Dylan did, too.

She was relieved when the minister stopped speaking, when George took her arm, said, "We're leaving now, Dolores. Jay will come out to Emerald Station later on."

He came that evening, as twilight fell. He was plainly tired, his face shadowed with fatigue, and with a new loneliness that tore Dolores' heart because she understood it so well.

223

He didn't mention the funeral, nor his father. He sat with them for a little while, and then excused himself, saying that he wanted an early night.

When he had gone up to the room Evanne had prepared for him days earlier, George said quietly, "I'm glad he's here."

"So am I," Jennifer answered. Her face tightened as she turned her gaze on Dolores. "And it goes without saying that you are, too, Dolly. You're making a complete, an absolute, fool of yourself, you know. Why, everybody can see it. Your heart in your eyes, and on your sleeve, too. You ought to be ashamed of yourself."

"I'm sorry for Jay," Dolores retorted, thinking that Jennifer had apparently already forgotten her apparent sympathy.

"Sorry for him," Jennifer jeered. "If that's all it is . . . well, then, we'd all look as mealy-faced as you do. But it's more than that. Why don't you admit it? Why don't you say that you're going to try to win him?"

"I'm not going to . . . to . . ."

But Jennifer didn't allow Dolores to finish. She cried, "Well, I warn you. He's mine. So hands off."

Jennings burst into uproarious laughter. "If only poor Jay could hear you, Jen. He'd pack up right now and get out. He'd feel like a stuffed doll being ripped between the two of you. And no man wants to feel like a stuffed doll, believe me."

"You were always on her side," Jennifer said, sweetly poisonous. "I don't see why. I'm as much a Kennelly as she is. You're uncle to both of us. At least I've always thought you were. But . . ."

"Jennifer, do be quiet," William cut in. He rose, went to the liquor cabinet. "You can be amazingly rude without even trying."

"So can you, though you try all the time," she retorted. She got to her feet. "I know what I want. And I'm going to get it. And if any of you get in my way, then you'd better watch out."

George glanced at her sideways, his mouth tight. His

hands massaged his bad hip, without conscious volition. He said, "Jay is a guest in our house. I suggest you keep that in mind. I don't want you to make him uncomfortable. And I don't want you to impinge on his privacy. If you do, you'll drive him away."

Jennifer shrilled, "Oh, no. Not you, too. Don't start acting the heavy patriarch the way David did."

George said heavily, "Just remember, Jennifer. I don't want you to drive Jay away."

Dolores, listening to the exchange, was struck by the tone in which George spoke. He was, as usual, deadly serious. She couldn't remember when he had been otherwise. But there was urgency in his voice now, too.

She suddenly found herself remembering that she had wondered at Jay's decision to stay in Emerald Station when he had, originally, planned to live with the Maradines. Lolly had been somewhat surprised by the change. Surprised and disappointed. Now Dolores wondered again. Why had he altered the arrangements? When had he altered them? She wasn't quite sure, but she thought it was some time after David's death. Could there possibly be a connection?

She didn't know. But it was odd. She could see no reason why he should have come to live at Emerald Station. But Jay always had good reason for what he did. Then he had one now, too.

She wondered what that reason was.

Chapter 23

It was, perhaps, because she was so aware of his presence, the immediate impact he had on the others, and on herself, too, that Dolores soon knew her suspicions were not the product of an overactive imagination. They were not the result of adolescent fear, nor the creation of years of unease, nor the flowers of grief at the loss of those she loved. There was a reality to what she kept concealed within her. She was able to observe that reality in observation.

Jay moved quietly among them, but was always watchful, she saw. He maintained the cool detachment which he had always had, yet he plainly observed each member of the family in turn. He divided his time impartially, spending an hour on a walk to the quarry to watch the men at work there. He rode out to hunt with William, and, separately, with Judd. He discussed architecture with Storr, the garden with Henry, cooking with Evanne. He took Dolores herself walking.

He didn't go into Bellingham, nor to the house in which, supposedly, he was to begin work on his laboratory. That he didn't was one more sign that he had come to Emerald Station for some purpose.

He sought something, or someone. She didn't know which, or why, but she was certain it was true.

The certainty lent a kind of stiffness to her moments with him. She couldn't quite put it out of her mind, though she tried, nor dissemble enough to hide it, though she tried that, too.

Jennifer noticed, said, "Why, Dolores, I begin to think that your silly infatuation with Jay is addling your senses, what there is of them. Not that I mind. But I hate to take unfair advantage of you. And the way you behave would turn off a stone lion much less a red-blooded man."

George drew her aside, looking grave. "Dolores, what's been wrong with you these last few days? Are you ill? Are you still scared about what happened on the road?"

"You should have more pride," William told her, his lips turned in a sneer. "Your man-hunger is showing. Why not act your age?"

And Judd, closest to her in age, and always before, closest in affinity, too, simply gave her disgusted looks.

But she found that the only way to avoid the peculiar awkwardness born of her suspicions of Jay was to avoid his company. So she retreated to her room immediately after dinner that third night since his arrival.

She closed the door firmly against the laughter that floated up from the lower floor, filling the galleries and hallways with mocking sound, and the gay foxtrot from the gramaphone that teased her with visions of Jennifer in Jay's arms.

Against that background, the empty silence in her room was very nearly unbearable.

She remembered her irrational terror when she suddenly ran from Storr, remembered Tim Stapleton shouting, "That's for the killer Kennellys." Words that Dale Row had used, too.

Now she wished that she had forced herself to stay below. She wished that she and Judd had settled down to a game of checkers. She could, then, have watched Jay observing each of them in turn. What was he looking for? Why did the thought frighten her so?

She wished that she could, simply, have allowed herself to stay in his presence, instead of running away from it.

But she had said she was tired, ignoring his protests, the protests of the others. Now she was stuck here alone. It would seem too odd for her to return, claiming a change of heart. Jennifer would sneer at her all the more.

She sighed, wandered out to the balcony. From there, too, she could hear the music, could hear the empty silence that surrounded her.

The thick stars were gleaming against the velvet blue of the sky. There was a wind astir in the trees near the river. A glow of golden light lay across the courtyard, and an occasional shadow moved through it, marking the passage of someone across the lower window. She watched, fascinated, when the shadows of a dancing couple moved by, spinning quickly through the light. It would be Jennifer and Jay, as she had imagined them only moments before. A pang of envy touched her.

She banished the feeling with the wry observation that she had given Jennifer carte blanche for that evening, and had no right at all to envy her.

She turned her back on the dancing shadow, and went inside. Her eyes looked huge and dark in the gold-framed mirror. Her curls seemed dull and limp. She gave herself a dispirited smile, and turned her back on her reflection to prepare for bed.

Soon after, with all lights out except the lamp on the night table, she lay back against the pillow, a book resting on her raised knees. She tried to concentrate, but the print blurred into pictures that had no relationship to what was written there.

David ... his face absorbed, standing in front of the portraits in the family room. David ... considering the Kennelly generations ...

His face became Jay's ... thoughtful gray eyes ... a square stubborn jaw ...

She didn't notice when the book slipped off her knees

228

and fell to the floor. Nor notice, even, when her eyelids began to droop and finally closed.

Jay . . . his expression . . . closed, careful . . .

She came awake with a sudden start.

The lamp at her side still threw pale light on the coverlet.

She sat up slowly.

The house was quiet now, the music stilled, the laughter silenced. It was late. The family had retired.

As she yawned, reached to turn out the lamp, there was a sudden dull thud from somewhere outside.

She paused, her hand in mid-air. She turned her head, straining to listen.

All was quiet for that moment, and then, quite clearly, the dull thud was repeated.

She rose, started for the door. Halfway across the room, she stopped again.

Now a whisper of sound had come out of the stillness, had risen slowly from the whisper of the wind in the trees. A whisper of sound that was horribly, terrifyingly, familiar to her.

She had heard it only once before in her life, yet she knew it instantly. She knew that though she had pretended to herself that she had forgotten it, she had been waiting to hear it again.

It was louder now. It came from behind her. The hoarse chuckling that was filled with the acid of hate. The hoarse chuckling that she had heard the night David died.

She swung around, lunged for the window. She went through it, and out onto the balcony into utter darkness, into the blindness of the night.

"Who's there?" she called.

And the hoarse chuckling came again, came, bringing a chill to her body, an instant of paralysis to her mind. Then, slowly, it was gone, fading away into silence.

She leaned over the carved iron railing, and below her, a shadow moved, moved then disappeared, and she stared down at it. Was it her own shadow? Was it the shadow of someone climbing the narrow ladder that led down from the balcony to the one below, and to the courtyard?

She saw nothing, heard nothing. She began to wonder if it would have been her own shadow, cast by some trick of starlight, disappearing when she moved without awareness. For now, nothing moved. Nothing was there. Both shadow, and laughter, were gone.

She retreated into her room, closed the window, then covered it with the draperies. She stood, irresolute.

She had been dreaming of Jay, she remembered. Had the laughter been part of the dream as it had seemed the time before? Could the moving shadow have been part of the dream, too? Had she awakened? Or was she still asleep?

Then, quite clearly, she heard the sound of a dull thud once more. She was awake. She had to be. She was totally certain of the sound she had heard.

It came from somewhere beyond her room, somewhere in the hallway, near the steps.

She waited, expecting to hear that wave of hoarse chuckling laughter again. But there was nothing.

At last, unwillingly, she went into the hallway. It was so much like what had happened once before, like what had happened the night that David died. She had heard a sound, gone to the hall then. She had seen nothing and returned to her room. And then the laughter had come, drawing her out to the balcony and the discovery of poor David's body.

She looked slowly into the shadows of the hall. It was empty. She glanced down the steps, and saw, on the dark of the carpet, an odd glitter of light, a winking, gleaming strand of light.

She stared at it, unsure of what it was that she saw, more out of disbelief than lack of recognition. For she knew what lay there. It was a strand of emeralds set in gold links. Her mother had given it to her the year before she died. She had never worn it.

What was it doing out here on the steps? It should be lying in the padded velvet of her jewel case along with her other necklaces and earrings. She couldn't remember when she had last noticed it, touched it. But surely it had been months ago.

Puzzled, she went down the steps. She knelt to pick up the jewels. Her fingers had just curled around the strand, accepting the chill of them in her flesh, when she heard a sound above her. She turned, looked behind her.

But she was too late. She couldn't move quickly enough. She couldn't save herself.

A huge, gold-framed portrait came sledding down the steps with unbelieveable force. Its heavy wooden frame caught her at mid-forehead, and sent her somersaulting backwards, into immediate darkness . . .

She opened her eyes into a painful brilliance.

There was light all around her, and voices, and somewhere close by, there was anguished weeping.

She moved her head slightly, and the brilliance became stronger, blinding her, glowing and fading with throbs of pain.

For a moment, she couldn't remember. She assumed that she had had a fall. She didn't know where she was, or how it had happened.

Then her vision settled, and the mind-clouding throbs receded, and the brilliance steadied. She said, "What a crazy thing to have happened."

George said, "Evanne, please stop making that noise and do something useful. What about some ice and a towel?"

The anguished weeping stopped on a sniff.

Jay leaned over Dolores. "Don't move yet. We'll get you upstairs in a minute."

She blinked at him, and the whole memory was before her, hanging between the two of them as if it were sketched lightly on a veil. She had an instant's fantasy that he could even see it, too. He must be able to see what she herself saw now so clearly.

There had been that awful laughter.

Then a sound had drawn her into the hallway.

She had seen the emerald necklace on the steps below and wondered what it was doing there.

She had gone down to get it, knelt in the dark, and heard some small sound once more. When she looked up, the heavy gold frame had come leaping at her, like some living, predatory beast, out of the dark.

"I'd like to know what happened," Jennifer was saying. "I think it's absolutely ridiculous. What was she doing down here? Dolly, Dolly, why don't you speak up? Why don't you tell us what happened?"

"Not now," Jay said. "This isn't the time for questions. Let's be sure she's all right. Let's . . ."

But Judd was kneeling beside her. He took her hand. "Dolly, what were you doing? Why did you get that portrait down here anyway?"

"Portrait?" she asked, bewildered. "What portrait?"

"The one in the frame," he said impatiently. "You can see it down there. But why you . . ."

"The gold frame," she said.

"Dolly, yes. Now why were you trying to carry it down here? You should have known much better. It's much too heavy for you. And besides . . . the middle of the night . . ." His rough voice held a beeseeching note, as if he were pleading with her to explain the unexplainable, to make sensible what was so plainly without sense.

"I wasn't carrying it down here," she told Judd. She turned to look at Jay. She whispered, "It came flying down at me. I hadn't touched it. I didn't know it was there at the landing."

"But what were you doing here anyhow?" William asked.

"I . . . I saw my string of emeralds on the steps," she answered. Remembering the chill of the stones on her fingers, she stretched out her hand to pick it up, to display it as proof that something extraordinary had occurred. It wasn't close by. She thought that she'd been holding it when she fell, but she supposed that she had dropped it. She turned to look behind her up the flight of steps. It should be somewhere, gleaming against the dark of the ug. But she saw nothing, and the movement had made her head throb again.

Judd left her side. He went slowly up the steps to the landing, and then, very deliberately, he turned and came down again. On each stair, up and down, he paused, his hazel eyes searching carefully. He didn't have to say anything when he reached the bottom where she sat huddled surrounded by the others. His face, his shrug, were eloquent enough.

Storr said, "You . . . you must have been . . . d–dreaming, Dolores. There's nothing there. And besides, what would your . . . your j–jewelry be doing on the steps?"

He was upset, she knew. The stammer that he had overcome years before was suddenly noticeable. She had seen his lips writhe and his throat tighten with the effort to control it.

She didn't have to try to answer him.

Jay drew her to her feet, held her protectively. "Never mind," he told her. "We'll talk of it later. Later on, when you feel better."

She nodded, leaned against him. As she started up the steps, with his strength supporting her, she saw the heavy gold-framed portrait standing against the bannister. A piece of the carving had been broken, and lay near by like a golden ear. She paused, stared at the face that some artist had painted a long time before. Gray eyes, dark hair, a lushly curved mouth. She knew the face though she had never seen it in the flesh. The portrait was of her Aunt Alicia, who had died years before she was born. The last time she had seen the painting was when she was a child. It was standing, face to the wall, in the attic. She had asked why it wasn't downstairs with the others, in the family room, but nobody had answered her. And she *had* soon forgotten about it until this moment.

As she went past it, she asked herself how Alicia Kennelly's portrait had come down from the attic to attack her on the stairs.

She asked herself whose laughter she had heard in the dark, and whose shadow she had seen on the balcony ladder.

233

Chapter 24

Her head ached. Her back was stiff and sore. She lay still, staring at the white ceiling.

She wished with all her heart that the pill Jay had given her the night before had kept her drugged and sleeping. In sleep there was escape, in consciousness none.

The familiar room was a cocoon of fear. The sampler framed in gold leaf on the wall, embroidered by her mother's hand, was suddenly a mockery. 'God Bless Our Happy Home.' Where was the blessing? Where the happiness?

Some evil, shrouded in shadow, walked the corridors of Emerald Station. She had sensed it all her life, sensed it deep in blood, and muscle, and bone. But now it was more than intuition. Now it was knowledge. Evil walked, and though she couldn't see its face, nor name it, she saw it clearly.

There had been the laughter the night David died. Cruel chuckling laughter had presaged his death.

And the night before, again, there had been the same laughter. That same sound as she went into the hallway,

234

went down to retrieve her jewels, and a hand struck out of the dark.

She had been led into a trap. It had been sprung, but something had gone awry. She should have been dead, as David was dead.

Someone had attempted to murder her, just as they had David.

She must discover why David had died; why she had been attacked the night before. She must see the face of evil hidden in shadow, and unmask it forever.

Killer Kennellys . . .

The words came back to haunt her. There was more justice in them than she had supposed. They had a meaning they had never had before. What had Tim Stapleton and Dale Row meant when they said them to her?

But who at Emerald Station was suspect? She could think of no one who must not be beyond suspicion. Yet she knew that if everyone was beyond suspicion, then everyone must be suspect.

It was a recognition that shocked her.

Had George, who had never wanted to be master of Emerald Station, suddenly changed his mind, decided that he did want to be? Could he, with his poor crippled hip, have managed to climb the fire ladder from the balcony? Could he have struck David down, brought the portrait from the attic?

Had Judd been so angry at David over school that they had fought? He could easily have managed the balcony ladder, the portrait, too. But would he have turned against her as well? Was his the laughter she had heard?

What about Storr? Did he feel that he, and he alone, should rule here? Was his interest in architecture only a facet of his love for the house and all it held? Was that love so deep and strong that he would murder David to gratify it? And if so, then why had she been drawn into the trap?

She could see no reason for Jennings to turn against David, against her. And it was the same for William. Jennifer had resented David's threat to control her behavior by controlling the funds he gave her. But had she resented it enough to commit murder once, to attempt it again for another reason? A reason that might involve Jay?

Jay . . .

She blinked away tears again, put her hands to her throbbing temples.

Why had Jay come to live here? Why had she felt it odd that he had made such a decision? Why had she sensed some purpose in him, his manner, since his arrival?

He had brought her up to her room, the night before, waving the others away. He helped her to the bed, then sat beside her.

She looked into his face, still bewildered by her fall, the sudden shock of it, and the realization of the danger around her, with the sounds of the chuckling laughter still in her mind.

He regarded her long, silently, and then he asked, "Want to tell me what happened, Dolly?"

"It was just as I said."

He hesitated. Then, "You saw no one? Are you absolutely certain that you saw no one?"

"No one, Jay."

"It's very important," he said insistently. "You know that. So are you sure?"

"I didn't see anyone."

He sighed. "The jewels were on the steps? It wasn't an illusion, some trick of the dark? A mistake that you made? They *were* there, Dolly?"

"I didn't imagine it, Jay. I didn't dream it."

He rose, went to the dresser. He brought her leather jewel case to her. "Have a look and see."

She touched the pearls, the necklaces, turned a few earrings over. "It isn't here."

He set the jewel case on the bedside table. He left her alone for a moment, then came back with the pill, a glass of water. "Take this and get some sleep, Dolly."

"Someone tried to kill me, Jay. To make it appear that I'd had an accident."

He didn't answer her.

She said softly, insistently, "It was deliberate, Jay. I'm sure of it."

He rose. "I think you should rest now. We'll talk about it tomorrow."

"Someone left the jewels there for me to see, and then took them away in the confusion after I fell," she told him. "It has to be that way."

"Tomorrow, Dolly. Close your eyes and go to sleep now."

She closed her eyes. She hadn't told him about the laughter that she'd heard that night, as well as the night that David died. She hadn't been able to bring herself to do that. Fatigue rolled over her in long dark waves. She didn't think she could sleep. But, in a little while, oddly, she did.

Now she was awake. She remembered that Jay had seemed to doubt her, had seemed to want to doubt her. She remembered that he had looked into the jewel case. Had he been expecting to find the emerald necklace there? Had he thought that would prove she had imagined the bait on the stairs?

She took the case from the table, opened it. On top of everything else, spread out carefully, she saw the emeralds.

She cried out, fear sharp and cold in her. Some time during the night a faceless shadow had come into her room, stood over her bed while she slept. Some time during the night that shadow had returned the jewels to where they belonged, and slipped away without awakening her.

Now there was a tap at the door. Evanne called, "Dolores, are you awake?"

"Yes," Dolores answered. "Come in if you want to."

Evanne was very pale. Dark circles ringed her blue eyes, and her lips seemed bloodless. The few streaks of red still left in her gray hair seemed to have faded to pale pink over night. She carried a tray with a pot of coffee, a stack of toast, and a tall glass of orange juice. She set it on the bedside table. "I thought you might like to stay in bed for a while," she said, not quite meeting Dolores' eyes.

"You shouldn't have troubled. I could have gone down and would have."

"How do you feel?" As she asked the question, Evanne filled a coffee cup, handed it to Dolores.

"Okay. Except that I'm groggy from the sleeping pill Jay gave me."

"Start with the coffee. It'll clear your head." Evanne's gaze was on the jewel case. "Shall I put it back where it belongs?"

"Yes," Dolores said. "Please." Then, "The emeralds are there."

Evanne put the case on the dresser, returned to sit in the chair close to the bed. "It's like old times, Dolly. Remember when you had the measles?"

Dolores nodded. She wondered why Evanne had no comment to make about the return of the jewelry. But aloud, she said, "Yes, I remember, Evanne. Breakfast in bed instead of at the buffet. And I think you're trying to spoil me."

"Spoiling never hurt a child, if it's done out of love."

"But how else could it be done?"

Evanne looked down at her hands. "Out of a sense of guilt, maybe."

"Guilt?"

"For not loving, Dolly," Evanne said.

Dolores sipped her coffee, answered, "I suppose," and waited.

She knew that Evanne had something to say, and would say it when she had found the right words. It was not a matter of spoiling at all. It was a matter of finding the right moment of privacy in which to speak.

At last Evanne said, "Dolly, I called the Maradines this morning."

"You didn't tell them . . ."

Evanne shook her head. "I'll leave that to George. It's his decision. Or yours, if you like. No. I called and spoke to Brooke because I . . . well, I think you should stay with him for a while."

"Stay at Maradine Mansion?"

Evanne nodded, her eyes averted.

"Because of last night?"

Evanne nodded again. Her wrinkled hands were folded together in a relaxed pose, but her knuckles showed white.

"But why?" Dolores asked.

"Dolly, listen to me. There are times when it is much the best not to ask questions, not to know even. Ignorance is, and can be bliss. There's been so much trouble in this house. So much wickedness ... I remember too well the way it was once, and I see those days come again. I'm afraid for you, Dolly. I want to see you safe."

"Trouble?" Dolores asked. "Wickedness? Hadn't you better tell me what you mean?"

She wondered if it was this that she had felt through her childhood, this what she had read in the exchanged looks of her parents, in their watching eyes.

Evanne's mouth thinned. She raised her eyes to Dolores. She whispered, "I told you. The less said the better. Too much was always said."

"And too much is mystery that ought not to be, and ought never to have been."

"You don't know, Dolly." Evanne rose. "Shall I pack a bag for you?" she asked, her voice rough with pleading. "Shall I get you ready to go to the Maradines?"

Was the trouble, the wickedness, connected with the town's animosity for the Kennellys? Was it the basis for it? Dolores knew there would be no use in asking Evanne. She would offer no answers.

"Dolly. Shall I?"

"No," Dolores said. "No. I shan't go. I belong here. I'm a Kennelly."

"You don't understand," Evanne answered.

"Then explain it to me."

But the older woman didn't answer. She went to the door, opened it. She looked into the corridor, then she turned back. She said in a hoarse whisper, "Trust no one, Dolly. Believe in no one. For your life's sake."

"But why?" Dolores cried.

"If I knew that, I'd tell you. I swear it. If I knew, and it would help, I'd tell you."

"They've nominated Cox," George was saying. "Now there's a real nothing for you. It took forty-four ballots to accomplish that pretty piece of work."

"I think Roosevelt is terribly handsome," Jennifer said.

William laughed. "You hear that, Jay? And it's for that sort of brilliant understanding that we've changed the constitution to give women the vote."

"Well, he *is* handsome," Jennifer retorted. "And that's more than you can say for most politicians."

"I like Harding. He's our kind of man," George said.

"A vote for him in Bellingham will probably go into the trash," Jay told him.

"A Kennelly vote for him will certainly go in the trash," Storr observed. "You should hear Stapleton on the subject. But I'm going to cast it anyway."

Jennings grumbled through his whiskers that he despised political talk at meals, and then asked, "How's Dolores?"

It was just like any other day, she thought. The family was gathered for lunch, making small talk over salad and cheese. She drew a deep breath. She couldn't stand in the hallway, lingering, eavesdropping, forever. Yet she felt an unpleasant reluctance to go into the room. For she knew that there would be a falseness in one of them, a falseness that would be hidden behind pretended concern. The same falseness that had made mourning appear where there must have been joy when David was buried.

She stepped into the room.

The conversation stopped, Jay saying, "Dolores, if . . ."

Every eye turned toward her.

She forced a smile. "Is there a place set for me? I didn't tell Evanne I'd be coming down."

Jay rose. "Do you think you ought to be?"

"Of course."

Judd held her chair for her. "Evanne wouldn't leave you out. Sit here, next to me." He grinned at her. "Are you recovered from your sleep-walking?"

She nodded. She had powdered the bruise on her forehead. It hardly showed. Her headache was nearly gone.

Judd went on, "George and I searched the stairs, and the corridors again, Dolores. We didn't find your jewelry. It just seems to be gone. Unless you made a mistake, thinking it was there in the first place."

She hesitated, then said, "It was in my jewel case this morning."

Jennifer gave her a spiteful look. "Naturally. Where else would it be?"

"Then you *were* mistaken," George said, frowning.

"I suppose I was," she agreed. But she knew that she had not been. The emerald necklace had been left on the steps to draw her there so someone could stand in the shadows and pitch the heavy frame down at her.

Jennings cleared his throat. "Well, Storr, I wouldn't let Stapleton change my mind either. I'm with you. Harding's our man all right."

It was the signal to ignore what had happened the night before.

Jay crumbled a roll. "Do you think he'll be good for the country, Jennings?"

"What's good for us is good for the country. You know that."

The conversation went on.

Dolores, listening, sensed tension in the others. A tension they seemed determined to hide. Plainly they didn't want to think of what happened the night before. They didn't want to face it. It was as if they had joined in a conspiracy of silence.

"It will be dark soon," Lolly said. "I'll walk you as far as the bridge."

"I'll come, too," Brooke offered.

"Oh, no you won't," Lolly contradicted him, protecting him as always, Dolores thought.

"Then suppose I drive Dolores," he suggested.

She suspected that he was uneasily trying now to make amends for what had gone on before.

She had come to him in search of information. He had listened, gray-faced, to her questions, and then, instead of answering them, he had parried them. He had said, "All this has nothing to do with you, Dolores. Don't even think about it. You're young. Fall in love. Marry. Forget the past."

She had said, "Uncle Brooke. It does matter. It's terribly important. That's why Evanne wanted me to stay with you."

"Yes, yes," he'd said testily. "I know that. But I have nothing to tell you. And Evanne is an hysterical old woman. Of course you can stay if you like. But . . ."

She would have argued further, but Lolly intervened. Brooke was tired, she said. Brooke needed to rest. He didn't know anything anyway, he insisted. Neither did she. In fact, there was nothing at all to know.

So Dolores retreated with as much grace as she could muster. She refused Brooke's offer to drive her home, and his offer to walk across the valley with her. Lolly insisted on accompanying her, and did.

They parted at the small wooden bridge that crossed the river dividing their two estates. Lolly turned to go back up the hill.

Dolores paused at the bridge railing, looked down into the clear water. Twilight sky was reflected there, a fleece of distant pink clouds. Her face was reflected there, too.

Her face. And beyond it, another. An open-mouthed face and staring hazel eyes.

"Oh, Judd," she screamed. "Oh, no. No! It's Judd."

242

Chapter 25

She clung to the rail, screaming into the swiftly gathering dark, and the sound rolled out across the valley to be lost in the distances.

But Lolly must have heard. She turned almost at the brow of the hill, and looked for an instant, and then seemed to fly back over the meadows.

Jennings came bursting out of the grove of trees, his plump whiskered face creased with alarm.

They surrounded her, held her, while she pointed below, incoherently trying to explain what she had seen there. "Judd," she wept. "It's Judd. Jennings, do something."

He looked down, then looked at Dolores. "Yes," he said soothingly. "Yes, I understand now. But you've imagined it, Dolly. Yes, yes. You have. You've seen a leaf, a log, something, but I don't see any ..."

And as he was denying it, with another glance toward the river, his voice faded. His high color went swiftly as all blood drained from his face. He let go of Dolly, and tore off his jacket.

By then, she was dimly aware of Jay and William. While she clung to Lolly and wept, the three men went into the river.

243

Eyes closed, face wet with tears, trembling, she could hear them thrashing, hear their shouts. She knew when they found Judd. She knew when they realized that they could not make him breathe again.

Lolly took her to the house, back into the awful shadows. Evanne put her to bed.

But she knew when they brought Judd home for the last time. She heard the heavy dragging footsteps, and the deep murmuring voices.

She listened, and wept, and asked herself what would happen next.

"We'll never know," George said quietly. "There's just no way to tell. We couldn't find a mark on him, and Jay did a careful examination. I know the coroner must have done the same. He probably considers that Judd committed suicide, but intends to be gentle about it by calling it an accident."

"No," Dolores exploded. "No. I'll never believe that. The coroner can say what he pleases. But Judd didn't kill himself."

"Then what?" William asked. "What will you believe? He was fully clothed. It's not likely he decided to have a swim that way, is it? So we can't assume that he had a cramp and went down. It just doesn't make sense. Except as a suicide."

She didn't answer him. She didn't know what to say.

She had heard no hoarse chuckling laughter when she stared into Judd's floating face for a terrible instant. She had had no sign at all that his death was the same as David's had been. The same as what her own was to have been. And might still be. Yet she knew that the shadowed evil had touched Judd, touched her younger brother, and taken him forever.

She asked herself how the others could not know. She wondered why they refused to see what she saw so clearly. There was murder in Emerald Station.

244

Jay asked quietly, "You heard nothing, Dolly? You didn't see anyone?"

She shook her head. "I didn't, but perhaps Lolly ... from where she was on the hill ..."

"No," he answered. "I've asked her. She didn't know anything was wrong until she heard you scream, and saw you staring down into the river."

Storr was staring out of the window. His blond hair was oddly disheveled. His shoulders sagged. His profile was clean and sharp, a replica of Gareth's profile. Then he turned his head, and looked at her. It was strange, she thought, how he seemed to change then. The face she saw was not a Kennelly face. For just a moment, she imagined a familiarity there, a familiarity with some stranger. She shrugged the thought aside. If, for an instant, he seemed a stranger, it was because a resemblance to his mother must have shown. The familiarity would be because, without remarking it, she had noted that resemblance before. Not that she had ever known his mother, who had died many years before she herself was born. But because she had seen that look on Storr's face at some other time. It was only then, momentarily, that she even remembered that she and Storr did not share mothers. She wondered if he ever thought of it. She had never heard him mention it, and she knew that he had loved Nealanna as his own.

Now he said simply, "I'm ... I'm going to miss him. We could have done a lot together. We planned to. I ..."

She winced, closed her eyes.

He said softly, "I'm ... I'm sorry, Dolly."

She didn't answer him. She didn't dare trust herself to speak.

But Jennifer said thinly, "I'm scared. Too much has happened around here. David first. And now Judd. I don't know about the rest of you, but me, I'm scared," and she burst into tears.

It was George who answered her. His face was white, the strawberry birthmark stood out on his throat. "We all are, Jen. You're not the only one."

245

The foreman's name was Perkins. She had paused to say good morning to him, to his crew, many times since they had begun work on the wall. Now the foundations in the area of the two granite pillars were finished. The quarried stone was piled nearby. Soon the labor of stacking and mortaring would begin.

Perkins was a young man with bold eyes, and red hair. "How is it going?" she asked.

"Fast enough, I guess. But too slow for my taste. I don't like being away from home, though I don't have a home to miss. But being here is not much good. Not for me, and not for my men."

"Here?" she asked. "Why is it different from any place else?"

"Bellingham. It's nowhere." His mouth turned in a sour grin. "And I don't like working where there's been two deaths in the house either."

She nodded, began to back away. She supposed that such workmen were superstitious, and she supposed he meant nothing by the remark, but she wished that he hadn't made it. And she was sorry that she had stopped to speak to Perkins. Now she didn't know why she had.

He went on, raising his voice slightly, "Blood tells. That's what they say in town."

"Blood tells," she repeated. A shiver touched her. She wanted to leave him, but she couldn't. She wanted to look away from his bold eyes, but they held hers.

"History," he said. "You can't get away from it. That's what bothers me. And the rest of the men. What they say in town. It may well be the family first. But what next? How about the rest of us that are here, just working here? Are we safe?"

The killer Kennellys . . . blood tells . . . each word was a painful beat of her pulse.

But she managed to say, "Mr. Perkins, I'm afraid that you listen to ridiculous gossip."

"Ridiculous? Well, maybe. But there's always a bit of truth somewhere in gossip. That's what my old mother used to say. Just a bit, maybe, but truth all the same. And

246

where there's smoke there's bound to be fire. You know it yourself."

She took another step away from him, then stopped again. "You're paid for your work. What you do on your own time is your business, but I'd strongly advise you against believing all that you hear."

"I don't have to," he grinned. "And I don't hear all that much. You'd think that I, and my men, too, have some awful disease at the least. We're avoided in town like the plague. I expect they're afraid it'll rub off on them. From the Kennellys to us to them."

She asked through dry lips, "What will rub off?"

"Why, you know. Whatever it is that afflicts the bunch of you, I guess. Whatever it is that blood tells."

She turned then, went slowly up the driveway past the stone lions, then past the fountain that threw a veil of glittering spray into the warm air.

Within it was quiet, cool. She strained for the sound of hoarse chuckling laughter, but heard nothing.

She went into the living room, sank wearily into a chair near the gray stone fireplace.

"Blood will tell," she whispered. But what would it tell, she wondered.

Was it possible that if she knew what that meant then she would know what evil concealed itself behind the granite walls of Emerald Station? If she knew why the Stapletons said the words Killer Kennellys, would she then know the threat that hung over her?

Was the answer to her present terror in Bellingham, and not here? Did the truth lie there beyond the ring of small hills, beyond the valley?

She had asked Brooke and he wouldn't talk about the past. She had asked Evanne and the older woman had shuddered and turned away.

Jennings and Storr both worked with Tom Stapleton on rebuilding the library. Perhaps through him, they would know. Perhaps she could get them to tell her.

But when she found Jennings on the balcony outside his room, and raised the question, he simply stared at her. "What do you mean, Dolores? What are you talking about?"

It was impossible to read his face, his squinting eyes. She said, "But you must know. Why are we so hated in Bellingham? What have we done? The library was burned to the ground deliberately two years ago. And now you're paying out good money to rebuild it. All right. That's your affair, I suppose. And you can do as you like. But why was the library burned in the first place? And much less important, but the same idea, why were the tires on my car slashed? And why did Tim Stapleton throw a tomato at me, and shout those awful things. What have the Stapletons got against us?"

"My dear girl," he said slowly, his heavy shoulders hunching as he sank more deeply into his chair. "You throw a whole ton of mad questions at me and stand there apparently expecting me to be able to answer them. But there's absolutely no sense in it."

"Jennings, you were here. You must know the truth."

"I know nothing. There's nothing to know." He got to his feet suddenly. "I'll go into town now. Do you want to come with me?"

She shook her head. "I have nothing to do there today."

"Nor have I, for that matter. But I like to get away from here once in a while."

"Then you feel it," she said.

"Feel it? Feel what? Dolores, You sometimes don't express yourself clearly."

"You feel the pressure . . . the . . ."

He cut in quickly, "I feel nothing of the sort. And you are far too imaginative for your own good. I always said so, and I say it now. You . . ."

"Perhaps I'm not imaginative enough," she retorted, and went in search of Storr.

He was leaning over his drafting table, but the pencil was still in his fingers, and he was plainly not at work. When he spoke, though, he carried on the pretense. He said, "I'm busy, Dolores. What did you want? Could it wait?"

It was one more sign of how he had changed in these past months, she suddenly realized. Storr had always had time for her before. He had not been too busy to teach her to ride, to swim. He had not been too busy to read to her. Though there was sixteen years between them, and during much of her growing up they had both been away at school, he had always been a devoted and loving oldest brother.

She said, "Storr, what's the matter?"

He simply stared at her, his green eyes blank.

"With you," she said. "I know something is. I can feel it. And the same is true of the rest of us, Storr. What is it? Do you know?"

He drew a deep obvious breath. His throat worked and his lips writhed, but when he spoke he had controlled his stammer. He said, "Nothing's wrong that won't pass. For everything does. Nothing that you believe in, or think you believe in, is real. And nothing is permanent."

"But you build," she objected. "You build things to be permanent. That's the whole point of it. To make them last forever."

"I build on sand," he answered. He looked at her directly then for the first time since she had come in. "But never mind that. What did you want?"

She said, "Storr, I was talking to Perkins a few minutes ago. He said ... he told me ... in Bellingham, they say the Kennellys ..."

Storr got to his feet, giving her his full attention at last. "What has Perkins got to do with what they say in Bellingham?"

"Well, he told me that he ..."

Storr cut in, "I don't want to hear what they say in Bellingham. This is Kennelly land here. This is Emerald Station. I won't have that filth whispered here. Not by Perkins, and not by you."

She cried, "But what filth? What is it? Why do they say blood tells?"

A rare fine rage flickered across his face. It changed

249

him. It seemed to make him another man, a familiar man, yet one that she couldn't quite identify.

He didn't answer her.

She remembered her terror the night she had run from him, run fleeing away from the trees to the road. She remembered Storr shouting after her, pausing to watch as the car came over the rise, and Tim Stapleton yelled, and threw the tomato at her, and the warm red juice staining her dress and shoulder the color of blood.

She drew back from Storr now. But he didn't seem to notice. He stalked past her and left the room.

She didn't know it then, but later she discovered that when he left her, he went directly to Perkins. He sent the foreman and his crew away. He paid them off, and told them to leave.

A peculiar silence hung over the house and lawns with the men gone. There was no more scrape of shovels, no more blasting in the quarry, no more sudden shouts, and no more laughter.

A day passed, then another. It began to seem as if the bad times were gone. David's name was not mentioned, nor was Judd's.

William drank steadily, his eyes too bright at nine in the morning, dull and hardly seeing by six in the evening.

Jennifer played the femme fatale for Jay, and pursued him openly, while he was openly watchful.

Jennings continued his visits to town, and Storr stayed at his drawing board.

It should have been soothing for Dolores, but instead of being comforted, she found that the very normalcy made her even more uneasy. She was obsessed with the knowledge that murder had been done, murder had been done twice, and was unrevealed, unavenged, unexplained. She was certain it would be done again. Her safety, the safety of the others, depended on learning the truth. But if truth was in Emerald Station she could not find it.

Her thoughts returned again and again to what Storr had done. The wall, barely begun, was abandoned. For he had sent Perkins and his men away. And he'd sent them away because Perkins had repeated to her what he had heard in town, what had been said in Bellingham for years. "Blood tells." Those had been Perkins' words. Would she understand why they were called killer Kennellys if she understood what was meant by that cruel 'blood tells?'

Was there something in the old gossip that would explain what had happened at Emerald Station? She was obsessed with that thought, too.

She went to the family room, stayed there for hours, studying the portraits of her mother and father, of her grandfather, and great uncle, of Faran and Avis. It seemed to her that those faces should be able to speak, even if not in words. But she learned nothing there.

Finally, she drove to town, after another of those unhappy discussions with Henry over whether she should go alone. She did, and stopped at Row's garage.

She had hoped to see the older man, Dale, but Dylan came out of the shed, smiled at her. "Trouble with your automobile?" he asked.

"Not that. I wanted to ask your father something. But I see he's not here."

"No. He's at home today. Not feeling well."

"I'm sorry," she said automatically. Then, "Perhaps you ... you could tell me, Dylan. Why do they hate us so? Here, I mean, in town. What have the Kennellys ever done ..."

His face changed. He gave her a long sad look. "It has nothing to do with you, miss. Go back to Emerald Station, and forget this town, and the Stapletons. Or better yet, just go far away, and forget it, and them, and Emerald Station, too."

"But I can't do that," she exclaimed. "I'm a Kennelly just like all the others."

"I can't help you," he said.

"You mean that you won't, Dylan. But I don't see why."

"My father feels the way he does for his own reasons," Dylan said. "But those reasons don't concern you. And

251

even if they did, I couldn't tell you them because I don't know them myself. All I know is, when he starts on the Kennellys, my mother won't listen, nor my grandmother, if she's there. It's the only thing they disagree on that I know of, but disagree on that, they do. As for the Stapletons..." He smiled faintly. "You must have gathered I'm no friend of Tim's."

"Yes," she agreed. "I saw that. I remember. But, Dylan . . ."

"Maybe they want that land back," he said. "It belonged to them once Tom Stapleton told my father a long while back. They could use half the valley for the little houses they're putting up. So maybe . . ."

"No," she said. "This is something that goes a long way back. What they say . . ."

He shook his head.

"Then what am I to do?" she asked helplessly.

"I've given you the only advice I could," he told her. "And I think you should heed it. Whatever there is between your family, and the town, or the Stapletons, has nothing to do with me. Or with you."

"They say blood tells," she murmured. "They call us the killer Kennellys."

"I don't listen, and never have." He paused. Then added, "You ought to go home."

A shiver touched her. She knew that he was right. She didn't belong in Bellingham surely. There was danger in the town, though she couldn't see it, just as there was danger in Emerald Station, which she couldn't see either.

She thanked him through dry lips, started the car.

Another one drove in. Tom Stapleton was at the wheel. She saw his profile, and then, quite suddenly, she thought of Storr.

It was Stapleton that she had seen in Storr's face sometimes. But that, she thought, was impossible. It couldn't be. Storr was in no way related to Tom Stapleton. The older man stared at her, recognition in his face.

She drove quickly away.

Chapter 26

But she didn't go home. She stopped, instead, at Maradine Mansion.

Lolly and Brooke greeted her happily. But their smiles faded when she asked, "Uncle Brooke, who was Storr's mother?"

There was a brief silence.

Brooke's thin face became pale, and Lolly's was almost angry as she said, "Why, Dolores, what an odd thing for you to ask of your uncle."

"Why is it so odd?" Dolores demanded. "We all know that he wasn't my mother's son. And it's never mattered."

"Then why should it suddenly matter now?" Lolly asked.

"Because . . ." Dolores turned to Brooke. "Please, if you know, tell me."

But it was Lolly who said, "Dolores, Storr is thirty-six years old. His mother died at his birth. To all intents and purposes Nealanna was his real mother. Why, from the time he was six, she . . ."

Brooke sighed, said, "Never mind, Lolly. Dolores understands about that. I'm curious to know, though, what's made you begin to think about this just now."

Dolores said, "I've just come from town. I happened to see Tom Stapleton. I had the feeling . . ." She let the words trail away.

Brooke had leaned back, closed his blue eyes. He said wearily, "So much time has passed. What difference can it make now?"

She didn't know herself. She knew only that she had seen a strange resemblance to Stapleton in Storr, that Storr had spent a lot of time working with Stapleton in rebuilding the library. She said, "Is Tom Stapleton related to Storr in any way? Is that why he hates the Kennellys so?"

Brooke said, "Storr's mother was Tom Stapleton's sister. She . . ."

"Extraordinary," Lolly cried, with plainly forced amazement in her voice. "I never even knew that. I was just a girl then, barely sixteen." She immediately launched herself into a tale Dolores had heard many times before. She told how she and Nealanna had come to America together. Nealanna as Gareth's young and beautiful bride. She as nursemaid to Jay and Doe Gordon. "Oh, those were such fine days," she ended, smiling happily. "Oh, yes, they were lovely days." She grinned at Brooke. "But not nearly as lovely as now."

Dolores had waited patiently through the whole story, her eyes on the portrait of the young and lovely blonde girl that hung over the mantel. She was, Dolores knew, Deborah Maradine, Brooke's sister who had died as a girl. Deborah had remained young forever, and Brooke was middle-aged. As soon as Lolly finished her story, Dolores asked, "But what happened to Storr's mother?"

"She went away," Brooke said after a moment.

"You mean that she died," Lolly said quickly.

Dolores looked from one to the other. "What was it?" she demanded.

Brooke said, "I think there'll be no profit in discussing this, Dolores."

254

"I agree," Lolly cried, "And besides, we must have some tea. Brooke, you look tired. I insist now, no more discussion. No more, I say." She clapped her hands at Dolores, suddenly the governess again. "I insist, truly. Tea, and quiet, is the program now."

It was impossible to continue, impossible to ask whether Storr's mother had died, as Dolores had always believed, and knew that Storr, too, believed, or whether she had simply abandoned Gareth and her infant son. It was impossible to ask if Tom Stapleton knew that Storr was his nephew, or if Storr knew that Tom was his uncle. It was impossible to ask why Tom Stapleton hated the Kennellys.

But while Lolly was pouring tea, Dolores said, "I heard today in town that Stapleton might have his eye on our part of the valley."

"He always has," Brooke said tiredly.

"But particularly so now. Because he could put new houses there."

Brooke shrugged. "It wouldn't surprise me. He's not a man willing to give up. But I shouldn't worry about it."

"That might be why Tim slashed my tires though, why he yelled at me that night. It might also explain that there seems to be more gossip in town about us than ever."

Brooke said, "I wish I knew what this is all about, Dolores."

She told him, "I don't even know myself, Uncle Brooke."

She didn't add what she was thinking. That she only knew it was important.

He gave her a relieved look. "Then forget about it. The less said the better. To anyone, Dolores. To anyone at all."

But it was not a question of forgetting. She could not, even if she had tried. And she would not try, she told herself.

She went home soon after.

As she drove under the big iron sign, past the broken beginnings of the wall, she shivered. It seemed that a cold wind reached down from the early summer trees to touch her.

Emerald Station. A place where creeping evil lurked in the shadows. A place where the past refused to die.

But she was a Kennelly. She belonged here. She had a debt to pay, a debt for her two brothers. Neither David nor Judd could rest in their graves until the truth was known.

But where was the truth to be found?

"I think," Jennifer said, smiling triumphantly, "that Jay will ask me to marry him soon. What do you say to that?"

Dolores fought to keep a pleasant expression on her face. She said, "When it happens I'll wish you all the joy in the world."

"Oh, come, don't pretend," Jennifer laughed. "I can just see it now."

Dolores shrugged. "Jennifer, think what you want to. I'm not jealous of you."

But it wasn't quite true. Her heart was sinking within her. She couldn't think of Jennifer and Jay married. The pain was too intense, too deep. She must conceal it, yet it was there, not to be denied. Jennifer in Jay's arms . . . Jennifer smiling up at him.

Dolores deliberately forced the picture from her mind. Whatever happened, she would have to bear it. Whether she could or not, she would have to.

But she wondered what she would do. Now, finally, facing the depth of her feeling for Jay, she was suddenly more frightened than ever. Was she to live all her life with the memory of a lost love? Was she to go on, alone and as heartsick as she felt at this moment?

Jennifer was saying, "This is one time, at least, when you won't get your way," with her eyes narrowed on Dolores' face.

"All right, Jennifer." Dolores turned away. "For your sake I'm glad."

"That's awfully nice of you, kid. But I don't care if you're glad or sorry. Though I know how you really feel.

But you were foolish to dream of him, Dolores. He's much too old for you in the first place."

"There are just four years between you and me," Dolores said, smiling. "So do you think Jay's age really matters?"

"Four years are a lot. But that's not all, of course. You're too ... well, I think you're just too much a Kennelly for him to take. Or for anyone else to take either."

"No more than you are, in fact," Dolores retorted.

"But you have that dark streak," Jennifer told her. "William and I take more after the Maradines ... our mother's side."

"And I take after my mother. She was a Yarrow."

Jennifer answered, but Dolores didn't hear the words. She was thinking of Storr again. Storr who was Tom Stapleton's nephew. Who was part Kennelly, just as she, and Jennifer were partly Kennelly.

Jennifer said, recalling Dolores' attention, "Well, in any event, I'll expect you to be my bridesmaid. Anything else wouldn't look right."

"Of course. We'll have a beautiful ceremony. Right here, in Emerald Station."

Jay, in the doorway, asked, "And who's getting married?"

Jennifer said very quickly, with a flush on her cheeks, "Why, we were just talking in general, Jay. The way girls do."

He looked at Dolores, amusement glowing in his gray eyes. "You'll need a beau or two before you think of it, you know."

She nodded, warm with the glow of relief at Jennifer's embarrassment. Everything Jennifer said had been fantasy. There was no need for pain. "At the right time, Jay, I'll have my beaux," she said.

"If she left Emerald Station once in a while," Jennifer said, "she might find herself a boyfriend. There's no one here, and no one in town that would do."

"Exactly what I was thinking," Jay agreed. He grinned at Dolores. "I've had a letter from Doe. She'd like you to visit her for a bit. She promises extravagant and interesting entertainment."

Dolores shook her head.

She knew why Jennifer would like her to go away for a while. It would leave her the field to make her fantasies real. She would be able to concentrate on Jay. She would be able to ensure the proposal about which she had just been speaking, but about which Jay himself had plainly not yet even been thinking. But why did Jay want Dolores to go away to see Doe? It wasn't the first time he had mentioned it.

"The trouble," Jennifer said, "is that Dolores has it, and it distorts and disturbs her. She won't face up to it, of course. So it's destroying her."

"What are you talking about?" Jay asked.

"The dark streak that some of the Kennellys have." Jennifer sighed exaggeratedly. "I don't really know where it comes from. But Gareth had it, and David, too."

"What nonsense," Jay retorted.

"It's true," she insisted. "And look at Dolores. You can see it in her."

Jay shrugged. "Doe would love to have you there with her for a while, Dolores. And I know it would do you good."

"Do my dark streak good?" she demanded.

"That's nonsense," he said. "I just said so." He gave Jennifer a sharp gray look. "And I shouldn't have expected you to say such a thing."

She pouted at him. "But I didn't mean any harm. I was just telling Dolores that she doesn't look herself, and hasn't for sometime. I was just telling her that she ought to get away."

Jay didn't reply.

Dolores felt his glance go with her when she excused herself and left him alone with Jennifer.

She managed to get to her room before the tears came. She fought them, but at last gave way. And finally, with the storm over, cried out, she determined that she would put Jay out of her mind. She would forget him.

Soon now he would leave Emerald Station, and more likely than not, he would take Jennifer with him.

Why had he come here in the first place? Was it to be near Jennifer? Had he thought that he could win her more easily that way? It hardly seemed reasonable. He would have courted her easily from town, from the house that he had still not remodelled into the laboratory as planned.

Why then had he moved to Emerald Station?

He came just days after David died. Was he, like herself, in search of the explanation for David's death, and Judd's, and the attack on her?

She shuddered. The evil was still loose, reaching out to doom another one of them.

That night at dinner George said, "Storr, I've been meaning to ask you for days ... why did you fire Perkins?"

"I had my reasons." Storr's green eyes seemed shuttered, watchful.

"But we can't leave the wall as it is," Jennings said. "It's an eyesore. Soon there'll be sightseers coming out from town to gawk at it. Tom was just saying the other day, and I know he meant it, though he was pretending to be making a joke, that he could let us have some men to finish it."

"He said the same to me," Storr said stiffly. "But I won't have his men out here."

"Well, we can't leave it as it is. There's months of work to be done before winter. If we're going to have a wall around the property, then we must go on with it soon. If not, then we'll need men to pull up the foundations, and fill the ditches in ..."

"Jennings, you can leave that to me," Storr said. "I'll handle it soon."

"But when?" George asked. "If what Jennings says is so, then ..."

"I wish you'd stop talking about it," Jennifer said petulantly. "I don't like the thought of that wall."

"We need something," Storr told her. "We've no way to protect ourselves otherwise."

"It closes the world out," she protested. "But it closes us in, too. I don't like the feeling of being closed in."

He smiled at her. "We're Kennellys," he said. "We're naturally closed in."

She retorted, "What nonsense. I don't believe that."

Storr shrugged. "What a pity. But it doesn't matter. Believe what you like."

William emptied his glass and said, blurring the words, "And that goes for everyone of us. For Storr, and George and Dolores, as well as for you and me, Jennifer."

It was late the next afternoon. She had just come in from a ride in the meadows.

Evanne met her at the door, looking worried. "Dolores, have you seen Jennifer?"

"Why, no, I've just gotten back."

"You didn't pass her while you were out? She wasn't at the river, or in the courtyard?"

"No, she wasn't. But what's the matter?"

Evanne twisted her hands together. "We spoke at lunch time. She didn't say she was going anywhere. Jay went into town with Jennings and Storr, I think. When they came back, Jay asked for Jennifer. I've looked all over. Henry has, too. He even went down to the quarry. We can't find her."

"Maybe she's at the Maradines. I'll . . ."

"I phoned them. She hasn't been there either."

Suddenly Dolores heart began to beat very quickly. Something had happened. She knew it in her blood and bones. And she knew that Evanne was thinking exactly the same thing.

"We'd better speak to George," she said at last. "I'll go up and get out of these boots first, and then . . ."

"I'll tell him meantime," Evanne answered.

Dolores ran up the steps, changed to a skirt and blouse. She heard voices below as she stepped out into the hall. She started down, but her attention was caught by a slender beam of light that lay along the top of the steps. She turned to seek out its source, and saw that the door at the top of the next landing was partially open. The door that led to the nursery floor, so long unused, and to the storage attic that was beyond it.

She went up the steps quickly, lightly, making no sound on the heavy carpet. She thrust the door fully open. The ceiling light was burning. Puzzled, she went on.

The first thing she saw in the hallway was the portrait of her Aunt Alicia. It stood against the wall, looking almost alive.

Then she saw Jennifer, who lay on the floor just below. Her eyes were wide, startled, as if death had caught her by surprise.

Chapter 27

"She's dead," Jay said quietly. He looked up, his eyes impersonal, professional. They touched Dolores, moved on to Storr, William, Jennings, then to George.

Dolores saw that the glance exchanged between him and George was long, significant. Jay was saying something with his eyes. George seemed to understand, for his face grayed, and he limped to the wall, leaned there for support.

William said, "But what was she doing up here? This is crazy, you know. Why would she come to this place? In front of Alicia's portrait, and . . ." He stopped himself suddenly. Then he cried, "And what did she die of?"

"I can't tell," Jay answered. He rose, stepped back from Jennifer's plump body.

Dolores, her small hand fisted at her mouth, whispered, "Don't you remember that she said she was afraid.of the wall? Of being closed in? Don't you remember that she said she was scared?"

Evanne took Dolores into her arms. "Hush, child. It won't do any good. Come away."

George's eyes were wide, dark with shadows, as if he

were struggling through a nightmare. "We're cursed," he mumbled.

As Evanne led Dolores away, Storr was saying, "We'll have to report it, though I wish we didn't. I'll go down to the phone right now."

Seven days had passed since Jennifer's death.

Dazed and disbelieving, Dolores had attended the coroner's inquest. He had found that Jennifer had died of heart failure. Why her heart should have stopped was unknown. Why she had gone to the attic and been before Alicia's portrait was unknown.

The small room had been terribly crowded, breathlessly hot, and as silent as a tomb, while he rendered his decision.

Afterwards, as Dolores, leaning on Evanne, followed Storr and William and Jennings from the office, there had been a wave of whispers.

She had felt them trailing after her, had thought that surely she must drown in them.

She could easily imagine the words. Blood tells. Blood tells. One more death at Emerald Station where the killer Kennellys live.

Jay had helped her into the car, patted her hand, said quietly, "Take it easy. We'll be away from this and back home in a little while."

She had trembled at the thought. Home. Home was where murder was done. Where evil walked in the shadows.

David. Judd. Now Jennifer.

Dolores didn't believe that Jennifer had died accidentally of heart failure at the age of twenty-four. She knew that Jennifer must have been murdered in some way which the coroner had not detected.

George. Storr. Jennings. William. And she herself. These were the last of the Kennellys. Must they all die to assuage some terrible hatred?

When the town was behind them, Jay said, "I want you

to go and stay with Doe for a week or two, Dolly. You don't look well. You need a change."

"Yes," Evanne agreed. "That's just what she should do, Jay. I was thinking of it myself. I . . ."

But Dolores whispered, "I can't leave them. I mustn't."

"You can't do anything here," Jay answered.

"That's right," Evanne said. "Nothing, Dolly. So you'd better just go."

"No, no," Dolores answered. "I mustn't leave, Jay."

"Why, Dolores? I can give you half a dozen good reasons for going away for a little while. You can't give me any for staying."

"Because I must."

Evanne made a sound that was a cross between a groan and a whimper.

Dolores went on, "I don't believe Jennifer died of heart failure. How could she have? She was young, healthy. It's just not possible."

"You can't know that, Dolly."

But she saw that his hands had tightened on the steering wheel. She saw how grim his mouth was.

"I know it hurts you to think about it, Jay. I know what you must be feeling."

He was silent for a moment, then he answered, "I was fond of Jennifer, Dolly. Just as I've been fond of all of you. But . . ."

"Jennifer was certain that you and she would be married soon," Dolores told him. "That day, do you remember? When you came in while we were talking about a wedding. It was her wedding to you we were discussing."

His mouth grew even more grim. "I had a suspicion that it might be. But Jennifer was somewhat premature, and incorrect, in her expectations."

"As anyone with a bit of sense would have guessed," Evanne put in tartly.

Jay made no comment on that. He went on, "I suppose I was unfair to her, and I'm sorry for it now, believe me. But I did have good reason for not disabusing her of her idea, Dolly."

Before Dolores could answer him, Evanne said impatiently, "It was no fault of yours, Jay. Jennifer had her ideas because she wanted to have them. Her reason was to hurt Dolly. She wanted Dolly to hate you, Jay. She wanted anything Dolly wanted, and always did. I remember when they were small, the tricks she pulled. I knew, we all did. From the time Faran and Avis died, it was that way. It's no good speaking ill of the dead, and I know it, but Dolly might as well understand it."

Dolores knew that Evanne was right. Jennifer *had* always plotted and planned and fought to be the center of attention. She had always used any means at her disposal to get what she wanted. And she had always felt, somehow, not quite at home, not quite a part of Emerald Station. But she was dead now. And, though no one had mentioned the word, the thought, Dolores was certain that she had been murdered. She had been murdered like David, like Judd. And this time, too, as when Dolores had seen Judd's face through the rippling current, there had been no chuckling laughter to warn her. There had been only Jennifer's still body lying beneath the still portrait of Alicia Kennelly.

Now Dolores asked, without looking at Jay, keeping her voice level, "Why did you come to live with us?"

"I thought I'd explained that a long while ago. The house . . ."

"That wasn't the real reason, Jay."

He hesitated.

She said, "David, Judd, and now Jennifer are dead. We are . . . we Kennellys live with danger."

Evanne said, "Dolly, you mustn't let . . ."

Jay interrupted, "I told you I think you ought to go away."

"Why?" she demanded.

"Dolly, I . . ."

"But you've told me nothing," she cried. "You, all the rest, tell me nothing."

"But perhaps there's nothing to tell," he answered quietly.

265

"Nothing happens without reason," she said. "Nothing, Jay. I'll find the reason. I'll learn the truth. I'll know why David and Judd and Jennifer died."

Beside her, Evanne buried her face in her hands and wept.

Since then, Dolores had begun to wonder. She remembered her fervent words, and Evanne's tears. She remembered the determination she had felt. In the quiet of the passing days, though, she had begun to despair that she would ever learn the truth. She had come to imagine that she would live with terror until, finally, on some dark night, the hand of evil would reach out and smash her as it had smashed the others.

Now she was curled in her favorite rocking chair in the kitchen. She watched Evanne preparing salads for dinner.

She said, "It's so different. I can hardly believe that there was ever a time when we were happy."

"There'll be happy times again," Evanne told her. "This house has seen its troubles, but they finally go."

"When do they go?" Dolores asked, sighing.

Evanne's blue eyes flashed up, then down to her work. She said, "Why, one of these days, you'll fall in love, and that fine man will take you away from here."

"I don't think I'll ever leave Emerald Station," Dolores answered.

"What nonsense. When you love a man you go with him."

Dolores thought of Jay. She had already found the fine man that she wanted. But, clearly, her hopes were never to be realized.

Aloud she said, "I'm a Kennelly, Evanne."

"You can make more of that than need be," Evanne said sharply. "You'd do well to forget you're a Kennelly, and remember that you're a woman. You must have what all women want. A husband, children . . ."

Dolores wondered. She thought of the new graves in the cemetery near town. Would there be another one beside them soon? Would she herself lie forever next to David and Judd and Jennifer?

Evanne said, "The family room. The portraits. All those papers accumulating. Pride. Too much pride. Yes, Dolly. It goes back a long long way. Pride. It can be good, of course. But it can be bad, too. Pride can lift up, but it can cast down, too."

"Yes," Dolores agreed.

"Pride shamed can cause sin," Evanne said quietly, her hands suddenly still.

"And that's a big subject," Storr said, appearing in the doorway, green eyes aglow and blond hair dissheveled. "Sin. What an odd discussion to have while you're slicing tomatoes, Evanne."

Dolores dreamed. The room was black and silent. The heavy walls rippled in the darkness. The white ceiling seemed to have disappeared, and the whole floor above, too, so that above, there was a wide empty tunnel into the sky.

There should have been air, but there was none. It was hard to breathe. The dark pressed down and down.

She struggled, fought, screaming soundlessly.

And it was suddenly not a dream.

She was wide awake. She heard the whisper of hoarse chuckling laughter, but there was only an empty blackness around her. Something held her firmly, her body, her head. She could not see. She could not breathe. She could not ... Pinwheels began to explode behind her closed eyelids. Pain pricked in her bursting lungs. The whispering chuckle became a sob.

She fought free, flinging herself from the bed, the pillow from her face.

She screamed, then screamed again.

The door to her room was open. The draperies billowed out before the window.

Even in that moment of fear, she thought of Jennifer. Jennifer lying on the floor before the portrait of Alicia, lying there with her eyes open wide, her face unmarked. And she knew how Jennifer had died.

Jay burst into the room, swept her into his arms. She

267

felt his lean strength envelope her. She clung to him, gasping, "There was someone here. Here in the room with me. A pillow on my face . . ."

"Wait." He put her away from him, and ran for the window. He stepped outside, his silhouette tall and dark against the faint gleam of the sky.

In a moment he returned. "There's no one out there now, Dolly."

"But the door was open. And the window. And . . ."

"Yes. You don't know who . . ."

She sank down on the edge of the bed. "No." She touched the small satin pillow with her foot. "This was over my face."

She leaned to turn on the lamp, her arm brushing momentarily against his. When she sat back, she looked at him. His face was blank, oddly blank.

She was suddenly even more frightened than she had been before. She was alone with him. She couldn't tell what he was thinking.

Suppose it had been he who bent over her? Suppose it had been his mad laughter that she had heard through the awful pounding in her ears?

"Go on," he said.

"I heard . . . a kind of chuckling. I was being suffocated. I remember thinking that probably Jennifer . . ."

"And you couldn't tell who it was, Dolly? Are you absolutely sure that you don't have any idea . . ."

Was the question too quick, too anxious? She asked herself. Was he frightened that she had recognized him? Was the man she loved the man who had just tried to kill her?

He must have read something of her thoughts in her expression, something of the horror she felt. He didn't touch her, but he said gently, "Dolly, it's me. It's Jay. You mustn't be afraid of me. I want to help you. I have to. Don't turn away from me now. Trust me as you always have. I'd never hurt you. You must know at least that much, Dolly."

She was suddenly ashamed of herself, all fear of him,

all suspicions gone. What horrible spell had Emerald Station cast on her that she should doubt him?

She breathed, "Yes, Jay. Yes. I know that much. I know I can trust you." She took a deep breath. "Jay, I told you that I heard laughing . . . it turned to a sob. And that was when I was freed. That was when whoever it was ran out."

"Laughter," he repeated.

"I've heard the same sound before, Jay. I never . . . I didn't speak of it. But the night that David died, and that night I saw the emeralds on the stairs; I heard it those times, too."

"Why didn't you tell me before?" he asked grimly.

"I don't know, Jay. I just . . ."

"And tonight you heard it again. But just as you were freed there was a sob?"

She nodded.

He didn't say anything. He smoothed the disarrayed sheets, picked up the small satin pillow and dropped it on the chair. Finally he told her, "Better go back to bed now, Dolly."

"You weren't asleep when I cried out, were you?" she asked.

"No. I had been reading. I was just coming up."

She nodded acceptingly. She told herself that she must believe him.

But when he had left her, and she had turned off the lamp, and gone back to bed, she wondered. She wondered that he would have been downstairs reading so late. She wondered if his had been the hands that held her, his the strength that had nearly overpowered her. She wondered if his laughter had changed to sobs before he fled from the window, climbed down the fire ladder to the balcony below, then come up the steps and into her room.

Storr said, eyeing her over his coffee cup, "Jay tells me you had some trouble during the night."

"I'm all right," she told him quickly. "It was nothing."

"I couldn't quite figure out what Jay was saying. Was it a dream? Or did you hear something that frightened you?"

"I don't want to think about it," she told him, but she was looking at George. He stood near the buffet, his shoulders slumped, his head averted. She said, "George? Are you all right?"

He turned his face toward her, and she caught her breath. There were rings, dark and deep, around his eyes, and his cheeks seemed to have hollowed in the past few days. He nodded at her, and limped to the table.

"Yes, Dolores. Don't worry," he said.

Storr cut in. "We ought to know what happened, if something did, Dolores. We can't just ignore . . ."

"There's nothing to know." She gulped her coffee, avoiding his direct and probing green stare.

Were his the hands that had held her?

Had her oldest brother leaned over her, hating her, determined to destroy her?

"I see," he said thoughtfully. "Well, maybe Jay exaggerated."

"Maybe he did," she agreed. She rose. "Excuse me, both of you. I have errands in town."

"Errands?" George asked sharply.

"Yes."

"But Henry could . . ."

"Henry wouldn't know what to get," she said casually.

George looked as if he had more to say, but she didn't give him a chance to. She hurried out, wondering if the anguish she saw in his face was the anguish of guilt. Could George have pressed the pillow to her face? Could he have made the climb on the ladder?

She took the roadster, smiling at Henry's reproachful look, and drove through the sun-filled valley to Bellingham.

If she knew why they were called killer Kennellys, if she knew why blood tells, she would know something of the truth. And that truth would lead her to the shadowy evil which threatened. That was what she had decided, and that was why she drove to the library site to see Tom Stapleton.

But he wasn't there. She got directions from a workman, and at last found his house.

It was a pretentious town dwelling, gray stone that was vaguely familiar to her, with turrets and balconies surrounding it. A brass gargoyle leered at her from the door knocker.

She touched it once, and the door opened.

Tom Stapleton stood there, staring at her. He was heavy-set. His face was brown, sun-wrinkled. His shaggy hair was half blond, half gray.

She said quickly, "I'm Dolores Kennelly, Mr. Stapleton."

"I know you," he said dryly. "I know all of the Kennellys."

"May I talk to you for a little while?" she asked.

"Why not? I'm not like some. I wouldn't ride a man down in the road. I wouldn't put myself above him. Talk if you want to then."

"I know that we've not been exactly friends. My family, yours . . ."

"No. Not exactly friends. That's right. But if it's about my Tim, then forget it. Boys will be boys. And he's high-spirited, and if you've any complaints, then . . ."

"No. It's not about that," she said. She drew a deep breath, plunged in. "Mr. Stapleton, why do you hate us?"

"For the wrong done me and my family," he said softly. "And I'll hate you all until the last Kennelly is gone from the valley and from the earth."

"The wrongs done you and your family?" she repeated. "But what . . ."

"My father's land stolen from him, and that was only the beginning. Then my sister Jane debauched and thrown aside, and gone. Gone, God knows where. For I was never able to find her. And I believe she never left Emerald Station. There's killing in the blood of the Kennellys, and blood tells." His eyes were blazing, his lips snarling with teeth exposed.

271

"You know then that Storr is your nephew. And do you hate him, too?"

"I do not."

"But he's a Kennelly," she said.

"He is not." Tom's snarl grew into a wide and ugly smile. "Not really a Kennelly, that is. Your grandfather never married my poor sister. Storr is a bastard. Though he didn't always know it. Even if he should have when David was named heir."

"You told him, didn't you?" she said, suddenly shivering with cold in spite of the warm sunlight.

"I did. We were together one day, going over the plans. I saw myself in him. I knew that he had to know. So I told him the truth. All of the truth."

She said, "You did a terrible thing when you told him."

Laughter turning into a sob . . .

Love turning into hate . . .

Tom Stapleton grinned at her. "I thought that he ought to know. After all, the Kennellys aren't the only ones in the world with pride."

Chapter 28

Unwillingly, she turned the roadster toward Emerald Station.

Blood tells . . .

The killer Kennellys . . .

Tom Stapleton had said those words so often over the years that he believed them.

She wondered if he realized just what he had done.

Because she was certain now. She had believed that if she knew the truth she would understand. She had the answer she had sought. But she didn't know what to do with it.

Storr would be there. She would have to look upon his face, remembering how she had loved him, yet remembering, too, what had happened.

David . . . Judd . . . Jennifer . . .

She must be next. Then George. Then William. Then Jennings . . .

All the legitimate Kennellys must die, so that Storr could be the only Kennelly.

Pain took her breath away.

She imagined him standing close behind David, in the

dark of the balcony, trusted, cherished. She imagined him shoving David down, and chuckling hoarsely in the dark.

She saw him with Judd, the two of them walking together. Judd listening while Storr spoke of his plans, a new addition to Emerald Station perhaps. And Judd's eyes filled with vision. Then the sudden powerful thrust that sent him spinning into the river near the footbridge.

Brooke had told her only a part of it that day. A single part. And what he had left out, perhaps for Storr's own sake, had been most important. He hadn't mentioned the illegitimacy that had stained Storr, driven him from a loving brother to a murderer. Leaving Brooke, she had walked with Lolly across the meadow, down to the bridge, and seen Judd's face looking up at her, hazel eyes wide, mouth gaping.

She imagined Storr outside her room, laughing, drawing her out. The emerald necklace set there to capture her attention, while he pitched the heavy frame at her from the shadows above. She could picture him afterwards, bending to commiserate with her, snatching up the necklace to return it to her jewel box while she slept.

She saw him holding the pillow to Jennifer's face until her struggling body was still, and then arranging it below the portrait of Alicia.

She imagined him bending over her, holding her, pressing the small satin pillow to her face, laughing until, suddenly, sanity returned and recognition made him sob and free her and run into the shadows.

She could, now that she knew, imagine all this. But she couldn't imagine just what he would do next. She didn't know what she must do.

Her hands trembled on the steering wheel. Her toe quivered at the accelerator. She didn't want to go home. She didn't want to look into the eyes so like her father's, eyes that concealed madness now, and hate.

But she drove on steadily into the fading sunshine.

She turned in past the crape myrtle trees, past the jagged rim of the partly-done wall. She parked under the porte-cochere, and went into the house.

274

The carved black masks seemed to leer at her as she passed them. She pulled off her small hat, dropped it and her gloves on the table, and then went on into the drawing room.

". . . oughtn't to have gone alone," George was saying. "She's not been looking too well. I'm worried about her, Jay."

"I'm back," she said simply, trying to smile at him.

But the muscles of her face seemed stiff, frozen. It was hard to act natural with the burden of knowledge of what must be done pressing her down.

Jay said, eyeing her, "You look tired, Dolores."

And Storr, rising, asked, "Did you get all your errands finished?"

"Yes, Storr. I did." She looked into his face, into his green eyes. They were oddly opaque now, bottomless and brooding.

Jennings cleared his throat uneasily, scratched his whiskers. "William, don't you imagine that we could have a drink?"

William nodded, but made no move.

Plainly, he, the rest of them, sensed the quality of tension, of terror, that she had brought with her into the big familiar room.

She waited, not quite knowing how to begin, what to say.

Then Storr said to her, "Dolly, you didn't do errands. You went to see Tom Stapleton in Bellingham, didn't you?"

"Yes, Storr. That's just what I did."

"Tom Stapleton?" George said. "Why? What was the point of that? Dolores, I insist that you . . ."

But Storr cut him off, "And he told you, didn't he?"

She nodded.

"The same thing that he told me," Storr went on.

Again she nodded.

"And then you understood it all, didn't you, Dolly?"

"I'm sorry," she answered. It was very hard to speak, hard to look at him. But, just as she'd had to answer him,

275

she had to keep looking at him now, looking into the opaque green of his eyes.

And for the first time she wondered why Tom Stapleton had told her the truth. Was it because he had known what must happen? Had he been able to foresee this awful moment? Had he hated the Kennelly part of Storr? Had he hated the Kennelly part of him so much that he wanted to see Storr destroyed? And was that why he had, in the first place, told Storr the truth of his birth? What purpose other than revenge could Tom Stapleton have had? Revenge which would destroy all the Kennellys.

"Yes," Storr said, taking a step toward her. "It was Alicia, you see. She came in the night and told me what to do. I was trying to fall asleep, but she came and whispered at me."

"Alicia ..." Jennings groaned. "But you were just a child then, Storr."

Storr ignored the words. He said, "She came and talked to me in the night, and then I ran and hid. And Nealanna came and saved me. My second Mama, you see. She saved me because she loved me. That made it so hard when I knew what I had to do. The flames leaped up, and singed her dress. She held me. Then Gareth took me away. They never told me why she went away. It was months before I knew Alicia died."

"The portrait," Jay said softly.

But Storr continued to stare at Dolores. "It was so hard. But I knew what I had to do. Never think it was easy, Dolly. But Nealanna died, and she was all I had. Though I never really had her. Nealanna died. Jennings and I continued to plan the rebuilding of the library. Tom Stapleton and I were going over it. I knew what he felt. I could sense it, smell it. It was an odor around him, that hate. An odor that has hung over all our lives for years and years. And then, that day, he said, 'You're no real Kennelly. Why do you pretend you are?' I told him that I was. Of course I was. I was Gareth Kennelly's son, and everyone knew it. And then he said, 'Is that so?' and laughed at me." Now it was Storr who laughed, a low hoarse chuckle that made Dolores' blood run cold. "He said, 'You ought to know the truth, my boy. You're the son of Gareth Kennelly's whore, who happened to be my sister. She disappeared when you were born. Those two were never married, and never could be. Do you really think that Neil Kennelly would have allowed his heir to marry a housemaid?'" Storr's eyes narrowed. "It was while he was talking that I could see the flames again. We were up in the attic, and Nealanna was holding me. I saw Alicia's face afterwards. I knew what she was, though they thought that I didn't. Just as they thought they could hide my bastardy from me."

"But Storr," Dolores said softly, "Why did it matter? Why does it matter? You're part of us, and always have been."

"It isn't so," he told her. "What Nealanna did for me was out of love. What Gareth did for me was out of shame. But they neither of them considered me a Kennelly. And Gareth proved it when he passed me over and made David heir. I didn't mind, I was even glad, until I understood the reason for it. But understanding changed that. Being a bastard, no matter what you say, kept me from being a Kennelly under law and in every other way."

"But it was only a piece of paper, Storr. A marriage certificate. What does that matter?"

"And where do you suppose my mother went?"

"I don't know," she said. "Perhaps she was ashamed, unhappy. Perhaps she went away and built a new life."

"Tom Stapleton thinks she was murdered. Murdered here at Emerald Station."

Jennings swore under his breath.

Jay moved closer to Dolores, and George pushed himself up, favoring his bad hip.

Dolores said, "Storr, you must be mad to let Tom Stapleton . . ."

Storr said, "Sometimes when Alicia comes in the night, then I'm mad." He chuckled hoarsely. "Then there's a mad part of me. The Kennelly part."

"No," she said. "No, Storr."

And now she was afraid.

His eyes were now longer opaque. They glowed at her, as if flame danced in them. His face was bloodless, shiny with sweat, though the room was cool. His big hands flexed at his sides.

He said, "I killed them, you know. David. Judd. Jennifer. I would have killed you, Dolly. But your curls ringed that small pillow, and you were Nealanna again. You opened your arms wide to me and hugged me when I was afraid. You welcomed me and loved me when I was finally brought home after wishing for it, and praying for it, for so long. I dropped the pillow and ran away."

He took a step toward her then, and she backed away.

"We'll help you," she said. "We'll find a way."

"You're afraid of me, aren't you, Dolly?"

"We'll help you," she repeated.

"You should be afraid of me," he told her. "And afraid, as well, of what's in yourself. We share the same blood. We are the same." He smiled at her. "If you were all dead, then I would be the only Kennelly."

Jay said quietly, "Sit down, Storr. We'll have to talk a little."

But Storr took another step. There was color in his face now. His eyes were a clear cold green. He said, "We ... we ... don't have ... any ... anything to talk about," with his lips twisting, and his throat tense, to force the words out. "Nothing."

He took another step. It brought him to the door.

Jay reached out to hold him by the arm.

Then Storr moved, but not slowly. He spun away, and into the hallway. His footsteps pounded into the foyer. The door crashed open.

Jay had started to go after him, but Jennings had yelled, "No, Jay. Let him go."

They crowded around the window. They were there when the roadster shot out from under the porte-cochere, and down the driveway.

It fled like a thing pursued past the stone lions and the fountain.

Then it leaped off the road, spun down across the smooth green of the lawn where Tim Stapleton and his girlfriend had once picnicked, and hurled itself head-on, at the half-done wall. For a moment, it hung on the jagged stones. Then it fell back, and burst into a great sheet of flame.

"It was George who suggested it to me," Jay said. "Right after David died, he came to me and told me that he couldn't believe it had been an accident. He asked me to move in, see what I could see."

"Then you did have a reason," Dolores said. "I knew there had to be some . . ."

"To protect you, among other things," he told her, his lips twisting bitterly. "Not that I was much good."

"But you were," she protested. "Just having you here must have changed things for Storr. Must have made him more wary." Tears stung her eyes. "It's so hard to believe, to accept."

"Let time help you, Dolly." His arms closed around her. "Let me help you, too."

She smiled at him through her tears. She knew that would be answer enough.

Chapter 29

The end of the year was coming fast, Dolores thought. The ring of hills around the valley was aflame with October color, and the rope myrtle blossoms had finally begun to fade. That morning the windows had been white with frost, though now, the sun gleamed brilliantly through the jagged shards of green glass that had been cemented on the top of the gray stone wall. It was nine years since she had returned from Bellingham, carrying the awful burden of knowing what Storr had done, and seen the madness blaze at her from his emerald eyes.

Now, Evanne, rocking in her chair, seemed to share her thoughts. "I like the winters less and less," she said, her voice thin and wheezing. "It's age, I suppose." Her narrow shoulders hunched under the blue shawl that matched her eyes.

Dolores smiled at her. "Don't speak of age to me, Evanne. You're doing fine."

"Fine, am I?" Evanne sighed. "Well, maybe. But I was a great deal finer in my prime, I think." She went silent then, seeming to sink into a light doze.

It happened often now, Dolores thought. Except for

that, one would never guess that Evanne was seventy-seven. That she no longer cooked, ran the house, didn't matter. She remained the rock on which the whole family depended. She was surrogate grandmother for the children, making dolls for Anna, and paper boats for Neil, and reading stories for seven-year-old Garan, the only one who considered himself too grown up, finally, to sit on her lap.

Evanne's head lifted. She blinked at Dolores. "Still, I would like to see them all again."

"Yes," Dolores agreed gently, knowing what the old lady meant.

"I won't understand it. Not until the day I die. I'll never understand why George did what he did. No, Dolly, you've gone over it for me a dozen times. But still, I don't understand."

"It was what he felt he had to do. We can't be judges of that, Evanne. Nor decide whether it was right or wrong."

"Nine years of silence. Never speaking a word. Without love. Without a future. Without marriage, and children. Dolly, it doesn't make sense to me." Evanne's thin fingers writhed together, and tears suddenly filled her eyes. "He is a Kennelly, and he can't have stopped being one. Even though he chose to."

Dolores didn't answer. It was a discussion they had had before. She found now, as always, that there was nothing she could add to what she had already said.

In the beginning, when she first heard what George intended to do, she had felt the same sense of disbelief. Time had given her acceptance, but not real understanding. As Evanne said, George was a Kennelly. He couldn't change that. But he had tried to.

She knew that she would always remember the afternoon he had told her what he intended.

It was just six months after Storr had died, and two months after she and Jay had been married.

George had asked her to come into his study, and when she had, he sat down behind the desk, as if it were a bar-

ricade between the two of them. Hardly a necessary bar-
ricade, she had thought at the time, since he had, over the
months, withdrawn so deeply into himself that she had not
known how to reach him. She supposed it was the result
of everything that had happened. But it was over now,
and there was joy in Emerald Station again, and if,
sometimes, she remembered the creeping shadows, she
would quickly turn to Jay, and his smile, and put them out
of her mind again.

But George apparently couldn't do the same. He had
said in a quiet heavy tone, "Dolores, I've been thinking
about this for a long time, though I've never mentioned it
before."

She waited, feeling the first uneasiness.

He went on, "I'm going to join the Church, Dolly. And
then, if I'm acceptable, I want to go into a Trappist
monastery."

She stared at him, barely able to speak. He had always
been serious, turned inward, more concentrated on his
books than anything else. But he had his responsibilities
... the family, Emerald Station.

He went on, "I want to take vows of silence, and spend
the rest of my life in a less worldly way than this one."

She gasped, "But George, you can't. You're a Kennelly."

He gave her a bitter smile. "And is that such a fine
thing to be, Dolly?"

Her small hands became fists. She leaned forward.
"Yes," she said. "Yes, it is. And you belong here with us."

"In a prison?"

"Our home," she told him.

"You sound just like father, saying almost his words."
George's smile faded. "Did you know that once, it must be
nearly eighteen years ago, I tried to run away?"

"*You* did?"

"I did. And of course, you wouldn't have heard of it.
Not even mother knew. I was at school then. I went down
to New York, in search of something. I beat a good tambourine then, though I've never done it since. That's where

Father found me. Shaking a tambourine with a Salvation Army group in front of Macy's Department Store."

"He brought you back?"

"Back to school. And that was the end of that. But not really the end."

"The once ought to have been enough for you," she told him.

"But it wasn't."

"I don't understand. Tell me, explain it to me. Why, why do you want to leave us and the world? What does it mean?"

He shrugged. "I can't explain, and I don't think I want to. Just let's say that I feel I've finished my work here. I've done what I set out to do."

She shook her head slowly. "No, George."

He turned in his chair, looked out the window. That day, too, the sun had blazed through the green glass that rose like jagged teeth on the top of the new wall. "I saw that job done. The wall. Emerald Station is impregnable now. With the river at its back, and the wall along the road, nothing can attack it now. Not from the outside."

A shiver touched her. "George, that's not why we built the wall."

"Then why did we?"

"Because of the . . . the trespassers," she said.

He grinned at her. "A boy and his girl had a picnic on the front lawn. William, out hunting, ran into a couple of poachers. Is that so great a threat?" He didn't wait for her answer. He went on, "No, Dolly. Storr and Jennings planned the wall. They knew what they were doing, and why."

"If you ask Jennings now, he'll tell you . . ."

"I know what he'll say. But it's what he feels that matters." George turned back. "And he feels much as I do. As William did."

"Oh, no," she protested. "William simply wanted a change. I suppose Jennifer's death and then Storr's . . . He'll be back soon. I know he will."

"Do you? I doubt that."

283

George had been right. William had returned only a few times in the past nine years for brief holiday visits. A few months earlier he had married, but he hadn't yet brought his bride to Emerald Station.

But George, that day in the study, had known only what his heart told him. He went on, "I doubt William will be back to live. And anyway, I won't be here to welcome him. I leave tomorrow, Dolly."

"But you can't," she cried. "You can't turn your back on your responsibilities and pretend they don't exist."

"I have another responsibility. Uncle Brooke will help you, and so will Jay. You'll be mistress here. I only hope that being so won't hurt you."

"I can't be," she said numbly. "I wouldn't know . . ."

"There's Jay remember." George leaned back, smiled. "It goes on, and needs very little managing. Grandfather Neil was wise, you know. And father, too."

She said, "But there's only the two of us left, George. How can you do this?"

"I have to," he said softly. "I wouldn't, except that I have to."

Why he had to, what it meant to him, she never knew. He was gone the next day.

He had written to her twice yearly in the nine years that passed. She had answered him with long letters about Jay, the children, the Maradines, and suggested that they exchange visits. He had ignored her comments about that, and had never seen Garan, Neil, or Anna. Nor, she had begun to realize, would he ever see them.

Now Evanne was saying, "And the others, too. William . . . why hasn't he brought us his new wife?"

"Oh, he will, Evanne. One of these days." But Dolores wondered. She had begun to believe that he, like George, had turned his back forever on Emerald Station.

"One of these days may not be soon enough for me," Evanne complained. "I'm old. Old, Dolly. I don't count on all that many days."

Dolores said quickly, "Stop that. I'm going to ring for

284

Dot to bring in the children. That will make you feel better."

"Winter," Evanne said. "I feel it coming."

"So you might. Since it's almost here," Dolores laughed. She rang for Henry, and when he appeared, bent, pink-faced, and with pale scalp shining through strands of thin red hair, she sent him to the nursery for the children. He hobbled off, as slim as he had been when young, but stiff with arthritis.

A moment later, Jennings came in. He was heavier than ever, his face florid, his whiskers thick and untouched with gray. He wore a tweed suit, and under it, a brown vest embroidered with gold that he had had for many years.

He dropped into a chair, settled his heavy bulk. "Is Jay back yet?"

"Not yet," Dolores told him.

"I can't see why he went. It's the same old thing, Dolores. It happens every once in a while."

"Jay doesn't seem to think so," she answered. "He's convinced it means the beginning of a big change. A serious change."

"I've heard that before. What's a recession or two? We've had them before, and will again. And besides, it won't affect us."

"He doesn't think it will. But he wanted to see some people, to know what's happening."

She was suddenly restless. She wished Jay hadn't gone to New York, and knew it was always that way. When he was gone from Emerald Station, she felt the weight of it, saw the creeping shadows again. Jay stood between her and memory, between her and fear. They had a good life, a good marriage. If it were possible, she thought she loved him more now than on the day they were wed. And he seemed to feel the same. She smiled faintly then, thinking of the most difficult time they had had. It happened a year before when she cropped her hair without warning him that she was going to. He hadn't spoken to her for two days, then he had confessed, "It does look good, Dolly.

285

But you look so young. So terribly young for twenty-nine."

Jennings was saying through pursed rosebud lips, "If it's a real crash, Bellingham will suffer."

She said quietly, "I don't care about Bellingham, Jennings."

"Of course," he agreed, but with a reservation in his tone.

She didn't pursue the subject. There was a brief silence, then Evanne said, "But, Dolores, you must care. It's there. It's always been there, and always will be. You can't pretend that it doesn't exist."

"It doesn't exist for me," Dolores said firmly. She understood Evanne's feelings. There was Moira Row, the Row children. They were part of the town for Evanne. But for Dolores herself the town held nothing but evil memories. She tried never to permit herself to recall them. She had determined that they would never touch her children.

"Anyway," Jennings said, "the library stands, and is used."

Dolores shrugged. Why he took satisfaction in that thought, she didn't understand. The library . . . her father's death, and Storr's madness . . .

"Dot's a town girl, and she's fine," Evanne put in.

There was the sound of scampering feet in the hallway.

Garan came striding in, importantly announcing, "Henry says that he'll teach me to drive the Rolls, if he lives long enough." He was tall for his age, very thin, all elbows and knees, with his father's jutting stubborn chin. But his hair was Dolores' own, very dark and glossy, while his eyes were hazel, like those of his Uncle Judd whom he would never know.

Evanne laughed, "Well, Henry might just do that. Have a look at me, and keep up your hopes."

"Me, too," Neil asserted, grinning broadly. "He's going to teach me, too." Neil had sandy hair, but his eyes were as dark, as tilted, as Dolores' own.

Anna, who at three tried to copy her brothers in all

ways, nodded her dark head vigorously. Then she brushed Neil aside, and climbed up on Evanne's lap, where she sat rocking, her thumb in her mouth, and her eyes wide with deliberate challenge.

Soon after, Jay arrived. He was grim-faced and there were shadows in his gray eyes. He sat down tiredly.

Jennings asked, "Well, how was it?"

"Bad."

"Then you'd say it isn't just the same old thing?"

"I wouldn't." Jay shook his head. "The market's in very deep trouble. Whole fortunes have been washed out today. There were two . . ." He stopped himself, glanced at the children. He went on, forcing a smile, "But it's going to be all right, Dolly. As far as we're concerned."

"I told you," Jennings crowed. "I knew it wouldn't affect the Kennellys."

"Who's the Kennellys?" Garan asked.

Jay answered, "Well, Jennings is, for one. And you, and your brother and sister, are half Kennellys."

"Aren't you a Kennelly?" Garan asked.

Jay grinned. "Of course not. You know that. I'm a Gordon."

"Then I don't want to be a Kennelly. I want to be a Gordon, too," Garan said.

So much for all those visits to the family room, Dolores thought. So much for the gilt-framed portraits, the banks of photographs, the shelves of memorabilia.

Evanne raised her head. She looked over Anna's dark curls. "But Garan," she said. "You don't have a choice."

And something cold touched Dolores, something cold made her shiver.

Dolores braked to a gentle stop. "I'll give you the ration coupons, and the list, Anna. And you can start getting the order together while I go to the post office."

Anna said, "Do you want to just sit here and wait? I'll be glad to do both. You look a little tired."

Dolores forced a smile. "I guess I am tired. The fourth month of pregnancy is when I always began to feel it."

"But you're not sorry, are you?" Anna asked, her sixteen-year-old face suddenly anxious. "I mean ... you don't wish it hadn't happened, do you?"

Dolores laughed softly. "What good would wishing be?" But when she saw the sudden sharp fear in Anna's face, she said quickly, "Oh, no, of course I'm not sorry. This new baby makes me feel young again, and your father, too."

"At least it takes his attention off the war news for a few minutes at a time," Anna said, sighing. "Honestly, the way he glues himself to the radio ... for the last year it's been just about impossible to talk to him."

"But with Garan and Neil both in the service, you understand."

"Sure, I understand. Only between his lab, and the radio ..."

Dolores smiled. "Men concentrate on the essentials. And so had we better." She touched Anna's shoulder. "Get going. I'll pick you up in a few minutes."

Anna slipped from the car, went into the shop. Dolores drove down the block, and parked the Rolls in front of the post office. She got out clumsily, then took a deep breath, resting, she told herself, before she went inside.

She was at her box, holding the two V-letters, drawing reassurance and joy just from the sight of the familiar sprawling penmanship of her two sons, when a voice said, "Mrs. Gordon ..."

She turned, looked into Tom Stapleton's faded eyes. She remembered that he had had blond hair, thick and shaggy. Now it was white. He had had a craggy bitter face, it was the same now, but sharper, thinner, scored with heavy lines.

She said, her voice shaking, "Good morning, Mr. Stapleton."

"Not for me." His hating smile broke the deep lines. "My grandson ... we've got a gold star in the window for him."

"I'm sorry," she said faintly.

"It's bad for a young man to die."

288

She thought of David, of Judd. She thought of Jennifer, and of Storr himself. They had all been young. But she said nothing.

"My boy Tim, he's half out of his mind. He was always a good boy, always a piece of me. Now he's lost his son."

"I'm sorry," she said again, and hurried outside, still clasping her two letters in her hand.

She got into the car, drove down the street. She sat at the wheel, waiting for Anna to come out, and breathing hard to fight the dizziness that assailed her.

She didn't notice time passing. She sat there hunched, and shivering. She didn't notice that Anna had come out of the grocery until the young girl gasped, "Mother, what's the matter?"

"You must get help," Dolores gasped. "Someone to drive me ..." The pain hit her then, and the cold sweat broke out on her face. She writhed against the seat, turning her head from side to side. Her bloodless lips moved in an incoherent whisper.

"Is something happening?" Anna cried.

"I think so," Dolores whispered. "I think ... someone must drive me. ..."

Anna looked up and down the empty street.

Dolores, watching through pain-blurred gray, saw her run into the store. A moment later, the young girl appeared. A man was with her. He trotted to the car, thin, dark-haired, her own age. She knew him.

He leaned close to her.

She whispered, "Dylan, will you help me?" and fainted.

Chapter 30

The window was a pale square against the gray of the sky. The room was filled with the scent of roses, which, somehow, didn't mask the odor of acrid medication.

Jay said quietly, "There was no chance at all, Dolly."

She nodded, brushed away the tears that overflowed her eyes and slid down her pale cheeks.

It was six days since she had miscarried in the Rolls on Maine Avenue. They had been able to tell her only that morning that the baby had been gone.

"And if Dylan Row hadn't been so quick, and given his own blood . . ." Jay's voice broke. "I couldn't have stood it if anything happened to you, Dolly. I need you."

She gripped his hand tightly. "I'll be all right. Just give me a little time. I know I'll be all right." Then, with a forced smile, she asked, "Tell me about the letters from Garan and Neil, Jay. I never had a chance to read them."

It seemed, then, that she would be able to put the loss behind her. But weeks passed, and then months, and then more months, and she didn't regain her strength, nor her interest in life.

Where her hair had been dark, just as it had been in her

youth, it suddenly developed two broad white streaks. Her eyes lost their glow and warmth. Her slender body became thin, emaciated, and without its former grace.

It was that year, when Garan and Neil went into the Army, and she lost the baby, that she began, suddenly to catch up with Jay in age. She was no longer just forty-two, she felt. She was old, old. And her thoughts, as always with the old, began to turn backward.

She would not think of Guadacanal nor Iwo Jima, when, finally, those assaults made black headlines in the newspapers. She would not think of Tobruk, nor, even much later, of Hiroshima. The years of the war passed, and Anna grew taller, slimmer, more lovely every day.

But Dolores thought of Evanne, who had died at eighty-three, in the midst of the Depression that the beginning of the war had ended. Dolores thought of Henry, retired now, and living out his days in a chair near the cottage they had built for him in the shadow of the wall where Storr died.

She thought of Storr, his tormented eyes, and his husky whisper, and how he had been driven mad by Tom Stapleton. She thought of the blood of Dylan Row that now ran in her veins. She wrote to George and waited for his answers, and to William, and waited for his.

She spent hours, though Jay begged her not to, in the family room, looking into her father's green eyes, feeling that they smiled at her from his portrait. She studied her mother's young and beautiful face, and wondered if she had ever felt what Dolores herself now felt. She asked herself about Holt Kennelly, and her grandfather Neil. Sometimes she heard herself say aloud, "Blood tells . . ." and shivered at the words.

The news that the war had ended did not touch her. The laughing celebrations in Bellingham, and on the radio, meant nothing to her.

But she became, very briefly, herself, when first Garan and then Neil came home. Both times though her apathy quickly returned.

When, in 1947, Jay closed the laboratory in the Gordon

house, Dolores knew that he was doing it for her. He wanted to be with her, no longer spending hours away in town at work that separated them. She was delighted that he should have done so, and, for a long while, she was once more herself again.

But then the apathy surrounded her, a dark cloud that lay upon her spirit.

Lolly and Brooke came to visit, and she could hardly talk to them.

Brooke said, "Dolly, you must get hold of yourself. You don't realize what you're doing to Jay. You have a fine family. You should be happy. You mustn't think of what you lost. But only of what you have."

"Lost?" she asked, not knowing what he referred to.

His thin face, wrinkled now, but still very alert, became a mask. He said, "Dolly, I refer to the child. But you . . ."

"Oh," she said. "Oh, that. But I never had the child." And she thought of what she had really lost. There had been David, and Judd. There had been Jennifer. And there had been Storr. And George . . . William, too.

But when William came for a Christmas visit with his wife Helga, and his son Davis, she found that she could spend only short periods of time with them. These three reminded her of the past, too, and a smile out of which had come the haunting words, "Blood tells."

One morning, at the end of the year in which Jay had closed the Gordon house forever, she awakened at dawn.

There was pale light filtering from around the edges of the drawn drapes.

She stared at it, bemused, and wondering what sound had pulled her so abruptly from sleep, or what dream had touched her and brought her awake.

Jay lay still beside her, his head turned away.

He was her life, she thought. Her love. He kept the shadows at bay. From the time he first moved into Emerald Station, he had become part of her.

She snuggled closer to him, then, because he didn't respond, closer still. But something was wrong.

There was no warmth in his body, no heat in his flesh.

She sat up, threw back the covers. She said, "Jay?" and leaned over him, and saw the blank empty stare of his gray eyes, and knew that he was dead.

Garan said, "Mother, this is Julia," and smiled.

Dolores nodded, "Welcome to our family, Julia. Welcome to Emerald Station. I hope you'll be happy here." But the dark, slanted eyes were blank. There was no emotion in her words.

Julia, tall, slender and as dark as Garan, said, "Oh, but I'm going to love it. It's a fantastic place. And there's really quite a lot we can do. With your permission, of course."

"My permission?" Dolores said. "Oh, you won't need that. Whatever Garan wants ... whatever you want ..." She looked out of the window, and saw the sun shine on the broken green glass on the lichen-covered wall, and shuddered, and shook her head.

"You're cold," Garan said quickly. "I'll get you a sweater."

But Dolores rose, walked out of the room, and heard Garan say softly, "Don't mind her, Julia. She can't help it. Ever since my father died ..."

Towards the end of that year, when Anna came home from school, she said, "Mama, you have to get out for a bit. I'll take you for a ride to town."

"Oh, no," Dolores said. "I've no desire to go to Bellingham."

"Oh, all right. Then we'll just ride over to see Uncle Brooke. Now that's okay, isn't it? You can't shake your head at that."

Dolores agreed that she would go to Maradine Mansion. She sent Anna for a light coat, and went outside to wait.

The sun made a gleaming veil of the fountain spray, and cast long big shadows of the two stone lions that flanked it.

She heard the car coming around the house from where

293

the garages were, and when it pulled up, she said to Anna, "Never mind. I find that I don't want to go after all."

"Mother . . ." Anna began.

"No, but thank you," Dolores said. She went inside, climbed the steps past the leering black masks, and went into the family room.

She thought that they were all there. All of the Kennellys. And she was with them. She and Jay, too. "Blood tells," she whispered aloud. "They all say that blood tells."

"You'll have to speak to Anna," Jennings said coldly. And then, "Dolores, are you listening to me?"

"I'm listening," she answered. "What about Anna?"

But, in fact, she wasn't attending, and when Jennings went on, she didn't hear him. She was thinking that both the boys were settled now. Garan had married his Julia, and she had filled their second floor apartment with strange-looking lightwood furniture imported from Sweden. Dolores supposed that it was attractive, but it seemed oddly out of place in Emerald Station. Now Neil had brought home Tanya, a pleasant young woman who would, surely, make him a fine wife.

There would be another generation of Kennellys. They, of course, considered themselves Gordons. But they didn't know. And she didn't know how to tell them.

If only Jay were alive . . .

She put her head back on the chair, and closed her eyes, and from the distance, she heard Jennings say, "Dolly, Dolly, what's the matter?" but she couldn't answer him, and the shadows moved in swiftly from the corners of the big room.

Chapter 31

Jennings' white head trembled on the thin stalk of his neck. "Anna, my dear, you do see a great deal of that young man, don't you?" he observed.

Anna said, "Why, yes. I do. He's very pleasant company, you know." She reflected that Jennings seemed very suddenly to have aged in these past months. Or perhaps that she was just beginning to notice what had been going on for a long time. Either way, the pink plumpness had melted from his face, leaving hard bones that showed beneath his white beard, and sunken eyes that glittered from under unruly white brows.

"You say he's pleasant company. I shouldn't have thought so." Jennings took a cigar from his breast pocket, examined it with careful squinting eyes, and then lit it. The gold lighter seemed to tremble in his fingers, the flame to dance dangerously near his whiskers. "I don't see what you could have in common with that young man."

"Lots," Anna laughed, studying the soiled tips of her saddle shoes. She was a slender girl, with small wrists and neat ankles, and a heart-shaped face that was dominated by great dark eyes. Those eyes of hers were like windows into her soul. They changed with her moods and feelings so openly that she had, lately, determined that she must find some way to control them. She considered that she was too old at twenty-two to allow herself to be read like a neon sign.

"Of course," Jennings was saying, "I suppose that there isn't a great deal to choose from in the locality these days. And you are a young woman. You must have your interests. But still, I should think the best way to handle it is to go off to Boston, even to New York. You could broaden your experiences there, couldn't you?"

She said gently, "I've not been home from school very long," and added sadly, "though I wish I'd come home sooner. Maybe, if I'd had more time with Mama . . ."

"You couldn't have prevented it, Anna. Never think so. You saw how she was. It was coming, coming. Every since your father died . . ." He sighed, then blew through his whiskers with a pout of rosebud lips. "It was so terrible a thing to happen to her. To die so young. Just like her mother Nealanna. Young. Too young. And I am seventy-five years old. And I go on and on. I begin to think I'll last forever, but am not charmed by the idea." His glittering eyes narrowed. "Though I'll admit to you now there was a time when I thought my end was about to come. I believed I'd be cut off in my young manhood, in my prime . . . the things I've seen, Anna," he finished vaguely. He was quiet for a little while, then suddenly he raised his head again. "But you do spend too much time in that town, Anna. And too much with your young friend as well."

She ran her slim hands through her loose dark curls, and a band of diamonds glittered from one of them. She gave it a casual polish on her plaid skirt, then grinned, "Now you aren't really going to lecture me, are you?"

He puffed on his cigar and looked at her through a veil of smoke. "I wouldn't presume. You've always been headstrong. Odd that people don't change. But they don't. I am not lecturing. I am telling you, Anna, that no good will come from your continual running off to Bellingham."

She told herself that nothing would be accomplished by becoming angry. She grinned again, "I do believe I've heard those words before."

"I'm sure you have. For a good part of your life. Ever since you grew up enough to go about on your own. I must say I don't understand the attraction."

It was very likely indeed that Jennings would not understand the attraction. He was an old man, quite content to stay within the walls of Emerald Station. But she knew that there was a time when he hadn't felt that way. She reminded him of it, saying, "You used to spend a lot of time in town, you know. What about the library that you and Storr built?"

Jennings winced. "Yes. I remember. I also remember that I learned better."

"The library still stands, and is still used."

"Burned down once," he answered. "Just before your grandfather died. Then Storr and I . . ." He stopped himself, and leaned sideways to mash the partly-smoked cigar in an ash tray. When he straightened, he said, "Just don't pass it by too often."

She sighed to herself. He could be persistent when he wanted to be. Yet good manners, and a very real fondness kept her from telling him that she would do as she pleased. Instead, she asked, "Tell me why I oughtn't to spend so much time in town. Give me a sensible reason."

"Because of things that happened long long before you were born, and things that happened even before your mother was born."

"I said a sensible reason," Anna laughed. "I can't be bothered with all that old nonsense."

"Perhaps you should be. I remember, when I was your age . . . No. I was younger than you. I was seventeen then, I think. Yes, yes, at seventeen, I felt much the same. Town was the flame, and I was the moth. I couldn't stay away from it. No, no. I had to test myself. Many's the time I tangled with Tom Stapleton. I had to test myself. I was a Kennelly."

"A Kennelly," she grinned. "The way you say that . . ."

She thought of the family room ... the place where ancestor worship flourished as in olden times. The familiar faces, one after another, peering out of the shadows.

Jennings was saying, "There's only one way to say it, Anna."

"And I'm a Gordon. Poor me," she grinned. "I expect that's what makes me so different. I'm a Gordon, and my father's girl."

"You're that all right," Jennings agreed, not sounding particularly pleased. "Clever like your father, and not easily swayed, not by man or the devil. But you're a Kennelly, too, and don't you ever forget it. You've got old Neil's blood in your veins, and Gareth's, as well as your mother's. Mind now, I know what I'm talking about."

She concealed her impatience. She knew that whenever he said he knew what he was talking about he was preparing to babble about the old days. One minute he would be talking about his father, about Neil, locking him in his room for three days, and accusing him of some terrible crime he hadn't committed. She supposed it was smoking a cigarette behind the carriage houses, though he, when questioned, always slyly evaded a straight answer. Another minute he would go into the tale of his wanderings for ten years. That would lead him to a maudlin description of the horrors of having always been alone, never marrying, never having children. But if she asked him why he hadn't, he would say, 'It was never meant to be.' He would tell her that he had learned much, but mostly that he was a Kennelly, and belonged in Emerald Station, no matter what his fate would bring him.

But now he surprised her. He said, "Oh, never mind that foolish business, Anna. Don't listen to an old man. Blood doesn't mean a damn thing. Nor does a name. But it's the young man that I'm talking about. Martin Milton. Do you mean to marry him?"

She burst out laughing. "Uncle, it may be that in your day a girl always married a man she dated. But not now. Not in 1948. No. Of course I don't mean to marry him. I don't mean to marry anyone right now."

"I see," he said, thoughtfully tugging his whiskers. "But still, propinquity makes strange bedfellows."

She laughed again, supposing that he expected it. He had made what was, after all, quite an up-to-date pun.

But he didn't seem to notice. "When there's no one else, and the time comes, a woman has been known to settle for second best. Or third or fourth. Just because it's the time."

"Maybe it's just not that time for me," she said.

"Maybe you don't recognize it now that it's here," he retorted. "And still, what am I trying to tell you? That you must get about in the world a bit before you decide on love? That seems rather reasonable advice from an old man to a young woman. But you know, Anna, what's reasonable isn't always right."

"You're certainly full of your homemade little homilies this morning," she told him.

"I'm leading up to something. But you refuse to understand. That doesn't disturb me. The old are never understood by the young. Nor the young by the old." He sighed deeply. "If only they were. Old Neil, my father, would have known me better then. He would have been able to read my heart. That would have changed everything for me. For my whole life. And I would have been able to understand his despair and his terror." Jennings stopped, withdrew a fresh cigar from his breast pocket. He lit it carefully, then went on, "But that won't help you, will it? Never mind. My advice—have experience before you choose your young man—such advice is meaningless. For you can not read the human heart, nor see behind the masks we all wear. You can not know those small mechanisms that determine what we are, and what our fates shall be."

"Why, then," she answered, "it's all just luck. Good fortune or bad, or both. So there's no need to worry."

"Perhaps. But I wonder." His glittering eyes were suddenly hidden behind drooping wrinkled lids. "Was it chance that brought Nealanna here? Was her arrival merely a matter of accident? I somehow doubt that. I know what my father was. I think Neil planned it. He must have. He was a ruthless man in his way, and he was determined to found a dynasty. Which is what he did."

She swallowed a yawn. She wasn't interested in these old tales. It was now that she found compelling. Now, and the prospects for the future, of course.

She had told her uncle the literal truth. She liked Martin Milton, and enjoyed his company. She was sure that it had nothing to do with propinquity, and it didn't matter to her if it did. She was determined to have someone to go about with. Someone from town. She had determined when she was sixteen years old that she would ignore the family's attitude toward Bellingham. It had nothing to do with her, she had decided, and she wouldn't permit it to guide her or deprive her either. Her mother, though understanding in most ways, had quite thoroughly disapproved, and was, Anna knew, always relieved when Anna had gone back to school, though she missed her youngest child bitterly.

Anna had been sixteen when Dolores had the miscarriage in town, and Dylan Row had helped take her to the hospital, had given of his own blood to save her life. Anna knew that she would never forget those moments.

Later, when Dolores was somewhat recovered physically, though not emotionally, Anna had persuaded Lolly Maradine to drive her to town, and had gone to see Dylan Row. His garage and automobile showroom took up a good part of one block on Maine Avenue.

Red and white and blue pennants danced in the breeze, but the big dim room was almost empty. She supposed it was the war. There would be no new cars to sell until it was over. But the garage itself seemed a hub of busy activity.

Dylan came to meet her, smiling. He was a slim man, with dark eyes, and dark hair heavily laced with gray. He said, "How are you, Anna? And how is your mother now?"

"I'm fine," she told him. "And mother is . . . well . . ."

"It'll take time," he assured her. "You mustn't worry,

300

Anna. Your mother is from good stock. She'll get over this."

"I hope so. And if she does it'll only be because of how you helped us. That's why I came. I wanted to thank you."

"Well, never mind that now," he said gently.

"We owe you so much," she burst out. "Why can't we be friends?"

He smiled at her again, tobacco-stained teeth showing under his long upper lip. "Why, we can, and we are." He went on quickly, "Did you know your father had been in, too?"

She shook her head.

A faintly wistful look crossed Dylan's face. He said softly, "You're very like your mother, you know." Then, as if recollecting himself, "Yes. Your father was in. For the same purpose."

"He didn't tell me," Anna had said. She thought that was exactly like her father. He was less affected by the aura of Emerald Station than anyone she had ever known. And it was like him, too, to do what he thought right in secret, without announcing it to the rest of the family.

"Your brothers are both gone into the service, aren't they?" Dylan was asking.

She nodded.

Beyond his shoulder, through the plate glass window, she saw an old man cross the garage lot. He was looking her way, staring. He was slight, with bent shoulders, and thin white hair. She saw the expression on his face, and found herself stepping back involuntarily, recognizing a cold and implacable dislike.

Dylan glanced behind him, said quickly, "That's my father." Then, without further explanation, he said, "I suppose your mother worries about the boys. I know I will. My son Dan will be going within a day or two."

"I've never met him," she said.

"No. That's right. He's twenty-two. He's been at State University for the past four years. But he wasn't able to quite finish. He will when he comes back."

301

She nodded, crossed her fingers, wishing Dylan and his unknown Dan good luck. There were gold stars in several windows of houses in town.

She burst out, "It's terrible to be a girl, Mr. Row. I feel so . . . so much that I must do something . . . anything . . . to be part of this, to belong to what everyone is doing."

"There's things for you to do," he told her.

"What things? Because I would . . . if only I knew . . ."

He shook his head. "I doubt your family would allow it, Anna."

"But why not?"

He asked, "For instance, do they know you're in town?"

"Mother's not well, and my father is concentrating on her." Anna grinned. "I guess I'm not really answering you, am I? No. They don't know. I walked across the meadow to the Maradines, and talked Lolly into bringing me in. She's parked outside now, probably stiff with disapproval still."

"Perhaps you oughtn't to keep her waiting too long."

Anna ignored his remark. With a sixteen-year-old's directness, she demanded, "Why do you think my family doesn't want me to come to Bellingham?"

"I'll leave the explanation to them, I believe."

She said, "I'm quite grown up now. I can make up my own mind."

"You can?" He was plainly about to say more. But he stopped himself at the slam of a car door. He said, beginning to smile again, "That'll be my son Dan."

"Then I'd better go," she said. "But thank you again for what you did for my mother."

She went toward the door, and just then it opened.

The young man standing there was tall, with dark hair and blue eyes. He had a good firm jaw, and a cleft chin.

He held the door back for her, smiled.

She thanked him, and then went on. He was a nice-looking man, she had thought then, who must take after his mother's side of the family, rather than his father's. And then she forgot about him.

She passed the hardware store window and saw a

printed placard. The Red Cross was holding bandage rolling sessions twice weekly, and knitting sessions twice weekly. Everyone was invited to participate, to do their bit for the boys abroad.

She made a mental note of the times of the meetings, determined to attend. She had done just that, but it had proven to be more difficult than she had anticipated.

"What were you studying there so long?" Lolly asked, when Anna returned to the car.

Anna explained.

Lolly had sighed. "I doubt that's a good idea." She started the car, sat up very straight, peering straight ahead over the windshield. "I doubt it, Anna."

"I think it is," Anna told her.

But when she mentioned it to her mother, Dolores had said, "No, Anna. I don't want you mingling with townsfolk. It wouldn't do."

"But why not?" Anna asked.

Her mother said obscurely, "It just wouldn't do. We've never mingled with them, and I don't want you to start now."

"I don't think we're so much superior to everyone else that we might get soiled by association with them," Anna protested. "And I think . . ."

"I'm not a snob. I just don't want you to." Dolores gave Anna a pale smile. It wasn't reflected in her eyes, Anna noticed. "Let that be my reason."

"I can't," Anna had cried. "It isn't a reason at all."

"I'm sorry." Dolores' eyes had filled with sudden tears. She leaned back, her hands folded in her lap. "If only Garan and Neil were home and safe. If only I knew . . . it could be a judgment on me. But for what sin? Why did it happen?"

Anna sighed. She knew that her mother was no longer thinking about her, but about the baby laid to rest forever in the Kennelly plot in the cemetery outside Bellingham.

Her father had given her permission, however, and a warning at the same time. "We're not well liked, as you'll soon find out. If you want to try it, okay. But you must be

303

forewarned. If you're offended, or turned away, then you'll have to accept that as an adult would."

"I'm sixteen," she retorted. "Of course I'll accept whatever happens as an adult would."

She was, in fact, neither insulted nor turned away.

But when she went into the church basement for the first time, she sensed an odd constraint in the woman who greeted her, and in those to whom she was finally introduced. She supposed, at first, it was because she was so much younger than they were. But she was soon disabused of that notion.

The woman who met her at the door said, "Everybody, this is Anna Kennelly."

"Anna Gordon," Anna said, smiling apologetically.

There was an instant of silence. Then the woman said, "I'm sorry. Anna Gordon, of course. You're Dolores Kennelly's and Jay Gordon's daughter. And we all know the Gordons, don't we?"

There were nods, faint smiles.

Anna went to work at the place she was shown. But as she bent her head over the great pile of bandages, she knew that everyone was staring at her. . .

Now Jennings said, "The trouble is, we just don't know." He pushed himself to his feet, stamped out his cigar. "Don't know. And ignorance is dangerous. It can destroy."

She asked half-heartedly, her mind still on the past, "What don't we know, Uncle?"

"Why things are the way they are," he told her. "We just don't know why."

Chapter 32

Much later she was to remember that Jennings had said that, and wonder. But now she answered, "Well, maybe some day we will know why things are the way they are," and knew, even as she spoke, that her words meant nothing.

The door opened just as Jennings tottered toward it. He stopped, and she thought, for a moment, that he would fall. It struck her that in a short time he had, not only seemingly aged in appearance but also increased in fragility.

Helga Kennelly looked in, as if not quite certain of her welcome. "Has anyone seen William? That husband of mine seems to have disappeared and I can't find him anywhere."

Jennings simply stared at her, saying nothing, while his mouth pursed in his white whiskers.

"I haven't seen William since breakfast," Anna told her. "I expect he's somewhere on the grounds. Did you have a look at the pool?"

"I did. And at the stable as well. I was sure I'd find him with the horses. But no luck. I'd walk down to the river and see if he's there, but I'm still uneasy about getting that far from the house." Helga laughed. "I know it's silly of me. But it's all so big, so awe-inspiringly big that I have the feeling I'll get lost and nobody'll ever find me."

"Hardly." Jennings peered at her plump round body as if to imply that she was too large to be lost, though he didn't at all disapprove of the possibility.

She was a woman in her mid-forties, and fairly tall, and she hadn't yet learned to accommodate her mannerisms to her change in figure. She swayed when she walked, and the sway became a jiggle of plump hips. She languished into a chair with a graceless thump. Her hair was silvered, worn in a high waved pompadour. Her blue eyes were heavily lined and shadowed. Her clothes were always just one size too tight.

It was all these, Anna supposed, that brought the look of disdain to Jennings' old face, as if he considered Helga not quite fit to be a Kennelly.

Now she had begun to pout.

Anna said quickly, "Let me change my shoes, and we'll walk to the river together." She glanced at Helga's spike-heeled ankle strap shoes. "Maybe you should, too."

"Is the going rough? Then, if it is . . ."

"Oh, not that bad. Just across the meadows. But low heels do make it easier."

"Then I will change," Helga answered. "I'll be right down."

When she had left the room, Jennings asked, "Has William said anything about when they will be going?"

"Going?"

"Returning to the Maine house, Anna."

"No. But I don't suppose it will be for some time," Anna told him. "Why do you ask?"

"Because I want to know," he said dryly. "When they came for your mother's funeral I believed it to be a matter of a brief stay. Now, and it's a full month later, they're still here."

Bewildered, Anna said, "But Emerald Station was always William's home, Uncle Jennings. He, and his wife

306

and son, have a right to be here. Why do you sound as if you disapprove?"

"I'm not Brooke Maradine and his Lolly either," he snapped pettishly. "I'll not pretend to what I don't feel."

"Why, Uncle Brooke's not pretending," she said. "At least I don't think so. He's fond of William."

"Fond? Certainly. But he must remember how it was. William and Jennifer. Faran and Avis' children. It would have been different if Faran and Avis hadn't died in the San Francisco earthquake, but die they did. And it changed everything."

He looked as if he were going to continue, but she said quickly, "Excuse me, Uncle, but I think I'd better go and change my shoes now. Helga will be down any minute."

It was as if he hadn't heard her. "Judgment. It falls hard on this family, Anna. Be careful, my dear. I've said the same to Garan and to Neil, but they laugh at me. They call me senile behind my back, and chuckle. And Tanya and Julia do the same. But none of them know, you see. If they knew, they would heed me."

She sighed, then grinned. She kissed his cheek. "Nobody laughs at you. We love you."

"Of course," he said quietly. "We all love each other. But that changes nothing."

She grinned again, slipped out. She wondered briefly what had started him off on that track. Then she forgot him and his words.

She hurried up the steps, past the leering old black masks and the great leather shield, without noticing them. They were so much a part of her life that she rarely even saw them.

Dot was just coming out of Anna's room. Once she had been the nursemaid, but when the children grew up, she became the housekeeper. She had been slim, quick, and full of laughter. Nearly twenty years older, she was much the same. Except that, at this moment, she was not laughing. She met Anna with a reproving frown, said, "Anna, why on earth did you throw all your jewels around like that? Were you looking for something special?"

"Throw my ..." Anna stared at her. "What are you talking about?"

"Come and see," Dot told her.

They went into the room together. The top of Anna's mahogany dresser glittered with necklaces and earrings. She said, "Why, Dot, that's the craziest thing. I haven't touched that leather case for months." She picked up a string of emeralds set in gold links. "This was mother's ... but you know, she never wore it."

"She didn't care for it," Dot said. "Nor for most of the other pieces. But never mind. If you didn't pull them out, then who did?"

"I can't imagine," Anna answered thoughtfully. "Unless Julia or Tanya wanted to borrow something, but they'd hardly ..."

Dot swept the jewelry into its case. "We'll have to see." She went to the window, looked out on the balcony. "It's good that you have the pool. Davis wouldn't have much to do if he couldn't swim."

"Yes," Anna agreed. "Which reminds me. I'd better get going. I'm supposed to meet Helga downstairs right now." She put on sneakers, hurried back to the foyer.

"I thought you'd changed your mind," Helga said, pouting at her.

"Oh, no. I just stopped to talk to Dot for a minute. And before that Jennings held me up."

"A very odd old man," Helga said, dimpling. "Do you know, sometimes when he looks at me, at William, and at our Davis, too, I have the most awful feeling. As if he were stripping us down to our backbones and peering into the vertebrae. And it gives me the willies."

"Oh, I think you're imagining things," Anna protested, though she knew just what Helga meant.

"I have no imagination," Helga retorted proudly. "I think that's one reason William fell in love with me. I gather that he grew up with more of that around him than he could tolerate. To put it kindly."

Anna laughed. "We all have our old family foibles, don't we?"

"And the Kennellys appear to have more than most. Another thing that gives me the willies is the family room. Imagine having your own little shrine . . ."

Anna didn't answer. They had, while talking, left the house, and crossed the back terrace. She was remembering when the stone paving of the old courtyard had been pulled up, and grass laid, and the yews planted, under her father's direction.

They were only a few steps into the meadows when Helga stopped, sighed. "Oh, this is silly, Anna. Why are we going to look for William? This is his home. He can surely find his way back. And I don't know that he went down to the river."

"You seemed rather anxious," Anna said dryly, wondering what would come next.

Helga dimpled. "Never mind. We'll let William take care of himself. He always has until now. I suspect he wouldn't appreciate my tracking him down with you."

Anna shrugged. "Whatever you say." She turned back toward the house.

It rose above her, a huge gray stone monolith. High up, at the third story, there were great smudges of black, smoke stains from the fire there had been many years before she was born. The scrolled and decorated balconies at each floor were linked by steel ladders. She remembered when she and Garan and Neil had climbed them like monkeys.

Now Helga touched her arm. "Tell me, Anna. Are you seriously interested in that Martin Milton boy?"

Anna repressed her impatience. It was the second time that day that her relationship with Martin Milton had been brought up. She considered it to be no one's business but her own, and she saw no reason why first Jennings, and then Helga, should make a point of questioning her about it.

But she asked, "Is that the real reason why you led me out here? Was looking for William just a pretense, Helga?"

Helga blushed to the roots of her silvery pompadour.

She stammered, "Well . . . no . . . of course not. Whatever would make you think . . ."

Anna waited. Since she resented this prying she wouldn't make it any easier.

Helga said, "But I *did* wonder."

"Why did you?"

"It's natural enough to wonder when a twenty-two-year old-girl dates a man, isn't it?"

"It may be," Anna agreed gently. "But I'll admit to you that I find your curiosity rather annoying."

"I'm sorry, Anna. I suppose it does seem very . . . very forward of me. I realize that we aren't very good friends, and that we hardly know each other."

Anna didn't reply. They were surely not friends, and though they were related by marriage, they had nothing in common. Even William, related by blood, was no more than an acquaintance. Anna had seen him for several brief weekends during her childhood. She had met Helga one Christmas, so long before that she barely knew exactly when it was, but she remembered that Davis, now eighteen, was quite awful as a little boy.

Helga said quietly, "Do you resent our being here, Anna? Would you prefer us to leave?"

"Why should I?" Anna said quickly. "You and William, and Davis have an absolute right to be here. A right, Helga. This remains William's home, you know. He is a Kennelly."

Helga groaned. "Must you? I've lived with that ever since our marriage. Every day, sometimes twice a day, for the last twenty years, William has reminded me that he is a Kennelly. Well, I'm a Harding. I couldn't care less about my family or his either. I tell you, Anna, it can be extremely annoying to have family names thrown in your face as the excuse for, and glorification for everything. I consider that the person is not a name, but a human being. And I wish William would realize that, too. Though I expect it's hopeless."

"It sounds vaguely familiar to me as a Kennelly

310

failing." Anna grinned. "And I couldn't agree with you more."

"But you haven't answered me," Helga told her. "I wish you'd say that you want us to leave Emerald Station, Anna."

Taken aback, Anna could only stare.

Helga went on. "I know this will sound very ungrateful to you and the rest of the family, but I don't mean it to be. It's just that I'm accustomed to being mistress in my own house. And it's what I like. Enjoy. Want. But William simply won't listen to me."

"Then you've told him you want to go home?"

Helga laughed bitterly. "You can be certain that I have. We were supposed to be here for just a week or so. When I remind William of that, he ignores me. And Davis sides with him. He loves it here. And he's fascinated by everything—even the family room. Though I can't see why." Helga's voice became wistful. "If you only know how beautiful our Maine house is. We have everything we need, and laughter, and music, and parties. We have gay times, I assure you."

"This is a difficult period for Emerald Station," Anna said. "Since my mother died, we've all been rather quiet, you know."

"Since your mother died, and before," Helga said. "It's always been like that here. I know. I can tell. It's as if you're all afraid to breathe. I must say it's an unpleasant feeling to live with."

"Afraid to breathe?" Anna repeated. "Whatever do you mean?"

Helga shrugged her plump shoulders. "If you don't know, then you don't."

Anna didn't answer. She walked toward the house, Helga trotting beside her. What Anna wouldn't acknowledge in words, she acknowledged in her heart.

Helga, in some deep quite way, had sensed something that was real. There was an oddness about Emerald Station that couldn't be denied. One could ignore it, but one lived with it regardless. Anna knew that it had always been that way. Her father had never been affected by it, she was quite certain, but her mother had been. So had all the others. Jennings, with his travels and returns. Garan and Neil. William. Dot, so long with the family that she was almost a member, was touched by it. Was that what had kept away her Uncle George, the one she had never seen, who had taken vows of silence, and written but not returned even for her mother's funeral?

Helga, the outsider, could see it clearly, feel it. But Anna would not admit that to her, nor to anyone else. She considered herself an extremely up-to-date, modern young woman of the forties. She refused to allow herself the weakness of deep dark feelings, or questions about the past. She didn't believe in intuition, nor in haunted houses. Yet she knew there was an oddness about Emerald Station, the lichen-covered walls topped with shards of green glass, the stillness of the empty valley.

"And the thing is," Helga said quietly, "Jennings isn't the only one. There's Tanya and Julia ... they seem to feel that we're interlopers, too."

"They shouldn't. I hope they've not been rude to you, Helga."

"Rude? No. Not rude. But if I should mention to Dot that Davis does like an occasional change from roast beef to something more ... more continental, why, Julia and Tanya stare at me as if I've uttered an obscenity."

Anna chuckled. "How did Dot look at you?"

"As if I'd just lost my mind."

"I'm afraid that's because she doesn't know anything more continental than roast beef."

Helga sighed. "Then I could do it myself, you know. Though my servants in the Maine house ..."

Anna cut in, promising, "I'll speak to Dot."

"Oh, it's not her. She's just the housekeeper. I know how to deal with the likes of her all right. But your two sisters-in-law ..."

"Oh, well, Helga, you know that Julia's pregnant, and it has made her touchy. And Tanya ... she's touchy by nature, I think."

"I suppose I am making too much of it," Helga conceded. "I wouldn't if William would just listen to me, and . . ."

"I can't do anything about it, Helga," Anna said quickly. "When William goes must be his decision. I've no right to interfere. Or to suggest."

"Well, I do wish your grandfather, or great-grandfather, or whoever it was originally, hadn't had such peculiar and old-fashioned ideas. Even for the time. William ought to have his fair share of the estate given him, and be free to do as he likes."

"That's just as it is now," Anna told her.

"No. Not quite. Because he has no control over the Kennelly fortunes. Your brother Garan does."

"But that makes no difference."

"Not to you," Helga said. "Nor to me. But William seems to feel that he must be here, just for that reason."

"He'd better speak to Garan about it. Though it won't do any good. There's no way to change it, even if Garan were inclined to. And I doubt that he would be. Emerald Station went to Gareth, our grandfather, then finally, to my mother, and then to Garan. While the income from the mines is divided, the rest stands. Emerald Station stands."

"Of course," Helga agreed. She laughed. "I can hardly see the whole house cut up into pieces and carted off by the various Kennellys and Gordons. But still . . ."

Anna said, "I'll try to see that you don't feel so much an outsider, Helga. That's the most I can do."

As they reached the terrace, Helga said timidly, "I hope I haven't annoyed you, Anna."

"Of course not. I'm glad you told me what you feel."

Helga said brightly, "And I want to tell you, I do like your young man. That Martin Milton, I mean. He seems very clever."

"He's a good attorney," Anna said briefly.

"Another attorney." Helga laughed. "We have a plethora of them, don't we? Old Brooke, and Garan, too. And now Martin Milton. And William wants Davis to go into the law as well. At least you should be sensibly advised in all things."

Anna didn't answer.

"Where do you go?" Helga asked. "I mean when you go out with him. There's not much to do in Bellingham."

"Not much at all." Anna grinned. "There's the Old Angler's Inn, and a couple of other bars. We split our time between them. Once in a while we go to New York to see a show."

"It sounds like fun," Helga said. "Maybe I could talk William into something like that."

"Maybe you could," Anna agreed, without much interest.

William and Davis stood on the terrace together.

Helga gave a small embarrassed giggle when she saw them. "There William is now. He must have been in the house all the time."

"Yes," Anna agreed absently, her eyes on the father and son.

They stood shoulder to shoulder. Both tall, though Davis was slender and William was extremely portly.

William was speaking, gesturing. Davis, his dark head inclined, listened, an oddly avid expression on his lean face.

Anna wondered what William was saying.

Chapter 33

Martin Milton was twenty-five years old, a big man, his body already verging on fat. He had crinkly blond hair that had begun to recede from his high forehead, blue eyes, and a cupid's bow of a mouth. He sat in the red velvet chair, and smiled at Anna, while he nodded attentively at Garan.

Garan was saying, "I was in Normandy, and that was plenty. I think this country has done enough for Europe. Maybe too much already. It's time we brought our boys back home, and forgot about those damn people. We've got a right to live, too."

His dark brows pulled down over his hazel eyes in a Kennelly frown, Anna thought, watching. He could have stepped out of any number of the portraits in the family room.

William said petulantly, "But we have our responsibilities, too, Garan. You act as if we aren't the world's only strong democracy. That gives us obligations."

"I'm tired of obligations," Garan retorted. "I think Truman's all wrong. We were better off when we remembered that we had our two oceans to protect us, and to hell with the rest."

"But it's too late for an isolationist stance now," William protested, his pink, jowly face hardening.

There was a moment of silence. Then Neil asked, "Were you in the service, Martin?"

Martin nodded, ran his hand through his blond hair. "Sure. In Italy."

"That so?" Garan asked. "And what brought you here to Bellingham?"

Martin grinned. "That was part of it. I mean, having been in the Army. I was at State U. before I went in. And I knew Dan Row there. Do you know him? He's the editor of the *News*."

"I know of him," Garan answered. "We're not acquainted, however."

Martin shook his head. "I tell you, this town is really something. I'll admit I don't understand it. Nor expect to. Not unless I spend the rest of my life here, and maybe not then either. The population is maybe six thousand plus whatever's in the bedroom community over in Bellingham Woods, the Stapleton development, you know. I'm not sure what that is. But half the people in town don't know each other. It's wild. Where I come from everybody knew what was cooking in everybody else's pot. And if they didn't, they knew how to find out."

Neil said, "That would hold for Bellingham, too," and grinned widely. "But Emerald Station isn't Bellingham. And we're not interested in the town. We value our own privacy too much."

"But how you can avoid ..."

Garan said coldly, "Well, of course, Neil, and Anna, and I, were sent away to prep schools, and then on to college. Which makes the difference, you know."

"It sure does." Martin drained his glass, looked sideways to Anna.

She reached for her purse, knowing that he was hinting that it was time they were on their way. But she didn't move quickly enough.

"So you met Dan Row in the service," Garan said. "And then?"

For a moment, Martin looked blank. Then he answered, "Oh, you mean about how come I came here to town. Yes, I'd met Dan. And then I was discharged."

"Before V-E Day?" Garan asked quickly.

"Well before then," Martin answered dryly. "I got a steel plate in my leg." He tapped his right thigh. "And I went back, as soon as I could, to State U. with the G.I. Bill helping me. When the war ended, Dan came back, too. We roomed together, saving money between us. We graduated, and he decided to come home. This was as good a place as any for me to hang out my sign. So that's what I did."

"Do you plan on staying here forever?" Neil asked.

"Forever? That's a long time, isn't it? People don't stay anywhere forever. Not any more." He grinned. "But I like the town, and if I can make a living here, then I'll stay on."

"You have enough work to keep you busy?"

"Enough to keep me eating, let's say. I've been lucky. Dan's father tosses some business my way. And . . ."

"You've made friends, of course. Besides Dan Row?" Garan pressed.

Martin said cautiously. "A few. I don't expect anybody to fall all over me, you understand."

Anna listened with amusement. Anybody could tell that Martin was a good lawyer, and would be a better one as he grew older and more experienced. He handled himself well. She hoped that he didn't mind the third degree that Garan and Neil had been putting him through. She had suspected that that was what was coming when Garan suggested that she and Martin have a drink with the family before they went out to dinner. She also suspected that Garan had passed the word around because the whole clan had gathered in the big living room.

Julia, heavy and uncomfortable-looking, was sitting in a straight chair with her legs thrust out before her, and

317

yawning behind her hand. Her straight black hair was pulled up into a knot on the top of her head, and held in place by two diamond pins. Her face was sallow, her eyes gray. She looked her age, which was twenty-five.

Tanya sat flexing her slim, beautiful ankles and looking at Neil sideways, her blue eyes glinting with suppressed laughter. She wore her auburn hair long, loose on her shoulders, which made her look younger than twenty-three.

Jennings puffed his cigar absently, and squinted across the room at Martin.

William and Helga sat side by side on the sofa, each with a stiff little smile, directed, not at Martin, but at their son Davis, who stood at the gray stone fireplace. His shoulders were squared, his dark head bent, and his dark tilted eyes moved slowly from face to face, following the conversation.

He was, Anna thought, a peculiarly intense eighteen-year-old in a family of peculiarly intense people. She wished some times that she could read his mind, know what he felt, believed in, thought.

Garan, asking, "Do you know the Stapletons personally?" caught her attention now.

"Personally?" Martin answered. "Hardly that. Though I know the old man. Tom Stapleton. He's quite a codger."

"Old men are always codgers," Jennings said angrily.

Martin flushed. "I didn't mean that. And besides, he's a great deal older than you are, Mr. Kennelly."

"Three years older to be precise," Jennings retorted. "A meager three years."

Martin did a good job of acting out surprise. "I never dreamed that, sir. I could have sworn you were in your late sixties. And I know him to be seventy-eight. He told me. He's told me several times, in fact."

There was a brief silence, and then Jennings asked coldly, "Did he tell you about the time we had the fight on the road out near Maradine Mansion?"

"Sorry," Martin shrugged. "He didn't mention that." He

318

moved his legs uncomfortably, looked as if he were about to rise.

Anna said quickly, "I think we'd better be on our way now."

"Yes," he said gratefully, getting to his feet.

But Anna had not been quick enough that time either.

Garan stood before her, cocktail shaker in hand. "You'll have one for the road, of course." He refilled her glass without giving her an opportunity to protest.

He went quickly to Martin, did the same.

Martin's sigh was open and obvious. He sat down, his eyes hooded.

Garan took his seat, asked softly, "And what does old Tom Stapleton have to say for himself?"

Martin answered, with a quick glance at Jennings, "Not very much."

And Jennings said softly, "I doubt that. I doubt it very much."

"There's a lot of feeling there," Martin said. "Your family and the Stapletons . . ."

"You got a small dose of it," Anna laughed. She put her head back on the seat, let the warm spring wind blow her curls back from her face. "I'm sorry I let you in for it, Martin."

"Don't be. I didn't mind." He slanted a look at her. "But it does make me curious, you know."

"About what?"

"Why your brothers don't like me. Nor your uncle."

"Oh, now, Martin, you mustn't . . ."

"Hold on. Don't think I take it personally. Because I don't. Not really. They don't like me because we date. If we didn't, I wouldn't even exist as far as they're concerned. Right?"

"I suppose so," she said unwillingly.

"So it's not me. And I doubt that it's just our dating either. After all, you're a big girl. You've a right to have some sort of life of your own. Then what's left?"

She shook her head. "You tell me, since you seem to have worked it all out."

"Not all," he answered. "But some. It has to do with the fact that they identify me with the town. With Stapleton. And with Row."

"I suppose so," she agreed. "But it doesn't matter."

"I know it doesn't. Except in their minds."

She straightened up, peered at him through the blue twilight. "You say it doesn't matter, but there's something in your voice, Martin. Something that intrigues me. You sound doubtful. I've never heard you sound doubtful before."

"Being positive is a lawyer's stock in trade," he answered.

"Maybe that's why Garan always sounds so positive," she said, "though he's never practiced law, except as it pertained to our holdings."

"You're terribly filthy rich, of course," Martin answered. "That may be part of it. Though I must say, Stapleton is pretty rich himself. Though he wasn't always, as he likes to remind me whenever we meet."

"Stapleton," she said thoughtfully. "Do you know that I've never actually spoken to him? Sometimes I can hardly believe that he's alive. It's as if he's a . . . well, a legend."

"You've heard his name mentioned," Martin said.

"But always in . . . lets say in whispers, or in quotation marks. Jennings sometimes. My parents once or twice. I know Dot's talked about him. She told me that his grandson died in the war, and his son Tim has become a pretty heavy drinker. But somehow . . ."

"In what connection did Jennings speak of him? Or your parents?"

"I don't know." She frowned. "Are you cross-examining me?"

"One good turn deserves another, Anna."

"I'm not responsible for what my older brothers ask you," she said more sharply than she intended.

"Of course not. I didn't mean to imply that," Martin said, sliding another sideways glance at her. "I was asking out of idle curiosity. Tom Stapleton speaks of your family occasionally, you know."

"What does he say?"

Martin hesitated, then, "Well, about the wall and the valley. Mostly an old man's mutterings. You can't take it seriously, you know. And he was terribly hurt when his grandson died, and now he's worried about his son."

She smiled faintly. "Martin, let me remind you that my question was, 'What does Tom Stapleton say about us?' "

He laughed openly, "You should have gone into the law yourself, Anna. You'd have done nicely at it."

"Thank you," she answered. "And the question?"

"Why is it so important to you?"

She hesitated. "I don't know why," she said at last.

"It goes back a long way. There was something between your folks and his. I gather it's your grandfather."

"Gareth Kennelly," Anna said.

"Yes. Gareth. And your grandmother. Her name was Nealanna, wasn't it?"

"Yes. It was." Anna paused, then, "But you know, I never knew either of them. They were dead before I was born. They're portraits to me. Portraits that hang in the family room along with the other Kennelly junk. And I have a brooch that I think belonged to my grandmother. Most of my family is like that. Unreal, you see. I had uncles and aunts I never knew. I knew their names, and I know that they lived in Emerald Station. For all I know their ghosts still wander through the place at midnight. But I can't believe they ever existed as flesh and blood. None of them mean anything to me."

"That's how we all feel," Martin said. He looked at his wrist. "We're going to keep Dan waiting."

"Oh? Are we meeting Dan?" She hoped that her voice was steady, that she hadn't revealed the sudden quick beating of her heart.

"Yes. At the Old Anglers Inn. He said he'd make it if he could. And I think he will. You don't mind?"

"Oh, no. That's fine."

"If it hadn't been for him, I wouldn't have met you. Or at least not right away."

She nodded, remembering. She had been in the post office, and started out, her hand tight around a thick packet of letters.

She collided in the doorway with a big bear of a man, and her mail shot away in all directions.

He apologized, bent quickly to help her gather the letters. When they both rose, red-faced and gasping, they collided again.

"It's fate," he said, laughing. "It has to be that. Neither one of us could possibly be so clumsy. And certainly not you."

Dan Row had appeared then, smiling. "It's Anna Gordon, isn't it?" he asked.

She knew him at once, though it was years since she had seen him. That time he had held the door to his father's automobile showroom open while she passed through. She had never forgotten what he looked like. Now she saw the change in him. His eyes were the clear hard blue of a summer sky. His face was lean and tanned. He had a square jaw, and a cleft chin, and a way of bending his head to her that was intriguing.

She said, "You're Dan Row. Welcome home to Bellingham."

"I've been back a couple of months, but thank you," he answered.

"And how are your folks?" she asked, remembering Dylan, his kindness to her, to her mother.

"They're fine." He turned to Martin. "It would seem that you've already met bodily, but let me introduce you. Anna, this is my friend from the war and from school, too. Martin Milton. A very good man to know."

Martin rubbed his blond hair, protested quickly, "That's the kind of introduction that turns a pretty girl off. Was it deliberate?"

Dan Row grinned. "No, Martin. So relax."

Martin said, "Then I'd like to buy you a cup of coffee, Anna. If I may. You'll join us, won't you, Dan?"

322

But Dan had an appointment at the office.

Anna watched him stride away regretfully.

Martin said, "I'm waiting to hear your answer. You'll join me, won't you?"

And she'd laughed, "Yes. Of course. I'll be glad to."

Now Martin asked, "Did you know that Dan's grandfather came from England, too?"

"No," Anna said. "I never knew his grandfather, though I think I saw him once or twice."

"Well, he did. At about the same time as your grandmother. And they were of an age, I understand."

"Is that so?"

"Yes. Dan told me. He also told me that his grandmother, as a girl, worked at Emerald Station." Martin grinned at her as he swerved into the Old Angler parking lot. "He likes talking about you, you know. That's how it happened to come up."

Chapter 34

"Anna," Garan called. "Is that you?"

She waved as Martin pulled out from the porte-cochere, then closed the door gently behind her.

"Anna?" Garan repeated.

She sighed. She didn't want to speak to him now. She wanted to go up to bed, to lie down in darkness and think of Dan Row. Tonight, for the first time, she had admitted to herself what she saw in Martin Milton. She was ashamed of it, but she had faced it at last. He was a friend of Dan's. And through him, she managed occasionally to see Dan. That was Martin's importance to her. Now that she had faced it, she must decide what to do. Should she go on seeing Martin? And thus be unfair to him? Or should she stop seeing him, and risk not seeing Dan either?

Garan appeared in the drawing room doorway, his silhouette long and dark against the dim light behind him. "Are you alone?"

"Yes," she said. "And I'm about to go up."

"I'd like a word with you, if you don't mind."

"Must it be right now? I'm very tired, Garan."

She knew the portentous tone, and she suspected that she knew what he had on his mind. She preferred to delay the discussion.

But he smiled. "You had a big night on the town? In Bellingham? It's hard to believe."

"If it could wait . . ."

"Just a few moments. Julia and I have been waiting up for you."

She dropped her light sweater on the cobbler's bench, and went into the drawing room.

Julia yawned widely. "Thank goodness you're home. If I had to stay up much longer I don't know what I'd do."

"You'd have another drink," Garan said sourly. "You and William. I don't know which of the two of you is worse. And he isn't pregnant."

"He looks as if he might be," Julia laughed. "And don't start in on me about my drinking. You want to talk to Anna. At least that's what you said."

Anna waited.

"This fellow, this Martin Milton," Garan said.

She sighed. "Oh, listen, we don't have to talk about that. Not now. You've already made me feel enough like a fool."

"I?" Garan sank into the easy chair near the fireplace and leaned back, stretching out his long legs. "I? I didn't do anything. I just asked him a few civil questions about his background. And you'll notice that he was evasive enough to leave me with no information at all."

She let her legs drop, and plopped down on the sofa cushions, sprawling comfortably. She thought that the trouble with her brother Garan was his pomposity. He was only four years older than she was, but it might well have been a generation. It was impossible to believe that he had ever been young. She would have blamed it on the war, except that there had been strings pulled, and he had spent the major part of his service well behind the lines.

"You got what you asked for," she said finally. "Or at least as much of Martin's background as you're entitled to."

He said, "You're an extremely wealthy young woman, Anna. You're somebody. You refuse to believe that, of course. I don't know why. I think it's father's influence on you. But just the same, you must think of that now."

"I don't see why. And particularly not why I have to think of it right now when I'm tired and want to go to bed."

Garan raised his eyes to the ceiling in a caricature of disgust. "Anna, honestly. You must understand. You can't be so stupid. If this man is courting you . . ."

"He isn't," she answered sharply.

Julia put in, "Well, you do go out with him, Anna. You have to admit that."

Anna said, "I'll admit nothing." She got to her feet. "And now, if you'll excuse me, I'm going to bed."

Garan's hazel eyes narrowed. He said gruffly, "But I don't excuse you. It's important that you understand. He's not suitable for you. You mustn't get yourself so involved that you are hurt, or cause hurt to him, Anna."

"I'm not any more involved than I intend to be. And I'll thank you to remember that from now on." She went to the door. "I appreciate your brotherly concern, but there's no need for it."

"We never, never, before this, have associated with people from town," Garan said stiffly. "You know that, Anna."

"I wish we did," Julia pouted. "I can stand a friend or two beyond Emerald Station. I hate being cooped up here all the time."

Garan gave her a sour look. "You have your friends. But they needn't be in Bellingham, and they won't be." He turned back to Anna. "And the same should hold for you. You know what Mother would say if she knew. You know perfectly well how she, and Dad, too, would feel."

Anna said tiredly, "But I am my own girl, Garan. I'll decide for myself."

He looked as if he would say more. She didn't give him an opportunity to. She went into the foyer, and caught up her sweater. She climbed the stairway to the second floor, then turned down the corridor to her room.

As she reached her door, she heard a faint click of sound, and paused, wondering what it was. But it didn't come again. She went into her room, yawning and stretching.

The balcony doors were wide open. The room was chilled with spring night air. She closed the doors, covered them with the heavy red damask drapes.

Then she heard a sound again. But that time it came from the sitting room, and called out, "Who's there?"

"It's me. Tanya."

Anna rolled her eyes ceilingward, said, "Yes, Tanya. All right. I'm coming. But what do you want?"

She returned to the sitting room. It had been empty a moment before when she passed through and into her bedroom. Now Tanya had taken a chair near the small hearth, balancing her neat ankles on the fender.

"I was about to go to bed," Anna told her.

"Oh. Well. I'm sorry." Tanya had made sure that her voice carried weighty disappointment at the rebuff. But she didn't move.

"Is something the matter?" Anna asked.

"I don't know." Tanya sighed, turned her auburn head to look at Anna. Her blue eyes were bright, excited. She said, "A funny thing happened to me this evening."

Anna raised her brows.

"I drove in to town. With Neil, you understand. Not alone. I wouldn't have dreamed of going in alone."

"Why not? Are you afraid of the bogey man?" Anna demanded.

"You certainly know why. Or ought to. The way Neil talks ... Why, when we first met, he told me all about Bellingham. And Maradine Mansion. And Emerald Station."

"That doesn't explain why you're afraid to go to town alone, but never mind. Tell me what happened to you," Anna said impatiently.

"I . . . well, Neil said I mustn't mention it. But he's so

327

funny sometimes. I just ... well, the truth is, I want to know what you think. It sort of scared me. I mean, you never do know. And Neil wouldn't explain. So maybe ..."

Anna said, gritting her teeth, "Tanya, what happened in town?"

Tanya stiffened, flung back her auburn hair. She drew a deep noisy breath. "All right, all right. I'll tell you. We drove in. Neil went into Moody's Drug Store. I waited in the car out front, and I could see him inside at the cigarette counter. I saw a man stop at the big lighted window, and peer in at him. He stood there for a few minutes, just staring, and then he turned and stared at the car. Then he came over to me. He bent down, an old man. I didn't know him. But he tipped his hat and said, 'You're a Kennelly, too, aren't you? Though by marriage?' And I told him I was Tanya Kennelly, Mrs. Neil Kennelly, to him and to everyone else. Well, he laughed a little. And then said, 'That's nothing to me. But if I was you I wouldn't stay there. I'd never stay in Emerald Station. Blood tells, you know. The killer Kennellys' blood tells most of all. So you'll have a taste of it before you die. Yes, you will. If you stay in Emerald Station.'"

A shiver touched Anna. Her hands began to tremble. But she said stiffly, "That's ridiculous. No wonder Neil told you not to mention it to anybody. You sound half-mad. Who was the man?"

"Just an old man," Tanya said. "Stooped, but I'll bet he once had been tallish. His hair was thick, white. And there was something so ... so ..."

"What did you say to him?"

"I told him I thought he was crazy, and he laughed, and walked away, leaning on his cane."

"And then?"

"Then nothing. Neil came out, and we drove back here. I told him about it. He became very angry. At me. Though I couldn't see what I'd done. But he was awfully angry, and he told me not to tell anyone. But I wanted to talk to somebody. So I came in here."

"Can you tell me what he looked like?" Anna asked.

"I did tell you. Stooped. White-haired. Old like Uncle Jennings. But thinner, straighter, and meaner."

"Could it have been Mr. Stapleton?"

"How do I know? I've never seen him."

"You probably have, but haven't known him," Anna said absently.

She was thinking of her dinner in town with Martin and Dan. Could old Mr. Stapleton have seen her at the Old Anglers Inn? Had he peered in through the windows from the dark of the street or parking lot, and seen her with the two men, and then wandered off to confront Tanya moments later? Would he have told Anna about blood telling and the killer Kennellys if he had crossed her path?

Tanya asked anxiously, "Do you know what he meant? Do you know why he tried to scare me?"

"*Tried* to scare you?" Anna laughed. "It looks as if he did."

"I can't explain it really, but he gave me chills. I'm still shaky. I can't tell you how relieved I felt when he walked away."

"I can imagine." Anna covered a yawn. "But I don't know what to tell you, Tanya. I'm sure he's harmless enough, just a little touched maybe. Anyhow, why don't you forget it?"

"That's what Neil says. Forget it. But, Anna, if something bad is going to happen, why then, I just don't want to be here."

"Nothing bad is going to happen," Anna assured her. "Except that if I don't get into bed I'm going to keel over."

Tanya got to her feet. "Then you're not worried about it?"

"No," Anna said. "Why should I be?"

Tanya shrugged. "You're as bad as Neil." She went to the door, turned back as if to speak.

But Anna never knew what she was going to say. Before Tanya uttered a word, a terrible explosion rocked the house. The walls seemed to shudder, the floor trembled.

Deafening thunder crashed down on the massive structure and rolled in great roaring echoes through the hallways.

Tanya gasped, "Oh, my God, what's that?" and clung to the door frame as if she could no longer stand up.

Anna, after one frozen moment, raced to the window. She threw back the draperies, and stepped outside.

As the great rolling echoes faded away, she saw a huge tower of flame leap toward the star-lit sky.

"It's the quarry," she said softly. "I'm afraid that something's blown up at the quarry."

By then, there were sounds in the hall.

Neil, ashen-faced and angry, grabbed at Tanya. "What are you doing here? What was that?" he demanded.

She couldn't answer him. Her teeth chattered, and tears spilled from her eyes.

"We'd better go down to the quarry," Anna told him. "And you can stop brow-beating poor Tanya. She had nothing to do with it. She was right here, talking to me."

"Talking to you! And I know about what. And now this! Now . . ."

Garan came running down the steps. "I've told Thomson to call the fire department."

"But you don't know what it is," William said. "It would be a good idea . . ."

"It's a fire," Helga cried. "Anybody can see. . ."

Anna ran down the steps. She had a sudden terrible feeling that she mustn't stand there, listening to these inanities while the fire climbed toward the sky.

The others had caught up with her by the time she reached the garage area.

Garan thrust her aside. "Let me drive. And I think you'd better wait here."

"I'm coming," she said, and climbed in beside him.

William and Neil got into the back.

As Garan got the car moving, Davis appeared in the headlight beams, waving his arms. Garan stopped, allowed him to get in, and then got under way again.

It took what seemed to be a long time to cross the

meadow toward the towering flame that lit both the arch of the sky and the spread of the fields.

Anna, peering forward, saw other car tracks there, tracks that cut into the delicate meadow grass. She whispered, "Garan, do you see them? Someone else has come this way, and not very long ago."

"It seems so," he said. "But I can't think why anyone would do that. And the gates were closed. They were, weren't they?"

"Yes. They were closed when we drove up. Thomson let us in. And I'm sure he locked up after Martin left."

She caught her breath. The fear she had refused to face had surfaced with those words.

Garan asked, "Anna, are you absolutely sure he left?"

"I saw him drive away. I came into the house. Oh, Garan . . ."

He said quickly, "Now wait. We don't know what's going on, do we?"

Davis said, "Listen, there's an old road, isn't there? One that comes in from outside?"

"No," Garan said. "There's no way in except through the gates."

Davis frowned. "But there is. I've been on it myself. Across the Maradine property, from their entrance to the highway . . . anybody could . . ."

"The river is in the way, you know," Garan told him.

"There's a place where you can ford the river," Davis explained.

Garan swore softly. "Then maybe some of the kids from town . . . we'll have to see . . ."

William said, "I hope not, Garan. I really do hope not. The Kennellys can't take any more. We . . ."

"Be quiet," Neil told him. "There's no need to panic. We don't yet know what's happened."

Anna sat forward on the seat, rigid, cold.

The towering flame was close now.

"Slow," Neil said. "We don't know just where it begins, Garan. I haven't been out here for a long while. And neither have you. Watch out for the quarry rim."

Garan nodded, braked suddenly. The headlights picked out tire tracks where the grass was packed down, then more tire tracks that swerved off into the darkness that edged the flame.

Garan opened the door, got out.

Anna followed him.

The others came with them.

Garan held her arm firmly as they went together toward the rim.

The fire had begun to sink. There was a sizzling sound of flame and water joining. Clouds of steam began to boil up.

They peered down into fading red light.

A white car lay on its side, nose pointed toward the quarry depths and covered with water. Flame danced along its hood.

Anna stared, gasped, "It's Martin's. It's Martin's car," and felt Garan's arms close around her.

Chapter 35

Anna turned away from the flower-decked gravesite, from the few, dark-clothed mourners who stood there, heads bowed.

She was conscious of the slanting eyes that watched her as she stumbled alone down the pebbled path toward where she had left her car.

She had not been able to stay at home. She had quarreled briefly but bitterly with Garan about it, crying, "We can't pretend it didn't happen. We can't pretend that it didn't happen *here*."

Garan's hazel eyes had become narrow slits. He shouted, "It's no business of ours. What was he doing, driving over the meadow? It doesn't make sense, and it never will."

"But Martin was my friend. And he died here, on our property, Garan. We do have some responsibility."

The word seemed to set him afire. His face turned red. "Anna, you listen to me. We'll have nothing to do with it. I don't want to hear Martin Milton's name mentioned in this house. Not ever again."

"I'll go to the funeral," she said finally, her voice cold, her words measured. "I'll go, and you can't stop me."

"I won't try to stop you. But I'll say this. You're making a mistake. And if you had any sense, you'd know it. You were there. You saw how it was when the volunteers arrived. You must have guessed what they were thinking when they pulled his body out."

She relived those terrible moments then, while Garan stared at her.

She, the family, had stood helpless, watching, as the pale light receded and then died away, leaving only the stench of burning rubber and paint, hanging like a shroud over the quarry, spreading slowly across the valley.

There were murmurings around her, Jennings' voice, and Davis', and Neil's. But she paid no attention to their words. She clung to Garan, weeping.

At last two fire engines came thundering across the meadows, casting blinking red lights in stunning waves across the scene. Men jumped down from the trucks.

Neil went to meet them, explained quietly.

Within moments, the men swarmed at the quarry rim with winches and chains and ropes. Their hard black hats gleamed with red light, and their uniform buttons flickered pink signals through the shadows.

Anna watched them, impatiently dashing away her tears. She sensed a cold animosity flowing from them toward her, toward the family.

She knew most of the volunteers by sight and name, had known them all her life. Fred Moody, who ran the Old Anglers' Inn, and his cousin John Moody, who owned the town's only drugstore, were both there. The post office head, Henry Carter, was handling the big grappling hooks. Bert Harris hauled out hoses. Yes, she thought, she knew most of these men, but they were strangers to her, and had always been.

Time, which seemed to have stopped at the moment of the explosion, suddenly began again with a rush.

Clanking and banging, the car was hauled up to the quarry rim. Bert Harris and the two Moodys cursed while they ripped away the crushed and broken door, and lifted out Martin Milton's body, crouching over it for a brief examination by flashlight before raising their faces to stare at the family again.

Then Fred Harris rose, came to where Garan and Anna waited.

"It's Martin Milton. He's dead. Was he visiting here?"

Garan started to speak, but Anna whispered, "Yes." She swallowed, cleared her throat. Then, "We were out this evening for dinner. He brought me home. Some time later I heard the explosion. We all ran out here. We ... I recognized his car from what I could see of it. I . . ."

A tall heavy figure appeared suddenly, looming over Fred Harris, thrusting him aside. "I'm Jim Arden." A big finger briefly touched the sheriff's badge pinned to his shirt. "Was Mr. Milton drunk when he left you?"

"Oh, no," she gasped. "Not at all."

"Why did he drive to the quarry?"

"I don't know," she answered, quailing at the strange hard note in his voice, but meeting his intent stare head on.

"Did you have an argument? Fight about something? Did you . . ."

"Oh, no," she told him. "No. Of course not. We'd made plans to meet tomorrow." She closed her eyes then, fighting back a new wave of tears. How could this have happened to Martin? Why had it happened?

Jim Arden grunted, then walked away.

She heard his loud carrying voice as he spoke to the other men. "All right. Let's pack it up and get out of here. It looks like it was just another one of those Kennelly accidents."

She had allowed Garan to lead her back to the house, too upset then to think.

But in the two days that followed, his words had echoed through her mind. *Another one of those Kennelly accidents.* The words terrified her, but she didn't know why. She didn't know what they meant. She didn't understand the peculiar tone of voice in which they had been uttered.

Another one of those Kennelly accidents . . .

They heard nothing more about it at Emerald Station. She waited to be questioned by Jim Arden again, to be called as a witness by the coroner, to be notified when and where Martin was to be buried. But nothing happened. It was as if there had been no terrible explosion, no great leap of flame, that night. It was as if Martin had never died.

She called Dan Row twice at the newspaper office. Each time he was out, so she left her name. He didn't phone her back. Finally, she called again, asked about Martin's funeral. Dan's assistant gave her the details.

That was when her argument with Garan began.

She told him that she was going, said, "You ought to come, too. As head of the family, you owe it to Martin."

"How did you find out about it?" Garan demanded.

"What do you mean?"

"You know exactly what I mean," he told her. "How did you know the funeral would be this afternoon?"

"I called *The News* and asked."

"Dan Row told you."

"One of his assistants told me," she said. And then, suspicious suddenly, "Why do you mention Dan Row now?"

Garan didn't reply.

She asked, "Did he phone me here, Garan?"

Garan shrugged. "He did. I told him you weren't available."

A hot angry flush swept up her throat to the roots of her hair. "You had no right to do that," she said coldly. "What must he think of me? To have heard you say that . . ."

"I only want to protect you," Garan told her. "And as for what he thinks, what difference does that make? He's just the editor of a small town weekly. He's nothing to you, or us, and we're nothing to him. I don't . . ."

"It makes a difference to me," she answered. She already knew how much Dan's opinion mattered to her. She couldn't bear to think that he might consider her cruel, heartless, that he might think Martin's meaningless death didn't touch her. Aloud, she said, "And I think you should go with me, Garan."

"No. And you shouldn't go either."

"I will go," she had answered.

So she had stood alone through the brief ceremony, and followed the short line of cars to the cemetery.

The Harrises were there, and the Moodys, and standing with them was old Tom Stapleton. It was seeing him that reminded her of what Tanya had said just before Martin's accident.

Tanya ... uneasy ... her blue eyes evasive. The old man had peered through the drugstore window at Neil, and then come to the car and spoken to Tanya. He had had a mean grin, she'd said, saying something about the killer Kennellys, something about blood that tells. Tanya had been frightened.

And now, oddly, seeing the old man look at her, Anna was frightened, too. She shifted her eyes to where Dan stood with his parents, and knew, when she stumbled away to her car, that he had seen her go.

She opened the door, slid behind the wheel.

Dan said, "Wait, Anna."

She looked up at him, tears burning in her eyes. She said, "I'm so sorry, Dan. I don't know what else to say."

"I know you're sorry." He paused. Then, "Thank you for coming."

She blurted, "What? How can you say that? Martin and I were friends, Dan. How can you . . ."

He touched her shoulder. "I would have understood if you felt that you couldn't do it, Anna. And when you refused to talk to me. . ."

"That was my brother's doing," she said bitterly. "Garan. He never even told me that you had phoned."

Dan said quietly, "Look, we can't stand here like this. Will you do me a favor? Will you drive in to town and wait for me at the Old Anglers' Inn?"

She nodded, started the car.

He said, "I'll drive my folks home first. But it'll be just a few minutes."

"I'll be there," she told him.

As she drove off, she saw him rejoin the group at the grave. She saw him bend his head to speak to his father.

She stayed in the car for a little while, powdering her nose, refreshing her lipstick, before she went into the Old Anglers'.

Fred Moody was already there. He had taken off his blue serge jacket, and put on a light blue one. He came toward her. "I saw you at the funeral, Miss Kennelly."

She said curtly, "Miss Gordon, as you know perfectly well."

A wave of red swept up his square face. His eyes glittered. He answered, "I do beg your pardon, Miss Gordon. It just slipped my mind."

Something in his hard intent stare reminded her of the night Martin died . . . the way he, the others, had looked at her then . . . Jim Arden saying, "Another Kennelly accident . . ."

She turned away from Fred Moody, twisting her black gloves in nervous fingers. It couldn't have slipped his mind that she was a Gordon. He'd known her, her parents before her, for years. He was the third generation owner of the Anglers', which once, according to what she had been told by Martin, had been a rather disreputable place. Tears came to her eyes with that thought. Martin had told her a great many things about Bellingham that she had never known before.

She was so sunk in her thoughts that she didn't see Dan approach her. He said suddenly, "Anna? Shall we go in?"

She nodded, swallowed hard, and followed him into the small coffee shop. It was shaded against the bright sun, and blanketed with huge potted plants that seemed to writhe against the walls.

They sat side by side on a small banquette, and Dan, after a few words of greeting to Fred Moody, ordered coffee. After they had been served, Fred Moody lingered, watching them from across the room.

Dan offered her a cigarette, and when she refused it, lit

338

one for himself. At last he said, "I'm sorry you had to come by yourself, Anna."

"That doesn't matter."

"I decided not to notify the Maradines. He's so old now, and very frail, and she's not in good health either."

"Yes," Anna answered. "That's why I didn't call them about it. Though I know Brooke was fond of Martin." She turned sideways to look into Dan's rugged face, his clear blue eyes. "What do you think happened, Dan? How could it have happened?"

He was quiet for a moment. Then he said, "That's what I was going to ask you, Anna."

"But I don't know," she said. "I don't understand it. It's just . . . just impossible. But it happened."

Another Kennelly accident . . . The words flickered through her mind for an instant. Then she forgot them. She had been over it so many times since that terrible night. She remembered Martin saying, "It's been a good evening, Anna," when she thanked him. She remembered him saying, "Let's get together tomorrow. I'll pick you up at seven. Is that okay?" and she had agreed. He had been starting off down the driveway when she went inside. There had been that intensely annoying conversation with Garan and Julia. When she had finally gone up to her room, Tanya had come in to mutter uneasily about Tom Stapleton's odd behavior. She was still with Anna when the explosion came.

Anna had tried, she didn't know how many times, to calculate how long she had been in the house before she saw the towering flame from her balcony window. But she hadn't been able to do it. She knew only that some time had passed. Too much time had passed, considering that she had seen Martin's car roll away down the driveway toward the gates. She decided that he must have stopped for some reason. Stopped in the dark, and waited. But what could he have been waiting for? Why would he have done that?

"How was he when he dropped you off?" Dan asked her now.

She remembered that Jim Arden had asked almost the same question. She said, "Why, you know yourself. You saw him only a little while before, Dan."

"You went straight home then?"

"Yes. Of course."

"He didn't have a nightcap on the way? You didn't ask him in?"

"No, It was late. And . . ." she hesitated, then went on bitterly, "I didn't ask him in because when he picked me up earlier, the family had gathered to give him a rather obvious and ridiculous looking over. I felt very embarrassed about it."

Dan nodded thoughtfully, dragged hard on his cigarette. Blue plumes of smoke filtered between his lips as he said, "They've called it an accident, you know."

"I assumed that." She shivered. *Another Kennelly accident* . . . "It *has* to be that, Dan. I just don't see how it could be anything else."

"I know," Dan agreed. "And it's so weird, really. He went through so much in the war. That leg wound of his was a real mess. And the action he saw. It was luck that he survived. To come here, because of me, and to die that way." Dan drew a deep breath. "He didn't have any family, you know. That's why I handled it all. I knew he'd have wanted me to."

She said wretchedly, "If only he hadn't met me, Dan."

Dan turned, stared at her, his blue eyes bright and hard, "Why do you say that?" he demanded.

Sudden fright touched her. She didn't understand its source. She knew only that she felt as if he had lunged at her, unexpectedly, dangerously. She found that she had pulled away from him, quickly, bodily, withdrawn, as if she had expected a blow.

He said, "Hold it, Anna," and put a big warm hand over hers. "I didn't mean to scare you."

She waited, looking at him, holding herself very still, though she couldn't control the quick hard beating of her heart.

"I wasn't accusing you of anything," he went on. "I just wondered what you meant."

She knew that it must be more than that. There had been something definite in his mind. There had been a depth of meaning in his quick question. But she said, explaining, "Dan, if Martin had never met me, he'd never have been at Emerald Station." She paused, swallowed. Then, "And he'd never have driven into the quarry either."

"That's the thing," Dan said. "I just don't see how he could have done it. How could he have gotten confused on the drive, lost his way."

"It's more impossible than you realize. Because you don't know Emerald Station. The driveway goes in a circle from the gates to the house and then back to the gates. There is a short gravel road that goes around the side of the house at the north end. It leads into the garage area, past the terrace and swimming pool. That road ends there. He went that far, just about to the garages, and then pulled off, into the meadow. We could see his tire tracks in the grass. There was a place near the quarry edge where it was packed down, as if he had stopped there for a while, and then there were more tracks ... swerving off ... off into space."

"Could he have gotten on the garage road by mistake, do you suppose?"

"The driveway is clearly marked with painted white stones. And he'd been in and out quite a few times before, both by day and night. So ..."

"Then you think he went that way deliberately. Is that what you're saying?"

"I just don't see how ..."

Dan asked, "Anna, you told me that Martin had met your family earlier. Could anyone have stopped him, talked to him, as he was driving away?"

She closed her eyes. That was the question she had dreaded, had known would come. It was the question she had been asking herself ever since the night Martin died.

Chapter 36

Martin would have stopped, talked to anyone who hailed him outside the doors of Emerald Station.

But who could have?

Garan and Julia had been waiting up for her. She had spoken to them for a few minutes in the drawing room. That would have been while Martin was driving away.

Tanya had come into her room, settled near the hearth, within moments, it seemed, after Anna herself had entered her bedroom.

But what about Jennings? William? Neil? Davis? Where had they been as Martin pulled away from the house? She didn't know. She couldn't imagine.

She tried to picture how they had been dressed when they gathered in the hallway after the explosion. But she couldn't remember. She tried to picture which direction each one had come from, but it was the same. She had been too frightened then to be observant enough to impress anything on her mind.

Dan was asking in a low hard voice, "Anna?"

She opened her eyes. She said steadily, "Martin had met the whole family, as I told you. He had briefly seen some,

342

like my uncle, and my sisters-in-law before. But surely you've no reason to imply . . ."

"I'm implying nothing, Anna. I'm just asking you about the possibilities."

"Yes," she agreed dully.

"And the answer to my question is also 'yes,' isn't it?" He rubbed his cigarette out in the brown clay ashtray.

"It could have been an accident, Dan," she said at last, trying to convince herself as well as him, knowing that it was vitally important that she believe it, and he believe it, too. "Just because we can't explain how it happened surely doesn't mean that it wasn't an accident. You do see that, don't you?"

He said gently, "Yes, of course I do see. But I'm afraid it's just not so simple. An accident can be explained, understood. And this . . ." He shook his head. "I wish I could accept it, Anna."

"But why? Why can't it be an accident?" She knew the answer. She could hear those words spoken at the quarry edge. *Another Kennelly accident*. What did it mean? Blood tells, Tanya had told her. Old Tom Stapleton had muttered at her from the dark. Killer's blood, he had said.

She felt as if her heart were shrivelling within her. Did Dan believe that she must be responsible? Did he think that she had somehow maneuvered Martin's murder? For if it were not accident, then it must be murder.

Dan said gently, "You were fond of him, weren't you, Anna?"

She nodded. Then, "Yes. You know that. As a friend."

"No really serious romantic . . ." Dan's voice trailed away, as if he had found that he couldn't put the question into words.

She said hardily, "Dan, you saw us together often enough. What do you think?'

"He liked you. He wasn't ready to allow himself any more than that just yet."

"Exactly," she agreed.

"And on your side?"

"It was the same with me. I'm not ready to be serious about anyone either."

She was remembering now that Jennings had questioned her about Martin. And not only Jennings. Tanya and Helga, too. Why had they all been so concerned about these casual meetings?

Dan was saying, "Then this much we know. He was happy in his life, in his work, and with his few friends. So he had no reason to deliberately do what he seems to have done."

She gasped, "But surely you didn't think . . ."

That had never occurred to her. That Martin might have committed suicide was as impossible to believe as it was impossible to believe that he had died by accident.

"I'm eliminating all possibilities as they occur to me, Anna. And that was the first one."

"But I've told you . . ."

"Yes. He didn't drive out that way on purpose. And he couldn't have done it by mistake, as you say. And I'm sure you're right. So . . ."

She stared at him. She had reached the point at which he now was earlier. She waited for him to put it into words.

Instead he said, "I'm sorry, Anna."

"No," she said, denying him, and herself. "No. We must be wrong. It can't be true."

Fred Moody appeared beside the table, holding a coffeepot. "More?" he asked.

Dan nodded absently.

Fred Moody filled the two cups, lingered to say, "Didn't have a chance to talk to you at the funeral. It's a shame about Martin."

Dan raised his dark head. "Yes."

"I was out at Emerald Station that night. I helped get him out of the car. A bad mess, it was."

Dan nodded.

"But how are you these days, Dan?"

"Fine. And you?"

Fred Moody grinned. "Me? I'm fine. I'm always fine.

Though I wish now I hadn't gone out to Emerald Station that night. First time it was for me, and last." He looked hard at Anna. "My grandmother, she was a seamstress when times were bad. She'd never go out to Emerald Station. She did her work for them, for the Kennellys, in the Gordon house right here in town. She always told us to stay clear of that place. And I will. From now on." Now he turned his attention to Dan. "But you ought to look after your health, you know."

Dan grinned. "I've never been sick a day in my life."

"Well, you could be. You never know when it'll hit you," Fred answered. "I mean, you never know what'll happen. Like to your friend Martin, for instance."

Dan's grin froze on his mouth. He said through it, "Thanks for the coffee, Fred. If I want any more, I'll ask for it."

Fred shrugged and walked away, looking back twice over his shoulder.

"I think I'd like to leave," Anna whispered.

"Not yet," Dan told her. "Drink your coffee then we'll go. I should have seen that coming, but I didn't. And we're not going to back down before the likes of Fred Moody, are we?"

"I do," she said. "I would."

"Your family wouldn't approve of that, Anna. They've lived here three generations now without ever backing down."

"I'm not a family," Anna said hotly. "I'm me. I'm Anna Gordon I want to be known for myself, considered for myself. I'm not a name, and a set of parents and grandparents. I'm a person."

"Yes," he said, laughing softly. "You're a person all right. But you're a product of a family, too."

She gulped her coffee quickly, thrust the cup aside. She folded her napkin, then said, "Going back to what you were saying before Fred presented himself . . . I said that what you . . . you implied can't be true. And I really don't see how it can be. I see no reason for it. I see no way it could have been done either."

"Not yet, you don't. But maybe you will some day, Anna."

"What do you mean?"

He pushed back the table, left some change on the cloth, then looked down at her. "I mean that I'm going to find out what happened to Martin. I have to know why, after all he went through, he ended up dying at Emerald Station."

It was impulse that led her to stop at Maradine Mansion.

She was on the way home, limp with reaction to the funeral, and the long talk she had had with Dan. She didn't want to face Garan's hard-eyed disapproval, nor Jennings' questions.

She turned into the big estate, rolled under the huge old oaks, and parked before the tall white columns.

She sat in the car, gathering herself for a moment. Sitting there, looking around, she noticed for the first time that the big old house needed a fresh coat of paint, the windows required washing. The grounds looked oddly untended and unloved. The Maradines were old, of course. But she knew that they still had pride of house and family. It was the war that had done it. Through those long years, help had been hard to come by. The available young men had gone either into the service or into the factories. The older ones couldn't manage the heavy labor involved. Even now, several years later, it was still difficult to run so large an estate. It was completely different at Emerald Station. The family had always brought their people in from elsewhere, from Boston or New York. They didn't rely on Bellingham to supply the labor needed. But the Maradines didn't want to do that, though they could afford it as well as the Gordons could. And perhaps, now that they were older, the Maradines just didn't care any more.

She got out of the car, went up the three white steps, and touched the dull brass knocker.

She waited, tapping her feet impatiently, until the door

opened. Emily Harris, the middle-aged maid, stood there, staring at her in open disapproval.

"I'd like to see my uncle and aunt," Anna said. "If it's convenient."

"They're not well," Emily answered. "You'd best come back some other time." The door began to swing shut.

Anna said coolly, "Would you please ask them? Since I'm already here."

And from past Emily's rigid shoulders, she heard, "Emily, who is it? Did I hear Anna's voice?"

"Yes," she called. "Yes, it's me, Uncle Brooke."

Emily frowned, muttered. She jerked the door back, her face stony. "In the living room then. If you insist."

Anna ignored her, started down the long hall.

Brooke came hobbling to meet her, leaning on the heavy black stick he had used for so many years. It was then, suddenly, that Anna realized she didn't know exactly how Brooke had come by his wooden leg, nor when. She had taken that, along with so much else, for granted. Now, in this time of questioning, she found she could take nothing for granted.

"My dear," Brooke said. "I'm so glad to see you." His wrinkled face shadowed for a moment. "You're on the way back from the funeral, I assume."

"Yes, I am," she said.

"Then come in. We'll talk." He turned to Emily, who stood waiting. "Will you tell my wife that Anna is here?"

"I expect she's napping," Emily said tartly.

"I think not," Brooke answered. He smiled at Anna, led her into the living room, and sank into a big plush chair, adjusting his bad leg. "Now. How about some sherry?"

"No, thanks. I just had coffee with Dan Row."

"Dan. A fine boy. He's made something special of himself, too. Editing the paper. A good job for him, I should imagine."

"Yes," she agreed.

"Martin's friend," Brooke said gently. "I understand Dan handled all of it."

"Martin had no family. There was just Dan." She

347

paused. Then she said, "He didn't phone you about it because he thought that . . ." She let the words fade. It didn't seem polite to speak of Brooke's age, his failing health.

Brooke said, "Yes, of course. I understand. He didn't want us to feel obliged to attend. But I knew about it anyway. Emily was brimming with details, you know." He raised his head stiffly. "Is that Lolly coming now?"

There was the sound of footsteps, footsteps scurrying away down the hall.

Brooke grinned at Anna. "Emily. She hopes for a morsel or two, I suppose. I imagine I sent her away with a bee in her bonnet that will hold her for a while." His grin faded from his thin face. "I would liked to have gone with you, Anna. I felt that I should. But Lolly's not too well, and I didn't think it would be good for her. But if I went, then she would, too."

"It's just as well you stayed home," she said gently. Then, "I spoke to Dan afterwards. He seems to feel that . . . that Martin didn't die by accident."

Brooke bent his head, silently regarded his black stick. His gnarled hands trembled on his knees.

She went on, "He thinks Martin was murdered, Uncle Brooke."

"The town," he said.

She asked, "What is it about us that they hate, Uncle Brooke? What have we done?"

He raised his white head. He said gently, "No, child. No one hates you."

"That night . . . when Martin died . . . Jim Arden said, 'It just another Kennelly accident.' His tone was so ugly, ironic."

Brooke sighed.

She whispered, "All these years, I've known something . . . something odd, and never faced it. The way the people in town look at me, talk to me. . . ."

Brooke folded his gnarled hands around his cane. He said through bloodless lips, "That has nothing to do with the present, Anna."

"And Tom Stapleton said something to Tanya about the killer Kennellys ... about how blood tells ..."

Brooke cut in, "Martin's death was a sad accident. Dan must be wrong."

"He may be. And I hope so," she answered, hearing the doubt in her own voice, knowing that though he ignored it, he heard it, too.

"Such a long time ago," he said quietly. "Why, it's amazing to realize how long it is. The days move so slowly, one by one. The changes are so small. Then quite suddenly, it's gone. Time is behind you. Your strength is behind you, your memory. It's all gone, and you don't know where it went. Nor how it happened."

She sighed impatiently, thinking of Jennings. This was how he would go on when he was asked a direct question. Or when he wanted to speak of something but didn't dare mention it directly. He would meander, and eventually he would get to the point. If he wanted to. But only if he wanted to. Well, she told herself. It didn't matter. She loved Jennings, and she loved Brooke. And if it took them both time to tell her what they wanted to, then she would take the time to listen until they did.

But Brooke's voice changed. The musing was going from it. He said sharply, "No, no, it's impossible. It can't be happening again. I refuse to believe it. I'll speak to Dan myself. I'll tell him. He's wrong. Poor Martin was confused. He was somehow lost in the dark. He probably never even knew the quarry was there." His words came to an abrupt stop.

Lolly walked into the room, leaning on two steel braces. She wore a light blue gown that was just a few inches from the floor. White lace framed her face.

Brooke rose, went to meet her. "Come, dear, sit down on a straight chair."

She ignored him, asked, "What are you talking about, Anna?"

Anna said, "Why, about Martin. The funeral ..."

"We mustn't," Lolly returned. "We've had enough of it. No more, I say. No more. I'll not have it." She turned her

349

pale face to Brooke. "Do you understand me, Brooke? I won't have it. Not for you. Not for me. I shall not go through it all again. I'm old now. I'm tired. I won't have it."

"We'll just have a bit of sherry," he said soothingly. "That's what we'll have. Now do sit down and smile, and stop dithering, and ask Anna how she's been and what she plans for the summer."

Lolly took the chair he offered her, and set aside the steel crutches. She forced a smile. "How are you, Anna?"

"I'm fine," Anna said quickly.

Brooke, she saw, had started for the cabinet but paused midway of the room to look up at the portrait that hung above the mantel. A young girl smiled gently down at him. A young girl with a heart-shaped face, and beautiful blonde hair parted at the center and drawn into curls at the nape of her neck. It was, Anna knew, Brooke's sister, who had died when he was hardly more than a boy. Now he stiffly turned away, went on to the cabinet, and took out a bottle.

"Now, tell me," Lolly was saying, "what *are* your plans for the summer?"

"I have no plans. I'll just be at home."

"You'll be at Emerald Station?" Lolly asked.

Brooke came with a small tray, offering tiny glasses of sherry that had been filled only with a sip or two.

Anna drank hers quickly, and rose to go. She saw the relief in his face, in Lolly's eyes.

As she left, she heard Lolly sob, "I'm too old, and so are you. I'm afraid. I can't go through it all again."

Emily was at the front door, her head cocked, listening. "I knew you'd upset them," she said angrily, and pulled the door open to usher Anna out, and then slam it hard behind her.

Chapter 37

She guided the car along the curves that led to Emerald Station, wishing that she had not stopped to see Brooke and Lolly. She knew that she had unwittingly managed to upset them both, and to no purpose. She knew no more now than when she had been so grudgingly admitted by Emily.

Then she told herself thoughtfully that her assessment wasn't quite correct. She did know a bit more, and that bit only served to increase her fear.

Lolly had sobbed, "I'm too old. I'm afraid. I can't go through it again." And Brooke, far from answering Anna's questions about the past, had not so skillfully avoided them, and then hurried her out.

Was it concern for Lolly that had made him do that? Or was it refusal to explain to Anna what she must know? And why was Lolly suddenly afraid?

The gray stone walls loomed up, topped with glittering shards of green glass. Green for Emerald Station. She wondered suddenly whose fancy it had been to add that touch, she wondered why he considered that those heavy walls must have such added security.

The gates were closed. She was quite certain they were locked now. She stopped, tapped her horn once, very gently.

Thomson came out of the cottage. She remembered when it was new, bare, and Henry had sat rocking on the porch. Now it was clogged with ivy and honeysuckle and hard to see against the green of the bushes that surrounded it.

Thomson swung the gate back, then closed it, and locked it again, once she had driven through. She stopped, and he came to the car, bent to the window.

He was middle-aged, bald, with a hard and weathered face, and a tall, thin, hard body. He had come to work at Emerald Station several years before as caretaker, gardener, handyman and groom. He did his work well, kept to himself, and though she had seen him some time every day since his arrival, she knew nothing about him.

Now she asked, "Thomson, the night that Mr. Milton had the accident, did you stay out here and wait for him to drive back?"

He shook his bald head. "No, Miss Anna. I thought he might visit a while. So I went inside, knowing I'd hear him honk for me when he was ready to leave."

"Then you didn't notice his lights coming back down the driveway?"

"No, I didn't see anything, nor did anything. Not until the car hit rock bottom and blew. And that's just what I told them, too."

"Told who?" she asked.

"That sheriff. Arden. He's asked me a couple of times. And some men in town. I don't hold with nosy questions, nor with answering them either. I told them what I knew, and that's nothing. Which is what I said."

She thanked him, drove on, up the curving driveway, under the porte-cochere and back around the house to the garage, the same path Martin had taken the night he died.

As she passed under the rim of the terrace, she saw Davis. He was standing on the wall, straight as an arrow, wearing black trousers and a long-sleeved black sweat shirt. Something about his stance, the lift of his dark head impressed her. Even after she had passed him by, pulled in to the garage, she saw him in her mind.

It was odd how little he resembled William and Helga, she thought, starting back to the house. He seemed more a Kennelly than his father. He looked like Gareth, who had brought his English bride to Emerald Station so long before. There was that same high hard look about the eyes, the same lean jaw. Though he was just eighteen and still had some of the unfinished quality of youth about him she was sure that when he was older, he would seem more Gareth's own grandson than either of his direct descendants did.

She climbed to the terrace and found him still standing there. He appeared to be so absorbed that he didn't notice her approach.

His slightly tilted brown eyes were focused into the distance. She turned, wondering what it was that he found so interesting. She saw the meadows that rolled off toward the quarry, and toward the river with its small bridge that led to the Maradine property. She saw the ring of distant hills blue with afternoon haze. She looked back at him. As she watched, he turned his head slowly. It struck her then that he was like a king surveying his domain. Or like a general studying the battlefield before a big campaign. She smiled to herself. Both were fanciful thoughts. Davis, if he could read her mind, would laugh at her, and she wouldn't blame him.

Now, suddenly, he seemed to start as he became aware of her.

She saw the quick closing of his face, as if a curtain had been drawn across it.

She said quickly, "I'm sorry, Davis. I didn't mean to startle you. I was on my way into the house."

He jumped lightly from the wall, landed beside her without a sound. "Was it bad, Anna?"

She stared at him.

"The funeral, I mean. I've never been to one. The folks were talking about it. Uncle Garan seemed to think it

353

would be terrible, and that you shouldn't have gone. Dad agreed. They've been in there all afternoon checking their watches and wringing their hands."

She said lightly, "They needn't have worried."

He sat on the wall. "Well, I guess you're pretty upset."

"Martin was a good friend," she said.

"Friend?" Davis peered at her. "That's not what I heard. They were saying you were going to marry him for sure. Then there'd be a Milton, a bunch of them, in Emerald Station eventually."

"They were mistaken," she said.

"Then you're not all that upset, I suppose."

"Not in the way they meant anyway. But it's not easy to lose a friend."

He was silent for a moment. Then, "You know, Anna, I like it here. I belong here. I'm a Kennelly, too."

"Why, of course you are," she agreed.

"I don't just mean by name," he said shyly. "I mean all the way. I can feel it, sense it. I belong with the paintings in the family room. I'm them, and they're me. And when I look around all I can think of is what could be done with the old place."

"I'm sure Garan would be glad to have your ideas," she said.

"Maybe. If we get to stay. Mother wants to go back to the Maine house the way we figured we would at first."

"But. . . ?"

"Dad doesn't want to go. And neither do I."

"That's interesting. I would have thought you'd find it boring here, Davis."

"Boring? It's a fascinating place." He grinned boyishly. "I guess, maybe, you don't think so. You take it for granted in the same way I take the Maine house for granted. And if you went there you'd find it more interesting than here. But for me . . . well, this is where history is."

"History, Davis? I don't know what you mean."

"I know," he said. "And that's so funny. Because you're part of it. I'm talking about *our* history. The Kennellys."

She smiled at him. "Oh, I see. Well, I suppose we do have a history, just as every other family does. But I never really thought of it that way."

"You should." He paused. "But maybe it's different for you. You're a Gordon."

"Yes," she grinned. "I'm a Gordon all right." She thought of her father. His gray eyes, and sweet sudden smile. She was a Gordon, though she mightn't look like one.

"Then that's what it is." Davis bent his dark head. "I wish I could get Uncle Jennings to talk about it. He must know it all. He's the oldest. He's sure to remember everything about the olden days."

"I'm sure all you need do is ask him," she said.

"I have, of course. But he always goes off into his travels. Chicago, all those places. I don't care about that. All I care about is Emerald Station. And he hardly tells me about that, except some mutterings about his father. Great-grandfather Neil, I guess that is."

She nodded.

"Of course there's Uncle Brooke . . . but he's about the same way." Davis looked into Anna's eyes. "It's frustrating. But I'll find out."

"What about your father!"

"Oh, he's willing enough to tell me what he remembers. About growing up with your mother, you know, after his parents died in the earthquake. But somehow he always ends up telling me about Storr. What a great architect Storr was, and how much of what's here now Storr designed himself."

"I guess that's so," Anna said. "But what else is there to know?"

"I'm not sure," Davis said. He laughed softly. "Maybe there's nothing else. But I'll find out."

"And I don't know what there is to find out," she told him as casually as she could. But she felt a shiver on her arms.

The killer Kennellys . . . blood tells . . . another one of these Kennelly accidents . . .

355

Had he somehow heard those words, too? Had Tanya been foolish enough to speak to him about what Tom Stapelton had said to her? It hardly seemed possible. Yet what other reason could there be for his odd curiosity about the past. She felt that he was too young to concentrate so hard on the past, and decided it might be better if William and Helga left Emerald Station with Davis after all.

Davis said, as if reading her thoughts, "I know I'll have to go away to school in the fall. My folks have it all planned. But there's the whole summer for me to enjoy here, and I intend to do it, too. And make the most of it."

She said, "I'm sure you will," and then excused herself and went indoors.

Dot came trotting from the kitchen. Her gray hair was disheveled, as if she had repeatedly thrust her slim fingers through it. Her eyes were anxious. "Anna, are you all right? Would you like a cup of tea? Will you lie down for a little while?"

Anna said, "No thanks. I've had coffee, Dot. And I'm fine. And I don't want to lie down."

"It might be a good idea," Dot said insistently. She slewed her eyes in a meaningful way toward the drawing room.

"The family?" Anna asked, grinning. It was like the old days, she thought. Dot and she in some small conspiracy against the others. But then her grin faded. The old days were gone.

Dot nodded. "Waiting."

"As usual." Anna dropped her bag and gloves and hat on the cobbler's bench, and saw Tanya's reflection over her own narrow black-clad shoulder. She turned slowly.

Tanya said, with a pretext of nonchalance. "Oh, there you are, Anna. Everything go all right?"

Anna nodded.

"I'm sorry I couldn't go with you. It must have been awful to be alone. But I didn't know . . . If I had though . . ." Tanya had a flushed, hot-eyed look, an embarrassed look.

"I doubt that Neil would have permitted it," Anna said dryly. "But it doesn't matter. I managed."

"Nobody said . . ." Tanya began. "I mean there wasn't any unpleasantness, was there?"

Anna thought of the glances she had felt on her at the gravesite, of Fred Moody's remarks in the Old Anglers' Inn. But she said, her voice steady, "Nothing happened that I couldn't handle, Tanya."

"Good." Tanya stepped back to allow Garan to take her place.

He moved past her as if he didn't know she was there. She flashed him an angry blue look and darted into the drawing room.

Garan said, "Anna, I think you ought to see what comes of your stubbornness. I have to ask you not to associate with anyone else in town."

"Ask and be damned," she said sharply. "I'll do just as I please, Garan."

He flushed, said, "You were always too hard-headed, you know."

"And I haven't changed," she flashed.

"Very well. Then I'll say no more."

"Thank you." She turned toward the steps.

Halfway up, she heard him say, "I wish you'd reconsider, Anna."

She went on slowly, not answering, not acknowledging that she had heard him.

She spent the next three days quietly, reading and walking, but mostly thinking. She half-expected to hear from Dan, but when she didn't, she wasn't surprised. She supposed that he was busy. Perhaps he'd decided that he could do nothing to discover the truth about Martin's death. Perhaps he'd even decided that she could not, or would not help him. She knew that she would eventually contact him. But that could wait. Meanwhile, she would watch, listen, try to understand the strange currents she felt in the house. Strange currents that were not new to her, but that now, for the first time in her life, she acknowledged and questioned.

She passed the family room one day, and heard voices, and paused in the open doorway.

Garan stood at a small inlaid table with Davis.

Beyond them both, the green eyes of Gareth, the dark eyes of Nealanna, watched from the walls. The others—Neil with his heavy mustache, Mary, old Holt—watched, too. Alicia seemed to laugh from within the mended heavy gold frame.

Garan held a small leather pouch in his hand. "The beginning," he said. "A token of what Neil found." He opened the pouch and a waterfall of bright winking gems spilled across the table top.

"The Kennelly stones," Davis breathed. "Then they're real."

"Oh, yes, they're real enough. We've always kept them. Since they're just a token."

Anna shrugged, went on to the kitchen. She curled in a rocking chair, remembering how often her mother had done the same, small hands folded in her lap, small feet tucked under.

The Kennellys had kept the gems as they kept everything. A symbol for the name, the place. The moldy tree trunk carved in the shape of a man that stood in the foyer. . . . the mildewed leather shield between the black masks over the steps. The guns that went back three generations. The very wall itself . . .

She sighed, then looked up at Dot. "How long have you worked for us?" she asked.

"Since I was a youngster. And don't ask me how old I was because if I tell you you'll figure out how old I am now. And I won't have that."

"But you do remember before I was born, don't you?"

"I do. I came when Garan was just a few weeks old. And the old lady was housekeeper still. Evanne, that was. God rest her. And Henry was about to do the chores."

"I remember them both," Anna said.

"Why, I should hope you do," Dot retorted. Then,

"What tales she could tell, if she only would. But not her. She had a mouth like a steel trap that's just caught it's prey. Many times I tried to pry a bit out of her, but she said no, better let it lie and die. And that's what it did, I suppose, whatever it was."

It was the next day, early. Anna had had her coffee alone, and stepped out on the terrace into the sunlight.

Jennings, wrapped in an old Black Watch plaid shawl, was squinting unhappily at the New York *Times*.

"Politics," he growled at her. "Dewey. Truman. It's all the same. The same I tell you."

"What's the matter?" she grinned. "Are you reading editorials again?"

"I'm trying to read columnists. They annoy me, child. They try my spirits and my soul. I think I'd do better to read the *Kinsey Report*. It might tell me more of the workings of man." He flung the paper down, leaned back and closed his eyes.

"You're broody," he said without looking at her. "You think I haven't noticed. But I have. I have noticed, and I don't like it. Anna. You remind me of my sister Alicia these days. You never did before. Never. And I don't like that either. I think you should go away."

She thought vaguely that he had, some time before, suggested the same thing. She asked, "Why do you think that, Uncle? And why shouldn't I remind you of Aunt Alicia?"

"Call it an old man's fancy," he grumbled through his whiskers.

She was about to answer him when she saw the riderless horse galloping across the meadow, empty stirrups flying from the empty saddle.

She rose quickly, asked, "Uncle, do you know who went out this morning?"

He jerked upright. "What? What did you say?" And then he pushed himself to his feet, stared as the big black stallion pounded closer, and he mumbled, "Oh, no. Not once more. Then it's real. It's true. I'm right. The past is alive again."

Chapter 38

She set out across the terrace at a dead run, shouting for Neil as she went.

He and William came from within the house, but through separate doors.

William ran from the kitchen, where, she thought fleetingly, he had probably been snacking and gossiping with Dot. Neil came from the game room. Julia and Tanya appeared on the second floor balcony.

Tanya climbed down the steel fire ladder as if she had done it many times before, but Julia clung to the carved railing, clumsy in her pregnancy, and cried, "What is it, Anna? Why are you screaming?" Her voice suddenly went shrill. "That's Garan's horse! Where's Garan?"

No one answered her.

Tanya ran back to the house, calling out, "Dot? Dot, go up to Julia. She needs you. Right away, Dot," and then darted back to the follow the others, Leaving Jennings alone on the terrace.

The jeep that Davis had so proudly bought a week before suddenly darted out of the garage with a roar. It jerked to a stop beside Anna.

Davis leaned out, his eyes bright with excitement. Momentarily Anna remembered how he had looked when Garan showed him the Kennelly gems. Then he cried, "What's the matter, Anna? What's the excitement?"

She threw herself into the high seat. "It looks as if Garan's been thrown. We have to find him."

"We can. This'll go anywhere," Davis assured her. He gunned the motor, shifted gears with an ominous growl, as Neil and William climbed awkwardly into the back.

They were hardly settled when the jeep went rocketing off. It bounced from rut to rut, hit dirt and rose, as it made long sweeping crosses over the meadows, and finding nothing to slow for, moved closer and closer to the border of trees near the river, and then to the river itself.

Anna, peering ahead through squinting eyes, saw the trampled grass first. "There, Davis," she said quietly. "Slow down now. Do you see it, too?"

"I see something. But I don't know what," he answered. He down-shifted so that the jeep coughed and slowed.

Just beyond there were deep hoofprints. A small bush was uprooted. The tall meadow grass was furrowed and ripped and stomped in a wide circle.

At its center, Garan lay sprawled and still. Too still.

Davis jerked the jeep to a halt, and then jumped out. "Let me, Anna. You'd better not go," he said quickly.

Neil and William followed him without speaking.

Ignoring Davis', "No, Anna. Please," she climbed down, too.

Garan lay on his face, his blue shirt and tan trousers streaked and dusty, his dark hair dusty, too.

William, grunting, bent down, turned him over.

His hazel eyes stared wide and blank from beneath the red yawning wound in his forehead.

It seemed to Anna that she must faint. She must escape. But she could not. All she could do was look in frozen horror at the red pool on the ground, the glistening red of the jagged rock that was near by.

Utter silence had descended on the valley. The river no

longer whispered. The breeze had died, and the trees was still. Not a bird sang. Not a bee hummed.

For moments, they remained as if transfixed, and then, at last, freed from some awful spell, they spoke, moved.

Anna said tonelessly, "We must get him back at once."

Davis took off his shirt, wrapped it carefully around Garan's bloody head. Then he and William lifted him into the jeep.

Davis got behind the wheel, waited for the others to get in.

Anna found herself moving slowly, as if her muscles responded only reluctantly to her will. Her face felt stiff and cold, almost set in concrete. Her eyes burned with unshed tears. At last, as Davis drove slowly back across the meadow to the house, out of the terrible silence, she whispered, "Oh, poor Julia."

Jennings' hoarse and broken cry was gone from her mind then. But very soon, she would remember it.

Now, as the jeep stopped below the terrace, Julia, leaning there, flanked by both Dot and Tanya, cried shrilly, "What is it? Did you find him? Did he break his leg?"

Anna said quickly, under her breath, "Neil, don't let her see Garan now. We must get her upstairs and to bed before we tell her."

But it was too late. From where Julia stood she had a clear view of the still body in the back of the jeep. She shook herself fresh of Tanya and Dot's restraining hands, and began to run awkwardly for the steps.

Anna raced to meet her, stop her, and block her way. She took the bulky figure into her arms. "We must get you to bed, Julia. Not now. You can't go down there. Don't wait a minute, please, Julia, for Garan's sake, we must get you to bed."

But Julia shrilled, "He's dead, isn't he? Now Garan's dead, too."

And that was when Anna remembered what Jennings had muttered through his beard, his wrinkled face turning dirty gray, and his eyes sinking suddenly into his head. A tremor of terror touched her.

362

Martin had been first.

And today Garan. . . .

She wouldn't allow herself to think. She didn't dare to. She led Julia carefully across the terrace and into the house. She cajoled her in wordless whispers, closing her heart and mind to Julia's shrill, broken cries, up to her room. There, while Dot phoned for the doctor, she persuaded Julia to lie down.

She stayed with her until Dr. Robinson had given her enough sedation to make her sleep, and then, leaving Dot to watch over Julia, with Tanya tagging at her heels like a lost puppy, she went downstairs with the doctor.

He was the second generation in his family to go into medicine and practice in Bellingham. She had known him since he treated her for chicken pox when she was five. Now he was an old man, with a small withered square face, and tired eyes.

He went into the room where Garan had been laid, and stayed there for what seemed to Anna to be a very long time.

She, and the others, waited for him in the drawing room.

When he appeared, he said, "I've made a careful examination. There's a very deep prefrontal fracture. I doubt that anything could have been done. He was thrown, or fell, it appears. He hit his head on a rock. Did you see one? Or something with a jagged edge to it?"

"It's there," Neil answered dryly. "We left it where it was."

"I'll fill out the death certificate," the doctor said.

No one spoke.

He went on after a brief pause, "It's an accident. That's plain, of course."

Anna couldn't tell if he had stressed the word 'accident', or if the stress had been only in her own mind.

Martin had had an accident. An improbable unbelievable thing happened to him that led to his death. And now Garan had died, extraordinarily, unbelievably, in his own way.

Again Dr. Robinson waited. Still no one spoke. Finally, he said, "Now then, Mrs. Gordon is somewhat hysterical. I'm sure you understand. She should be all right. It will pass. The body protects itself in times such as these. But make sure she has plenty of rest. Otherwise she may face a second tragedy. There's a coming child to consider."

Anna wondered if he had heard, listened to, understood Julia's wild accusations. If he had been able to piece together the sum of her disjointed cries.

For the word Julia had used as Anna helped her up the steps was not 'accident.' The word she used was murder. "Somebody killed him. I know, I know," she'd cried through bloodless lips. "It was murder, I tell you. Garan would never fall or be thrown. He was murdered. And we're all going to die."

Anna turned away as Neil and William discussed arrangements with the doctor. She went quietly from the room, and then outside. She crossed the terrace and hurried down the steps, and then into the stables beyond the garage.

She found Thomson grooming Garan's horse. He was rubbing the long arching neck hard with a towel, a towel that was grimy and stained. The horse moved restlessly as she approached.

Thomson said, "Careful, Miss Anna. He's uneasy, you know. He feels that something's happened and doesn't like it."

She nodded, watched as Thomson quickly folded the towel, tossed it aside, and then moved, so that his narrow shoulders abscured the saddle that hung on the stall peg.

"The horse isn't injured himself, is he?" She asked finally.

Thomson bent his bald head to her. "Right as rain. Not a scratch on him that I could find." The moment the answer was out, he looked as if he regretted it. He hurriedly added, "Not that I looked all that carefully. There was no reason to . . . I just . . ."

"You washed blood off his neck, didn't you?" she asked levelly.

He didn't answer her.

"And there's blood on that saddle, too." She had noticed that before he moved to block it from her sight.

Thomson said quickly, "Well, some, though not much. And I don't believe it was a rock at all. I think Garan must have hit a tree limb at full gallop, and it unseated him. Nothing else could have the way he rode. You know that, Miss Anna."

"Yes," she said. "I know that."

But she didn't believe that Garan had been struck, while at a gallop, by a low-hanging tree limb, though that would explain how he could have bled on the horse before falling to the ground.

She saw what had happened quite differently. She saw a rock, jagged, hard, spinning through the sunny still air. She saw it strike Garan, and the blood spurt, and his unconscious body dropping over the saddle, the horse's neck, to leave its trail of blood, as it fell to the ground. She saw the evil design of murder.

Martin. Garan.

She could imagine no connection between the two deaths. But there must be one, she told herself. There had to be.

Thomson said softly, "I wish you hadn't noticed the blood on the saddle. It doesn't mean anything, and the less said the better, Miss Anna. You know that I'm right. The less said the better."

"Yes," she agreed. As she turned, left him, she sensed that his sharp eyes stayed with her until she had climbed to the terrace.

There she looked up. The long narrow balconies, connected by their fire ladders, hugged the face of the house, partly obscuring the great black smudges on the stone. Smudges left by the fire that had ravaged the top floor so long ago. The bright pots of petunias and dwarf roses, cultivated assiduously by Thomson, kept the eye from noticing the old scars. But they were there, noticed or not. All the old scars were still there, she thought, as she went inside.

Dr. Robinson had gone, but the family was still gathered in the living room.

Neil was saying, "But think of how it will look. You just can't do it, Uncle. Imagine what people will say. And there's absolutely no need. You heard the doctor with your own ears. There's not the slightest . . ."

Jennings stood with his back to the fireplace, leaning on a cane with both gnarled hands. "I am not interested in what people will say. Nor in talk. Not in yours, or theirs, or anybody else's. Including the good doctor himself. I have spoken to Brooke and to Lolly. They are agreeable. In fact, they extended the invitation themselves. And without my prompting. They'll be here shortly, and when they leave I'll go with them."

"What's this?" Anna asked. "Where will you go, Uncle?"

"To Maradine Mansion," he said tartly. "And don't you start in on me, too. I'm old enough to know my own mind, and I know it. And I shall not spend another night in Emerald Station."

Davis gave a great hoot of laughter. "What are you running away from? Why are you scared? You don't even ride horses."

"That'll do," William said shortly, and the boy subsided, though a look of amusement remained on his face.

Anna said gently, "Why, Uncle, I think you must do as you like."

"And I shall," he told her. "I've left before. I can leave now, too. I may not have another chance," he added darkly.

She wondered then why he had left the first time, why he had suggested that he might not have another chance. But there was no opportunity to ask him. She knew that he would explain nothing to her with Neil and William standing and listening with such open disapproval, with Davis whistling silently between his teeth, and Helga frowning and wide-eyed in the corner, and Tanya sobbing softly into a lace handkerchief. She knew that she would have to question Jennings alone.

366

But it was days before the right time came, and by then a great deal more had happened.

Garan was buried on a gray Sunday morning.

Anna clung to William's arm, fighting back tears. They had disagreed about so much. He had grown pompous, serious, had taken his duties as master of Emerald Station too much to heart. She remembered his reverent face as he showed Davis the old Kennelly gems, and Davis' shining eyes. Garan and Davis in the family room. But he was her brother, and only twenty-six years old, and now he was dead.

The Maradines had come, with Jennings between them. The rest of the family stood huddled together, and somewhat apart from them, a few people from town.

The cruel and the curious, Anna had thought, quickly averting her eyes. But then, after the service, Dan and his parents came to speak to her.

Dan had called the afternoon it had happened. He'd said, "Are you all right, Anna?"

"Yes," she'd told him. "But I can't . . ."

"I'd like to see you," he'd said.

"After the funeral, Dan. Not just yet . . ."

"All right. It can wait until then, I think."

The sound of his low, warm voice had strengthened her somehow, but it had frightened her, too. The implication in his words frightened her.

But now he smiled as Dylan Row said, "I'm sorry for your troubles," and as his mother nodded, moved her lips soundlessly.

She remembered the day that Dylan had helped her mother, and given his own blood. She remembered the day that she had gone to thank him and seen Dan for the first time.

She said, "Thank you both for coming."

Dan took her hand. "Easy, Anna. I'd like to come out and see you. Some time in the early evening. Will that be all right?"

"Yes," she answered, and promptly forgot his question

367

and her reply, as William drew her away, led her back to the big limousine.

So she was surprised when he came, arriving at twilight.

She had heard the gate signal, and wondered who was waiting to be let in. Soon after, she heard his voice at the door, asking for her.

"This house is in mourning," Neil said coldly.

"Anna expects me," Dan retorted.

It was then that she remembered. She hurried to meet him, her heart beating quickly.

Neil smoothed his sandy hair and gave her an open look of reproof as she led Dan out to the back terrace.

The two of them settled in the deep wooden chairs. She sat so that she had a clear view of the balconies, of the rows of petunias, and the scars of the old fire. He sat opposite her.

He said, bending his dark head, "I wanted to see you because . . . because I know how hard it is for you now."

She thanked him, supposing that he considered a condolence call an obligation he must fulfill.

Then he said quietly, his clear hard blue eyes meeting hers, "But it was much more than that, Anna."

She caught her breath, suddenly frightened again.

He went on, his voice deep, quiet, in the falling twilight. "You realize, of course, that this is the second time in weeks that death has struck Emerald Station, and that both times the circumstances have been somewhat odd."

She folded her hands in her lap, whispered, "Dan, you know that these things *do* happen."

He smiled faintly. "Then you believe that things go in threes? A pleasant superstition under the circumstances, isn't it?"

"No, Dan," she said quickly. "It's just that I can't believe. . . ." She let the words trail away. She found that she couldn't lie to him. What he was saying was what she had thought herself. Martin and Garan had both been murdered. She couldn't deny it, yet she couldn't admit it either. She looked past his watchful face to the house, to the bright splotches of color on the balcony railings just above.

It was very nearly dark now. But she saw that something seemed to flicker there, a touch of movement, the wind perhaps. Something scraped faintly. And then, very slowly, one of the ceramic pots tipped forward into a dark blurring spin.

She stared, hypnotized, as it arrowed toward her. Then she heard Dan's exclamation. At the same time her chair was kicked back, kicked away from under her, so that she fell, sprawling. She fell, and the pot exploded just where she had been only moments before.

Chapter 39

He said, "Anna! Anna!" in a strange, breathy voice.

She blinked dizzily. There was a red strain on his shoulder. He was bleeding. He had been hurt.

She rose toward him, and at the same time, he bent to her.

The red stain became a bright blossom falling away from him. A bright petunia blossom . . .

"Anna!" he said again.

"Yes, yes, I'm all right. Dan." She stopped. She looked up at the balcony again. The darkness had fallen, but there was light from Tanya's window. There was a single empty place in the row of ceramic pots. An empty space, and a dark ribbon that must be a dangling rope. "It's amazing . . . the way it . . ." She gave it up, shaking her head.

He helped her to her feet. "You're sure you're not hurt."

"I'm sure, Dan."

His big hand was closed around her shoulder, fingers biting into the flesh. "But you could have been," he said gently. "You *do* see it, don't you? You *do* understand?"

Her lips felt cold, stiff. Her hands trembled. She tried to steady herself. She said finally, "It must have just fallen. Perhaps it was pushed out of line somehow. Perhaps . . ."

"Martin died last week. Garan died two days ago. And now this."

It was no use to try to deceive him. She knew what he meant. She knew what he must be thinking. Ever since Martin's death, Dan had been wondering, questioning. His questions had only grown sharper when Garan died. Now there would be no stopping him.

It was no use to try to deceive herself either. *Just another one of those Kennelly accidents . . .*

He kicked the broken pot aside, and righted the chair she had been sitting on. He pulled it close to the house, so that she was protected by the balcony above. He moved his own chair beside hers, and then sat down. It was dark, shadowed. She couldn't see his face, read his expression.

"Anna, are you going to pretend that there's no connection between those things?"

"There may be," she admitted cautiously.

"Do you know what it is? What it could be?"

She shook her head.

"Think, Anna."

"I've tried to, Dan. But it's no use. I just don't understand. I'm not even sure that I believe it. It seems . . . it just seems unreal, impossible."

"But it *is* real, and we have to find out whatever it is," he told her. When she didn't speak, he went on. "I told you before. I'm determined to find out what happened to Martin, why he died. I owe him that much."

"Yes," she said.

But Martin had had no connection with Emerald Station, except that he had taken her out a few times. He had picked her up and brought her back. And listened, amused and patient, while the family questioned him.

"I don't think I can do it in town," Dan was saying. "Though I've asked enough questions there to fill a book."

She made a protesting sound.

He said quietly, "Don't worry. I didn't start any talk.

371

Though I don't see how there could be more talk than there already is. What I mean is that I didn't add any new fuel to it. And I won't."

"Talk," she said softly. "And what do they say?"

"The same thing they've said for sixty years."

"The killer Kennellys," she whispered. She leaned back, closed her eyes. She remembered when she had gone to roll bandages in town. She was sixteen then. The women had stared at her, whispered. She remembered the dying flame in the quarry, the men hauling the chains to the rim, staring at her, whispering . . .

"Whose room is that?" Dan asked. "The one where the light is. Where the . . ."

"Tanya's," she said. "But she wouldn't have . . ."

"How do you know?" he demanded.

She didn't answer him. She thought of Tanya's fear of old Tom Stapleton and his words. She leaned back, closed her eyes. "No, Dan. She's afraid, too." Then she remembered what Jennings had said that day at the funeral.

"Anna, you must come away from there."

She told him, "I can't, Jennings," and turned away.

"Tanya's not the only one who's afraid," Dan was saying. "What about your uncle? Why did he move to the Maradines?"

"How do you know that already?"

"Everyone knows it in town. My mother heard it from Emily somebody or other."

"The Maradines' housekeeper."

"I suppose," he said absently. "Your uncle was right though. And he had his reasons. I wish you'd do the same."

She shook her head.

"After what's just happened, do I really need to try to convince you, Anna?"

She said, "I belong here, Dan. I must see it through to the end."

The words shocked her. What was she saying? Why did she belong in Emerald Station? She was a Gordon. She could do as she pleased. But suddenly, she thought, I'm a Kennelly, too. That's why I have to stay.

Dan got to his feet, saying, "Then I'll see it through to the end, too, Anna."

It was late. The house was finally still.

Anna paused before Julia's door, listening. There was no sound from within. She wondered uneasily if Julia was all right. She had, since her hysterical outburst after Garan's body had been brought back from the meadow, been unnaturally controlled. She had become quiet, unsmiling, the pallor of her face stressed by sudden new lines under her dull eyes and bracketing her mouth. Her grief was open and unassumed, and Anna never doubted it for an instant. But now she sensed in Julia something far beyond grief. It was not a quality to which she could accurately put a name, but some empathetic intuition told her that Julia walked with terror. With the same terror that Anna herself felt.

There was still no sound from within. No sound, no movement, no sighing breath.

Anna eased the door open. The room was dark except near the bed where a lamp spilled pale yellow over the golden birch of the table and the champagne shade of the rug. Even in her choice of color and style Julia had shown a need for escape from the shadows of Emerald Station. She had made of her rooms an oasis of brightness in the dark of the rest of the house.

Julia's mouth sagged open, her arms flung wide. Her body bulked high and unwieldly under the light coverlet. A stringent odor was noticeable. Anna's nose wrinkled. It was the smell of whiskey. Julia had found a way to go to sleep at last. But what would it do to her?

Anna backed out, eased the door shut, and went on to her own room. Poor Julia had always been more fond of whiskey than was good for her. Garan had often reproached her about taking that one extra drink that took her beyond sociability to sullenness. And now, in fear and grief, she had taken the extra drink which had taken her from sullenness to unconsciousness.

Anna knew that she would have to do something. To protect Julia, to protect the child that sheltered in Julia's anguished body as well.

But what could she do? she asked herself, as she crawled tiredly into bed. How could she help Julia, the whole family, when she didn't even know how to help herself?

She had seen the pot move, shift, tilt. She had stared at it in disbelief. Later, when Neil and Tanya were downstairs, she had gone to check the balcony outside their window. The thin black rope dangled where she had spotted it before, and on its end there had been an iron hook. She had understood instantly how the pot had been tilted. She had known then beyond a doubt what had been intended. If it hadn't been for Dan, there would surely have been another accident at Emerald Station. Another unexplainable accident. Another death.

She shivered, pictured Dan. He was stubborn, strong, inquisitive. He would never let go now. Never. Never. Not until he learned the whole truth. And she was no longer sure that the truth should be known. Perhaps it would be better to let come what may, to allow time and events to unravel without interference. Perhaps to know the truth was to be destroyed.

She drifted into sleep, remembering the touch of Dan's hands as he drew her to her feet, held her, his head bent so that his mouth was only inches from hers, only inches but not touching, not quite touching. . . . .

She put on a sleeveless blue dress. She caught up her purse, and threw a sweater around her shoulders when she heard Dan's voice in the lower hallway. Dot was with him.

She ran down the steps past the black masks without noticing them. Her eyes were on him, and when he looked up, smiling faintly, her heart seemed to catch for a moment. The hours since she had seen him the evening before, since the ceramic planter had come tumbling down at her out of the shadows, had been long, drawn out, and

374

empty. She had struggled through them, frightened by what had happened and by what might come, but always looking forward to now.

"Ready?" he asked.

"Yes. But let's have a drink with the family first," she suggested.

"They're on the terrace," Dot said, looking amused, and somewhat quizzical.

Anna knew that the older woman was wondering why she wanted to subject Dan to a meeting with them, but she had her own reasons.

She led the way outside.

Davis sat on the wall, his long arms folded around his legs, surveying the sunset-dyed meadow.

Tanya sat close to Neil, her hand on his arm, as if in restraint or protection, and Julia lay back in a green chaise, her eyes unfocused and unseeing, as she stared over the rim of her glass.

William's portly body overflowed a small iron chair, and near him, Helga sat with her silver head bent and her plump shoulders sagging.

She looked up, dimpling in appreciation of an attractive man.

The others greeted Dan without warmth.

Then Neil said, "I didn't expect to see you tonight."

Dan smiled easily. "Didn't Anna tell you that we're going to have dinner with my folks?"

Neil stiffened so openly that even his sandy hair seemed to bristle.

Anna spoke before he could. She said, "I don't explain my comings and going, Dan." And then to Dot, "I'd like a small sherry, Dot. And I think Dan will have Scotch."

Dot went inside, the same quizzical look on her face, and Dan went to sit on the wall next to Davis.

The younger man turned his head slowly, stared him up and down, in what, if he hadn't been that age, would seem to be a peculiarly insolent manner.

Neil said quietly, "Anna, I don't mean to embarrass you,

375

but you're forcing me to speak of this. Do you think it's a good idea to visit the Rows?"

Dan raised his brows, grinned.

"Why shouldn't I, Neil?" Anna asked.

"We're really quite respectable family," Dan said.

"Of course," Neil agreed, but without conviction. "I didn't intend any aspersions. We here all know what fine people the Rows are. But I'm troubled about Anna. All her life she's been determined to go where she wasn't wanted. I remember . . ."

"My folks invited Anna, and they do want her," Dan said quickly.

"But it serves no purpose," William put in. "We're Kennellys. And fraternizing isn't . . ."

Dan's grin widened. He answered, "But we're not speaking of opposing armies. We're speaking of families which have known each other for generations."

Dot brought Anna her sherry, served Dan his drink, passed the tray of small hot canapés, and then disappeared again.

Neil waited until the door had closed behind her, then cleared his throat. "Anna, I know you don't really believe it yet, not understand it either. But now that Garan is dead, you should realize that I'm head of this family."

Davis, Anna saw, turned his head stiffly, regarded Neil with an intent stare.

"It's not going to be easy for me," Neil went on. "Though I'm trained for it, I suppose, as Garan was. Still, the circumstances . . . I'll need your help. All the help you can give me."

"Of course." She smiled, finished her sherry and rose. "But I'm still going to dinner at the Rows with Dan. And I'll go to town when I please, and for what I please, in the future as in the past."

Julia made a sound that was a cross between a groan and a laugh.

Tanya said angrily, "I think you should consider Neil, and the rest of us, too, Anna."

376

But Anna answered only, "I'll do what I think is right," and then, "Shall we go now, Dan?"

It had been a pleasant hour. Now they were having coffee around the big kitchen table.

Anna felt comfortable and at home here. She had played a small game with herself during the meal. She had, knowing that she was being ridiculous, pretended that Dan had brought her to meet his parents for the reason that most young men brought a girl to meet their parents. She would liked to have believed that he was interested in her, in Anna Gordon, that he no longer thought of Martin when he looked at her. But to believe that would be to make the mistake of confusing fact with wish.

Dan's father pushed back his chair, leaned his elbows on the table. His smile laced his face with wrinkles. "We're old friends, Anna. So I'll speak freely."

"Dan said you had something to tell me," she answered.

Dylan went on, "What it means, I'm not sure, Anna. But for your own safety, I think you must know it."

She thought of Martin's death, of Garan's. She thought of what had happened the evening before. She remembered her hypnotized stare as the ceramic planter began to tilt. Her own safety . . . she waited.

"There was, way back, something between our two families. I don't know just what it was. I'll tell you the little I learned though. Your grandmother was named Nealanna Yarrow. She married your grandfather, Gareth, in London, and came here with him. Not long after, my father came here, too. His name was Dale Yarrow, and he changed it to Row some time after he settled here. He married Moira, the daughter of Evanne Borden, who was the housekeeper at Emerald Station." He paused.

Dan's mother, plump and blue-eyed, moved silently, refilling the coffee cups.

Dylan shook his head. "My father was violent on the subject of the Kennellys until the day he died. He, and his crony, Tom Stapleton, spent many a joyful hour discussing their separate hates. My mother would have none of it,

377

and I can remember them sneering at her when she said they were wrong, evil, in their ugly speculations. But I remember, too, that there was something she held back, some fear, or memory of fear, that she never explained." He stopped then.

Anna said thoughtfully, "Fear or memory of fear. Connected with the Kennellys. With Emerald Station."

She thought of what Tom Stapleton had said to Tanya. The killer Kennellys . . . blood tells . . .

Dan said quietly, "That fits in with old Stapleton's maunderings. Yes. I've heard him myself, Anna."

She didn't answer him. She was suddenly thinking of Jennings' anguished, 'It's beginning again.'

In the face of her silence, Dan went on, "There are records available, Anna, I've studied them. I've been to the cemetery and checked the dates on the tombstones. I see a pattern emerging though I don't know what it means. History seems to be repeating itself somehow."

Again she remembered Jennings' saying, 'It's beginning again.'

Softly, Dylan said, "Stapleton had a sister named Jane. She worked at Emerald Station. She disappeared one day and was never heard of again. There was a girl named Deborah Maradine. Brooke's younger sister. She was murdered, by a tramp, it was said, but the man was never found. Neil Kennelly died in a hunting accident, and then Alicia, sometime later, hanged herself."

Another Kennelly accident . . . Anna shivered. She thought of the family room. The faces looking down at her from the walls . . .

Dylan continued, "And it went on. In the next generation, David Kennelly died in a fall. Judd drowned, and Jennifer, though very young, had a heart attack. Storr died in an automobile accident. And now . . ." He let his voice trail away.

She raised her eyes to his. "Yes. I see."

Dan said, "You should leave Emerald Station, Anna. I'm convinced now that Martin was murdered, and that

Garan was, too. Something's begun that isn't finished. Remember what happened last night."

She drew a long slow breath. "I do remember. But I can't abandon the family, Dan."

"Not even to save your life?"

She didn't answer.

He said, "Anna, you must have some protection. Surely you see that."

She did see it, and clearly. But she couldn't run away from the danger, whatever it was.

He sighed, exchanged a look with his father, then, his mother, a look that said, "That's what I was afraid of." Then he said, "I want to move out to Emerald Station, Anna. I want to be there with you."

She lowered her eyes lest he read too clearly in them a reflection of the emotion she felt. To have him close by, to see him every day . . . it was not protection she was thinking of then. Only the sweetness of it. But she knew his only interest in her was her connection with Martin. It was through her, he thought, that he would learn the truth.

She said aloud, "I don't see any way that we can manage that."

He smiled faintly. "We can," he said. "If you're willing to announce your engagement to me."

Chapter 40

She felt a revealing heat rise up her throat and into her cheeks, and knew that she was blushing.

Dan said quickly, "Just a pretext, of course. Don't you see, Anna? How else could I come there, be there, with you?"

"I . . ."

He went on. "It's not just about Martin any more. You must understand that. There's something else. And I know it's serious."

She waited.

"The talk in Bellingham, Anna. It's always been there. All these years. But now, since Martin died, and then Garan . . . now it's turned ugly. Worse than ugly. We have to do something about it."

"And I agree," Dylan Row said firmly. "It's time there was an end to the old business. And the only way to end it is to learn the truth of what's happening."

The truth, she thought. But perhaps, to learn the truth would be dangerous. Perhaps it would destroy her, her family. And yet, she knew there was no answer to the Rows. They were right. And there was no other way.

She said, "All right, Dan. If you think it's a good idea, and a workable one."

He grinned at her. "It won't be as difficult as you seem to believe."

"That remains to be seen," she answered.

They left the small house just off Maine Avenue a few minutes later.

On the way back to Emerald Station, he outlined his plans. "We'll tell them tonight, Anna. I suppose there'll be some static about it, but we'll ignore it. I'll wait a couple of days, and then move out. That way I can have a good look around at the quarry and where Garan was killed, and at the balconies, too."

"But what of your work at the paper?"

"I'll have my vacation now as far as anyone else is concerned. My assistant will carry on. And I'll drive in for a couple of hours each day to make sure it goes right."

"I suppose you can do that," she said thoughtfully.

"I can. What worries me is whether we can carry it off, make it seem the real thing to the family."

She didn't answer him. She couldn't.

"But I think we can manage it," he went on.

The valley was wrapped in darkness. Their headlights made a long white tunnel through the heavy shadows. He stopped at the gates under the big scrolled sign. He tapped his horn.

Thomson came out of the cottage, appearing suddenly from the lush growth of ivy and honeysuckle. He peered through the railings at the car, then unlocked the gates.

Dan drove through slowly, stopped as Thomson signalled him, bent his bald head at the window to ask, "Will you be coming back right away? If so, I'll wait here."

"I'll stay on for a while," Dan told him. "I'll let you know when I come down again."

Thomson nodded, turned back to his cottage.

Anna thought, but didn't say, Thomson's question was a result of what had happened to Martin. Now the caretaker was determined that he have some idea of when

381

to expect a guest to be leaving. So that, if it should seem too long to him, he would be forewarned of trouble.

Dan drove on, parked under the porte-cochere.

They went inside together, holding hands.

There was, she saw, a faintly embarrassed smile on Dan's face. The right kind of a smile, perhaps for a man about to announce that he intended to marry the daughter of the household.

It didn't go quite as Anna had anticipated. For there were loud voices from the drawing room.

Neil was saying, "But it was in the top drawer of my desk. In my study. Now it's gone."

"You're probably mistaken," Julia said, slurring her words. "How long has it been since you noticed it?" She wore a chiffon hostess gown that billowed around her, and long diamond earrings, but her black hair was disheveled, with wisps hanging limply around her pale face, and her gray eyes were dull.

"I'm not mistaken," Neil retorted. "I'm not an absent-minded old man. I brought it back from Germany with me, and I've had it ever since. Tanya will vouch for that."

"Yes," Tanya said. "It's true. He did bring it back. And he showed it to me. And I know it was there."

Dan raised questioning brows at Anna, but she shook her head. She didn't know what they were talking about. She knew only that Neil was angry, perhaps even frightened.

She led Dan inside.

All conversations stopped. Every eye in the room beamed total suspicion at her and at Dan.

She forced what she hoped was a gay, and excited smile. "What's the matter? I could hear you very nearly halfway to town."

Neil said heavily, "I think we won't discuss it now."

But William shrugged his heavy hunched shoulders. His eyes were grim in his red face. "His gun is missing. You'd think it was the diamonds the way he goes on. We've been listening to him rave for hours. As for me, I never saw his damn Luger, nor expect to."

382

"Well, somebody did," Neil said harshly. "And I want it back."

Davis, leaning against the gray stone mantel, narrowed his eyes. "Don't look at me. I don't need your gun. What would I do with it?"

Helga cried, "Why, of course, Davis, what would you do with a gun?" in a happy voice, and smiled at Dan.

"Have you asked Dot?" Anna asked. "Maybe it's in the gun room with all the other . . ."

"It's not," Neil told her. "I looked."

Dan tugged at Anna's arm, reminding her of what she had to do now.

She made herself smile up at him. She said, "I think this may be what you could consider a typical family scene, Dan. I hope it doesn't frighten you off."

He grinned widely. Then answered, but looked at Neil, "Since I'm soon to be a part of the family I'd better get used to it, hadn't I?"

Julia's eyes widened. She gasped, "What? Anna, what does he mean?"

"You?" Tanya cried. "You?"

Neil said, from between clenched teeth, "Are you implying that you and Anna . . ."

She cut in quickly, "Neil, all of you, Listen. Dan and I are going to be married." She held up her hand at the quick exclamations. "Just wait. We haven't yet decided on the date. But it will be fairly soon, I think. We don't see any real reason to delay. Now, I hope you'll all be happy for me."

If there was any joy at the announcement, it didn't show.

The silence that followed her words was heavy with disapproval and with shock.

At last, Neil said, with a flicker of embarrassment. "I see. Well then . . ."

Helga's dimples had disappeared from her plump face. She said softly, "But I was so sure you were going to marry Martin . . ." She stopped, swallowed. "I mean, all

383

the time, when you were going with him, I was so sure . . ."

And Julia smiled blearily. "This certainly calls for a toast. Davis, why don't you route out Dot and ask her to see about some champagne."

It was a relief to be alone.

Anna brushed her hair, feeling the tension in her body begin to ease. To be alone, away from the family . . . Neil and Tanya, William and Helga and Davis, Julia . . . that was the family now.

And one of them might already have killed twice, killed twice, yes, but tried three times.

Killer Kennellys . . . blood tells . . . that was what old Stapleton had called it. And Dylan Row had pointed out a pattern too sharp to be ignored. A stain passed from one generation. . . .

With Garan's death, Neil had become master of Emerald Station. Could that have been a motive for fratricide? But what of Martin? What of the attack on her herself?

She put the brush down wearily.

She was in danger. She knew it, and Dan knew it, too. He had kissed her gently, a parody of a lover's kiss, she had thought at the time, and then left her.

Neil had waited until the door had closed behind him, and then said angrily, "I suppose there's absolutely no use in trying to talk sense to you. You're addled, Anna, and always have been."

"No use," she smiled. "I've made up my mind. I'm going to marry Dan Row."

She wished it were true. She would have given much to know that what she said wasn't pretense.

Helga put in, "Why, if she loves him, Neil . . ."

"Keep out of it," William told her. "You don't understand. You never could. You're not a Kennelly."

"Neither is she," Davis said quietly. "So I don't see what the fuss is about."

Anna smiled at him, rose. "There's no fuss. Dan and I will be married, and that's the end of it."

"One more mistake out of so many mistakes," Neil said heavily.

"I'm sure it isn't one," Anna told him.

Helga smiled, patted her silver pompadour. "You see? She's in love. When a girl's in love . . ."

William growled, "Oh, shut up, Helga. Love has nothing to do with it. For her to marry a Bellingham man is . . . why it's. . . ."

Anna laughed. "Well, what is it, William? What do you call it?"

"Treason," he said. "We've been at odds for so many years. Yes, you're betraying. . . ."

"Emerald Station is not an armed camp attacked by maurading pirates," she snapped. "This is 1948. We are civilized people, educated people. Now, will one of you tell me, if you can, why we're supposed to be afraid of the people of Bellingham."

And she remembered Tom Stapleton's words, and Tanya's face when she had repeated them.

"Afraid?" Neil said. "Who claims we're afraid? It just won't do. We have a tradition to uphold. We have our pride. The Kennellys . . ."

She said, "Spare me. And remember that neither you nor I are Kennellys. It's time to forget that nonsense."

"Oh, no, wait," William cried, his face purpling, a vein throbbing obviously in his forehead. "That's a pretty cavalier way of dismissing your family and its traditions."

She said, "I no longer consider that as important. The rest of you can do as you please. All I know is that nothing has been accomplished by taking that tack. And we've tried for three generations." She waited, then added, "And on that note, I'll say good night, and go to bed."

She had felt the angry silence follow her up to her room, follow her as if a wave of it crept at her heels, at her ankles, threatening to rise and drown her.

But these four walls, this old and shining furniture

385

heavy with wax, had always been her refuge. It was now, too.

Neil's gun was gone. It was a frightening thought. As she considered it, she remembered that someone had opened her jewel case, turned out the necklaces and earrings and left them scattered on her dresser top.

It seemed now as meaningless a thing to do as it had seemed then. As meaningless as taking Neil's gun from his desk. But was that really meaningless?

She prepared for bed, turned out the lights, and opened the draperies at the windows. The spring night was still, sweet. An angle of moonbeam lay across the foot of her bed.

She snuggled the pillows behind her and folded her arms behind her head, and watched it move slow, creeping closer, as she thought of Dan.

She remembered when she had first seen him. A tall, lean, half-smiling boy who opened the door of his father's automobile show room. She had wished then that she knew him. Had she, in some odd way, at an immature sixteen, already guessed what he could be to her? She remembered, too, that she had seen his grandfather, Dale Row, looking at her from outside, looking at her with a hating smile.

Now she reminded herself wearily that Dan was nothing to her, in fact. He was using her, and not pretending otherwise. He felt that he owed the memory of Martin Milton the truth of the destruction that had befallen him. To believe that he had any other interest in her would be to deceive herself. And there had already been too much deception.

Yet as she drifted into sleep, she was smiling. She dreamed that he bent his head to kiss her cheek, and she was smiling . . .

The sound that brought her awake still lingered in the room. A faint aftermath of something she had heard through her sleep, and only partially identified. But now, as she listened, it faded away under the noise of babbling voices.

She imagined that under the babble she could still hear, faintly, the dimming crack, and the clatter of splintering glass.

She climbed from the bed, found robe and slippers, in a single swift movement. She swept her black curls from her face as she ran for the hall.

There were lights below, and the voices grew louder, more shriller. She raced down the steps.

Neil's study doors were open. The overhead light was brilliant, almost blinding, and cast a merciless glare on the shattered balcony window behind his desk, on the long furrow across the mahogany top before him.

He was saying, his hazel eyes glittering, "I was just trying to do some work. I heard something. Don't ask me what, and threw myself aside. I threw myself aside, but only just in time."

William's face was purple again. "Somebody obviously took a shot at you, Neil."

Anna's hand went to her mouth. She felt her eyes widen. "Shot at you, Neil? Are you sure?"

Davis got up from where he had been kneeling near the wall. Wordlessly he held out a bit of flattened metal.

Tanya wailed, "I can't stand any more," and crumpled into a chair, with Helga leaning over her, whispering.

"The balcony," Anna said. "It was from the balcony, wasn't it? You're quite sure?"

Davis pointed to the shattered glass, then went to it. He swung the window open and stepped outside. His exclamation of surprise was clearly audible within the room.

He was white-faced when he returned.

"What did you find?" Neil asked.

Davis offered a small white linen handkerchief, and Anna gasped, "But that's mine. How could it have gotten out there? I've not been on that balcony for months."

No one answered her. She felt the sweep of quick glances that touched her and then fled away. She knew that they were all remembering her quarrel with Neil only a few hours before. She wondered if they were remembering, too, her quarrel with Garan before he died.

"I think," William said deliberately, "that we had better make a search right away. Now that we know why Neil's gun was taken, we'd better find it, and lock it up. Come with me, Davis. Neil, you stay here and catch your breath. We'll have a quick look around."

Davis and William went out into the hallway. Anna heard their footsteps on the stairs. She heard the muffled sounds from above as they walked down the corridor.

She said softly, "I think we should check with Thomson. Maybe he'll know if there was anyone at the gate, if there were any intruders around."

Neil didn't answer her, but Tanya sniffed loudly, and Julia said, "We'd already have heard from him if he'd seen anyone."

Helga added, "We'd better wait until William and Davis come back. Perhaps ... perhaps the less said the better, and the fewer who know the better as well."

They stood in empty silence.

William and Davis returned within moments.

They were both ashen-faced, grim.

But Davis' eyes held glints of excitement, small embers that seemed to burn in bottomless depths.

He held out his hand, and the gun glinted evilly in the light. "It was on Anna's balcony," he said softly. "And its been fired."

Chapter 41

There was a moment of stillness.

Anna felt as if she were sinking in it, drowning in the emptiness that was so full of terrible but unspoken suspicions.

She remembered what Dylan Row had told her about the Kennellys in those long ago years before her grandparents married. She remembered what had happened before her parents had married. And now, in her own generation . . .

At last she said, looking at Neil, "You know better. Whatever it is that you're thinking, Neil, you know better than to believe that I . . ."

He said stiffly, "I'm not thinking anything, Anna."

Tanya cried out, "But how it got up there is the question. What was that gun doing on Anna's balcony? And what was her handkerchief doing just outside this room?" Her accusing blue eyes said for her what she would not put directly into words.

Anna supposed it was what they were all thinking. She had quarreled with Neil over Dan, and she had stolen his gun, shot at him from the balcony, and then fled to her room.

That someone had done it, she knew. But she had not. And in fact, her argument with Neil, after the announcement of her engagement to Dan which had provoked it, had come after Neil said that the gun was missing.

At last Neil said, "Helga's right. We'd better say no more about it." He opened his hand to Davis. "Let me have that. I'll see that it's safely locked away."

Davis gave it up reluctantly, it seemed to Anna.

Tanya wiped tears from her eyes, said, "We should call Jim Arden. We should find out what happened. We have to know who did it, I'm afraid, Neil. I'm afraid that something'll happen to you, too."

"We can't call the sheriff out here," he told her impatiently. "Can you imagine what it would sound like, for God's sake?"

William agreed gruffly. "Of course we can't. Think, Tanya. The Kennellys . . ."

Anna turned, left them still standing together. Standing together, she thought, and banded against her in terrible suspicion.

She went to the kitchen to phone the cottage.

Thomson answered sleepily. She asked if there had been anyone at the gates, if he had heard a car, had any reason to believe that anyone from the outside had entered Emerald Station that night.

He assured her that he had heard nothing, and then, his voice suddenly sharp, asked, "Why? What's wrong, Miss Anna?"

"Nothing," she said wearily. "I'm sorry I awakened you. Better go back to sleep."

"There was nobody here, not after I let Dan Row out," Thomson said, yawning.

She thanked him, hung up.

She knew that she must call Dan, but she decided to wait until morning. She was sure that no more would happen that night.

She went back to bed, but found sleep impossible.

The shadows that filled Emerald Station seemed to loom closer, blacker, reaching out with chill tentacles to claim her.

Martin had died.

Then Garan.

She had been attacked.

Now Neil had been threatened, too. And the circumstances seemed to point to her. It was plain that an attempt had been made to incriminate her. To make the others suspect her, and turn against her.

One of those in the house had planned Martin's death, then Garan's. Then hers. He had been successful at the first two, unsuccessful at the third. So another attempt had been made, this time on Neil. And Neil had escaped it. But if he had not, would his death have been made to appear an accident, too? He had survived, but she hadn't escaped the blame, she knew. Was it hoped that she would flee Emerald Station now? Then only Neil would be left. Neil, with William and his family, and Tanya and Julia.

Could he have staged this attempt on himself? If so, why? Was he so opposed to her marriage to Dan that he would try to drive her away, try even to destroy her?

What reason could William have for wanting to kill Neil? To try to kill her, to try to drive her away?

Garan . . . Neil . . . herself . . . The three Gordons. But then why Martin?

A shiver touched her. They were Gordons. But they were half Kennellys, too. And was the Kennelly half of these Gordons cursed? The bed seemed to quiver beneath her.

She watched dawn filter around the edges of the closed draperies. She was filled with relief to know that the night was finally over. Her thoughts had taken her in aimless circles of suspicion and fear, had plodded through avenues of questions that seemed unanswerable. Yet there must be answers, she knew.

When the room turned pink with sunrise, she got up. She dressed in blue jeans and a white shirt. She brushed her curls.

She supposed that no one, not even Dot, would be up yet. But she was anxious to begin the day. She would have coffee, she decided. She would wait until she could call Dan and tell him what had happened. Then, when she had spoken with him, perhaps she would know what to do. If there was anything to do.

She made coffee in the kitchen. She had just begun to drink it when Dot came in, yawning and stretching, to say reproachfully, "Why didn't you wake me up, Anna? I wouldn't have minded." And then, bustling to the refrigerator, "You need more than that. What about waffles? I'll make you a quick . . ."

"No thanks," Anna said hastily. "I'm not hungry."

Dot gave her a worried look. "You don't eat enough to keep a bird alive. It's bad. A girl needs her health and strength."

She didn't say what for, but her tone made it obvious. There was some special, but unmentioned reason, why a girl named Anna Gordon needed her health and her strength.

She gave Anna another worried look, then sat opposite her. "That was a bad thing last night, Anna. I'm scared. I'll admit it."

"I suppose that was the general idea," Anna said. "To scare us. If not worse."

She thought of the handkerchief on the balcony outside Neil's study, the gun on the balcony outside her bedroom. To scare the others, implicate her.

She glanced at her watch. It was still too early to call Dan. If only the time would pass . . .

"You should go and stay with the Maradines the way Jennings did," Dot told her. "It'd be all right. If you just got away from Emerald Station for a while."

"That's what Dan said, too. And his father."

"Then listen to them," Dot urged her. "I know what I'm talking about. And so do they."

It would be good to sleep beyond the glass-topped walls of Emerald Station, good to be free of the lurking shadows, to leave behind the faces that looked at her from the portraits in the family room. Yes. To think of it was to breathe more freely. But to do that meant to avoid the truth.

She said, "I can't go away, Dot. I have to see it through."

Dot hesitated, then asked in an anguished whisper, "Even if ... even if something more so awful happens that you ... you ..."

"It won't," Anna said firmly. Much more firmly than she felt. For she wasn't sure. She felt as if she were wandering in the dark, as if great mazes surrounded her, and there was no sign toward the entry or exit. It had begun, she thought, a long time before. The exit was now. It must be. But the entrance was in another generation. In Nealanna's and Gareth's ...

She said only, "Dan's probably coming out today, Dot." And taking a deep noisy breath, "To stay with us for a while."

Dot's blue eyes widened within their mesh of wrinkles. "Anna ..."

"I've not spoken to him yet this morning. It's too early. But when I tell him what happened last night ..."

"Neil ... the others ... What will they say? You know how they feel, Anna."

"The days of the grand old patriarchs are over," Anna answered. "And Neil isn't one, can't be. I don't intend to give him a chance to say anything, nor the others either." She grinned faintly. "After all, he's my fiancé. If I want him here with me, I have that right."

"But ..."

"Dot, don't argue. Please. Just get a room ready for him."

Dot nodded, turned her mind to the necessary practicalities. She considered, suggested one room, then another. At last they settled it, and Dot promised that Dan's accommodations would be ready for him whenever he came out.

He arrived just a short hour after Anna phoned him. He

393

listened silently while she described the events of the night before.

Then he said, "I'll go home and pack a bag, Anna. I'll be out as soon as I can. Just tell the family I'll be here, and sit tight. My arrival will give all of them something to think about. And that's good."

It turned out to be a long hour. She found that waiting for him, even for the short period, was difficult. She had to remind herself that what they were doing was pretense. She told herself that she wasn't in love with him, nor he with her. They were, simply, working together to learn the truth of Martin Milton's death, and Garan's death. To learn why she and Neil had been attacked. To discover what evil walked loose through Emerald Station.

But still, having told Neil that Dan was coming out to live for a while, having seen his face go stony, and heard his, "Anna, you musn't," she went to the window to watch for him.

Thomson had turned on the fountain. Its spray was golden against the sky. The stone lions were long black shadows. She couldn't see the road itself. But she could see the gate, the tall scrolled iron sign over it. She was still there, watching, when the sun flashed on the car windshield.

She went outside, and was there, waiting for him when he drove under the porte-cochere.

He smiled at her. "All right? Nothing new, is there?"

She shook her head.

"How did they take the news?"

"I only told Dot, and then Neil."

"And?"

"He seemed more stunned than anything else. He said I couldn't do it. And I said that I had asked you to come out and stay, and that it was done. And that was that."

Dan bent close to her, patted her cheek, said, "Well, I don't suppose he decided to relax and enjoy it. But maybe he decided good grace was the better part of valor in this instance."

"Maybe." But she was doubtful. She suspected that Neil

had decided to wait and tell Dan directly that he was unwelcome in Emerald Station, as unwelcome there as anyone from Bellingham would be.

She soon found out that she was wrong.

She and Dan drove back to the garage, where he left his car. Then they walked back to the house across the terrace.

Dot showed Dan where to put his things, and when he was finished, he joined Anna. They went into the breakfast room together.

Neil looked up from a chaffing dish of kidneys, said, "Oh, hello, Dan, come and join me."

"I've eaten, thank you," Dan answered, giving Anna a covert look. "But I'll have some coffee."

"Of course." Neil gestured to a chair. "Have a seat. Help yourself. That's how we do it at this time of day."

Dan sat down, and Anna joined him.

Neil brought his plate to the table and took his usual chair.

Julia yawned, said, "Has Dot made you comfortable, Dan?"

"Oh, yes. She certainly has. I've a room on the top floor. A beautiful view. I never realized how fine the scenery is in the valley."

Tanya said, "I don't like the top floor. It gives me the willies, and always has. I keep thinking I smell smoke up there, the smoke from the old fire that Neil told me about."

"It's long gone," Neil said stiffly, openly annoyed with her for having mentioned it.

"But it would still be awful to be trapped there," she said.

"There are plenty of ladders down," Neil said. And then, "You must get Anna to show you through the whole of the house, Dan. It holds a lot of history. The Kennellys go back a long way."

"So they do." Dan laughed softly. "As a matter of fact, so do we all."

Tanya chuckled. "Thank you, Dan. You'll be a nice and

refreshing addition to the family, I think. At least it'll be nice to have new blood."

"All families need new blood occasionally," William said.

Davis put in, "But that depends on the blood, doesn't it?"

Anna sat back, relaxing. It was plain that whatever opposition the family felt, they would all attempt to conceal it. They would play kind hosts, and attentive relations to the man they thought was her new fiancé. At the same time, mixed with her relief, she felt a strange uneasiness. She wondered why the pretense. She wondered what they thought it would accomplish to pretend that Dan was a welcome guest, a welcome prospective member of the family.

It troubled her, too, that no one had mentioned what had happened the night before. It was as if they had made a compact to pretend that there had been no shot in the night, that no one had looked at her with accusing eyes.

At last she could no longer bear it. She took a deep breath, said, "I've told Dan about the attack on you, Neil."

There was a dead silence.

Then Julia laughed. "Why, Anna, of course you did. And that's why he turned up so quickly, isn't it? He wants to make sure nothing bad happens to you, and I can't blame him. This is a mad house, and a bad house, and the sooner Dan knows it and takes you away from here, the better it will be for all of us."

When she had stopped, Neil said heavily, "I suppose you felt it necessary, Anna. But we must forget all about it. There was no harm done, after all."

Dan said, "But there could have been harm done, Neil."

Neil shook his head, said stubbornly, "I think the best thing to do is forget it. Yes, the less said the better."

Was that the way the family had always dealt with its problems? Anna found herself wondering. Had they always swept them under the carpet? Had they always hidden them from the outside, and from themselves at the same time?

"You're like an ostrich," Tanya told him bitterly. "You won't look, you won't listen. But don't you realize that you might have been killed? You might be dead right now?" Her voice shook, and her auburn head trembled on her slim neck. "What about me? Don't you care about me? How do you know that I won't be next?"

Julia sighed, "Oh, Tanya, you insist on being the center of attention. Nothing has happened to you, and nothing will." Tears glinted in her eyes. "If I can stand it, and I'm trying to as hard as I can, then I don't see why you have to become hysterical."

William cleared his throat, patted his pink forehead with a napkin. "What an unseemly conversation. There are some things one just doesn't talk about." His eyes were fixed firmly on Dan.

Dan said, "I'm not exactly a stranger. You needn't think that I'll repeat in town, or anywhere else, what I hear in Emerald Station."

William's plump face reddened. "I didn't mean to imply any such thing."

Dan deliberately emptied his cup, put it down. "Want to take me on a sight-seeing tour?" he asked Anna.

. . . She was standing at the top of the stairs. It was very dark. Not a glint of moonlight cut through the shadows. Then Dan was there, bathed in white light. He looked up at her, his face grave. "It's a mistake," he said. "We should never have done it. It was a mistake to fall in love, Anna. We must pretend that we haven't. Love is dangerous. Love can destroy us. Can you pretend that we haven't fallen in love?"

"I can't," she told him. "I won't. Because it's true, you see. It's real. I'll never give you up, Dan. No matter what they do to me, I won't give you up."

"Maybe that's why Martin died," Dan told her. "Because you wouldn't give him up. Could that be why, Anna?"

She was about to answer him. She was forming the words on her lips. Then she heard a sound. Someone moaned behind her. She turned slowly . . .

She opened her eyes, stared into the darkness. The dream had been so real, she thought. She must remember it. It was important. As if . . .

She heard the sound again. A long quiet moan of pain. And she hadn't dreamed it. She had heard it through veils of sleep, and awakened to hear it once more.

She threw back the sheets, and got up, reaching for the lamp, then withdrawing her hand.

Let the bedroom remain dark. The sound was from further down the hall, not from in here.

She took her robe, slipped it on, and went out into the corridor.

Again she heard the moan. She knew the voice, and knew from where it came.

She gasped, and made quickly for the room at the head of the stairs.

Chapter 42

The groans were louder here, and mixed with not quite clear words.

Anna threw open the door.

The room was filled with a strange and wavering light, and in the shadows it cast, Julia, on her knees near the bed, looked like a half-mad witch woman muttering incanations to awful gods.

"Julia!" Anna was instantly beside the older woman. "Julia, what happened? What's wrong?"

The not quite clear incantations became a terrified plea. "Anna, help me!"

Now Anna saw that the flickering light came from an old-fashioned lantern. A kerosene lantern. It sat on the floor before the big double doors that led out into the balcony.

The flickering light . . . Julia on her knees, huddled over the fullness of her belly, and clawing at the big chair near the bed . . .

"Somebody was here," she moaned. "Here in the room with me. The lantern. You do see it? I didn't dream it. It's there. It woke me up. And it sat there, blinking at me. I couldn't stand it . . . I got up, and the chair . . ."

Anna switched on the bedside light. Instantly the flickering was gone, although the lamp remained where it had been.

Now she could see that the chair had been moved. It had been pushed across the room leaving long dark tracks in the nap of the green carpet. The chair was an obstacle positioned to block Julia when she rose. The lamp was the bait to draw her, half-asleep and frightened, out of bed. She was supposed to fall, to miscarry, to lose her baby. Garan's baby. The new Gordon.

Evil had once more reached out of the shadows to injure the innocent.

With those thoughts in her mind, Anna acted. She grabbed a blanket from the bed and wrapped it around Julia's shoulders. She said, "Stay where you are. I'll get Dan. We'll take you in to the doctor. But just don't move."

Julia's thin fingers caught her wrist. "Anna, don't leave me alone. Don't leave me. I know someone's out there, waiting. Somebody wants to destroy me. I'm scared. Don't leave me alone. "

"Just for a second," Anna promised, pity twisting her heart. "Wait until I can get Dan." She drew her hand away, patted Julia's shoulder, and hurried out. In passing she gave the smoking kerosene lamp a quick look. Where had it come from? Who had put it there? How long had it waited in Emerald Station to be used for this wicked purpose?

Behind her Julia wept quietly, clinging to the chair as desperately as she had clung, moments before, to Anna's wrist.

"Hurry," she whispered. "Dear God, help me. There isn't much time."

Julia's baby was born two hours later in Dr. Robinson's office. It was a boy, too premature to survive the shocks it had received. It took two choking breaths, and then it died.

Mercifully, Julia was unconscious at the time.

Anna looked at the tiny body, and turned away in a grief too deep for tears.

Julia would have to be told. Anna dreaded the moment.

Dan said quietly, "Anna, you know that there's only one thing we can do for Julia now."

"Yes," she answered. "Find out who did this to her. And find out why."

She had, in those terrible moments after she summoned Dan, told him only a little. On the anxious drive into town she had told him a bit more.

Now, in the doctor's quiet waiting room, he said, "I want you to tell me every single thing that Julia said to you when you found her, and every single thing you saw."

She sagged in the straight chair. "I heard her moaning, and went down the hall into her room. It was full of that weird flickering light. She was on her knees near the big chair. You saw it next to her bed, and the tracks that showed it had been pushed there. She said she woke up and saw the light in front of the balcony doors. She was frightened, and got up. She fell over the chair . . ."

"Where did the lantern come from?" Dan asked.

"I don't know. But I suppose it's been around for years. Probably stored with a lot of other junk in the sheds behind the garages. I know, years ago, I saw some like it."

"Someone brought it into the house, of course," Dan said, his voice grim. "The same someone that stole Neil's gun, and then fired it at him, and left it on your balcony. The same someone who pushed that flowerpot at you."

She knew that Dan was right. And she knew, beyond any doubt, though sickened at the thought, that that someone, was related to her by blood, was determined that all the Gordons die. But, once again, the certainty brought her back to Martin Milton. Why had he been killed? Was it only because she had been going out with him? Was their innocent friendship a threat she didn't understand? Or was it because he had seen, learned, some small fact of which she was unaware, that had made him a danger?

Had William, returning to Emerald Station after all these years, determined that he would be master there? He was a Kennelly, and had the Kennelly pride. She'd seen him in the family room, smiling up at the portraits of his forebears. Did that mean something? Was silver-haired, dimpled Helga only pretending to want to return to her Maine home to cover some pathological determination to be mistress of the house? Was young Davis, so much like his grand-uncle, involved? Was it possible that Tanya, feeling overwhelmed by the others, had managed to do these things, trying to destroy the others so that she, as Neil's wife, would have absolute control?

Anna shuddered within herself, sick at being enmeshed in such speculations, but knowing that it was in them that she would find the answers she sought.

Dan took her hand. "You're terribly tired. Let's go get some coffee. We'll come back and see Julia in a few hours. I'm sure Dr. Robinson will see that she sleeps at least that long."

They went out into a cool spring morning. The sun was bright, the air scented. Dew sparkled on the trees, glistened like the Kennelly diamonds, she thought.

They walked the few blocks to the Old Anglers' Inn in silence.

There Fred Moody greeted them sourly. He served them coffee in a still-empty breakfast room full of dusty potted plants. Then, lingering with them, he said, "I hear you had some more trouble out there."

She simply looked at him.

"Brought in Julia, didn't you? Garan's wife? Brought her in to Dr. Robinson in the middle of the night."

Dan said crisply, "The grapevine in this town puts me to shame, Fred."

"No grapevine that I know of," Fred answered. "Remember I've got people working for me, and they come in pretty early. One of the Morris girls helps me out in the kitchen. She saw you stop. What's wrong?"

"Julia had a miscarriage," Dan said.

Fred's lip jutted out. "Is that right?"

Dan nodded.

"What happened to the baby then? It was pretty early, wasn't it?"

"It didn't make it."

Fred's complacent knowingness softened a little. "That's too bad. And Julia?"

"She's resting. She ought to be all right."

"Good that we've still got Dr. Robinson with us," Fred said. "He's an old man, and when he goes we're going to be in trouble. Nobody wants to set up shop in a town like this these days. But him, he's seen a lot, knows a lot. He could have told you, anybody in this town could have told you, that there'd be more trouble."

Dan's dark brows pulled into a frown, his jaw hardened. "What's that supposed to mean?"

"If you know the history of that place, and you ought to, you'd understand. And you'd watch out, too."

"I know the history of my family," Anna said coolly. "And I don't know what you're talking about."

Fred gave her a narrow grin. "You don't want to, girl. And I don't blame you a bit." He turned to Dan, "But you, you ought to have better sense. Martin Milton died out there, didn't he? Burned to death in his car in the quarry. And then Garan fell off that stallion of his and busted his head. The two of them in accidents. But Kennelly accidents are an old story around here. And there's some that have long memories. So they know ... they know ..."

Another Kennelly accident, Anna thought.

But Dan laughed. "You and your old wives' tales."

Fred sniffed. "Well, maybe. Only your grandfather, Dale Row, didn't think so. Nor did your grandmother, Moira, for all she wanted to, and wanted to stand up for the Kennellys, too, being as her mother lived out there." Fred shrugged. "It's none of my business. But I'll tell you what I told your father last week when I got my new car. I told him if I was you, I'd be damned careful. And now

403

that you're engaged to one, and you've moved your stuff out there, which looks pretty funny, I'd be even more careful." With that, Fred turned and stalked away.

Anne said softly, "Maybe you should listen to him, Dan. Maybe . . ."

Dan grinned at her. "Okay. I've listened. I don't know any more than I knew before. I'm not interested in his dire words of warning. I'm only interested in knowing who is responsible for what's happened."

"But you did go back and check the records, the burial dates, Dan. You did take me to see your father."

"Yes," Dan agreed soberly. "And believe me, I see something there. But we'll find the truth in the present, and not in the dead past, Anna."

"Martin," she said. "And Garan."

He nodded. "And Julia now. As well as you."

But she had to remind herself then that she musn't trust him too far. He was, after all, no matter what he had just told her, interested solely in learning about Martin's death. He wasn't in love with her, and she musn't allow herself the deep joy of thinking that he was. When this was over, they would go their own separate ways. They would never see each other again.

He said gently, "Anna, don't be afraid of me. I won't ever hurt you, you know."

"We don't know what will happen, Dan."

He rose, dropped change on the table. "Let's go back now, Anna." And as she followed him out, "We don't know yet. But we will know, and soon."

They started back toward Dr. Robinson's house. A big gray car pulled up beside them. A tall and hunched elderly man swung the door open, got out clumsily, and blocked their way.

"Good morning, Mr. Stapleton," Dan said. "How are you?"

"Old," Tom Stapleton quavered. "And getting more so all the time."

A young girl got out of the driver's seat, smiled uneasily from under a mass of blonde curls. "Grandpa, we'd better

404

go on now. These people don't really want to talk to you."

"But I want to talk to them," he said sourly. And then, smiling a narrow smile at Anna, "the younger generation has no respect. No respect, I say. Won't listen, don't listen. Are you that way, too?"

"I hope not," she answered, meeting his gray eyes.

"Told you ... no ... no, it wasn't you. That other one ... the wife ..."

"Anna Gordon is my name," she said quietly. "I think you mean my sister-in-law. Tanya. Neil's wife. She said that you spoke to her one night."

"Told her. Yes. All of you. You don't know. But it's happening again, you see. Oh, I hated them. Him. Yes, I admit it. I did. I did. And still do, though most of them are dead and gone. But it's murder, you see. In every generation. Murder unpunished and hidden. It should die. The Kennellys. . . ."

Dan's fingers curled around Anna's arm. He said evenly, "That's pretty wild talk, Mr. Stapleton."

"Grandpa," the blonde girl cut in, shuffling her sneakers. "Grandpa, I think it's time we got home."

Tom Stapleton ignored her. He stared at Dan. "Wild talk, is it? A lot you know. Smart whippersnapper, they tell me. Garage too good for you. Automobiles too good for you. Make the paper, that's what you do. But your grandfather was my friend. Good people, the Rows. Too good for the likes of the Kennellys. But pride . . ."

"Grandpa . . ." it was a wail now.

"She went away. That's what they told me. Gareth said it, with Nealanna standing there beside me. Told it to me to my face. Went away, he said. And was never heard from since. He took the boy, I'll give him that. And they raised him. My nephew, he was. Storr. I had a few words with him later. Years later, that is. Poor boy, he cracked his car and died on the Kennelly walls."

"Grandpa . . ."

"I'm coming," the old man said. "Don't pull and tug at me. Don't interrupt me." His eyes focused on Anna. "You ask Jennings," he mumbled. "Tried to buy me off with the library contract. Oh, that was years ago. As if that meant anything to me. Just a chance to cozy with Storr. Not that I meant anything special to happen. And not that I know what did. But Jennings must know. Away he went, afterwards. His blood too thin for them maybe. Well, he lived on, and the others didn't. Alicia, and Storr, and the others. They didn't live to be old, did they? And neither will you, poor girl, for all you say you're Anna Gordon."

Dan asked coolly, "Why not, Mr. Stapleton? Why shouldn't my girl marry me and live to an old age right along with me?"

"Why, it's in the blood," Tom Stapleton said. "Blood tells. I've said it all along. You ask Jennings. Or any of them. Ask the Maradines. They know, too."

Jennings had said, 'It's beginning again.'

Lolly had cried, 'I can't go through it once more. I'm too old.'

"Grandpa ..." The young girl pulled at him, and he grinned, a narrow, hating grin, and allowed himself to be put into the car.

His granddaughter slipped behind the wheel and drove away quickly.

"I never realized the old man was senile before," Dan said quietly. His big hand cupped her elbow. "Come on. Let's get back to Dr. Robinson's and see how Julia is now."

She said, as they went down the block, "I don't think he is senile. He was trying to tell us something."

"Do you know what?"

"I can make a few guesses. Much the same that your father was saying, what you saw in the burial dates, I suspect." She paused to take a shuddery breath. "I think he was talking about murder in three generations, Dan. Gareth ... Storr ... the others he mentioned. My uncle would know."

Dan said. "He might. He's about the same age as Stapleton, wouldn't you say?"

"About. Give or take a few years either way. Though

Jennings seems . . . seems less worn somehow. But that may be simply the life he's lived."

Dr. Robinson was at his desk when they went in. He looked up, his bulldog face sagging into lines. "She's awake," he said quietly. "I've told her."

Anna asked, "Will she be all right? How did she . . ." The memory of her mother's long shock at the loss of her baby came flooding back now. Poor Julia . . .

"She took it quietly. I think she already knew somehow." Dr. Robinson leaned back in his chair. "I hope that you'll approve of what I've done, Anna. I took it upon myself because I believed it to be necessary. This, coming after the shock of Garan's death, is too much for Julia. She's talking pretty wildly about what happened to her last night. But it's natural for her to see causes outside of herself. Natural for her to be terrified, too. Anyway, I've arranged for her to be transferred to a convalescent home for a month or so. She needs special care, and rest, and a less burdened mind. She doesn't want to return to Emerald Station, and I heartily agree with her that that would be a mistake at the present time. So . . ."

"Of course it's all right," Anna said. "You must do what you think best for her. I'm very relieved. I didn't know what we should do."

She saw Julia a few minutes later.

Julia's face was dead white, her eyes very large in her hollow-cheeked face. She said, "Anna, I was always afraid it would happen, and it did." Her hands clenched at her sides. "And you shouldn't go back either. You should get Dan to take you away, far far away. There's a wickedness bred into that place. Because of what I don't know. But save yourself from it, Anna. Go away and build a new life."

Tears clogged Anna's throat. Julia believed in Dan's engagement to her. Julia believed that Dan loved her, that the two of them could build a good life together.

There was nothing to say, no way to explain.

Anna bent, kissed her sister-in-law's cheek. "Never mind about Emerald Station. Just think of yourself, take care of

407

yourself. I'll visit you soon. And if there's anything you want, let me know."

"I don't want anything, "Julia said dully. "Except Garan back, and the baby. And it's too late for both of them. Now I just want to stop being afraid."

"I don't know anything about it," Jennings said stiffly. There was a white line around his rosebud lips, and a faint tinge of pink on his cheekbones above his whiskers. "I was just a boy. Seventeen, I think. Yes, yes, to be exact, I was seventeen. My father and I had a falling out, and I left. While I was away, oh, I guess it was soon after, my father died in a hunting accident. One of those things that happens sometimes, though he knew his guns. And some time soon after, I guess it was, Alicia died, too. While I was away though. So that's all I know. She died. Oh, yes, there were others. In every generation there are bound to be deaths, aren't there? Nobody, and no generation, lives forever. No family either. And the Kennellys are almost gone, aren't they? I mean . . . I'm an old man. And there's William and Davis. I don't count George. George musn't count in this, you see."

George, Anna thought, her mind quite blank. George Kennelly? And then she remembered. He was the uncle who had become a monk, taken vows of silence even before she was born. He had written when notified of her mother's death. But he hadn't come to the funeral. As far as she knew, he had never returned to Emerald Station since the day he first left it.

"And Storr," Jennings was saying. "Don't ask me about him. He was mad, you see. Just mad. And perhaps . . ."

Lolly cried, "Now, Jennings, you mustn't say that. Nobody really knows."

"I suppose," he grumbled.

Brooke's blue eyes were fixed on the portrait that hung over the fireplace. The portrait of Deborah Maradine. Still looking up at her, he said gently, "Never mind. Never mind now." And to Anna, "You see, it's no good raking up the past."

"Even if it explains the present?" Anna asked. "Even if we must to survive?"

"I, the rest of us here," his white head inclined toward Lolly and Jennings, "we know nothing of the present, Anna."

"But Jennings does," she insisted. "That's why he moved over here, isn't it? To get away from the present in Emerald Station?"

"Peace and quiet for old bones," he mumbled in his beard. "That's why I moved to Maradine Mansion. And if you had sense, and wanted that for your young bones, then you'd do exactly the same."

Chapter 43

"Madness?" William said, his florid face suddenly full of deeply scored lines. "Madness? Among the Kennellys? Why do you ask about that, Anna? What are you leading up to, or implying?"

"It was something Tom Stapleton said," she explained. "You see, we ran into him when we were going back to see Julia. And he . . ."

The lines smoothed out suddenly. William even smiled. "That senile old man? It's amazing that he's still walking around. You'd think by now he'd have forgotten his old grudge, something about the Kennelly land being his father's once."

"He still seems to do pretty nicely," she told William.

"Until he opens his mouth," William retorted. He rose then, stamped into the house.

Anna looked at Dan and shrugged. "That wasn't much help, was it?"

"We didn't expect it to be easy, Anna."

"And maybe we're wrong," she said. "Maybe there's been nothing but a series of weird accidents. What the town people call Kennelly accidents. After all, Dan, what

Jennings said is true. There are deaths in every generation, aren't there?"

He didn't answer her. He got to his feet, lean, tall, and somehow, she thought suddenly, dangerous-looking. "I want to go out and see the quarry," he said. "And the place where Garan fell. And the sheds where the kerosene lamps are stored."

They walked across the meadows together. She stumbled once, and he caught her, smiling slightly.

The shock of his touch, his closeness, made her breathless. The long held back feelings she had had for him rose up to claim her. In another time, another place, love might have been real, not pretended. In another time, another place . . . She reminded herself that she must expect nothing from him. It was a painful thought. She found herself stumbling again. Once more he steadied her.

"You're tired, aren't you? Suppose I make this tour on my own?" he suggested.

But she insisted on going with him.

Afterwards, when they had reached the quarry, and stood there at the rim, looking at the scummy water, the fire-blackened stones, she was sorry.

It was the first time she had been there since the night she heard the explosion, saw the flame tower toward the dark of the sky. The memory of it, dulling with time and distraction and fear, became sharp again.

She imagined Martin driving away from the house, and someone waving him down, whispering. She imagined Martin turning off the driveway into the gravel lane that led to the garages, turning again, directed by someone, to jolt across the meadow.

Now she showed Dan the place where the car had stopped, where the tracks veered away into fatal emptiness. She showed Dan where the car had been hauled out, where Jim Arden had stood saying, 'Another of those Kennelly accidents.'

Dan, grim-faced and quiet, surveyed the area through narrowed blue eyes. At last he said, "Now Garan . . ."

Slowly she led him to the grove of trees near the river.

She showed him the spot. There was nothing to be seen now of Garan's blood.

Dan studied the area, then shrugged. "Let's go back to the house. I want to spend some time with the family, Anna. I think that may be a lot more useful, after all."

"But why?" she asked quickly. "Have you begun to suspect any one of them in particular?"

"Not yet," he told her.

"But you must have some idea ... who? And why, Dan?"

But Dan said nothing. He turned, walked quickly through the trees. She followed him, hurrying to keep up with his long determined strides.

She dressed carefully that evening, not allowing herself to consider her motive, nor even to think of Dan, though certainly the thought of him was there in her mind, as it had been since she first saw him before he went away to war, as it had been ever since he had introduced her to Martin in the post office doorway.

Her gown was white silk, with long full sleeves and tight cuffs. It was narrow at the waist, and belled out just below her knees. She brushed her hair high into a waved crest at the front, and smoothed it into long waves at the back.

On an impulse she didn't pause to examine, she took from her jewel case a string of emeralds set in gold mountings. As she held it, she remembered that Dot had found all the jewels scattered on the dresser. She saw now that that small and unimportant act had been the beginning of what had followed. Someone had crept into her room, studied her jewels? Why?

She sighed, and hooking the emeralds around her throat, she remembered her mother wearing them. She was sure that her grandmother had worn them, too. Emeralds from Emerald Station, named for the original place so far away. They felt oddly cool to the touch, and the light glinted on them. They reminded her now of the green glass atop the wall that surrounded the estate. The

412

wall that made of Emerald Station a prison harried by its past.

When she went downstairs, she found that the others were gathered on the terrace having drinks and observing the sunset.

Dan rose to greet her, a smile on his lips, an approving look in his blue eyes. She wondered if he were acting for the benefit of the others.

Tanya, in flame red piqué, stretched out her long beautiful legs, and said enviously, "You're wearing the emeralds, Anna. I can't remember that you've ever bothered with them before."

"I don't often," she answered. She took a seat beside Dan, accepted the drink that he offered her.

"You should," Neil told her. "They were made to be worn. I can remember when Mother wore them. She walked like a queen. I suppose Grandmother did, too."

"Nealanna looked like a queen," Dan said. "I've just been in the family room, studying the portraits. I have the feeling that she was an extraordinary woman."

"I suppose she was," Neil agreed. "And Gareth an extraordinary man."

"But they weren't the ones who got the mines," Davis said suddenly, from his usual perch on the wall. "It was the old man, Neil Kennelly." His dark slanted eyes narrowed, glowed with a reflection of sunset. He leaned forward, his mouth quivering. "It was Neil. Neil Kennelly. It all goes back to him. Emerald Station is his."

"Sure," Neil agreed negligently. "He began it all right. But we're here now."

But Davis didn't seem to have heard him. He went on urgently. "It was Neil Kennelly who built Emerald Station. The Kennellys ..."

Helga chuckled, "Oh don't go off on that, Davis. We've heard enough of it in our lifetime. Why, your father gave me chapter and verse a million times starting the day I married him. And you get the same reading."

William grunted, "History."

And Davis smiled.

And that was when Anna knew. She, who considered herself a down-to-earth young woman, was suddenly seized by intuition. Seized, and given new sight by it.

She knew. 'It was the Kennellys'. . . Those were the words Davis used. But he, his father, were the only Kennellys left. Except for Jennings. And Jennings was old, with no heirs. All the rest of the family were Gordons, descended from Dolores Kennelly and Jay Gordon. They were part Kennelly but named Gordon. Garan, his infant son. Neil. And Anna herself. There was where death had struck, and succeeded, struck, and failed.

She clutched her glass in cold fingers, nearly holding her breath. But failure would not be accepted. There would be more. There had to be.

But what about Martin?

And once again, intuition whispered. She understood at last.

She looked sideways at Davis, and saw that his avid eyes were fixed on her. She kept her face as blank as she could, but she knew as if she could feel it as a touch that his gaze was on the emeralds at her throat.

Davis had thought she was going to marry Martin. He had told her so himself. He had been surprised when she said, after Martin's death, that she had been no more than a friend to the big blond man. So Martin had had to die, lest a new name be brought to Emerald Station, a new name, and eventually, new heirs. Then Garan had had to be killed. Garan Gordon, the master here. And the boy who might have been master after Garan. And Neil . . .

Her heart gave a sudden hitch. If she were right, then Dan was in danger, too. Anyone who might stand in the way of Davis Kennelly lived with death hanging over him like a big black shadow.

Davis Kennelly . . . eighteen years old . . . with that hard look of pride about his face, in his eyes . . .

She drew a deep breath. Now that she knew, she knew it was time for desperate measures. Neil, Tanya, Dan, she herself, must somehow be protected. But how? What could she do?

414

She sipped her drink cautiously, pretending to a nonchalance she didn't feel. There must be some way to force Davis to show himself, to prove that he, and he alone, was responsible for the terror at Emerald Station. There must be some way ...

And then Dan said, deliberately and slowly, "If you didn't isolate yourself here, you would know that not everyone regards the Kennelly name with so much favor. There are people who consider it a curse."

There was a brief silence.

William heaved in his chair, and Neil sat frozen and still, his hazel eyes sharp.

At last Davis laughed. "Some people will say anything at all. We're above that, you know, and have always been. But if you're afraid of all that, then you don't belong in Emerald Station."

William got to his feet, refilled his glass and went to stand next to his son.

Neil crossed his legs, and uncrossed them, and finally, with a look of satisfaction, said, "I've ordered a television set. It'll be the first in the area. Probably the first within a couple of hundred miles."

"A television set?" Tanya repeated. "What on earth do we need that for? It's just a silly toy. Nobody'll ever pay any attention to it."

"You'll see," he told her. "When you get your first look at it, you'll have the surprise of your life."

"I'd much rather have a strand of emeralds like those Anna's wearing," Tanya retorted, tossing her head.

"You've all the jewels you need and more," he answered sharply.

"But not emeralds," she pouted. "Julia had the earrings. And Anna the necklace. And she hardly ever wears it. If it were mine ..."

Anna saw her chance then. It came as a breathless burst of certainty within her. She smiled widely, said, "I wear it for special occasions, Tanya. And this is one of them."

The others looked at her expectantly. She saw Dan's

415

eyes touch her, a faint worried frown beginning to grow between his brows, his lean body suddenly stiffening. She wondered if he knew, if he understood what she was about to do.

She went on, "Dan and I are going to be married tomorrow."

There. It was out. It was done. She had set the trap, and now she must wait to see if Davis stepped into it. Or if and it could be, she knew, she was completely wrong.

Davis only blinked at her, a smile on his lips.

Neil said heavily, "I don't understand you, Anna. You've barely announced your engagement. I don't see why you don't wait for a little while."

"And it's hardly suitable," Helga put in, her plump face wrinkled with disapproval. "Not after all that's happened. Why, Garan is hardly cold in his grave. And poor Julia . . . And so soon after Martin died . . . What will people think? What will they say?"

"There won't be a real wedding. Not in the sense you mean it," Anna answered.

"Of course not," Dan said, smiling. "It certainly isn't time for that. We've decided though to ride over to the county seat, go to a justice of the peace. It will be a very quick and discreet affair."

"Oh, I see," Helga muttered, as if she didn't know what to say next.

William's florid face creased in a smile. "Then let us wish you the best of luck, Anna. And congratulations to you Dan."

"Its really a rather odd thing to do," Tanya complained. "Why, when Neil and I married we had . . ."

"Never mind," Neil cut in. "This is Anna's affair and Dan's. I presume they know what they're doing. Or think they know." His voice suggested that he believed they did not.

But that was all it suggested, Anna thought. She couldn't tell if the announcement had set his brain whirling with bright schemes to prevent a marriage he

416

didn't approve of. She couldn't tell that about William or Davis either.

If she were right, then she must not expect any reaction from Neil or William. But there was none that she could see in Davis either. He was silent, his profile, dark and straight, turned at an angle to her. Once again, she thought of him as a king, surveying his acres. Perhaps that was what he felt. That he, as a Kennelly, had a right to Emerald Station, a right he could share with no one else. Not even with those direct descendants of Neil Kennelly, who, without the name, had Emerald Station now.

There was no time to explain to Dan, no time to tell him why she had done what she had.

Dot announced that dinner was served, and they went, in a group, into the dining room.

The candlelight flickered over the long table, danced on the Royal Crown Derby china and crystal glassware, the heavy silver. These were the things that Anna had grown up with, taken for granted. Were these what Davis wanted for himself, she wondered.

She stole a glance at him. His dark eyes were fixed on the candles dreamily. She wondered what he saw in the dancing light, what visions drew him.

Neil was saying, "Now that Dewey's going to be president, we'll see some changes."

"The election hasn't been held yet," Dan told him, smiling. "You may wake up one morning to find that you have an unpleasant surprise."

"Surprise? Impossible," Neil snorted. "The county's fed up with the Democrats, and with Truman, too. We all want a good solid Republican in."

"Maybe." But Dan was plainly skeptical.

"It has to be," William said. "It's time we brought our boys back from Europe. All those garrisons mean nothing bu expense and further trouble for us."

"Politics," Tanya pouted. "Isn't there anything else to talk about?"

Helga chuckled. "I agree. But it's always the same when you get a bunch of men together."

"Just as," Davis said, "when you get a bunch of women together, they talk about clothes."

"Not true," Tanya told him. "You've not heard me, or any of us mention clothes. Not once, since you came here."

"But you're different." A teasing grin twisted his mouth. "This is Emerald Station. That's different, too. So here you talk about jewels, the way other women talk about clothes."

Helga said thoughtfully, "You're going to miss it, aren't you, Davis. When you go to college in the fall, You're really going to miss it."

"I might not go," he answered. "The fall is still a long way off."

"Just a few months." She was staring at him, her plump face full of dismay, the forkful of food halfway to her mouth. "But what do you mean you might not go? Do you realize what strings your father had to pull to get you into Yale? Don't you know what ..."

He said sullennly, "All right. Don't get in an uproar. I didn't say I wouldn't go. Only that I might not. Who knows what'll happen between now and then? Who can think that far ahead?"

"I can," William said brusquely. "You'll go, just as we've always planned."

Davis grinned. "I might be drafted, you know."

"You won't be," William told him.

Anna wondered how William could be that certain. Then she wondered what Davis thought might happen before the summer was over.

Dot brought in coffee and dessert, halting the discussion of Davis' future. When she had gone, it was not resumed, much to Anna's relief.

Later, Dan walked her up the steps to her room. On the way, he paused at the black masks that hung on the wall. "Where did these come from, do you know?"

"I think from Africa," Anna told him.

418

And Davis leaned over the bannister to say, smiling, "Neil brought them back from the diamond fields."

It was, Anna thought, another proof of his obsession. If he was the one . . . And she wasn't sure any more. How could she be absolutely sure?

In the privacy of her sitting room, Dan said, "Your announcement about tomorrow came as a surprise to me. But I'm pleased to hear it."

"You *do* understand," she said hastily. "You seemed to pick it up quickly."

"I think you decided to precipitate a crisis. To make something happen. I didn't want to spoil it for you. But hadn't you better tell me what you had in mind?"

"For a little while, listening to Davis, I thought I had the answer. I'm not sure any more."

"The Kennellys," he said softly.

She nodded.

"Yes. I think so. But you must be very careful, Anna. We don't know from which direction it might come."

"I'll be careful," she said.

"And I'll be looking forward to tomorrow."

A blush burned in her cheeks. "Dan, you mustn't pretend with me. You know that I only meant . . ."

He bent down to her. "Never mind," he said. "We'll concentrate on tonight. Tomorrow will take care of itself." He kissed her lightly, smiled, and left her.

She was determined to stay awake, to listen, to observe. If anyone in the house were to move about, she wanted to know it. She had, hopefully, set in motion what might reveal the truth. She must be prepared to deal with it.

She changed to sneakers and jeans, and sat down to read Mailer's *The Naked and the Dead*. But she found that she couldn't concentrate. The words blurred before her eyes. The very stillness of the house seemed to whisper in her ears. It was moments before she realized that that whisper was not of the house's stillness, not creaking floors, nor sighing walls. It was sound.

She leaned forward, switched off the lamp beside her.

The room was plunged into utter darkness.

Chapter 44

The sound came again.

That time she was able to identify the direction from which it had come. The balcony outside of her bedroom.

But she sat very still, waiting.

Whoever was there must feel safe, assured. That quick killer must move with confidence to the moment of unmasking.

She wondered where Dan was. They had, she realized suddenly, made no plans. But she was certain that he would be somewhere close. He understood the risk she had taken.

Unless ... suddenly her heart contracted. She forgot her fear for herself, for what was to come. Suppose a sudden hand had come out of the dark? Suppose Dan lay still, silent, unable to move? Suppose ...

A faint glimmer of light made a path across the rug at her feet. She knew that the balcony draperies had parted. She rose and waited again. Then the light was suddenly gone. She knew that meant the draperies had been closed once more.

Someone was in her bedroom.

Straining, she heard the faintest of breaths, the whisper of a careful footfall.

She tiptoed soundlessly to the door, reached inside and switched on the overhead chandelier.

Brilliant and blinding light drove the shadows away in that instant.

Davis stood hunched, all dressed in black, between one step and another. He stared at her, his eyes wide and glistening.

She said softly, "What are you doing here, Davis? What do you want?"

A rope dangled between his big hands. He let it slide between his fingers and fall to the rug. He said, "Were you waiting up for me, Anna? You should have been asleep long ago. You should have been in bed and sound asleep."

"Yes," she answered. "I was waiting." Her heart thudded hard against her ribs. Where was Dan? Did he know that Davis was up, walking, staring at her with entranced and glistening eyes?

"You were waiting," he laughed, and there was no mirth in the sound. "Then you know."

"I do know," she repeated.

"You're not like the others," he complained. "The others ... they ... they made it so easy. Too easy. There's no amusement without challenge."

She saw the madness that had driven him. Old Tom Stapleton had been right in a way. There *was* madness here. The madness that came from pride.

William ...

And this corrupted boy who was his instrument.

"They made it easy," Davis said again. He leaned against her dresser now, his body loose and slender.

"Yes," she agreed. "They didn't suspect you, did they?"

"No. There was nothing to suspect, after all. I'm just a kid, Anna. A kid doesn't count. Not even if he's a Kennelly. The only real Kennelly in Emerald Station. Martin ... he was driving away. I stepped out into the driveway. He stopped to talk, of course. I told him I had something to tell him and got in the car, too. Then I knocked him on the head with a flashlight. He went out. I was afraid Thomson was still hanging around, but he didn't see anything. I drove to the quarry, and pushed the car over, and headed back to the house. It was as simple as that."

She watched fascinated, as his fingers absently moved on her dresser top, settled on the jewel case and opened it. She watched as he hooked the emerald necklace around his neck. It glittered on his black sweater. It glittered like the glass atop the gray walls outside.

"Simple," she agreed finally, swallowing the sickness that rose in her throat. "So simple."

"I couldn't let you marry him, Anna. There were already too many others. There's already been too much thinning of the blood. It's the Kennellys that matter. That's all. Nobody else. You can't be one, not ever, and if you marry and have children, it would be the same thing all over again. My mother said you were crazy about him, and you'd get married soon. Julia thought so, too. So I had to stop that. And afterwards I saw that I'd gone about it wrong. There was still Garan, still the baby coming. There was still Neil. But it had to be only the Kennellys."

"So you killed Garan," she said softly, keeping her eyes away from the rope at his feet. She hoped that she could keep him talking, interested, obssesed with explaining. That way only could she save herself, the others.

"Oh, yes, I did kill Garan. He was riding through the grove. I knocked him off the horse with a rock. My aim is good. I'm a baseball player, you know. So he fell, and I made sure he was dead. I let the horse run, and got myself back to the house."

"And then drove the jeep to help us go looking for him," she said.

"Well, I had to do something."

"Once your aim wasn't so good," she reminded him. "That time you pushed the flowerpot over on me."

"It wasn't planned. Just an impulse. Otherwise I would have made it," he told her in a petulant voice. "I just happened to step out on the balcony near Tanya's room, and saw you and Dan sitting there, and my hand set the rope before I knew what I was going to do."

"Like when you stole Neil's gun, and then used it on him, and made it look as if I might have done it."

He smiled faintly, and stroked the emeralds at his throat. "Oh, that was window dressing. I wanted to scare you."

"The way you wanted to scare Julia, I suppose."

He nodded, and his shining eyes slid away from hers. "She shouldn't have been pregnant," he said quietly. "It was ridiculous to make more Gordons. There were already too many Gordons for me to get rid of. Don't you really understand it yet?"

"I think I do," she said. "It goes all the way back, doesn't it? If you stand in the family room, you can see it, can't you?"

"I did see it there," Davis agreed. "But my father told me, too. Always, all the time I was growing up, he told me. There was old Neil, and he died. Gareth was his heir, and Faran was his younger brother, my grandfather. If Gareth had died, Faran would have been the head of the family But Gareth didn't die. My grandfather did instead, in that earthquake in San Francisco. And Nealanna and Gareth raised my father and my aunt Jennifer. But then my father went away, because of all the things that happened, and Jennifer died, too. So we lost it all. The Kennellys lost it to the Gordons. Because your mother married one. And it was the end for us. Unless I could win it all back."

"But you can't, you know," she said conversationally. "You can't possibly do that, Davis. Even if you do manage to . . . to . . . kill me now. For there's still Neil, you know. And there's Dan. Dan will never allow you to get away with it, Davis. The family will know what you've done, and the whole world will know it, too."

He said, "Never. I've got it all planned."

"Have you?" she asked gently.

He smiled.

"Remember. There's Dan."

"Sound asleep in his bed," Davis retorted.

Elation swept her. He hadn't harmed Dan. Dan would be somewhere about, perhaps within arm's reach, listening. But where was he then? Why didn't he make himself known? She didn't allow herself to so much as glance toward the balcony, didn't allow even the slightest cringe toward the door behind her. She kept her attention firmly focused on where Davis stood, staring at her with a hot light in his eyes.

He swooped suddenly, and when he straightened he had the rope in his hands again.

"Yes," he said. "It's all planned. I'm going to kill you, Anna. I'm sorry. But it has to be."

She answered, "And then? What happens after that, Davis?"

"Then?"

"How will you explain it? How will you get away with it this time?"

"Oh, that. I think it'll look like suicide. That's probably the best way. And everybody will believe it because they know that the Kennellys are mad."

"But the Kennellys are not mad," she said softly. "Only you are."

"No," he said. "I'm not. I'm just, and fair, and trying only to do what has to be done."

She let herself smile, though she felt that the horror, the fear within her must rise up and overwhelm her.

He said roughly, "Oh, that breakdown was nothing. I didn't think they'd ever even told you about it. Sometimes boys . . . when they hit fifteen . . ."

"What breakdown?" she asked quickly.

His eyes narrowed. "They didn't tell you?" Now he grinned at her. "No, of course they didn't. But it doesn't matter. It was over long ago. Only that's why we hardly ever came here, came home, afterwards, I mean. Until I was well again."

She said, "Davis, you'd better . . ."

And the coiled rope in his hand suddenly flicked out at

her. It whistled through the air and grazed her shoulder. At the same time, the overhead light went out.

In total darkness, she heard the rope's whistle again, and dropped to hands and knees.

A lithe shadow seemed to lunge past her, and she knew Dan's presence. She sensed him there with her in the dark of the room.

Davis cursed. There was the thud of bodies coming together, and thrashing.

She rose cautiously, crept to the wall, and found the light switch.

The chandelier bloomed with light.

Davis and Dan were locked together, a tangle of frantic arms and legs.

William came pounding into her sitting room with plump Helga after him. Neil, followed by Tanya and Dot, crowded in, staring in amazed silence.

But William roared, "What's going on here? I tell you, you must stop it. Dan, Davis . . . Stop it, and . . ."

Helga cried, "Davis! What is he trying to do to you?"

Anna said, through dry lips, "Dan is trying to save my life."

"Save your . . ." William stopped, stared. His eyes bulged in his red face. The pulse beat visibly at his temple. "Save you . . ."

Davis raised his dark head, grinned. "You're just in time."

"Let him go, Dan," William ordered. "What do you think you're doing? You may be Anna's fiancé, but you're a guest in this house. How dare you . . ."

Dan glanced at Anna.

She said softly, "It's a long story, William. Dan and I have been listening to it. We can corroborate everything that Davis admitted. I imagine that you already have guessed part of it, somewhere inside yourself, though maybe you weren't willing to face it."

But Helga's plump face crumpled. "I was so afraid," she wailed. "I've always been so afraid. It was as if he were possessed. I kept thinking . . . Davis . . . what's wrong with the boy? And I wouldn't let myself think any more."

"You knew," Davis snarled. "You knew what I was doing."

"No," William cried. "Davis . . . you can't believe . . ."

"It was for us. For the three Kennellys," Davis said. His head went back, and his body arched. His heels drummed on the rug next to the rope he had dropped. Suddenly his eyes went back in his head, and with a consulsive jerk, he went limp.

Dan rose, said, "You'd better get him a doctor right away."

Dot, weeping and shuddering, ran into the hallway.

Neil said, "Dan, are you certain?"

Anna answered, "We both heard him."

Ashen-faced, Neil turned to William. "What shall we do?"

"Get him out of here," Tanya screamed. "Just get him out of here, that's all."

Anna, starting toward her, heard a sudden quick movement. She swung back. She saw Davis on his feet, eyes wide and glistening, as he plunged toward her.

Dan interposed his body, shunted Davis aside, and tried to seize him. But Davis gave a great yell. He bowled his mother over, and leaped for the balcony, tearing the drapes aside as he rushed into the dark.

Helga sobbed, struggling to rise.

William lurched forward, shouting hoarse but incomprehensible words.

But over their voices, Anna heard, very distinctly, a faint scraping sound, and then, a gasp. A gasp that became a deep hollow terrible thud.

She knew instantly what had happened.

She turned, fled from the room. With Dan at her heels, she raced down the steps and out to the back terrace.

Together they found the place where Davis had fallen from the fire ladder. His limp and sprawled body was lifeless, his eyes dull.

Dan put an arm around her shoulder, held her close.

"I'm sorry I waited so long," he said quietly. "But we had to hear it all, Anna. We had to know the truth."

She nodded, leaned wearily against him. They knew the pathetic truth, and Davis was dead.

Sobbing and whimpering, Helga came out into the dark on the balcony. William lumbered beside her.

Dan said quickly, "We need help, William. Don't look. Don't look, Helga."

But William, standing over his son, screamed "No, no," and then, with a lurching step, he crashed over the balcony and lay unmoving on the ground.

Neil knelt beside him, touched his throat and temple, then said quietly, "It's over, Anna. William is dead. The Kennellys are dead."

The sun glinted on the brilliant green glass at the top of the wall. It had been Storr's fancy, Ann supposed, that the green glass would symbolize the green emeralds of Emerald Station.

The gates closed gently.

Thomson stood there, his bald head bent, waving.

"He'll be leaving soon," she said. "They'll close up the house, he and Dot, and then it will be finished."

"Yes," Dan agreed. He turned slowly into the road that curled across the valley toward the ring of blue hills and Bellingham.

"Neil and Tanya will go to the Maine house with Helga for a while. She mustn't be alone. And then they'll see," Anna said. "We'll have to find out how Julia is, and what she wants to do."

"It will settle itself with time," Dan said.

She nodded, but didn't speak. The pretense was over now. This was the day on which she had said she and Dan would be married. Instead it was the day in which she and Dan became strangers again.

The night before Dot had called Dr. Robinson and Jim Arden.

There had been hours of the kind of controlled confusion that officials seem to bring with them. There had been depositions to make and sign. Arrangements to be discussed. Dan and Anna hadn't had a moment alone until now.

Dan slowed for the familiar curve. Something made her look back. Emerald Station stood high on its slope, blank windows glinting in the sunlight. The fountain still sprayed a veil over the two stone lions.

She swung around, thinking that she was glad to be going away. She would forget the shadows that had reached for her. She would forget them when she left them behind.

"You're not sorry?" Dan asked. "It was the only way, you know. It had to end, Anna."

She had looked back only once. She knew that she would never look back again. She said, "No, I'm not sorry. I'm glad, Dan. I'm glad that it's ended now. It should have been a long long time ago."

He directed the car around the bend, and without turning, she knew that Emerald Station was gone from sight.

He put a hand on hers, and slanted a blue-eyed look at her. "Anna," he said, "I'm not the kind of man who enjoys changing plans."

"Changing plans?" she asked.

"This was to have been the day we were going to get married. Do you remember?"

"Yes. I remember, but that was . . ."

"It was real, Anna. It always was. From the first time I saw you. You'd been in to talk with my father, and you were leaving. I held the door open for you, and watched you hurry away, and wished I had time to know you."

She said, with the joy blooming in her, "But Dan, I didn't know. I never even thought . . ."

"I did. And never stopped. Even when I introduced you to Martin. He understood pretty quickly, and was just waiting to see what would happen. And then too much happened. It was never the right time to speak up. But that's over. And the end of Emerald Station is the beginning for us."

She closed her eyes and leaned against him. "Beginning," she whispered. "That's a very beautiful word."

THE HAVERSHAM LEGACY
A TROUBADOUR SPECTACULAR

Daoma Winston

The saga of a powerful, passionate family whose riches concealed a mesh of corruption, bloodshed and madness, this is also the story of Miranda Jervis, who left her mother's seedy boarding house to claim a share in the dazzling Haversham inheritance – and began the stormiest era in all that family's troubled history.

'A wonderful gothic, full of jewels, flowers, love, envy, murder, childbirth, suspense and intrigue . . . a fiery tale that should find a wide audience.' *Publishers Weekly*

WICKED LOVING LIES

A TROUBADOUR SPECTACULAR

Rosemary Rogers

From the innocence of a sheltered Spanish convent to the splendour of a Sultan's harem . . . from the intrigues of Napoleon's court to England on the brink of war . . . and the wilds of Louisiana.

WICKED LOVING LIES is the story of two people whose paths were destined to cross and recross through revolution, war, captivity, in a saga of intrigue and desire. One, Dominic Challenger, roving sea captain. The other, Marisa de Castellanos, the golden-haired beauty whom he had once captured and ravished.

Another epic story of passion and adventure from the bestselling author of SWEET SAVAGE LOVE.

SWEET SAVAGE LOVE
A TROUBADOUR SPECTACULAR

Rosemary Rogers

The historical romance that has sold 2,000,000 copies.

BELLE of the sparkling Paris salons and the ballrooms of New Orleans.

REBEL on the sweating, dusty waggon trail to Mexico.

WILDCAT fighting for freedom in the tawdry whorehouse.

GYPSY swirling to the sensuous rhythms of the flamenco.

KILLER of the man who stripped her naked and auctioned her.

MISTRESS to the handsome renegade who needed her courage and her body – but not her love . . .

SWEET SAVAGE LOVE the stormy, passionate story of Virginia Brandon, bold, impetuous, beautiful – swept from an elegant social life in 19th century Paris into the violence and savagery of Emperor Maximilian's Mexico.